THE WITNESS

THE WITNESS

THE WITNESS

Jane Bidder

Published by Accent Press Ltd 2015

ISBN 9781783751372

Dedications

The Witness is dedicated to my children, William, Lucy, and Giles.

Also to my husband.

Acknowledgments

I would like to thank Teresa Chris, my agent; David and Iain for their legal advice; Betty Schwartz as always; my cousin Finni Golden for an extra eye at the proof-reading stage; and all the team at Accent Press.

PROLOGUE

It was all down to timing and what you saw – or didn't see – in life. If Daniel hadn't come home early that night, it wouldn't have happened. None of it. They could have gone on leading their ordinary lives and the girl (not to mention the youth) could have continued hers too.

You can't think like that, said the policeman when she had got to know him better. Oh but she could. Maybe that's what made her different. Maybe that's what had started all this in the first place.

ONE

The dog heard Daniel's arrival before Alice. How did animals do it? Their previous Labrador had been the same. Ears alert, stiffened body waiting at the bay window, keenly looking down the drive towards the gate, a good few moments before she herself heard her husband's expensive tyres crunch the gravel.

For a second, Alice's chest dipped a little in the realisation that her own day was at an end. No more listening to Radio 4 peacefully, or pottering round the garden, secateurs in hand, without someone requesting a cup of tea or demanding to know why the phone bill was so high.

You only had to look at the print-out to see how steeply it had risen since Garth had gone off on his latest gap year. Not that Garth bothered to phone *them* much. Every now and then, she received the odd email from Peru or Perth or, recently, a South Pacific island called Vanuatu which she'd had to look up on Google. Why didn't someone tell you, when your baby was born, that one day he would saunter off into the unknown and not look back?

"Down, down," she said slightly irritably to Mungo who was now pawing at the back door; a rather pretty stable design in Farrow and Ball duck blue which she had painted herself, to fill in the hours.

Glancing in the mirror, Alice gave herself a taut little smile. Apart from that smudge of earth by her mouth – weeding could be such an intimate business! – she might just about pass one of her mother's critical observations. Blonde hair loosely tied into a knot at the back (she liked to do that in the summer but

3

preferred it loose when colder). Pale blue eyes which looked better when they had a thin line of kohl beneath. Pearl earrings, that Garth had brought back from his first gap year in Thailand and which had annoyed Daniel. ("Why don't you ever wear the expensive ones I've bought you? God knows what kind of disease you might have caught from some street market tat.")

The memory made her smile more naturally at herself in the glass. For a minute, she caught a glimpse of the old Alice. The one before it had all happened. The girl she yearned for – yet feared for – at the same time. The one who was now replaced by this perfect prefect image in the mirror before her; immaculate on the outside but damaged irrevocably within.

If it hadn't been for Daniel, she would have been lost. Yet at the same time, he was unwittingly destroying her with his impossible expectations. "He's given you safety," she reminded herself, before walking towards the old coach house where her husband was parking the car. As she did so, she recalled, wistfully, the pony days which had preceded Garth's discovery of ska, punk, and girls. "Be grateful. You owe him that."

Mungo was frantic now. Leaping up at Daniel in his dark blue suit as though his master had been away for weeks instead of a mere ten hours. Daniel himself, she observed, looked tired. It wasn't an easy commute to Exeter. They could move again, her husband had suggested when he'd unexpectedly been seconded to Cornwall. But no. They both loved their seaside home which they had found when Garth had been twelve; more or less the same time that Daniel had accepted there weren't going to be any more children. A move from London to the south-west, had seemed like a good way to banish any regrets while pushing useless recriminations to one side.

And so it was. If it hadn't been for her garden – so much bigger than the one in Clapham – and the sea, with its never-ending fringed scalloped waves with maritime sighs that reminded her of the soothing white music she used to play when Garth was a baby, she might not have survived.

"You're early," she said, standing on tiptoes for a kiss. Only on the cheek of course. Sometimes, when Alice thought about it (which she tried not to do too much), she could barely remember any *other* kind of kiss between them. Then she added. "You smell nice."

Indeed he did. There was still a faint whiff of the morning pine cologne about him although the rest of her husband bore traces of a hard day's graft. Teaching wasn't what it used to be, he was always telling her. Too many Aims and Objectives which bore capital letters as an indication of their importance on the annual review.

"My last seminar was cancelled." Daniel gave the dog an affectionate pat. "Thought we might go out to dinner, if you like."

Dinner? Years of looking after Garth and making sure that he had not only completed his homework but that she was also well acquainted with his texts in order to have intelligent conversations about Chaucer or practise French conversation on the school run, meant that Alice was not very good at spontaneity. Even though Garth was away on his second gap year now – Durham had, very understandingly, agreed to another deferral – she had created a carefully crafted routine to replace the one that she missed.

Up at 6.30 to make Daniel's breakfast. Days spent gardening or playing tennis at the club where she had made most of her friends, or, if the weather was bad, at the new glossy gym in Plymouth. (Not that she needed to. Her figure, despite having had a child, remained almost embarrassingly girlish.) Once a month, there was Book Club which could be entertaining, when not poisoned by internal factions. Why did book clubs sometimes bring out the worst in people, instead of the best? And walking, which was always a good way to blast the cobwebs out of her head. She and Mungo loved exploring the coastal path which had, rather amusingly, become a rather fashionable thing to do amongst her old London friends. One, despite doing it for charity, admitted it was more of an excuse to 'get away from home'.

How else did she fill her day? Ah yes. Mending broken china; something she still described as a 'hobby', feeling too embarrassed to call it a business. There was also the occasional foray into Garth's room with its garish posters on the wall;

clean-smelling air without the usual whiff of BO; and too-tidy floor and desk. Even though it hurt to go in, Alice found it mildly reassuring – as though her son's possessions were waiting for him to return just as she was. What else? Preparing dinner of course; a ritual which, to her shame, had all too often become, since Garth's departure, an elaborate TV tray affair in front of a good box set.

It was a pattern that she and Daniel had fallen into as if by some unspoken agreement, in order to rescue the conversation from the 'How was your day' banalities. A pattern which she clung to like the orange lifebelts strung along the sea front.

Now she regarded the prospect of tonight's restaurant dinner with apprehension. How would they manage without the support of television to fill in the long conversation gaps between courses? She could see it now. Daniel would talk about the latest drive to recruit foreign students (necessary to fund the coffers) and she might chat about tennis or her book or that little jug which was proving tricky to repair. Both would feign interest in the other's snippets.

Indeed, usually, dinner out was an ordeal to be reserved for anniversaries and birthdays. Was this why Daniel had suggested it? Alice racked her brain as they walked past the bed of lupins she had been weeding that afternoon – such wonderful rich heads of purples and pinks! – to ensure that she hadn't forgotten a special date.

It seemed unlikely. Ever since she had married Daniel, she had become one of those organised women whom her mother despised so much. The type who wrote down exactly what they gave friends and family each Christmas so they wouldn't present a similar gift next year. The sort who not only had a birthday book but also remembered to post presents well in advance in case the post played up.

If she was in control, Alice kept reminding herself, nothing could ever go wrong again.

"Is it a special occasion?" she now asked as Mungo zoomed into the house before them, returning with one of Daniel's shoes as a welcome-home gift.

Her husband frowned at the left brogue; creased by the dog's enthusiasm. "Does it have to be, in order to dine out with my wife?"

Instantly, Alice knew she'd made a mistake. It was so easy to do so when your marriage was made of egg shells, papered over with Designer Guild paint, television suppers, and unspoken recriminations.

"Of course not." They were in the kitchen now with its honey pine dresser, studded with Emma Bridgewater botanical mugs hanging from cup hooks. On the marble island in the middle sat a bowl of plums from the garden. One, she noticed irrelevantly, had a hole where an animal had worked its way in and might still be there; drowning in juicy flesh.

The image made her shudder.

"That would be lovely." She glanced at the Victorian clock over the Aga with its mahogany surround and large digits, from which she'd taught Garth how to tell the time. Only five o'clock. Mungo had already had his afternoon walk; usually she gave him another good run at about six before Daniel got back but if they were going out for an early supper, she'd need to do it now. Otherwise he might not last. Mungo was a bit like Mum. Both acted younger than their age. Both were inconsistent. All over you one minute; distant the next.

"I'll just whip round the park while you have a shower, shall I?" she added. Daniel always liked to head for the bathroom when he got home. Wash first. Then dinner, followed by the papers, a little music perhaps, and an early night. Sometimes, when Alice considered the amalgamation of their set ways, she could persuade herself that it was these which constituted a firm marriage and that the 'other' part, as they called it in old-fashioned novels, wasn't necessary. After all, lots of people their age didn't have sex any more. There had been a survey about it only the other week in *The Times*.

"A walk? Good idea." Daniel was, she could see, still tense around his mouth from her reaction to his invitation to dinner. It wasn't until after they'd married that she'd learned how to handle these moods which could go as quickly as they had come. "Mollify and distract." That's what her mother had advised years ago. "Works for temper tantrums and for

7

husbands," she'd added with all the certainty that came from having added a long marriage to the list of her achievements. Now Mum wore widowhood almost as a badge of honour. "In my day," she was fond of announcing to whoever would listen, "we took our vows seriously. Even if we weren't particularly happy."

Whatever she might think of her mother, Alice told herself, there was no doubt that the mollify and distract technique could be very effective in smoothing troubled waters. "Cup of tea first?" she suggested, putting on the kettle. Daniel nodded and Alice wondered, not for the first time, if his students could see past that handsome jawline and fair looks to see the real Professor Daniel Honeybun.

"Second thoughts," he now said, his firm voice slicing through her movements, "I'll put on the kettle myself." He glanced at her cut-off denim jeans, still muddy from the garden, and blue sneakers. "Why don't you go for that walk now? We'll go out as soon as you're back and changed.'

One of the reasons they had bought their house in this sought-after seaside town, not far from Plymouth, was because of the park. It went on for miles, weaving its way inland as though purposefully trying to distract tourists from the sea like a jealous sibling.

Alice varied her walks. The beach first thing in the morning when she would jog along the front, nodding a cheery hello to the other runners whilst plump, screaming seagulls pecked at leftover fish and chips thrust into bins by the tourists. The park at lunchtime. Sea in the afternoon. Park again in the evening. On the lead in winter and off if it was summer when she could see the dog clearly.

When they'd first got Mungo, the vet's assistant had advised them to walk him a lot. "It's the ones that don't get enough exercise who misbehave," she had warned them. Yet, sometimes, Alice suspected that it was *her* who needed to get out, more than the dog.

Now, as he ran in front of her eagerly chasing the ball (no wonder her right arm, though slender like the rest of her, bore traces of muscle!), Alice felt a welcome peace seeping through her. It was so beautiful with the river running through it. The grass, freshly cut by the council, smelt as fragrant as the Chanel which she always wore. Number Five, she would say when asked although she had skirted, for a time, with Number 19 before returning guiltily, like a repentant wife.

Incredible really, she thought, putting up her hand to shield the sun from her eyes, that it was already early evening yet it could be the middle of the afternoon. So light! So summery. And yet, at the same time, quite empty. Earlier, when she'd been here at lunchtime, there had been the usual coterie of mothers and pushchairs with toddlers clutching the sides or else riding their trikes, wobbling precariously on stabilisers. The memory, as usual, had made Alice's heart lurch, recalling Garth's early years and her mother's warning to 'make the most of it because it doesn't last', even though at the time it had seemed to go on for ever.

Now, as Alice threw the second ball – two were advisable because it encouraged Mungo to come back – it felt as though she was almost on a stage set. No one else was around, save a young couple sitting on a bench just over there, under a clump of willow trees. It was quiet too. Unusually so.

The girl had auburn hair, she observed. About the same age as Garth, perhaps. Very thin, willowy and almost nymph-like in stature. What was she wearing? From this distance, it looked like a very short black skirt under an orange T-shirt. Still, that's how girls dressed nowadays, wasn't it? The other day in the shopping centre, she'd seen a young teenager – surely no more than twelve – wearing laddered tights under blue denim shorts, begging for money. The extent of homelessness, even in a city like Plymouth, often shocked her. Where had that girl's parents been?

Often, Alice had secretly imagined what it would have been like to have had a daughter. She would have called her Victoria, she'd decided. Vicky for short although her daughter would have spelled it differently with an 'i' because she would have been adventurous. Able to stand up for herself. Not like Alice.

Meanwhile, the boy, who seemed older, wore a leather

jacket and was sitting on the bench, legs outstretched, looking out across the park but not in a searching manner. More of a nothing-to-do-way.

Alice recognised that. Sometimes when she went for a long walk with Mungo, she took a break and sat for a while; wondering what Garth was doing and trying not to text because everyone said that you had to let go at that age.

Had the couple just had a row, wondered Alice? They were just sitting there, side by side, without even touching or, as far as she could see, talking. It struck her that this could be her and Daniel in an hour or so's time, facing each other in a restaurant, searching for something to say. Why couldn't he just have come back later as normal so they could have their usual TV supper (the chops were already marinating in honey and ginger in the fridge although she supposed they would last until tomorrow) and then they would have been saved that painful non-conversation.

"Other ball," she instructed Mungo who had come up clamouring for the second. "Find the other ball first."

It took him a while to find it amongst the newly mown grass cuttings by the river and, when he did, Alice realised the bench was now empty. The girl was walking gracefully – almost floating – towards the hedge that ran between the park and an old cottage which Alice had often admired; not that anything would ever possess her to leave their white Regency townhouse which she had taken such care over; with its mix of old and new; original fireplaces and flagstone floors covered with rich red and gold rugs from Liberty.

Meanwhile, the auburn-haired girl was moving very slowly; very deliberately. Almost as though in a film. Extremely straight. Quite erect with a certain out-of-world air that one could not help but admire. If this had been evening, one might have been forgiven for imagining she was a ghost.

Curiosity made Alice wonder if the girl had got up from the bench in a huff. A lover's tiff perhaps. Or maybe the couple were merely friends and she was walking back home from college. Then again, she didn't appear to be carrying a bag of any description. Nor had she left one on the bench.

Alice noticed details like that. You should be a writer, a teacher had once said at school. But when she had ventured to mention this to the sixth-form careers 'department' (a plain, uninspiring room, manned by a part-time woman with tight grey curls), she was told that it was 'very difficult to get in' and that she'd be far better off as an English or art teacher – leaving the path clear for other more deserving would-be novelists. In the event, neither had happened.

The girl was kneeling down now. She appeared to be looking for something while the boy was standing up, quite straight. His eyes were fixed in the same direction as earlier, not moving, as though he was a figurehead on a ship. Alice was close enough to see these things although not quite close enough to be certain. It looked like the girl was putting a plaster on the boy's knee. Indeed, his trousers were, she was pretty certain, on the ground and the girl's mouth was …

A hot red flush crawled over her cheeks. Surely not. It *couldn't* be. Not here in the park where there might be anyone around. Besides, it didn't fit with the girl's appearance. She'd seemed so young. So graceful. Too insubstantial for something as basic as lust.

Confused, unsure what to do, Alice glanced around, aware she was shaking. Surely someone else could step in. Stop them. But the park was still deserted save for her and Mungo who was worrying at her for the second ball.

"Ouch! That hurt. Bad boy," she said out loud as his teeth grazed her hand. Throwing it in the opposite direction from the couple, she tried to walk on but her gaze was curiously drawn back, Lot-wife style.

Oh my God. Alice, who didn't like to use His name (it seemed wrong when you were a regular at Evensong, a service which she found far more soothing than the more informal, modern-worded morning service), found herself moving closer to the couple; drawn by an invisible force.

The girl was lying on the ground now, her legs clearly up in the air in a v-shape. The boy was on top. His head down. There could be no doubt now. She could even see a small bluebird tattoo on the girl's slim neck.

Something had to be done. Didn't the couple realise they were in a public place? Any minute now, some mother with a gaggle of children on their way to Cubs or back from the beach after a late day out, might come across this ... this spectacle. It could traumatise them for ever!

Alice's right hand closed over the mobile phone in her pocket. She could call the police but, then again, might that not be as traumatic for the girl as it had been for *her*, all those years ago? Could she really inflict on her the same horrors that had stamped the old Alice, on the cusp of womanhood?

Besides, supposing this couple were in love? What if they had just got carried away? What if Garth was doing something similar with a girl on a foreign beach? Would she really thank a stranger for reporting them?

Better, surely, that she made her way back. "Home," she called out to Mungo. It was one of the few words he obeyed, providing she had sufficient treats in her pocket. Swiftly slipping the lead over his head, she took a left over the bridge, heading for the short-cut. Just as she reached the furthest point of visibility, she glanced back.

The couple were still on the grass in the same position. At the main gates, she could see someone else entering. On a bike. Good. Let that person deal with it then. Breaking out into a jog, Alice felt the heat still searing through her body along with an icy feeling, as though she had flu.

"You were quick." Daniel was already dressed in his smart brown hound's-tooth patterned sports jacket; catching up on the paper in the spacious kitchen which had doubled up as a den when Garth was little, with its squashy sofa in the corner. Now it was her 'office' where she took calls from clients, carefully noting down their needs in the little black book on the small lavender and pink mosaic-top table, which she'd made herself at a crafts workshop.

"Was I?" Alice glanced at the clock. It felt as though she had been out for an age yet it had only been twenty minutes.

"Did you run?" Daniel took in her hot, dishevelled appearance with a look that might either be amusement or disapproval. It was hard to read his mind nowadays; a criticism which he, ironically, had thrown at *her* the other month.

"Yes. No. Sort of."

She ought to tell him, Alice thought, as she busied herself, putting out fresh water for Mungo and scooping out his evening ration of dry food. But that would mean mentioning the 'sex' word. Why spoil the evening before she'd given it a chance? "I'm just going to have a shower. Won't be long."

Then she heard it. They all did, including the dog who tore past to the window, barking furiously. The sound of a siren. In London, it had been so familiar as to be unremarkable. The whirring of rescue helicopters was another matter. They were used to that here – amazing how people ignored the Danger sign on the cliff edge. But sirens were unusual unless someone had slipped in the high street and broken a leg, as had happened last month to an old lady from church. The snap, apparently, had been audible.

"Sounds like something's happened in the park," said Daniel looking out of the window. He squinted as he tried to focus; time and time again, she had to remind him to wear his new tortoiseshell glasses. Vanity or forgetfulness, she wondered. Both played their part in her husband's life. 'Did you see anything when you were there?" he added curiously.

"No." Alice heard her voice coming out like someone else's. Just as it had done all those years ago. "No. I didn't."

It was wrong to lie. How many times had she told Garth that? But far worse than the mistruth, was that strange feeling down below her waist, that had started when she had first seen the couple and which was still there now.

An excitement mixed with a disgust that made her want to gag.

Would the past *never* go away?

TWO

The day had started as it always did. The noise through the paper-thin wall that divided Kayleigh's room from Mum and Ron's. When he'd moved in last Christmas, there had been different noises. Like next door's cat which screamed every night.

"That's no bleeding cat," scoffed her friend Marlene who'd become really superior since her implant at the Family Planning Clinic; always showing off the tell-tale line at the top of her arm. "That's them having it off."

That was sick. Really sick. Every time Kayleigh looked at Ron with his stomach heaving over the top of his dirty black joggers, she felt ill. How could Mum allow *that* near her?

But the sounds had changed recently. Instead of cat wails, it was Mum crying. "Stop it, Ron," Kayleigh could hear her mum pleading. "Stop."

Marlene (who always got stroppy if you called her Marl*een* instead of Marl*ane-er*) explained that's what you said when you wanted more. It was called 'playing hard to get'. But in the morning, Mum would appear in the kitchen, trying to look away as she spoke, to hide the fact that she had one – if not two – black eyes.

"That's not good," Marlene conceded, applying another layer of lip gloss in the school toilet. "Unless she likes it that way."

How could anyone *like it that way*? But it was true that when Kayleigh came back from school that afternoon, Mum was humming along to her iPod. "Get yourself something from the

15

chippie," she'd said, pressing a two-pound coin into her hand. "Ron and I are going out tonight."

Kayleigh didn't dare point out that two quid would barely buy a bag of chips let alone a bit of batter. It was enough that Mum was OK again. But, the following morning, the bad sounds were there once more. And so it went on in a pattern as regular as the bruise/smile duet on Mum's face. In the last few weeks though, Kayleigh had noticed something different. Ron had started getting up earlier than Mum, even though he could have stayed in bed 'cos he was on 'bleeding benefits'. (His words, not hers.) It was him instead of Mum who was putting on the kettle when Kayleigh came in to make herself some toast before school. And he wasn't always wearing his jogger bottoms.

"Your stepdad prances about in the nood?" asked Marlene, almost dropping her lip gloss in the toilet at school. She pronounced the word 'nude' like they did on that American high school programme on Sky. Kayleigh missed it now there wasn't any money to pay the subscription.

"Not exactly," Kayleigh had said nervously, flicking back her hair while debating whether to have it shaved down one side with pink streaks like Marlene. "He was wearing boxers, and 'sides, he's not my stepdad."

It was true. Ron was only the latest of several 'friends' that Mum had brought home for as long as she could remember. One day, Kayleigh told herself, she'd try to find her real dad. She'd even asked one of the teachers at school about it. The problem was you needed stuff like his exact date of birth. When Kayleigh had summoned up the courage to tackle Mum on the subject, she'd received a clip on her ear. "Why the fuck do you need to know that kind of shit?"

So that had been that.

It didn't stop her dreaming though. "Dreaming's important," said the same teacher who took her for English. Not 'took' as in nicked. Or 'took' like 'taken' which was a word that kept coming up in that book they were doing by a bloke called D.H. Lawrence that made the boys snigger 'cos women were always being 'taken' by blokes. Just 'took'.

If pressed, Kayleigh would have to admit she had a bit of a crush on Mr Brown, whose first name, Marlene had discovered through looking in his bag when he'd gone out for a minute, was Joey. He had soft brown hair that he tied back in a ponytail and his kid's name was tattooed on his arm. *Jade*.

If there was one thing that Kayleigh had learned from Mum, it was that you didn't break up other people's families. 'Sides, she didn't even know if he was interested.

Back to the morning. Sometimes when Kayleigh recalled the evening of June 9th, she told herself it was the day that her life began. Or ended. Often it was hard to tell the difference. She'd written those lines down in her latest English essay and received a 'Very astute' comment written in the margin. She'd needed to look up the 'astute' bit and had memorised it on the Notes bit of her pay as you go.

Shit. That reminded her. She'd run out of credit.

When the usual cries of 'Don't, Ron' filtered through the wall, Kayleigh slipped out of bed (which took up most of her bedroom) and headed for the shower. There used to be a proper bathroom in this place, Mum was fond of moaning. But the council had turned it into her bedroom and put up the shower cubicle in a corner of the kitchen instead, behind a plastic curtain. At least there was a separate toilet but Kayleigh didn't like using it after Ron. Usually she'd hang on until school where your shoes didn't stick to the ground with piss. Or worse.

It was when she emerged from the shower ('emerge' was a new posh word that she'd picked up from this D.H. Lawrence bloke), that Kayleigh realised Ron was already there again, putting on the kettle and wearing those garish boxers with rolls of flab surfing over in waves. Flushing, Kayleigh wrapped the towel around her but not before Ron's eyes had taken her in. Looked right at her, he did. From the bluebird tattoo on her neck (a present from Mum on her last birthday) right down her body.

Where were her jeans and her underwear? She'd left them right here – could swear it on her nan's grave if she knew where that was. Kayleigh's eyes darted around the kitchen, moving from the pile of greasy plates still in the sink from last night's takeaway to the torn lino by the microwave that didn't work after Callum (who hadn't been around since last summer) had put his trainers in to 'dry off'.

"Looking for these, are yer?" leered Ron.

To her horror, Kayleigh saw that he was holding her stuff up in the air with a broad grin on his face. Was this some kind of game? Marlene would kill her. She'd lent her that bra 'cos Kayleigh's didn't fit any more and Mum didn't have any money to get her another. When she got to sixteen, it would be all right. She'd try to find a job to earn her own pocket money. But round here, no one would employ you if you were under-age. ("Too many kids nick stuff when they're working," Marlene had said knowledgeably. "Then the bosses like can't do nothing 'cos they're not meant to hire kids that young.")

"Please can I have them back?" Kayleigh pleaded. "They don't belong to me."

Ron's eyes glinted. "Your boyfriend give them to you, did he?"

"No." Kayleigh felt the humiliation searing through her. "I don't have one."

He was moving towards her now. "You telling me that a pretty girl like you doesn't have a bloke?"

Deftly Kayleigh stepped aside. She didn't want to be rude – Mum had given her a beating the other week for giving Ron lip – but he was getting close. Too close.

"Not so fast. If you want your clothes back, you're going to have to be nice to me. Not act all innocent, like." He leered. 'I've always had a thing for gingers.'

What was he doing? Disbelievingly, she felt his huge fat hot hand tugging at the towel. "FUCK OFF!" she heard herself yell in a voice that wasn't hers at all.

He lunged towards her but this time, she was faster. Picking up a knife, she brandished it at him. "If you touch me – or hit my mum again – I'll kill you," she hissed. "Got it!"

He began to laugh. A horrid scary throaty laugh. "Think you can threaten me, my girl? Just watch this."

Quick as a flash, he tore the knife from her hands but in the scuffle, the blade nicked his arm, causing a thin trickle of blood to ooze out.

"LITTLE COW. LOOK WHAT YOU'VE DONE NOW," he yelled, grinning. That wasn't fair. Mum would think it was her. Then his eyes grew cold. He was going for her! Instinctively, she ducked and dived for the door. Hugging the towel round her, Kayleigh tore down the two flights of steps – ignoring whistles from some lads across the block – and legged it up the next floor to Marlene's.

"What the fuck ..." said her friend, her voice trailing away as Kayleigh flung herself inside.

"It's Ron," gasped Kayleigh.

Marlene's voice hardened. "Warned you, didn't I?"

"You try living there." She flopped down on the green velour sofa, still hardly believing she'd made it. "It's bloody impossible."

There was a rolling of eyes. Kayleigh got the feeling that Marlene was enjoying the drama. "No good moaning. Let's get practical. We'd better find you something to wear for starters." Dragging her off the sofa, her friend led her into her room, reeking as usual of jasmine incense, and handed her a pink g-string. "You can have my school uniform today if you want. I'm bunking off." She grinned, and Kayleigh suddenly noticed a silver tongue stud which hadn't been there yesterday. "Seeing Pete, I am."

Then her tone softened as she took in the shivers which wouldn't stop even though Kayleigh knew she was safe now. "Calm down. Tell you what. Why don't you bunk off school too and come with us? Pete's got this really cool friend. Quite fancy him myself, I do."

Kayleigh thought of her school bag which she'd left behind in her rapid exit from home, and the essay inside on this Roger McGough, which she'd stayed up late to finish. Would Mr Brown believe her if she told him she'd done it but "left it behind".

Everyone else came out with that excuse. She couldn't bear to disappoint him. Kayleigh had never bunked off school before but surely it was better than letting Mr Brown down.

"OK."

Marlene grinned again. "Cool." She opened her wardrobe which had a double mirror on the doors and loads of clothes inside (so lucky!) and threw over a short black skirt and orange T-shirt. Both were much more revealing than her usual jeans and top but she didn't like to say anything. "Let's go then. Pete's getting a car from somewhere."

"From a garage?"

Marlene laughed loudly. "You're so naive, aren't yer?"

Mum said the same. Not in an amused way like her friend but with raised pencilled-in eyebrows and that exasperated edge to her voice. That reminded her. "What if Ron tries to hurt Mum when I'm gone?"

Marlene rolled her eyes again. "Your mum can look after herself from what I hear. 'Sides, where is *she* when you need her? Now are you coming or not?"

The car – a really cool red sports design – could only be started with a metal coat hanger. Kayleigh had a strong feeling that this wasn't legal.

Meanwhile, she was terrified that Ron was going to come after her still and kept looking over her shoulder to check. "We'll go to the seaside," Marlene's boyfriend had announced. With any luck, thought Kayleigh, it might give Ron time to calm down before she got back that night.

Marlene's chap – Pete – was very tall and thin with a tattoo of a cockerel down his neck and a silver stud in his right nipple, poking through a hole in his brown T-shirt. The more Kayleigh tried not to look, the more her attention was drawn to it. Had it hurt when it was done, she wondered? The bluebird had been as painful as shit and she didn't even like it. Its face was all squashed. But Mum would have been right narked if she'd said so.

Suddenly she became aware of Marlene's bloke slowing down on the edge of another estate on the other side of the city. "You'll have some company now, love." Then he dug Marlene in the ribs and laughed.

"I'm not sure," began Kayleigh …

Wow!

Kayleigh could feel her jaw dropping as a man came out of one of the downstairs flats and walked towards them. It wasn't that he was tall (in fact, he was medium height). Or that he had a soft ponytail like Mr Brown. Or even that he walked in a confident way like he was a celebrity. It was the way he was looking straight at her like they'd met before.

"Kayleigh?" he said, though it was less of a question than a statement. "Hi. Marlene's told me all about you."

Then he actually took her hand and kissed it. She thought she was going to die! Not in an awful way. But in a D.H. Lawrence way or even a Roger McGough one.

"Really?" she squeaked. "That sounds like a line from a book I'm reading."

Quite why she said that, she didn't know. Instantly she felt really stupid. But Frank – 'Call me Frankie' – seemed to think she'd just said something really, really clever.

"You didn't tell me your mate had brains as well as beauty, Marlene," he said, sliding into the tiny back seat behind her so that his leg pressed hers. Kayleigh didn't know where to look or what to say.

Instead she just closed her eyes and knew that she'd remember this day for the rest of her life. A bloke actually fancied her! Not the kids with spots and gelled-back hair who were always yelling out names on the estate.

Ging-ger! Freckle-face! Skinny tits!

But a really good-looking bloke who was a proper man. Someone who'd sort out Ron.

He was saying something to her now in the back. "I can't hear because the roof's down and there's too much noise from that lorry," she wanted to explain. But it wouldn't look cool. So instead she nodded and hoped that was the right thing. It seemed to be, because he looked quite pleased.

"The trick with boys," Marlene was always saying, "is to make them feel good about themselves. Then they stay with you."

Right now, Kayleigh wanted that more than anything. She might only have just met Frankie, but already there was something about him with that quiff of black hair, soft Irish accent, and dancing green eyes (the same colour as hers!), that reminded her of a hero in some poem that Mr Brown had read out loud in class.

Mr Brown! Oh my God. They were passing the school gates now and there he was. Walking in, books under his arm, in charge of a group of younger kids. Even from this distance in the car, she could see that he was frowning in her direction. He'd recognised her. Knew she was bunking off.

Too late to tap Marlene's boyfriend on the shoulder and ask him to stop. Pete was already shooting off – surely too fast – and was soon on the dual carriageway leading to a place she'd never heard of.

That was the thing about living in a city without a car. You didn't get out much. Mum was always going on about that. As the road spread out in front of them with hills sprouting up on their side, Kayleigh's excitement took over from that nagging worry about letting down Mr Brown.

"There's nowhere to bleeding park!" Marlene's boyfriend didn't look as annoyed as his words suggested. "Tell you what, we'll drop you two off here and find you later."

But Kayleigh hardly heard him. Instead, her eyes were fixed on the turquoise blue line in front of them. The sea! Far, far away in her dim memory, she could remember walking along the beach with a man holding her hand. Had it been her dad? Mum refused to talk about him, apart from declaring every now and then that he'd been a "waste of bloody space". But just the thought that this might have been *the* place where she and her father had been, made her jump out of the car with excitement.

"Someone's eager," said Frankie grinning.

He was older than she'd thought. Not just eighteen or nineteen. More like twenty-something. She could see that, now that they were walking side by side. Suddenly Kayleigh felt really nervous: especially since Marlene and her bloke had just driven off in the car and left them. She hadn't expected that. Why hadn't her friend said goodbye?

"What time will they be back?" she asked, her mouth dry as Frankie reached for her hand. It felt warm. Firm. Grown up.

"When they're ready." He looked down on her. "Don't

22

worry about that. Just enjoy yourself." His admiring glance and smooth way of talking almost made her feel attractive.

Drunk with gratitude, she gripped his hand as they walked past a mum with a toddler in a pushchair. The woman was quite old. Nearly as old as her mum who was thirty-nine next month. Kayleigh had been sworn to secrecy on that one in case Ron found out. He thought she was only thirty-two.

"Do you want kids?" she suddenly blurted out. Why had she asked that? How bloody stupid.

Frankie threw back his head and laughed. She liked that. It made her feel warm and good about herself; not stupid the way she usually did when someone laughed at her. "Why? Want one, do you?"

A hot flush spread over her face. "Not yet. But one day maybe."

He shrugged. "Might be OK, I suppose." He pulled her down onto a bench where an older woman was eating a sandwich, scattering grated cheese all over her lap while seagulls strutted, hoping for crumbs. In the distance, she could see surfers bobbing in the sea. It felt like she was in another world. Hardly daring to breathe, Kayleigh felt Frankie's hand slowly creeping round her waist and cupping her left breast. The woman eating the sandwich made a tutting noise, got up, and walked off, leaving the gulls to scatter in disappointment.

"Silly cow," commented Frankie laughing. Then his hand went down towards her waist.

She stood up, remembering the girl at school who'd got into trouble on her thirteenth birthday. "Not yet. It's too soon."

Appalled by her words, she waited. You've got to please a bloke, Marlene had instructed. And Marlene knew what she was talking about. Wasn't that why Kayleigh had been so flattered when she'd been chosen as her 'special mate' at school. Yet here she was now, breaking all the rules she'd learned.

Frankie would go now. She'd lost him.

"Too soon?" he repeated, breaking out into a broad grin. "You're a one, aren't you? Marlene said you were different. Don't remember what you said in the car, then?"

Kayleigh flushed. "I couldn't hear you. So I just said yes

because I didn't want to look daft."

Something crossed over his face. "I get that. Respect counts for a lot, doesn't it?" His Irish lilt made her want to hang on to every word. It was like recognising a song you didn't know you knew until you heard it. "I like you, Kayleigh. Know that?" His hand reached out and automatically she flinched in case he was going to hit her like Mum or Ron.

But instead, he stroked her hair, twisting it gently round his fingers. "I've never gone for gingers before but yours is different. More like a pale-red gold. Goes with your emerald eyes." He was so close she could smell the beer on his breath. Kayleigh closed her eyes in ecstasy. A real man! Just what her father would be like; whatever Mum said. In fact, she wouldn't be surprised when she found him (as she would one day) that he was a prince or someone famous. Didn't Callum always say that she was different from the rest of them?

"You're something else, aren't you?" The soft Irish accent stroked the air between them. "But you know what, me darling? You need something to help you relax."

Darling? No one else had ever called her that before! It sounded so smooth. So amazingly American, like she was in a film. Then Kayleigh felt Frankie pressing something into her hand. A small white pill: a bit smaller than an aspirin. "Knock it back," said Frankie lightly.

She hesitated, remembering that stuff that Callum had told her about tablets and not letting any bloke buy you a drink. "You're too naive, sis," he was always saying. "Christ knows why, in this place. Maybe you do it to block the rest of us out. You don't belong here, know that? Should have been born somewhere posh where people read the kind of books you've always got your nose in. Still, you don't have to worry about anyone hurting you. Not while I'm around."

Then he had gone, leaving a hole in her life that even Mr Brown and her dreams of finding an absent father, couldn't fill.

"Go on." The voice beside her was urgent, extracting her memory from the past. Before she knew what was happening, Frankie had picked the small white pill out of her palm, put it on the end of his tongue and kissed her.

24

His mouth was so warm. So soft. Yet hard at the same time. Really different from that horrible wet sloppy mess from the kid on the corner who then told all his mates they'd had it off when they'd only snogged. It had been horrible anyway. Their noses had kept colliding.

So this was what it should really be like! The wonderful realisation made her feel both powerful and weak at the same time. When they finally drew apart, she could feel something go down her throat. Not just the saliva. But something else. Something small and hard.

"What will it do to me?" she asked, nervously.

"Chill you out." His hand was reaching into his pocket and she saw he was popping another pill out of a silver foil sheet and knocking it back himself. A woman gave him an odd look as she walked past, carrying a kid with a bucket and spade.

"Mint," he said out loud. "Want one, anyone?"

Kayleigh found herself bursting out into loud peals of laughter. Frankie was right. Already the magic tablet was making her feel more relaxed, although that might have been psychological. That was another word which Mr Brown used a lot. For a moment, she had a flash of his disappointed face as they'd driven past school. Then it went. Her legs felt light. It was like walking on air.

"Tell you what," said Frankie, squeezing her bottom. "Why don't we take a walk."

The world had suddenly become a nicer place. Green one minute and pink the next. At least, that's how it seemed. A great sense of peace came over her as they sat on a bench. At least she thought they did. But after a few minutes, it felt like they were hovering over it like a seagull. Then down again.

"I want you to kiss me," said Frankie from a distance.

So she did.

"Not like that."

Then he took her by the hand and they floated towards a hedge. A blonde woman with a dog was staring at them. She'd do anything to be blonde instead of ginger, Kayleigh thought.

"Nosy cow," said Frankie's voice. It tinkled like church

bells. Trust the bleeding council to put us near the bleeding Catholics, her mother was always saying.

He told her what to do. It should have been disgusting but it wasn't. Was she doing it right? He was just standing there, looking away but then his body began to judder.

"Stop," he said urgently.

Then he laid her gently down on the grass. He smelt of cigarettes and sweat. Suddenly, a memory of the morning shot into her head. "Ron," she whispered, feeling her throat close with panic.

Frankie paused above her. "Was he your old boyfriend?"

"No. He's my mum's. And he scares me. He tried to touch me this morning."

Her words came out like swollen stones, reminding her of that numb feeling at the school dentist.

"I promise you, me darling," said Frankie stroking her hair, "that if you are nice to me, this Ron will never be able to hurt you again."

THREE

The whole town was talking about it. Even though she had lived here for years, Alice still found it hard to accept how parochial this place could be, compared with London.

The smallest things seemed to make it to headline status in the local paper. The other week, there had been half a page about a child's trike being stolen from outside the library.

Now it was much more dramatic.

"Flagrant display of al fresco sex in local park"

That was how the *Seaway Herald* put it. It didn't just make the front page. It carried on to the Letters column where the word 'disgusted' was used in abundance. They must have worked fast to get it into print. It had only happened two days ago.

"Weren't you there at around that time?" asked Daniel, who never usually read the local paper. He lowered his new glasses: a cutting-edge design which he had spent ages choosing; stuck in middle-age denial over fading eyesight. "Amazing that you didn't see anything."

This would have been the time to tell him! But for some reason, Alice, who was topping up the marmalade pot at the time, dropped the teaspoon which Mungo of course, immediately dived for. And in the confusion between mopping the floor – something she was quite fastidious about as she hated that sticky feeling you got if your shoe picked up something mucky – she didn't actually contradict him.

Afterwards, of course, it was too late. It would look odd, she told herself, to say, 'By the way. I forgot to tell you that I saw a couple having sex in the park. Before we went out to dinner. That's why I picked at my food in the Italian and we came back early. It wasn't because I had a headache at all. It's because I couldn't sit there and make banal conversation after seeing *that*. Surely you understand that, more than anyone else."

But instead, Alice remained silent; paralysed by guilt and shame.

Embarrassingly, when she went to Book Club that evening, they were all talking about it. "Unbelievable that anyone could do such a thing in broad daylight," declared Monica, a thin, sharp-forehand player from the tennis club, who was also in the book club crowd.

Janice, who was the nearest that Alice had to a best friend since moving down here, dug her in the ribs. "Probably just jealous! Can't see *her* having it off much, can you?"

Alice had prickled with discomfort. Sex, in her view, was something too private to discuss. A bit like money. Yet perhaps this was one thing she should have mentioned. It would have been so easy. Something casual, like "Actually, I saw it". Or maybe "You'll never guess but ..."

Yet she had let the moment slide, just as she had done with Daniel; fearful of all the questions and the blushes on her part. Perhaps it was just as well, she told herself. A revelation at book club might get back to Daniel. Besides, there were some – maybe like prickly Monica – who might even think she'd made it up, to get in on the act.

The following day, Alice tried to hide her 'should she have said something or shouldn't she?' angst with work. Mentally, she'd already put aside this week to repair a delicate early Victorian cup which had been dropped, causing the pink and green handle to become brutally separated from the main body. "Do you think you can do anything about it?" its owner had pleaded, after finding Alice through her advert in the parish magazine.

Alice had started mending china soon after Garth had started secondary school and found that the day needed filling with more than tennis or reading or walking the dog. It went some way towards filling her creative frustration at having dropped out of her Fine Art degree so many years ago.

Then a chance workshop on china restoration, advertised on the noticeboard outside an art shop, changed her life. The tutor, a friendly woman favouring ankle-length floral skirts and a rather messy birds'-nest hair style, had filled her with a passion she hadn't known possible. "I see it as restoring a piece of history," she had told the class, which – Alice noted with relief – was dominated by women in her own age group, each searching for 'something to do'.

The history reference had struck a chord. At school, she'd had a teacher who had spoken fervently about "us all having a piece of the past inside us which could, in turn, shape the outcome of the future". Perhaps this was her chance!

She also, as she discovered, had what the flowery workshop leader described as a 'real knack'. To her surprise and delight, Alice's fingers proved quite adept at gluing the missing piece into place. Janice, who had gone with her for company before dropping out, hadn't been so impressed. "What a performance! I simply don't have the patience."

But it was this quality, combined with a sense of purpose, that had encouraged Alice to practise on her own grandmother's rose-patterned china and then, after a few months, to quietly take on commissions.

Three nights after the park incident (which she was just beginning to put out of her mind, thank goodness), she was just sealing the broken handle to the cup when there was a knock on the door.

How annoying. Alice hoped it wasn't one of Daniel's cronies from the Parish County Council. Another custom, which she still found hugely irritating, was the frequency with which locals simply turned up on the doorstep instead of ringing to see if it was convenient.

"I'll get it," called out Daniel, amidst Mungo's enthusiastic barking.

She bent down to open the top right door of the Aga to check on the fish pie that she'd made earlier, using salmon from the harbour shop. The cheesy top layer was bubbling nicely. Hurry up, she thought, listening to the voices at the front door.

"Alice."

Daniel's voice had various tones to it – most of which she had learned to read during their married life. This one had an edge to it, which normally accompanied a discovery of an unpleasant variety. The time when he'd discovered a rolled-up cigarette in their son's bedroom, just before Garth had embarked on the second gap year, had been a case in point.

"Alice, there's someone here who wants to talk to you."

Daniel's voice preceded his entry into the kitchen. Someone was behind him. A tall man with neatly cut dark hair, wearing a uniform. Alice's mouth went dry as she took in the helmet under his arm. For a minute, she was eighteen again.

"Don't you dare call the police," her mother had said. *"Don't you dare."*

The visitor was holding out his hand for a handshake. "Sorry to bother you in the evening. My name is PC Black. Paul Black. I wonder if I might have a word."

Horrified, Alice glanced at Daniel who showed no sign of leaving. Any possibility of pretending that this was a parking offence of some kind or even a potential client (might a policeman be interested in mending broken china?) was hopeless in his presence.

"What's all this about, Alice?" asked Daniel, in a low voice.

"I'm not sure," she said faintly, desperately hoping for some last-minute reprieve. Perhaps he really *was* here for a parking misdemeanour, although she couldn't recall one. Once, Alice had been caught parking on a double yellow line for all of two minutes while she'd nipped into the chemist to get something for a teething Garth. The resulting ticket had shamed her into never doing it again.

Right now, Paul Black was looking at her intently. He had very blue eyes, she noticed irrelevantly. So blue, they should surely belong to a woman. His hair matched his name. At any other time, she'd have found this intriguing.

"I've been told that you might be a possible witness in the park case," he said. His voice was gravelly-deep and reassuring; rather like an articulate presenter she secretly admired on the radio whom her husband despised for his political beliefs. He also had the kind of weather-beaten skin, she noticed, that suggested a man who surfed or walked a lot. An explorer with a strong, rugby nose rather than a policeman.

There was a similarity too with a dark-haired Steve McQueen crossed with one of the old Bonds. And there was something about those almost boyish features, despite his age (forty-something at a guess) which reminded her of Gordon.

"Rubbish," snorted Daniel. "she didn't see anything. Did you, Alice?"

No, she was about to say. But then those blue eyes fixed on hers and there was something about them – so clear and penetrating – that the only possible answer was to tell the truth.

"Yes," she said, with a clarity that reminded her of the day she had said her wedding vows to Daniel. Her voice had rung out in the stone church, in direct comparison with her groom's quiet measured reply.

His face had been steady then. Trusting. Ready to shoulder the responsibilities that marriage would bring. Ignorant of the emotional baggage that his new wife was bringing with her. Now, however, Daniel's eyes registered shock. His forehead was wrinkled with disbelief. His hands, she suddenly noticed, were clenched at his side. Small, even though he was quite a tall man. Neat. Confused.

"You told me you hadn't seen anything," he said, in a steely tone.

Mungo, as if sensing his distress, got out of his basket and plodded across the kitchen floor, eyes fixed on his master as if to say: "I'm on *your* side here".

Alice found herself picking up the cup she had been mending, putting it down again, and then picking it up again. The repair was almost invisible; only she and its owner would know the crack was there unless an expert was present.

Just like her body.

"I was embarrassed," she said at last. "That sort of thing makes me …"

She stopped, aware of Daniel's tight expression. An image of their two separate beds, pushed together to look as though they were one but each with their own tucked in sheets, came into her head.

"That sort of thing makes me feel rather awkward," she continued lamely. The policeman's clear blue eyes seemed to flicker momentarily. Sympathy perhaps? Or curiosity. Or maybe nothing. Perhaps she'd just imagined it. What had he said his name was? Paul Black. That was it. It sounded clean cut. Memorable. Able to tell right from wrong even if those around him fudged the boundaries.

"How did you know?" Alice asked, leaning against the Aga for its warmth. She began to shake, despite the fact that it was unusually hot. Hadn't she been complaining for weeks that the Aga made the kitchen stuffy and that they really ought to get a conventional oven as well, just for the summer months?

"Someone saw you." The policeman glanced down at his notes. "A bike rider who thought she recognised you."

What bad luck. "Then she's a witness too."

"Unfortunately not. She, like you, was embarrassed about coming forward but it turns out that she didn't actually see what …"

He paused for a minute.

"… See what happened. But she did think, from your location, that you might have witnessed more."

Location? The use of such a distant, official word, disappointed her. Such official jargon didn't seem to marry with those sky-blue eyes which were pinning hers down again, as though seeing right through her.

"So it was this woman who reported it then?"

"Not exactly." PC Black gave a wry half shake of the head. "We had an anonymous tip-off about ten minutes earlier. However, the caller used a pay as you go and we can't trace it." Those blue eyes were fixed on hers again. If this had been a social situation, Alice might have imagined he was attracted to her. If only he knew.

"So you see, Mrs Honeybun, you are our only witness."

There was a pause during which Alice almost wanted to giggle. When she'd first met Daniel and he'd told her what his surname was, she had shot him a 'you can't be serious' grin. Later, when he'd proposed, she actually wondered if she could bring herself to live with such a name (so quaintly old-fashioned and yet suggestive at the same time) for the rest of her life.

Now, more than ever, it seemed highly inappropriate.

"I can't tell you how important that is," continued PC Black. "The man in question, Mrs Honeybun …"

Spontaneously, she interrupted. "Please. Call me Alice."

Daniel's eyebrows rose but she didn't care. She was in too deep now.

"The suspect, Alice, is a well-known character around here. He preys on young girls – usually rather naive ones – by giving them drugs so he can take advantage of them. Slippery sort. Until now, we've never had a witness."

He shrugged. "We can't force you to give a statement. But I would urge you to give it serious thought." His eyes glanced at the pictures of Garth on the kitchen dresser, studded amongst china cups and plates and hand-written invitations to dinner which now seemed inconsequential. "I don't know if you have a daughter but, if you do, imagine what it would be like if she had been taken advantage of …"

"That's quite enough." Daniel's voice cut in. "This is emotional blackmail. If my wife doesn't want to give evidence, that's up to her. Besides, I'm not at all sure you ought to be telling us all this. Isn't it confidential?"

A daughter. If she had a daughter …

Alice's mind went back to the day Garth had been born. How grateful she had been at the time that he hadn't been a girl. Thank God, she had breathed to himself. A boy would never, ever, have to go through what she had.

So why did she still occasionally yearn for a daughter who would have the guts to defend herself? To do what she had failed to do. She could have taught her. Trained her. Made her strong. Victoria. A daughter who would be everything she wasn't.

"It's all right," she heard herself say before Paul Black could say any more. Instinctively, she knew that he probably shouldn't have told them about the man and the drugs and the underage girl. But equally, she could see why he had done it.

33

This was her chance now, Alice told herself. To stand up and be counted. To claim back what was rightfully the girl's. Innocence. Not in terms of sex because that was too late. But to take the moral high ground. The earth that had been ripped from between her own feet all those years ago.

"If I do give a statement," she asked, deliberately not looking at Daniel, "will you give me protection? I don't want a brick through our window."

She tried to make it sound like a joke but secretly hoped this man would understand what she really meant. I don't want someone leaping on top of me in the dark and trying to rape or kill me.

He was nodding. "We will."

"How can you say that?" demanded Daniel angrily. "If my wife has to go to court to give evidence, this man will see her from the dock. He and his friends might track her down. And all in defence of some slut."

Alice's legs turned to jelly. Gripping the back of the kitchen chair to steady herself, she forced herself to look at Paul Black's face. It was tight with anger.

"I'm sorry you think that way. Regarding your concerns over security, it is possible that your wife would not have to go to court at all if we are able to tell the defence we have a witness. The hope is that the man in question will then plead guilty."

If. Maybe. Do this and you will be all right. Refuse and I will tell your parents you've been a bad girl. Slut … slut …

"I'll do it." Alice's voice sliced through the taunting words in her head. "Would you like me to come down to the station with you?"

There was a brief flicker of surprise. After what he'd just said, he seemed more like a Paul Black than a PC Black. More human. He knew, she thought gratefully. He knew she was different from her husband.

"We could take the statement here, if you like." He glanced at the Victorian pine kitchen table with its turned legs and aged knots that spoke of an earlier time when wars had been waging; long before her own.

Here? Amidst the green and cream trays, each neatly laid for a TV fish pie supper? Not of course, that she had an appetite any more: a feeling which she suspected that her husband shared from the look of distaste on his face. *Slut ... slut.* She knew it. Despite his words through the years, that was really what he thought of her too.

But Paul Black was already taking out a pile of papers and pen from his briefcase. Somehow she hadn't expected a policeman to carry a bag that looked more like a civil servant's. "Mind if we sit down? I'd like to start at the beginning. What did you see first?"

She could remember as if it had happened that morning. "They were sitting on the bench. A young girl with long wavy, auburn hair. I noticed that because it stood out. Rather pre-Raphaelite if you know what I mean."

"One of my favourite periods, actually." So he understood art too! The discovery gave her confidence. It was always easier to talk to people who liked the same things. Just as it was easy to grow a wall between you and someone who didn't.

"The man," she continued, "appeared a bit older."

"What colour hair?"

"Black. I think." Alice felt hot with confusion and embarrassment. "Then the girl stood up and moved as if in slow motion to a hedge. He followed her. She ... she bent down. I ... I thought she was putting a plaster on his knee ..."

Sweating, she glanced up at her husband. Daniel's face was dark. "You don't have to do this, Alice."

The policeman's hand stopped. Disappointed. As though she'd personally let him down.

"*You want to do this, Alice.*" That's what the other man had said to her all those years ago. "*I can tell. You want to do this.*"

"I want to do it," she said. Quietly. Firmly. "Please Daniel. Do you mind leaving us alone for a bit?"

FOUR

The steps outside the shopping centre were cold to sit on. Hard too. Her bottom would have ached if it hadn't been so numb. Funny really. When Kayleigh had been younger, she'd rather fancied the idea of going camping like those clean, smiley families you saw on telly adverts. But now, after spending her whole first night outside, without any shelter apart from a bit of the shopping centre roof overhead, she'd gone well off the idea.

"Ought to be here in the bleeding winter," sniffed a girl on the step below, poking her head out from a ripped sleeping bag. Kayleigh had been eying the latter with envy all night. It seemed like the height of luxury. Yet only three nights ago, she'd had her own bed. Even the thin wall dividing her from the 'No, Ron' sounds now seemed preferable to this.

Kayleigh's stomach began to rumble. So loud that the girl on the steps below, with the pink hair and black baggy combat trousers, heard it. "Hungry, are yer? Have to wait a bit till breakfast, you will."

She began to feel more hopeful. "Does someone bring something round then?"

The girl began to laugh so raucously that it turned into a throaty cough; exacerbated perhaps by the fag she had in her hand. ('Exacerbated' was a word she'd used in the essay for Mr Brown that would probably, she realised with a pang, never get handed to him now.) "You're a right one, aren't you? But in a way, I suppose you're right. Play your cards right and someone will give you summat to eat but you've got to wait until this place opens."

She jerked her patchily shaved head up towards the shopping centre. "Fridays are a good day. You get a lot of women here. The posh sort. They're the best. I got a fiver from one last week. Better than the bitch who palmed me off with a bleeding chocolate croissant."

"Didn't you want the food?" asked Kayleigh, puzzled. She'd give anything right now to have a bite of a chocolate croissant. The very thought made her drool with hunger.

The girl snorted with derision. "It can't bloody well buy you gear, can it?" Then her face seemed to soften slightly. "Here." She handed up the tail-end of her cigarette. "Take a drag if you like. Make you feel a bit better."

Kayleigh, hesitated but only for a minute. When Callum had given her a fag years ago, she hadn't been able to stop choking. "No thanks."

The girl's face hardened. "Suit yourself. You're new, aren't you?" She gave a hollow laugh, followed by another coughing fit. "You'll soon learn."

Learn? The only place where Kayleigh wanted to learn was school. This time last week, she'd been getting ready for school; eager to see Mr Brown and finish her poetry essay. How was it possible, wondered Kayleigh, wrapping her thin arms around her knees and rocking back and forth to try and get some heat pulsing through her veins, for life to change so fast?

Closing her eyes, she allowed the events of the last few days to run through her mind. It was how some writers wrote, Mr Brown said. They saw their lives as a film. One scene after the other. The trick was to mix the good with the bad. That way, you got your reader hooked.

It had hurt quite a bit, like Marlene had said. But it had felt really cool at the same time. "I'll look after you," Frankie had said just before he had got on top of her.

The grass felt soft. Softer than her own mattress at home. His lips were soft too. Much softer than she had imagined.

Her body was floating. Kayleigh had never learned to swim. Mum had always said there was no bloody need when you lived in a tower block. But she felt as though she was swimming now. And the lights! They were everywhere. Blue and pink, silver and gold. Bursting like fireworks all around.

It had been like that ever since Frankie had given her that tablet. Were the two connected? Maybe. Maybe not. Perhaps the lights were in her head because she was finally having sex.

"Is it wrong to have it off, sir, when you're not yet sixteen?" a girl in her English class had asked Mr Brown a few weeks ago.

There had been a general titter but it hadn't been a totally daft question, Kayleigh had thought. They were doing *Romeo and Juliet* after all and the heroine (not to be confused with 'heroin', as one of the boys had suggested), was still really young.

"Legally, it is." Joey Brown was looking out of the window when he spoke. But then he turned and looked at her. She could swear it, even though it was the other girl that had asked the question. "But some people would argue differently if they were really in love."

Right now, on the grass, Mr Brown didn't seem so important. It was Frankie, she wanted. Frankie who was moving up and down inside her and telling her that she was beautiful. Beautiful? With her ginger hair and freckles? It made her feel like a princess.

It would be all right, now. Kayleigh knew that for a certainty. He wouldn't let Ron try it on again. He'd tell Mum what a scumbag her bloke was. And if Mum wouldn't have her back home, she and Frankie could set up their own place together. Maybe one day, they might even be able to afford one of those amazing houses on the side of the park with proper drives for a car.

The thought struck her, through the lights and the music – which had come from nowhere – that she didn't know what kind of job Frankie had. When she'd asked, in the car on the way over, the others had roared with laughter as though she'd said something really funny but stupid at the same time.

Kayleigh hadn't liked that. It was one of the reasons why she'd taken the tablet that Frankie had offered on the bench. She hadn't wanted to look daft. It was also why she'd done what he had told her to by the hedge. And she'd been right, hadn't she? Look at Frankie now, gasping and calling out. She'd got him. Kayleigh felt a wonderful sense of power spreading through her.

The music got louder. Slowly, Kayleigh realised it wasn't music at all. It was a siren. God knows how she could have got that wrong. You heard it enough times every day on the estate. The fireworks were beginning to die down in her head now. As for Frankie, he was pulling himself out of her and scrambling into his jeans.

"Where are you going?" she called out, suddenly frightened.

"Leg it."

For a minute, she thought he was asking her to do something with her legs again.

"Show me."

Frankie threw her a look she hadn't seen before. It was like the glance Mum gave her when she didn't want her around. "You having me on? For fuck's sake, Kayleigh. Just leg it."

Then she realised. Run. He wanted her to run. But why? Hadn't she just been giving him a good time? Her heart sank. Maybe she'd been hopeless after all. Marlene always said that the first time wasn't much cop. You had to practise.

"You were my first, Frankie," she called out as he began to run. "I'm sorry. It will be better for you next time, I promise."

But he was off. Skimming over the grass, hanging on to his shoes, past a woman with a bike who was staring at them. Nosy cow, just like the other woman with the dog. Miserably, Kayleigh looked around for her clothes. Where had they gone? Then she became aware of someone standing over her. Bleeding hell, it was a cop. With pink lipstick.

"Put this round you." She was holding out a blanket. "Go on. Cover yourself up. Quickly, before someone sees you."

Her voice was thin and scratchy, like the blanket. She was speaking into a machine hanging from her pocket now. Despite her blurred state, Kayleigh wondered if it was a Dictaphone. Mr Brown had one of those. They were great for writers, he said, if you wanted to remember something when you were walking along. Mr Brown was writing a novel. He had told her that once, when she'd gone into school early one day and found him scribbling away at his desk.

But the policewoman wasn't writing a novel. Not unless it was about Kayleigh's life. The thought made her giggle. The more she tried to stop, the worse it got. The air was coming out of her in big spurts like she was belching, just as Ron was always doing.

"Think all this is funny, do you?" The woman glared at her. Thin nose, observed Kayleigh, but cool, long eyelashes. You needed to notice things like that, Mr Brown was always saying. "Do you realise you've just committed a criminal offence?"

Kayleigh froze. If there were two words that she knew, it was those. The very ones that the cops had used when they'd come for Callum last summer and found stuff under his bed; including a special hole inside his trainers.

"How?" she demanded but her tone felt thick and the word didn't come out very well.

"How?" The policewoman pointed to her. "Look at you. Stark naked under that blanket. Do you think it's all right to have sex in a public place?"

"It seemed OK at the time," Kayleigh heard herself saying. Suddenly she didn't feel like laughing any more.

"Gave you something, did he?" asked the policewoman, a bit kinder this time. "To make you do it?"

Briefly, she hesitated. If she told this woman about the pill, Frankie might get into trouble. Then he wouldn't be able to look after her. They wouldn't be able to have kids and live in a nice house overlooking the park with a proper drive for a car.

"You can tell me," said the policewoman. But there was an edge about her voice which Kayleigh didn't trust.

No comment. That's what her half-brother had said when they arrested him.

"No comment," said Kayleigh.

The policewoman's face hardened. "Don't try and protect him, Trust me. He's not worth it."

How did she know? Had she slept with him too? Just then, another policeman arrived, breathing fast like he was out of breath. "Got him. He's in the van."

Kayleigh's heart sank. They'd arrested Frankie? Now he'd think she'd split on him.

"What's your name, love?" The second policeman was talking to her more nicely than the first.

"Kayleigh," she said, reluctantly. There didn't seem much point in hiding stuff; not now the police were here and the fireworks had faded and Frankie was nicked in the van.

"How old are you?" he added.

His blue eyes were hypnotic. His hair as black as Frankie's. "Fifteen."

There was a sharp in-drawing of breath from the woman. "We've nailed him then. We've finally nailed him."

What had she meant, Kayleigh kept wondering as they put her in the back of the car, still wrapped up in the blanket. (Her own stuff, they said, had to go in a special bag for 'evidence' even though she tried telling them they really belonged to her friend Marlene so they mustn't muck them up.)

But she didn't like to make a fuss in case it got Frankie into more trouble. Where was he, she wanted to ask, as the car stopped outside a police station. It wasn't like their local one where her half-brother had been taken. This one had a view of the sea behind.

Someone gave her a cup of tea in a proper mug that had an outline of Kate and William on it with the words Royal Wedding written below. The rim had a chip. Kayleigh wished she'd nodded when asked if she took sugar but she was scared of being a nuisance. It might annoy them even more.

She was a good girl. Everyone knew that. Her mother told her that all the time, especially when she shut herself in her room to give Mum and Ron some 'privacy'. But she'd said it in a way that suggested that only saddos were 'good girls'.

"Come in here, Kayleigh, can you?" said someone else. It was the same man from the park with those very clear blue eyes that looked at her as though he either fancied her rotten or could see right through her. He opened a door that said 'Interview Room' on it and then allowed her to go through first like a real gentleman.

Either way, there was no way she could hide the truth. Not with eyes boring through her like that. The door opening had made a difference too. Mr Brown let women through first. She'd seen him doing it the other week with one of the women science teachers. It had impressed her. Looked like it had impressed the teacher too.

"I'd like you to tell me, Kayleigh, exactly what happened."

So she did; least, as far as she could remember.

When she'd finished, she could swear she saw tears in the policeman's eyes. Maybe he was a bloody good actor like her dad had been. At least that's what Mum was always saying.

"So he didn't force you?"

She shook her head.

"But he gave you a pill?"

She nodded.

He glanced down again at his pad of paper and she began to wish she hadn't told him all that stuff in the car about growing up without a dad. "Life hasn't been easy for you, Kayleigh, has it?"

A large lump formed in her throat.

"It's been OK."

His fingers played with the pen in his hand. They were long thin fingers and the nails were clipped quite short. Kayleigh glanced down at her own which bore traces of the black varnish that Marlene had lent her. When she had enough money, she was going to buy some remover pads.

"I'm beginning to wonder if we've done the right thing." He seemed to be talking to himself. "We've called your mum. She'd coming down here with your stepdad."

Kayleigh felt fear mixed with anger. "How did you find her?"

Those eyes held hers. "Her number was on your phone in your pocket."

"He's not my stepdad."

"Really?" There was a slight frown. "Your mum called him her husband."

Kayleigh heard her voice rise. "She says that about all of them."

Then she stopped. Bloody hell. That was her mother's voice outside. Now she'd had it.

"We can't just let you go," the policeman said gently. "You could be charged, you know. But if you promise to go back quietly with your mum and not get into any more trouble, we might manage to keep your record clean."

Those clean fingers were still firmly clasped round the pencil which he was tapping now on the paper. Not writing anything. Almost stabbing the words he'd just written. Least, that's what it looked like. "There's just one thing. We'll be using your statement to testify against Frankie Miller."

Miller? Was that his surname? It had a nice ring to it. Frankie Miller. Kayleigh Miller. It was a good game to give a kid. Not something stupid like *Long* which made the boys snigger at school.

Long face. Long ass.

"But you still might have to go to court if he refuses to plead guilty."

Go to court? Face Frankie, who would think she'd grassed on him? Tell the court what happened? "But it was a private thing," she said urgently. "Between him and us."

The blue eyes went cold. "Not when it's in a park. It's illegal, Don't you see, Kayleigh? Some kid might have seen you. You might have traumatised him – or her – for life."

Then he stopped as though he'd said too much. "Just do what I say, Kayleigh. Be a good girl. Or we'll have to hold you here."

"Mum will kill me," she wanted to say. But she stopped. Maybe going home was better than being put in a cell.

She was wrong. As soon as they got back, Mum started. *How could you do something so stupid? If you want to have sex (and God knows you've waited long enough – I was beginning to think there was something wrong with you), couldn't you have the decency to do it behind a bush instead of out in the open?*

But it was Ron who she was really scared of. He'd be there, she knew. Ready.

Sure enough, the following morning, when she came out of

the shower, there he was; his white floppy belly protruding over his boxers. "So I'm not good enough for you, am I? You'd rather have some druggie instead?"

Swiftly, Kayleigh pulled out the kitchen knife she'd taken into the shower with her. "Don't you dare talk about Frankie like that. And if you try to touch me," she hissed, "I'll kill you."

"What's going on?"

It was Mum, all pink-faced in her see-through market nightie that showed her breasts, heavy and drooping. It wasn't the first time Kayleigh had seen them and each time, she fervently hoped her own wouldn't end up like that.

"Your daughter was about to stab me," roared Ron.

"Only because he was trying it on with me," said Kayleigh nervously.

"No." Mum's face crumpled. "You didn't, did you, Ron?"

Kayleigh almost felt sorry for her.

"'Course I bleeding didn't." He pointed to the knife, still in her hands. "Can't you see what she's got there? It's not the first time either." Then he waved his bulky arm. "Look at these cuts. She did that yesterday but I didn't want to upset you."

"Yes, because you tried to touch me up then too."

Mum was looking from one to the other. With a horrible sinking feeling, Kayleigh realised she didn't know which one to believe. "I'm telling the truth, Mum," she whispered.

Ron slammed his hand down on the kitchen counter. "Fine. Believe the little bitch. I'll just go and then who do you think will pay the bills or shag you?"

He made to storm past but Mum caught him. "Please, Ron, stay."

Then she looked at Kayleigh as though she didn't know her. "You'd better pack your stuff."

Surely Mum couldn't really be saying this?

"But you promised the police that I'd be at home."

Mum faltered. "That was before this."

Ron shot her a triumphant look.

"Just for a few days," whispered Mum when she came in to Kayleigh's room with some plastic bags to put her bits in. "He'll have calmed down by then."

45

If she'd had a dad, Kayleigh told herself, she could have gone to him.

If Callum wasn't Inside, she could have gone to him too. "I might only be your half-brother," he'd yelled out when they'd taken him away, "but I'm always here for you as long as you're here for me."

If she wasn't scared that Frankie might be mad at her, she'd have tried to visit Callum, wherever they'd put him. But Mum wouldn't tell her. "That one's a bad influence," she sniffed. Mum, Kayleigh knew, was just jealous of the special relationship she had with her brother.

Still, there was always Marlene.

It took her friend a while to come to the door and when she did, her face was cold as she took in Kayleigh's carrier bags in each hand. "Don't tell me you want to kip here."

"They've thrown me out. Ron says I tried to have it off with him."

She'd expected Marlene to laugh but instead she stood there, crossing her arms on the second floor landing of the flats. "And did you?"

"'Course not." Kayleigh couldn't believe what she was hearing.

"Well you did with Frankie and now he's copped it."

A horrible tightness crawled over her. "What happened?"

"They've nicked him. Bastards wouldn't even give him bail."

Kayleigh was a bit hazy when it came to prison procedure. Hadn't Callum pleaded innocent? But he'd still got eighteen months even though she had jumped up in court when they'd read out the verdict and screamed that he was a good, kind brother who didn't deserve it.

"What does that mean?"

"He's got to stay Inside till the hearing, stupid." Marlene frowned and Kayleigh could see a large angry zit above one of her brows. "My Pete blames you. It was your statement, apparently, that helped to nail him. There was a bleeding witness too."

Poor Frankie. It wasn't fair. He'd been carried away, just

like her. He loved her too. She knew it. As soon as he got out, she'd explained how the policeman's eyes had made her talk and then it would be all right again.

Hopefully.

Below them, some kids were shouting something and then pointing up at her. "Can I stay? Just for a bit?"

Marlene looked hesitant. "I dunno. Pete would kill me but he's away for a few days on some job."

"So he's living here now?"

Her friend nodded, rather smugly. "Mum's new bloke has got a place of his own so she said I could stay here. Up to me who comes round." Then her smile went tight again. "You'll have to clear out before he gets back, though. Blames you, does Pete. Pity you didn't keep quiet, isn't it?"

Kayleigh went to school for the next two days though Marlene didn't bother. She felt sick, she said, and indeed she did look a bit rough. 'Course, Kayleigh offered to stay at home and look after her but Marlene said she was better off alone and 'sides, she could watch telly.

At least it gave Kayleigh a chance to explain what had happened to her essay to Mr Brown. "My stepdad tore it up after … after we had an argument."

Mr Brown flicked back his long brown fringe and gave her a lovely sympathetic look that made her feel warm inside. "Everything all right? Only the head told me that social services had been in touch. I gather there was some trouble." His voice dropped. "In a park."

Kayleigh went beetroot red. Now he'd think she was a slag like the others. "I'm OK," she said quickly.

Mr Brown nodded although he didn't look convinced. "Good. Glad to hear it. Let me know if you need to talk sometime, won't you?"

She remembered his words when she got back to Marlene's and found the door locked. "Go away," hissed her friend through the flap. "Pete's back early and if he sees you, he'll be mad with both of us."

"But I haven't got anywhere to go!"

"Try your mum again."

She didn't want to but what choice did she have?

This was funny. Her key wasn't working. In desperation, she rang the bell. No answer though she swore she could see a curtain twitching.

Now what? Maybe the local library? After all, she had an essay to write tonight on how poetry could make you feel happy. For a couple of hours, Kayleigh lost herself in some stuff written by someone called Carol Ann Duffy. She'd like to meet her one day. She said just what Kayleigh was feeling inside, but with better words.

"I'm sorry," said the librarian's voice just when Kayleigh was right in the middle of her third page. "But we're about to close."

Her words filled Kayleigh with panic. For a moment, she considered telling the librarian (a nice woman though she didn't care much for that maroon cardigan) that she didn't have anywhere to go. But then they might take her back to the police station. So, picking up her bag, she walked towards the automatic door in a way that suggested she was going home to an ordinary family where they all sat round the telly with trays on their knees instead of eating chips out of bags.

Instead she went to the shopping centre where she wandered round for another hour, looking at all the clothes she couldn't afford to buy and dreaming of the places she'd wear them too. Those leggings would look good at a Great Cynics gig. And that skirt would be really cool when Frankie got out of prison and they could go out to a posh restaurant.

Kayleigh had never been out to dinner in her life but she had imagined it so many times that it felt like she had. 'Vivid imagination,' her reports always said. Was that a good or bad thing?

"We're shutting now," said one of the security guards, sharply.

Ten o'clock. There had to be somewhere to go.

"Need somewhere to kip?" said a voice.

It was a girl with pink hair and baggy black combats. "Me too. If we wait round the back till they shut up, we can sleep on the steps. It's not too bad in the summer."

And that, thought Kayleigh ruefully, was how she'd ended up here.

Her new friend was wrong about the breakfast. There were plenty of women going past but not one had offered to give her some money. She should have gone into school but Kayleigh felt so cold and weak with hunger that she didn't have the energy.

"Here, have some of mine." The girl in black combats tore off a piece of pizza and handed it to her. "Go on. It's fresh. Well almost. I skipped it."

Skipped it?

"You know. Got it from the bin outside the pizza place. There's boxes of stuff there. Most of it untouched."

"Does it ... I mean could it have a pill inside?"

The girl stared at her. "You're weird. Why would it do that?"

Kayleigh thought back to the pill on Frankie's tongue. "I don't know."

Then the girl leaped to her feet. "I'm going to have a wash."

Her heart leaped. "There's a bathroom here?"

The girl laughed. "Sure. It's massive. The local leisure centre. You can have hot showers if you've got £4.20."

Kayleigh thought of the empty purse in her school bag. "Maybe see you later." Never admit your weaknesses, Callum always said.

She closed her eyes after that. It was easier. You could shut everything out and dream. Maybe if she stayed here long enough, her father might come along. You heard of coincidences happening like that. Someone would have told him what had gone on or maybe he got someone to spy on her to make sure she was all right. He'd save her and take her back to his home and ...

"Excuse me."

Kayleigh was suddenly aware of a tall, very elegant woman bending over her with long, blonde hair tied in a loose knot. Bloody hell. Just look at those beige trousers and cream linen jacket. Must have cost a bleeding fortune.

"Excuse me," repeated the woman, staring at Kayleigh's hair and then the bluebird tattoo on her shoulder. "But aren't you the girl from the park?"

FIVE

After she'd made her statement to the policeman with the clear blue eyes, Alice had expected Daniel to have had a go at her. Not physically of course because he wasn't that kind of man or she would never have married him. But verbally.

If words had been weapons, Daniel would have been an excellent swordsman. Came with the job, she'd always told herself. An academic tended to choose his sentences carefully, like picking exactly the right oranges from a supermarket shelf: another of her husband's irritating traits.

"*Why didn't you tell me you had seen the whole thing happening?*" he might have asked.

Or "*Why don't we talk any more?*"

Maybe "*Were you involved? Is that why you kept quiet?*"

Instead, anger made her get in first. "You called me a slut," she hissed, as soon as the door had closed behind Paul Black.

He'd stared at her as though she was mad. "I did not. I might have said the girl was one but ..."

"There's no difference!" The words burned out of her mouth. "Don't you understand? It's how you really see me."

"Alice, please."

She pushed him away as he approached. "Don't. Don't touch me."

Instantly, he stood back as if burned. "I'm not going through all that again," he said quietly. "Nor am I going to ask why you felt able to tell the policeman about the events in the park even though you haven't told me. So I will wait until you are ready to explain in your own time."

Then he had glanced at his watch: a rather superior type that she had bought him for a significant birthday a year earlier, hoping that the quality would make up for the holes in their marriage. "I'm going to walk Mungo now and then have an early night."

Sometimes they both took the dog on his last walk of the day; usually down to the sea front. If it was a filthy night, there was no need to talk (such a relief). And if it was clear enough to admire the moonlight glinting on the water, they could hold a neutral conversation about how lucky they were to live in such a lovely place.

But that night, there was no such invitation. Instead, Alice was left behind in the kitchen to freeze the fish pie, which now neither of them felt like having, and wonder exactly what she had done.

She was a witness! Well, a potential one. If the boy in the park refused to admit his 'crime', it would be tried at court and she, Alice, would have to go in the box and describe out loud exactly what she had said on the statement.

The horror of doing so made her blush hotly all over. What would people in the court say when she explained that initially, she'd thought the young girl had bent over to put a plaster on the boy's knee.

But it was true.

She had.

"You don't have to give a statement," Paul Black had explained (it felt odd to call a policeman by his surname, let alone a first name too.) "But if you don't, there's a strong possibility that the man will get away with it again."

When he'd put it that way, she'd had no choice. If someone had been there for her, all those years ago, Alice told herself, she might have been capable of living a normal life right now.

Meanwhile, she couldn't stop worrying about the young girl. "What will happen to her?" she'd asked, before Paul Black had left. "She won't be arrested, will she?"

"Possibly. Possibly not. Sometimes, if a girl is underage, like this one, she's allowed to go back home as long as she has someone to live with."

The thought of a fifteen-year-old *not* having someone to live with was almost too shocking to contemplate. When her son had been that age, he'd been barely able to get out of bed for school without her nagging and cajoling. Daniel had accused her of over-protecting him and he was probably right. Perhaps that was why Garth had never settled.

"There are plenty of girls out there like that, you know," the policeman had added as she'd seen him to the door. Then he'd glanced around at the original watercolours on the wall; the rich red and blue rug on the polished floor and the Wedgwood bowl on the mahogany table.

Clearly he thought she came from another world.

"I know," she wanted to add fiercely. "I was one of them."

The words were so loud in her head that for a moment, she wondered if she had actually said them. Indeed, he had been so kind and understanding when she'd faltered over the embarrassing parts of the statement, that Alice felt closer to him than she had done for a while to anyone. The temptation now, to tell Paul Black about her own life, was so strong that she had to hold herself back.

After all, not even Daniel knew everything.

So he had gone. And then her husband had gone out with the dog, only to return and go straight to bed. When she had finally crept in an hour later, he had turned away; leaving her to lie motionless, staring up at the ceiling and wondering what the hell she had done.

A witness! Until now, it was a term she had simply read about in the paper or heard on the radio. This was new territory. One which she had never expected to find herself in. The effect was uncomfortable yet inexplicably exciting at the same time.

As for the irony, that was irrefutable. Was someone playing a trick on her, wondered Alice, sitting up in the dark with pillows propped behind her after giving up on sleep. Was some unknown force providing her with the chance to be strong in a way that she should have been all those years ago?

Alice was tempted, later that week, to tell her friend Janice over their usual weekly game of doubles. Tennis at Ladies' Morning was invariably more of a social occasion than a competitive match. Often they all ended up chatting over the net about who was doing what. Frequently they forgot the score.

Not surprisingly, the conversation still centred around what was being called the Park Sex Scandal. If this had happened in London, Alice told herself, hitting a particularly weak backhand, no one would have thought twice about it. But for some reason, the story had actually made it into a one-paragraph item in *The Times*.

"Seaway, recently voted amongst the top ten beauty spots in Britain, was thrown into uproar by a couple who had open-air sex in the park during the afternoon."

"Why bother writing about us?" asked Alice, nervously.

One of the other 'girls', as they called themselves, piped up. "Apparently it's the silly season for news, when not much is going on. That's what my husband's cousin says." She blushed. "He works for a news agency and was staying with us when it all happened."

So that explained it. Shakily, Alice hit a shot straight into the net. "Sorry," she said to Janice. "I'm not concentrating."

Janice giggled. "Nor me. I keep thinking about that couple. Everyone criticises them but I wouldn't mind a bit of spontaneity now and then. The last time Brian and I did it outside was on our honeymoon." She brushed past her on her way back to the baseline. "We actually did it on the beach! Seemed frightfully daring. Since then, we've always had a bit of a penchant for sex in the open. That's why Brian bought a summer house for our twentieth anniversary."

She waited, clearly waiting for a mutual confidence in return. What could she say, Alice asked herself? There was no way she wanted to tell Janice that she and Daniel hadn't had sex since Garth was conceived.

Thankfully Monica had started to serve on the other side ("Are you two ready or are you going to natter all day?") and she was saved from having to reply.

As for that statement, several nights of not sleeping had made her wonder if she should have made it in the first place. It hadn't been fair of Paul Black to emotionally blackmail her like that: to declare, more or less, that if she didn't give evidence the young man might get away with it again and another girl could be hurt.

Maybe, Alice told herself uneasily, she had done the right thing. But at what cost? Daniel was hardly speaking to her because she'd lied *"although why I still don't know"*. No point in telling him that she didn't fully know herself; it was far more complicated than that. Just as bad, everyone else would be asking exactly the same question if – when? – the case came to court.

"Great shot," sang out Janice.

Alice always played well when she was upset. Maybe, she told herself, the best course of action was to ignore it. Hope the case didn't get that far. Paul Black had given her his number and promised he would let her know what happened. He'd also warned her that this could take 'weeks'.

In the meanwhile, she'd just do what she did best. Distract herself to stop thinking about the past.

Since that first china workshop, Alice had learned to channel any disappointments in life (Garth's reluctance to go to uni and Daniel's ever-increasing distant air) into the restoration of cups and bowls and saucers and anything else which had become smashed, often due to carelessness.

But this particular little rosebud cup had been one of her biggest challenges. The handle was a pretty curved shape which had taken a great deal of care and – she felt embarrassed to admit – a certain skill to reunite with its original resting place.

After returning from tennis, Alice checked it again. It certainly seemed firm enough. Ready to return to her client. The old lady was delighted when she rang. "Thank you so much, my dear. Yes, I'll be in this afternoon. Are you sure it's not too much trouble to drop it off?"

"It's all part of the service," she replied, glad to have the chance to get out of the house. Since the incident, as she called it in her head, its walls had begun to close in on her. She avoided the park, too, which felt sullied because of what had happened. Instead, she took Mungo for walks in the buttercup meadow on the hill, now that the beach was out of bounds for dogs until October.

Mrs Davies – or Joan as she was pressed to call her – insisted that Alice came in. "I've just put the kettle on, dear and besides, we can test it out, can't we?"

She held the cup lovingly in her hand. "It means a great deal to me, you know."

Alice felt the usual glow of pleasure. This wasn't the first time a client had told her this. It was only sensitive people like Joan Davies who went to the trouble and expense of having something mended. Others might just bin it with only a hint of regret. There had to be a link there with how you dealt with life's memories.

"So silly of me to drop it," continued the older woman, as she carefully measured out three teaspoons of loose tea into the pot. Her wrinkled hand, studded with liver spots, shook slightly. "But I was thinking of him, you see."

She said the 'him' bit as though Alice should know whom she meant.

"Your husband?"

The old lady shook her head. "Not Bernard, bless him. No. I'm talking about my first fiancé."

She looked straight at Alice with a direct gaze that reminded her of the policeman's. "Have you ever been in love? So badly that you can't eat or sleep?"

Alice thought back to a younger Daniel who had taken her out to dinner on their first date and escorted her back home, giving her a chaste kiss on the doorstep of her rented flat. There had never been any passion. No tingling of spines or goose-pimples down the arm.

If there had, she might have been too scared to have married him in case she got hurt again. Just as she'd been hurt by Gordon. Although whose fault was that …

"Not many people have," continued Joan Davies, who thankfully didn't seem to be expecting a reply. "But Gerald was different." Then she looked down at the little cup. "This was part of an engagement present. There was a whole set once but the rest got broken over the years. Thank you so much, my dear, for bringing it back to me."

What happened, Alice wanted to ask as they sipped their tea and talked of other things like the weather and that funny comedy on television that they both agreed was 'hysterical', even though Daniel thought it 'inane'.

Then, after Mrs Davies had paid her – something Alice always felt rather awkward about as she did it for the love rather than the money – she unexpectedly clutched Alice's hand with her own slim one. "I used to tell people, even my husband, that Gerald died. The truth was that he left me for someone else."

Alice was stunned. It seemed hard to equate this old lady with a young girl who had felt so humiliated that she had lied and kept a secret for all these years.

Then she took Alice's other hand, holding both at the same time. "Gerald wasn't really a gentleman, you know. But I didn't regret it for a moment." Her eyes shone. "He taught me things that my poor husband couldn't have imagined in a lifetime."

Were old people really meant to say things like that? Alice thought of her own mother, whose life revolved around the bridge club, and who had welcomed Daniel with open arms because "he will balance that silly imagination of yours".

Mrs Davies' eyes were looking more serious now. "If you ever get the chance, Alice, take it." Then she smiled knowingly. "Something tells me that you haven't found true love yet. No, don't say anything. I'm rather good at reading people's faces."

Then she reached up and kissed her cheek. "Bless you, my dear. And good luck."

The words rang round Alice's head all night. If you ever get the chance, take it. But what if you *did* have the chance and you couldn't take it because of what had happened to you in the past. Something so shameful that no one would believe you. Something that, every now and then, she wondered if she might have misinterpreted, just as her mother had insisted.

Had it just been in her head all those years ago?

Was it possible she'd misread the signs?

"You're up early," said Daniel, when she joined him for breakfast at 6.30. Even Mungo, who wasn't an early riser, was still in his basket by the Aga.

"I couldn't sleep. One slice or two?"

"Two please."

He seemed less distant this morning. More normal. Then again, it was always easier to talk to each other out of bed, rather than in it. Routines like the making of toast and topping up the butter dish were soothing. Reassuring. Normal.

"I'm sorry about ... about not telling you," she said, tentatively as they sat opposite each other at the table. "I was embarrassed, that's all."

Daniel continued spreading the butter on his toast. "That's all right."

"No, really. I don't want you thinking I hide anything else."

He was putting the spoon in the marmalade now, carefully taking care not to stain the red-and-white spotted tablecloth while still not looking at her. "It doesn't matter if you do. Not really."

His eyes lifted to hers finally. They were expressionless. "After all, it's not as though we have that kind of relationship any more, is it?"

Her mouth went dry. "What do you mean?"

Daniel pushed his chair back and got up. The consequential scrape on the quarry-stone tiles echoed the nerve-tingling apprehension in her head, "We're like a brother and sister who happen to have an almost grown-up child."

He said it in such a casual manner that she wondered if she had heard right. "No we're not ..."

"Alice." He took her hands in his briefly. The shock of the contact – unexpectedly warm yet cool at the same time – threw her. "It's all right. I've accepted it."

Never before had they been so open with each other. Daniel's cruel, candid words had the effect of ripping off a plaster, brutally, fiercely without warning, to reveal a festering wound underneath. Scared, she stared after his retreating back as he made his way into the hall where his briefcase waited.

"What about your toast?" she called out, realising as she did so, the banality of the question.

"I'm not hungry any more. Give it to Mungo."

Then he was gone, leaving her with so many thoughts and memories and fears rushing round her head, that she simply had to get out. The hills with the dog. And then maybe a trip to the shopping centre in Plymouth. Anything to distract her from the unsettling conversation that she and Daniel had just had.

It was easy to park at this time of the morning. The younger mums were all doing the school run. Older ones, forced into lives of their own, had gone back to work or were doing what she normally did. Playing tennis. Walking the dog. Making a hobby into a 'little job' that didn't interfere with the giving of dinner parties or weekend breaks now families were older and there were fewer financial obligations.

Money hadn't really been a problem for them, thought Alice slightly guiltily as she fished in her purse for some change for the car park machine. Moving out of London had enabled them to buy a bigger house and have some money left over. Her small inheritance from her father had helped too, although she would have given anything right now to have Dad around. Of all people, he was the one who had initially believed her story.

"Let me sort this out," he had declared. But then he had fallen ill – something that Mum had accused her of precipitating through 'stress'. It was a subject they never spoke of now.

Alice shook herself. Don't go down that road, she told herself. Distraction. That's what the counsellor had said: the one she had seen at university, before dropping out. And why not? Perhaps she would try on that blue dress again. The one she had seen the other day but not bought on the spot. That was her trouble, perhaps. Too careful. Unable to have the passionate affair that old Mrs Davies had. For a moment, the policeman's clear blue eyes came into her head. He had looked at her. Really looked at her.

Sure. Because he had wanted her to do what he said. Didn't they all?

Blue dress. Think of the blue dress. It would be perfect for Janice's forthcoming birthday barbecue. Locking the car, Alice headed for the shopping centre steps. The doors hadn't quite opened yet. There were people waiting. Other women like her, looking at their watches; even though they might have all the time in the world on their hands.

There were a couple of teenage kids too, whose filthy clothes and wild hair suggested they had been there all night. How awful. Poor things. What, she wondered, were the circumstances that had led to them spending a night out in the open?

Dear God, may Garth be all right. During their last Skype call, two weeks ago from Thailand, she'd asked him where he was staying. "On the beach, Mum. Don't freak out. Everyone does it."

Did they? It was all so different from her day when gap years were still new. Usually you went straight into a job or did VSO to help others – not lounge around the rest of the world, looking for yourself, as Daniel scathingly put it. Then she noticed one of the young women stretching out. There was a natural poise about her. An elegance which seemed at odds with the girl next to her with rougher, more common features.

The first girl looked almost ethereal despite the small silver stud in her lower lip. In a strange way, she reminded her of a gently freckled wood nymph or one of the figures in a pre-Raphaelite painting: a style that Alice adored. She was fiddling with her auburn dreadlocks (more like pale red-gold actually) as though trying to brush them out. As she did so, Alice noticed something on her neck and again on her shoulder. A pair of bluebirds.

Bluebirds. Just like the tattoo she had noticed that evening. *Don't let your imagination get the better of you, Alice.* Yet the hair was so distinctive! So too was that natural grace; that seemingly unconscious way of floating rather than moving, which Alice would have loved to have possessed herself.

"Excuse me," she said, hardly believing these words were coming out from her own mouth, "but aren't you the girl from the park?"

SIX

For a minute, Kayleigh wondered if the beautiful blonde woman leaning over her was an angel. They'd done angels last term when Mr Brown had told them about the Romantic poets. It had inspired her to borrow a book about them from the library and 'read more widely'; a phrase that her English teacher used quite a bit.

Angels didn't just belong to the fiction shelves, apparently. You could get them in real life. Some people swore by a Parking Angel who helped them find a space. Kayleigh found that hard to believe. Then again, she found it hard to imagine herself ever affording a car.

One book declared that everyone had a guardian angel who helped you in terms of trouble. All you had to do was think of it very hard and then ask it to visit you. Kayleigh had tried this when Mum came out of her room with a bigger shiner than usual but nothing happened.

Another angel book, which she took out at the same time, declared that there were loads of angels around, pretending to be ordinary people. Maybe this explained the woman bending over her now, smelling like the perfume counter at their local Boots where Marlene was always 'trying stuff out'.

But then she'd spoken. "Excuse me. But aren't you the girl from the park?"

The beautiful woman's words sent a shot of fear through her. She'd been recognised! All the humiliation and terror and hurt of that day came rushing back. Scrambling to her feet, Kayleigh made to take off but the woman put a hand on her arm. "Please

61

don't go. It's all right. I'm not going to call anyone. I just want to know if you're all right."

Glancing across the step, she saw that her new friend appeared to have gone. Good. So she hadn't heard. "I'm OK," she retorted, pulling her thin cardigan around her.

There was a frown across the beautiful woman's face. "Have you slept here all night?"

Kayleigh shrugged as though it was no big deal but inside she felt uncomfortable. She whiffed a bit. The way you did when you hadn't washed or cleaned your teeth before going to bed. She was always very careful to do that. But there hadn't been a shower room here; just a public toilet with pee on the concrete floor that she'd tried to step round. And there was no way she had enough for the leisure centre her new friend had mentioned.

Maybe the woman could smell her. Perhaps that frown on her face was due to distaste rather than pity. "You must be cold. Hungry too."

Her voice was posh but soothing too. It reminded her of a story that she'd found once. It had been in the kids' section but you could get some really good books there. This one had been about an enchantress (a really cool word that she'd written down in her book) who had given a kid called Edmund some kind of Turkish drug.

Unfortunately, someone had ripped out the last few pages so she didn't know how the story ended. But now she couldn't help wondering if this woman wasn't to be trusted any more than the enchantress in the book.

"Maybe this will help."

Kayleigh found a note being pressed into a hand. Bloody hell. She'd only once seen a red one when the police had come round and found that plastic bag under her half-brother's mattress. There had been loads of twenties as well but they had all been taken away apart from a couple that Mum had managed to sneak away.

"Have you got anywhere to live?"

Kayleigh wanted to tell her about Mum throwing her out and Marlene not wanting her because her bloke was mad about

Frankie being in the nick. But if she did that, the woman might shop her for sleeping rough.

So she said nothing, looking away but still clutching that fifty quid really tight.

"Please. Take this."

Another fifty? No. Disappointingly, she found a small card in her hand. It had a picture of a rose tea cup and saucer and the words *China Restoration* followed by a mobile number and a name. *Alice Honeybun*. She almost laughed. What kind of name was that?

"If you need me," continued the woman, "just give me a ring".

Then she stood up and looked down at Kayleigh but not in a way that made her feel dirty. This look reminded her of the way she'd seen a mother tenderly help her kid when he'd fallen over and hurt himself on the street the other day. (Her own mum would have just yelled at her, she'd thought at the time.)

"What's your name?"

The question slid in so neatly that she found herself replying. "Kayleigh."

"Kayleigh," repeated the beautiful woman as though savouring the word in her mouth. "Nice to meet you. And remember. Call me if you ever need me."

"I hate my name. I always wanted to be called Victoria."

The woman started as though she'd said something shocking. Maybe she had. Kayleigh had never told anyone this before, not even Marlene. But it was true. If she'd been a Victoria with blonde hair, her life would have been different. She just knew it.

"Why?" said the woman urgently. "Why do you want to be called that?

Kayleigh shrugged. "I just like it."

The woman's face softened. "Me too."

For a minute, she looked as though she was going to say something else but instead she shook her head, like she was disagreeing with herself and went. Up the stairs and into the centre which was open now. Kayleigh watched her standing at the automatic doors and glancing towards her. Then she just melted away. Maybe she had been an angel after all. Who else could have seen her in the park?

Then a vague image of a blonde woman with a dog came back to her along with Frankie's words. "*Nosy cow.*"

Had that been her? If so, maybe she had been responsible for ringing the police and getting poor Frankie arrested. In fact, perhaps she was calling them, right now and they'd come and get her for being a vagrant. That's what had happened to the kid in the flat next door when he'd run away last year.

"Give you anything, did she?" asked the girl with pink hair, suddenly returning. Kayleigh nodded, keeping her hands tightly closed around the fifty-pound note so it couldn't be seen. Otherwise she might lose it the way her half-brother had lost his to the cops.

"Enough for a double whopper and fries, is it?" pressed the girl.

Kayleigh felt guilty. Her night neighbour had been good to her. She ought to share the money; or at least some of it. "More than enough."

The girl grinned. There was a big gap at the side of her mouth where a tooth was missing. "Great. Let's go then, shall we? I know this cafe where you can get a butty and a cuppa for next to nothing if you play your cards right."

Kayleigh hesitated. It was Friday. The last day of the school term. She'd like to explain to Mr Brown why she hadn't handed in her essay. Then again, how could she go into school, looking like this?

Glancing down at her jeans, she could see they had bird poo down them from the pigeons earlier that morning. Just as well Frankie couldn't see her like this or he wouldn't fancy her. Frankie! Her heart lurched. She hoped he was all right.

"OK," she said, getting up. "Let's go."

Her new friend's name used to be Di. She'd been christened Diana after the princess but didn't like it 'cos it hadn't done William and Harry's mum any good, had it? So she'd decided when her mum had thrown her out that she was going to change her name. Posy sounded more exciting.

She said all this in between mouthfuls of the bacon sarnie which Kayleigh had paid for out of Alice Honeybun's crisp fifty-pound note. She had put the change carefully into the side pocket of the rucksack that Marlene had thoughtfully provided her with, before telling her she had to leave.

"What's the centre?" asked Kayleigh, sipping her tea which was very sweet. Maybe she'd got Di's, or rather Posy's, by mistake.

There was another 'are you mad' stare which made her feel really daft. "The centre's where you go if you haven't got anywhere else to kip." Kayleigh tried not to look as she spoke. It reminded her of Ron, who was always eating with his mouth open, making her stomach churn.

"Then why didn't you go there last night?" enquired Kayleigh, hoping that this wouldn't be treated as a daft question like the others.

Posy wiped the back of her hand across her mouth, leaving a tomato sauce stain across her cheek. Kayleigh had a motherly desire to reach over and wipe it off. Instead she sat and waited patiently. This was, she was beginning to learn, the way to handle this new friend of hers.

"'Cos I'd been using, that's why."

Using? Using what?

One of the boys at the table next to them, looked across sharply. "Got any stuff on you now?" he said in a low voice, looking round furtively. "'Cos I know someone who would pay good money for a bit of skunk."

Skunk? Kayleigh's ears pricked up. Callum, her half-brother had used that word. It had been something to do with the stash of notes under his bed. And some other stuff as well.

"No, I ain't." Posy scraped back her chair and stood up. "I'm clean now. Have been for twenty-four hours." She shot a glance at Kayleigh who was pretending not to listen; another trick she'd learned from living with Mum and Ron. Anyway, she was still savouring the last of the bacon butty. It tasted amazing after being hungry all night.

"Where are we going?"

Marlene used to say there were two kinds of people in life.

65

Leaders and those who liked to be led. 'I'm the first and you're the second' she had announced firmly. Sounded OK to Kayleigh. She didn't want to be the one with responsibility. It would be too easy to go wrong.

"To the centre." She pulled Kayleigh up by the sleeve. "They'll have me back once I've done my piss test. And if we can get there early, they might have a bed for you too."

A bed?

"It's not as though you've got anywhere else to go, is it?"

"But won't it be expensive?"

Posy laughed. "This ain't the bleeding Hilton we're talking about. The centre's got charitable status, like. That means you can live there free 'cos some geezer has had a prick of conscience and coughed up some money to help the less fortunate like us. But if you do want to splash out on a bed somewhere else, you've got your own money, haven't you?"

Kayleigh felt the pocket of the rucksack where she had put the change from the butties. It felt flat. Heart pounding, she unzipped it. Empty.

"It's gone!"

A feeling of dismay coupled with inevitability went through her. She hadn't deserved the money in the first place so maybe it was right that someone had taken it. Alice's card with the phone number wasn't there either.

Kayleigh looked at Posy. Her face seemed genuinely surprised. The bloke at the next table, near where she'd put her rucksack on the ground, wasn't there any more. "Maybe it was him or one of his mates," sniffed Posy. "You've got to be careful on the streets. Now come on. Before you get anything else nicked."

The centre was a small concrete building at the back of a dirty-looking church made of grey stone. It looked a bit like a squashed-up bus shelter but bigger. Posy rang the bell with an assurance that suggested she did this regularly. "It's me," she said through the speaker. "Posy."

"Don't you mean Di?" said a voice.

Posy sniffed. "Told you, didn't I? I've changed my name, no

matter what my paperwork says."

"Have you changed your habits too?"

The voice sounded like that of a serious young man. "Yes," replied Posy sullenly.

"Then you can come back, but we'll need to do a test first."

"All right, all right."

The door swung open to reveal not a young boy but a middle-aged man. He had a kind face, she noticed with relief. "I've brought a friend with me," announced Posy airily.

The man gave her a welcoming smile. "Hi. I'm Brian. What's your name?"

Kayleigh thought for a moment of telling him she was a Victoria. It would give her a new start. Maybe then, no one would be able to find her.

"It's Kayleigh," stepped in Posy firmly as though she wasn't there. "Don't know her second name. We've only just met. She was on the steps of the shopping centre." Her eyes hardened. "Where you made me spend the night."

Brian's voice was even and calm. "I didn't *make* you Posy. But you know there's a no drugs or smoking rule here." His gaze turned back to Kayleigh. "Do you do either?"

She thought of the pill in the park that Frankie had given her.

"No," she replied, crossing her fingers behind her back.

"Good. Then you don't mind doing a test then?" He led the way down a corridor covered in stained green carpet squares that reminded her of Mum's bedroom. The thought made Kayleigh feel both homesick and angry.

There was a lounge too with deep armchairs that a boy was sitting in, headphones plugged into his ears. Another boy, a bit older, was sitting in the other. He looked up as she passed and gave her a friendly nod. Kayleigh's heart began to feel a bit lighter. This was a bit like boarding school! She'd read about those places in a book from the library and wished with all her heart that she'd been allowed to go to one, far away from Mum or Ron.

"We need you to sign a form," said Brian. He was wearing brown corduroy trousers, she noticed. Classy. "How old are you?"

"Sixteen," said Kayleigh swiftly.

"You're sure?" His eyes were on her. "Because if you're younger, we need to inform your parents where you are."

"I don't have a dad. Just a mum."

Why did that still hurt when she said it, even though she'd never even seen her father?

Brian was writing something down. "Any trouble with the police?"

"No." She crossed her fingers again.

"That's good." He pushed across a form to her, inviting her first to sit down at his desk. It wasn't neat like Mr Master's desk at school but not untidy at the same time. She liked that.

The writing on the form swam in front of her eyes for a moment.

"You do know your date of birth, do you?" asked Brian.

What did he think she was? Stupid?

"'Course I do."

"That's good." He was nodding encouragingly. "Because not everyone does. Right, now when you've done that, we'll show you to your room. You'll need to share with Posy but that's good because she'll be able to teach you the ropes."

"Bleeding hell." Posy kicked the wall with her shoe. "I didn't know I was going to have to share or I wouldn't have brought her with me."

"Come on, Posy." Brian's brown eyes looked disappointed. "You know it's the ethos of this centre to encourage people to share."

"Ethos?" Posy snorted. "What's that when it's at home?"

"It's a sort of motto," said Kayleigh quickly. "Or principle."

Brian was giving her a respectful look. "It certainly is."

"Who's a smart-ass, then?" Posy tossed her head so that her long fringe covered only one eye instead of both. "Come on then. I'll introduce you to the others. Not Sam though. She's having her stomach pumped out."

She spoke like this was quite normal.

"Will she be all right?"

"Sure. Happens all the time." Posy nudged her hard in the ribs so Kayleigh winced. "Thought you came from the estate."

I do, Kayleigh wanted to say. But I'm a good girl. I don't want to be like the others or like Mum. Yet if she said that, Posy would think she wasn't cool. She needed a friend. After all, who else did she have now?

They had a really great evening. The boys in the television lounge were friendly, asking her where she had lived last and if she liked ping-pong. "They're trying to get into your pants," hissed Posy. "Be careful, unless you like that sort of thing."

Kayleigh thought of Frankie. It was difficult to remember exactly what had happened but it had seemed nice until the sirens had started. She certainly didn't want to repeat the experience with one of these lads. It was Frankie she loved and there was no way she was being unfaithful.

Where was he now? Please may he be all right and not as mad at her as Marlene said. She'd had to tell the policeman what happened. Surely Frankie would understand that.

When it was time to go to bed, Kayleigh tossed and turned for a bit in the bunk below Posy. It was quite a comfy mattress compared with her own at home but she couldn't sleep with the moonlight streaming in through the curtain. Would Mum be worried now?

Maybe she should have told her where was. On the other hand, Mr Brown was always telling them about the importance of putting both sides of an argument in an essay – Mum had put Ron first before her, hadn't she? When she was a mother, she would never do that.

In the morning, when they came down to breakfast in the canteen, there was cereal all nicely laid out with milk in a real jug and not a carton. Just like a proper hotel. Not that Kayleigh had ever been to one but Marlene had, once, and was always talking about it. It had been in a place called Minehead. One day, when she and Frankie were married with a baby, she might get him to take her there.

"What do we do next?" asked Kayleigh when they'd washed out their own plates afterwards.

"You'll need to see Sandy," said Posy knowledgeably. "She's on morning duty. She'll help you find a job. Got your national insurance number, have you?"

Kayleigh was about to say that she didn't and that actually, she couldn't work because she was really fifteen and not sixteen. But then she saw a tall, thin angular woman approaching, wearing jangly bracelets and earrings. "Kayleigh? Kayleigh Long?"

That wasn't the surname she'd put on her form. How did she know her real one?

The thin woman's lips tightened. "I'm afraid you haven't been telling us the truth, have you?"

She felt a nasty twinge of unease.

"We checked out your details with the police – something we do as a matter of course – and found that you are actually fifteen, not sixteen."

The woman's face looked like a sorrowful horse that Kayleigh had stroked once during a school trip to an inner city farm.

"You've been in trouble too, haven't you?" continued the woman, looking quickly behind her.

Then she saw him. The same policeman who had nicked her in the park. Standing by the door, helmet under his arm. "Hello, Kayleigh," he said with those clear blue eyes that really freaked her out. "Can you come this way for a minute?"

He led her into a room where – fucking hell – Mum was waiting. And Ron too. "What the bleeding hell d'you think you've been doing, my girl?" he yelled, leaping up and trying to grab her.

"That's quite enough." For a minute, she was glad the policeman was there to intervene. He turned to her. "Thought you'd like to know that your friend Frankie has pleaded guilty which means he will go to prison for a bit. I have to say it makes our life much easier. What we have to do now is decide what will happen to you."

He gesticulated towards a thin woman in a blue suit, sitting in the corner of the room. "This is Susan. She's going to be your social worker."

But his earlier words were still ringing round her head. Frankie was going to prison. Because of her. She'd let him down. She should never have told them what happened in the park.

"I'm afraid we have another problem too," continued the policeman. "The girl who brought you here says you stole some money."

"I did NOT!"

"Fifty pounds," continued the policeman, looking at her with that gaze that made her feel he could see inside her head. "She said you took it from a woman outside the centre and that you spent it all."

"She's lying!" Kayleigh could hardly believe it. "It was a present."

Ron snorted. "Sure it was."

Slowly, the truth began to dawn. So Posy had stolen the money. Not the boys. How could she have been so stupid?

"We've got a witness who says she saw you take the money," said the policeman heavily.

"Who?"

"Another of the girls sleeping rough."

Kayleigh snorted. "You don't believe her, do you?"

Those blue eyes looked sad. "I warned you after the park, Kayleigh. You only had one more chance. You're going to have to come down now to the station to be cautioned and maybe charged."

What? Most of the kids on the estate had records. It was why they couldn't get any decent jobs. That couldn't happen to her. It just couldn't.

The woman with the jangly bracelets, chipped in. "We also need to talk about care proceedings."

Care? Kayleigh knew about that all right. Hadn't her own Mum been in care for years? She was always talking about it.

"Mum," she called out. "Don't let them do this."

But her mother was just looking at her, stony-faced. "I don't want her," she muttered, turning away.

A long time ago, before Ron, Mum had had a boyfriend who was quite nice really. He had encouraged her to join a running club that was free for kids on the estate.

She hadn't forgotten how to do it.

"Stop her," called out the woman with jangly bracelets.

But she was off. Out of the window and down the street. Running as hard as her legs could carry her.

SEVEN

When Daniel got home that night, Alice told him about coming across the girl at the shopping centre. Her initial anger over his use of the word 'slut' had cooled. All these years, she'd known deep-down that 'the incident' as Mum sometimes called it, must have been her fault. So was it any wonder that Daniel thought badly of her?

Now her anger was replaced with fear. Daniel was right. She should have told him immediately what had happened in the park. So it wasn't surprising that he was now being so cool. Maybe he might even leave her …

Occasionally, in the last few years, Alice had fantasised about living alone. No one to shoot her reproachful looks because she didn't care for sex. No need to feel embarrassed if a passionate scene came on television or one of their friends told a raucous story at a dinner party that everyone else thought funny apart from her. No one to run around after in the home, in an attempt to make up for what was missing in bed.

But now, with Daniel's face set like stone – not to mention the fact that he'd started coming home much later than usual without attempting to give an excuse – Alice began to feel horribly insecure and scared.

What if he'd found someone else? No. That was impossible. Unlike her, Daniel was incapable of deception.

Supposing he'd had enough of her? Now that might be understandable.

How would she manage on her own? Not just financially, her own money from the china 'business' would barely have paid the phone bill. But emotionally too.

It had been a wake-up call and one, which Alice told herself, had come not a moment too soon. So it seemed right to tell him about the girl on the centre steps.

"You just bumped into her?" Daniel's face clearly showed he didn't believe her. "You didn't go looking?" He shook his head. "I know you, Alice, better than you realise. You were worried about her, weren't you?"

The softer tone in his voice flooded her with gratitude. So she was forgiven! "Yes. Now I've seen her, I can't stop thinking about where she's spending tonight and how she's coping. She's not some cheap tart, Daniel. She's a nice kid. I could tell."

The words came out in a rush even before she'd taken Daniel's light summer jacket and hung it on the row of hooks above the Victorian wooden settle in the hall, that had once belonged to her mother-in-law. "Her name's Kayleigh. She didn't tell me her surname. Or why she was sleeping rough."

Daniel shrugged. "Some people like it. There are places for these people to go, if they want a proper roof over their heads."

Were there? Once, Alice had had a furious row with her friend Janice's husband at a dinner party, when he had declared that 'the homeless had a choice'. You couldn't generalise in that way, she'd retorted. It had led to a distance between her and Janice for a while.

Now she was disappointed that Daniel had the same attitude. After all, wasn't his university keen on promoting pastoral care? That had certainly been the message in its recent prospectus which had carried a flattering photograph of her husband above the blurb for the English department.

Not that she was going to say anything. This was a time for rapprochement, not further arguments. "If you say so," she shrugged. "But she looked cold. And hungry."

Her back was to Daniel now, as she poured his pre-dinner scotch while keeping an eye on the cheese sauce at the same time. Alice always took care to make a fuss over dinner. It was the least she could do, given that she was so severely lacking in the other wifely department.

"How much did you give her?" said Daniel's voice.

She wasn't going to lie. Not again. "Fifty pounds."

"FIFTY POUNDS?"

"It was *my* money." Alice gave the sauce a sudden defiant stir.

"That's not the point." He stood beside her; the heat of his presence forcing her to look up. To her relief, his face registered concern rather than annoyance. "You do realise that she'll only go and spend it on drugs or drink, don't you? You've given her fuel for her habit. Made it much worse."

When he put it that way, Alice could see that she had in fact, been really silly. "I just kept thinking of Garth," she whispered. "If he was cold and hungry somewhere, I'd want someone to help him."

Something changed in her husband's face. Their son, who had promised faithfully to email 'regularly', hadn't made contact for nearly four weeks now. Daniel was as worried as she was. Alice could tell. The friend whom he was travelling with had his phone switched off too. Gap years, she'd begun to think, should be banned on the grounds of parental mental health.

"I can see that," he now said softly. Then he drew her to him, ignoring the spatula in her hand. "But we can't look after every waif and stray, can we?"

Sensing that something was going on, Mungo leaped up just as Daniel tried to hug her. It provided Alice with an excuse to break away. *Don't touch me. Don't touch me.* "Goodness, I've got cheese sauce on your shirt! Here, let me wipe it down."

Fussing, to hide her terror over the near-hug, she began sponging down the stain. "It's all right. Leave it."

Daniel's cool tone showed he wasn't fooled. Why, oh why, can't you show me any affection, he might as well have said. Can't you put the past behind you after all these years? But how was that possible when she was no better than the girl in the park?

"Perhaps you'd better contact your policeman," he said sharply, taking a place at the kitchen table and watching her strain the green beans (fresh from the garden) that were to go with the chicken in its cheese sauce. "I'm not sure it's legal for a witness to give money to a defendant." He gave her a hard look. "You might be in trouble."

Paul Black had given her a phone number after she'd made her statement. "It's just in case you think of anything else you'd like to add," he'd said as she'd looked at the card with a mobile number on it. "Or if there's something that's troubling you." His blue eyes had locked with hers. "Our force prides itself on looking after witnesses."

"*Should* I be worried?" she'd asked nervously, recalling her concern over bricks through the window? But now she thought about it, it could be worse. What if this youth in the park, who had such a nasty reputation, had a go at her?

Hadn't she read with horror, over the years, about awful attacks on women (rarely men) who'd had acid thrown at them? True, it was often in relation to 'honour' killings, rather than middle-class, middle-aged women like her about to give witness. But even so ...

And now, she had this other thing to worry about. A simple donation to a homeless girl. A rather large one, admittedly. Yet wouldn't anyone in her position have done the same?

"Paul Black speaking."

Alice hadn't expected him to pick up the phone on a Saturday morning. But Daniel's suggestion that she might have broken the law had worried her so much all night that she'd simply had to do something.

She'd leave a message, she told herself, so he could then ring her back on Monday morning. The sound of his deep voice – rather more educated than one might expect for a PC, although she felt awful just thinking that – both threw her and was reassuring at the same time.

"It's Mrs Honeybun speaking," she said. "Alice," she then added, remembering that she'd rather rashly and inexplicably suggested he called her that during the statement taking; even though she'd once reprimanded someone from a call centre for doing exactly the same.

"Hello." The last part of the word rose slightly in the air;

more like a greeting between good neighbours than policeman and witness. Did he speak to everyone like that, wondered Alice? Perhaps it was a tone he adopted to wheedle the maximum amount of co-operation out of people.

"You said I could ring if I had anything to ask," she said, feeling like a criminal herself. How awkward it was, talking to a policeman! Irrelevantly, she found herself wondering if her MOT was up to date. Janice always claimed that if she found herself driving behind a police car, she would pull in and let it go on ahead. They always find something to get you for, she'd announced with the authority of one who had six points on her licence. They need to do it to get their bonuses or stripes or whatever they get nowadays.

"The thing is," continued Alice, wishing now that she hadn't rung at all. "I think I might have done something rather stupid."

"To do with the case?"

There was a definite hint of alarm in his voice.

"Yes," she admitted, feeling really scared now.

"Tell you what." He sounded solidly brisk. "Why don't we talk about it over a cup of coffee. I'm in your area at the moment. How about that new place on the corner by the ice-cream kiosk."

Coffee? With a policeman? In full view of her friends who would be in town shopping?

"I won't be in uniform," he added as though he knew what she was thinking. "In fact, I'm just about to come off duty."

Totally thrown, she floundered silently for an excuse. "I don't want to bother you. Not if it's in your free time."

"It's no trouble at all. Besides, there's been a development with the case. I was going to contact you on Monday anyway."

Luckily Daniel was at the golf club, playing his usual Saturday morning round. It meant she could explain later. Say something casual like "*Guess who I bumped into?*" Or maybe "*I happened to see that policeman by the ice-cream kiosk so we had a coffee together.*"

No, Alice rebuked herself. Hadn't she promised not to hide anything else from Daniel? It was a promise she had made many years ago but she'd gone and broken it over the park business. It wasn't going to happen again.

She'd just tell him the truth at lunchtime when he got home, Alice decided as she cycled down to the front. She loved her bike; enjoying the wind through her hair. Stubbornly she refused to wear a helmet for this reason despite the statistics which Daniel was always spouting. Besides, it calmed her nerves, which were something that always seemed to need calming; especially now Garth was roaming the world.

As she entered the coffee shop, Alice was relieved to see that she didn't know anyone else there. In fact, she almost didn't recognise Paul Black. His black hair, that had been unremarkable the other evening – perhaps because it had been flattened by the helmet – was rather jauntily brushed to one side. He was wearing a green-and-brown checked shirt that looked very similar to a Burberry which she had bought Daniel the other month. And he had a pair of smart casual cords. He was also reading the T2 section of *The Times* which was one of her favourite bits. Instantly she felt better. "Almost like one of us," she could just hear Janice saying. Much as she liked her friend, she could be an awful snob.

"Hello," he said, for the second time that day. Face to face, it sounded different. Warmer. It struck Alice, rather bizarrely, that an outsider might think they were embarking on a blind date. The absurdity of the situation made her want to giggle.

"Something funny?" he asked, seemingly amused. There were laughter lines round his eyes, she noticed. So despite the serious conversations they'd had to date, Paul Black had a sense of humour. Interesting.

"Funny?" she repeated, thinking briefly of her husband's laugh, which was more of a reluctant smile. "Not really." Then, in case he thought her totally mad, she added. "Nerves actually. I sometimes laugh when I'm nervous."

"Me too," he said swiftly.

Really? Yet he appeared so confident. Perhaps he was just saying that to make her comfortable – cosy up to her to ensure she didn't back out as a potential witness. It was the way they worked, wasn't it? At least she'd recalled something similar on

The Bill which she used to watch when Daniel was out late.

"What would you like?" he continued as the waitress materialised beside them.

Paul – it felt weird that policeman had first names –ordered peppermint tea too, she noted with surprise. "My husband says it's not tea," she found herself saying.

"Exactly." His eyes twinkled. "Much better for you. Nice cups, aren't they? I like the colour. Fuchsia pink as my mother would have said."

A man who noticed colours. She liked that. Yet it was unusual in her experience. She glanced at his left hand. It was bare. No sign of the tell-tale, recently divorced white mark, either.

Maybe he was gay, she told herself, appalled by her own thoughts. Just because a policeman scrubs up well, drinks peppermint tea, and notices colours, that doesn't mean he was (as her own mother coyly called it) 'otherwise inclined'.

"You said you were worried about something," he said, when they had their drinks in front of them and had chatted for a bit about Thailand which was, according to the paper in front of them, one of the top five hot-spots for this time of year. They had both been there, it transpired, although if Paul Black had gone with someone, he had taken care not to use the word 'we'.

"Yes. Yes, I am worried." She nodded tightly as if agreeing with herself; wishing stupidly there was another reason for their meeting. Her companion was really rather easy to talk to. He listened carefully and then commented in a manner that complemented what she had just said instead of putting her down, as Daniel did all too often.

"I saw the girl from the park yesterday. At the shopping centre. She was on the steps. It was very early and I think she'd been sleeping rough. So I gave her fifty pounds."

His blue eyes were locking on hers again. Part of her wished he wouldn't do this. It was really unnerving. The other part felt glued to his in return. "You gave her fifty pounds," he repeated.

She nodded, her mouth dry. "I know it was rather a lot but I felt … well worried about her."

And guilty too, she added to herself, for having split on her.

In her nervousness, she took a gulp of peppermint tea which went down the wrong way, causing her to splutter. So embarrassing! His hand shot out and patted her back. Instead of recoiling, as she normally did when someone touched her, she felt grateful.

"All right?" he asked solicitously.

She nodded. "Yes thanks. Sorry."

"Not at all." He smiled briefly. "Can't have one of our witnesses expiring in front of me. They teach us the Heimlich move as part of our training but I've never had to put it into practice. Besides, I think that's for something solid that's got stuck. Not liquid going down the wrong way."

"I wonder," she began, "what people in the cafe would say if you hit me? They might not realise you were actually trying to save me."

He frowned. What on earth had made her share that thought with Paul Black; a man she barely knew? Hastily, she tried to explain. "It's so easy to misinterpret things, isn't it? To see something that isn't what it looks like?"

He nodded. "I know exactly what you mean."

Her chest fluttered with relief. Yet at the same time, she felt suspicious of herself. Why was she able to speak so openly to this man?

Then his eyes took on a steeliness she hadn't seen before. "So you definitely *gave* Kayleigh that fifty pounds?"

The way he said 'gave', sounded as though he thought the girl might have snatched it off her.

"Of course. Daniel – my husband – said I might have broken the law by helping someone I'm testifying against."

"Did you discuss the case?" he asked with an edge to his tone.

"No." Her denial rang out loudly.

"Good." He seemed satisfied. "The thing is, Alice ..." His eyes searched hers again. "The thing is," he continued, "the man in question has admitted he's guilty. So you won't have to go to court to testify. He'll simply get a custodial sentence."

Relief flooded through her, followed by a wave of concern. "But what about the girl? Will she go to prison too?"

"Probably not. She'll get a caution and maybe go into care as she's underage." He looked down at his coffee. "It appears her home life isn't what it could be. It's very hard for kids like that"

His empathy surprised her. Not for the first time she wondered if he should be so open. "There's something I need to tell you," she said, twisting her paper napkin with embarrassment. "My husband … when you came round … what I'm trying to say is that I was embarrassed when he called Kayleigh a slut."

Slowly, he stirred the froth in his coffee. His reply seemed to take an age. Finally, his gaze met hers. "You know what, Alice? The sad thing is that these girls really do blame themselves, even when it's not their fault. It can affect them for the rest of their lives." His voice took on a hard angry edge. "I've seen it happen, again and again; usually because someone has destroyed their self-esteem."

"I know, I know," she wanted to say. Instead, she made herself swallow hard; wanting to speak but not daring to in case she burst into tears. He understands, she thought, what it's like to go through something like this. He just doesn't realise that it happened to me. Instead, he thinks I'm a nice, middle-class woman who has no idea what it's like to be abused or believed or to feel guilty, because somewhere along the line, she must have inadvertently shown willing for a man to have taken advantage of her.

For a while, silence lay between them like the red-and-cream gingham tablecloth; bursting with chequered squares of unasked and unanswered questions. Then, just as she was going to say something – anything – to puncture the deafening emptiness, he spoke. "There's something else," he added, still toying with the froth on his coffee. "It so happens that I saw Kayleigh myself this morning before I went off night duty."

Alice's heart stopped. "You saw her? Was she all right?"

"She was in a centre for the homeless."

Thank goodness. So at least she had somewhere to sleep. Alice herself had scarcely been able to rest last night, thinking of the girl out in the cold with nowhere to go.

"Turned out she'd lied about her age. So we brought her mum along and one of the social workers."

His face turned to hers, with that reproachful expression she sometimes saw on her own in the mirror. "One of the other girls in the centre had accused her of stealing fifty pounds. Unfortunately, when we asked her about it, she ran off."

Shocked, Alice almost dropped her cup so that the tea slopped over into the saucer. "Where is she now?"

Paul Black's blue eyes locked with hers. He was worried too. She could see it from the way his pupils were flickering. "That's just it. We don't know."

"So who was that handsome man you were having coffee with this morning?"

Janice's voice rose above the general chitter-chatter of the birthday barbecue. Monica from the book club turned round and stared. Alice's heart missed a beat. So she'd been spotted! Then again, what did she expect in a place like this?

"Just a friend." She tried to sound casual, searching through the crowd for Daniel, fresh back from the golf course with Brian; hoping he hadn't overheard Janice's question. There hadn't been time to mention the coffee to her husband or think of an excuse to explain why she'd felt it necessary to have a social coffee with a policeman who, as Daniel kept saying, had been far too pushy over that statement business.

Nervously, Alice smoothed down her new dress. Already she'd received several compliments on its deep peacock-blue colour with a pretty scalloped neck; the one she'd bought after seeing Kayleigh on the steps the other day. At the time, Alice had been stricken with guilt as she'd handed over her credit card. How could she spend nearly a hundred pounds when the girl outside didn't have anywhere to stay the night? Part of her had wanted to bring her home although, of course, that would have been out of the question.

She still felt guilty. But despite this, Alice's lips twitched to imagine Daniel's reaction. If he'd thought that talking to Kayleigh was breaking the law, giving her a bed for the night would probably be a grave felony. Still, in the scheme of things, it was less grave than having coffee with a handsome policeman who didn't, she had to admit, fit in with her general stereotype picture of a policeman. Whatever that was.

"You're smiling," said Janice, her eyes narrowing. "Alice Honeybun! Are you seeing someone on the side?"

"Of course not."

Shocked and embarrassed she glanced at twice-divorced Monica whose attention was thankfully being taken up by a heavily charcoaled chop and one of the few single men at the party. "He's a client," she added, not sure why she was lying. "I'm trying to mend something for him."

That much, at least, was true.

Janice's eyes were gleaming with mischief. "I'm not sure I believe you."

"It's a bit more complicated than that." Alice had spotted Daniel now; he was swigging back a beer with Brian. He'd better not have too many or he'd have to leave his car here and come back with her. Trapped conversation was something that only other lonely wives understood. "Listen, Janice. I'd be grateful you didn't mention you saw us until I've told Daniel."

Janice looked worried. "You're not in any trouble, are you?"

Alice hesitated. Only for a moment. But it was enough.

"You *are*," breathed Janice.

"Actually it's someone else who's in trouble." Alice's eyes took in the beautiful herbaceous borders, trying to distract herself. "And I'm worried for them."

Janice touched her arm. "Dear, kind Alice. Just make sure you look after yourself. By the way, I'm glad to hear that son of yours has finally got in touch."

"He has?" Her heart leaped with disbelief and relief.

"Didn't Daniel tell you? Your Garth texted him when they were on the golf course."

Elbowing her way through the party, Alice grabbed her husband's arm. "Why didn't you tell me about Garth?" she demanded. "I've been worried out of my mind."

Daniel, to be fair, looked repentant. "Sorry. I meant to but it was right in the middle of the match – I shouldn't even have had the phone on ..."

"Is he all right?"

"Fine. I told you he would be." His voice made her look as though she'd been fussing.

"Where is he?" Her questions shot out like starved bullets.

"Got some budget flight to South America, apparently. He's short of money of course …'

South America? After Thailand? Alice was aware of a touch of envy amidst the tidal wave of relief. "You will put some in his account, won't you?"

"Already done. Not too much but just enough to get him by. I've told him to get a new phone too. He lost the last one. Now listen, Brian, about what we were saying …"

Alice wandered out on to the lawn, feeling hurt. Why hadn't Garth texted *her*, instead of Daniel? Didn't she mean anything to him any more? Getting out her phone, she checked it. No missed calls from her son. Only from her mother.

At seventy-three, Mum was still very elegant and took great delight in knowing that she looked a good ten years younger. Unlike many women of her age, she'd got away with keeping her hair (blonde like Alice's) in a shoulder-length bob. She was stylish too. Thanks to a well-preserved figure and a knack for searching out bargains, she was able to wear couture jackets and tailored trousers with an ease which many of Alice's own friends couldn't muster.

"I like to keep young," she would often say, waiting for someone to say "But you *are* still young." Yet at times, Alice wondered if Mum was jealous that she was no longer her daughter's age. How ironic, she also frequently thought, that they looked so alike. At home – an apartment in a nearby gracious, upmarket retirement village – Mum had a collection of silver-framed photographs on the now unused piano. Visitors sometimes had to look closely to check who was who. The innocent seventeen-year-old Alice with the happy, unsullied smile on her face bore a startling similarity to her mother at the same age in the frame next to it; taken on the evening she had met Alice's father at a Conservative ball. The two could almost have touched hands; indeed an onlooker might be forgiven for thinking that they were close.

Yet the truth, Alice thought grimly, was very different. Since 'the incident', they were more distant than they had been before. Neither side had been able to forgive the other. Still, that didn't take away a grown-up daughter's obligation to keep an eye on an aging parent. "Mum? You tried to ring me, I think."

Her mother's clear, rather aloof tones rang out as Alice stood in the part of the garden where Janice and Brian's twin boys – the same age as Garth – had had their swings. Now it was replaced by an elaborate bespoke arbour, made by someone who exhibited at Chelsea. Life moved on. For other people at least.

"Yes dear, I did. It's about Uncle Phil."

There was a soft thud as Alice's wine glass fell onto the grass, splattering red wine over her new dress. The voices behind her swelled up like waves in her ears. There was a bitter taste in her mouth.

Bile.

"What about him?" she breathed.

"He's not well. Terminal lung cancer, poor man. But he wants to see you."

"See me?"

"You heard me, dear. Now don't start getting your silly ideas again. He's an old man, Alice, whom you wronged and embarrassed all those years ago. Perhaps he wants to forgive you for all that fuss you caused, before he dies. You owe him that. Don't you think?"

EIGHT

Kayleigh ran until her chest throbbed too much to go on and she almost fell over a loose kerbstone. Eventually, when she was sure no one was behind her, she stopped briefly by a newsagent where a youngish woman was shepherding two young children inside, encouraging them to hold her hand. A good mother, Kayleigh observed enviously. Kind but firm. Kept her eyes on them the whole time, she did.

Not like her own mum.

Then she started running again. As her feet hit the pavement, they made a thudding sound. "Strong," they seemed to say. "Strong."

They were right. That was just what she needed to be. Somehow, she'd find somewhere to sleep. Maybe a different shopping centre. She'd also find out – maybe through Marlene's boyfriend – where they'd put Frankie. Then she'd visit him and explain that the policeman with the staring blue eyes had made her give a statement.

"I still love you," she'd tell him. "I want to have your baby and get married."

Then he'd put his arms around her and tell her it would be all right. "As soon as I get out of here, we'll find a place together," he'd assure her.

Be strong, strong, sang the pavements.

By mid-afternoon, Kayleigh still hadn't got anywhere. Apart from a few more shops in little clusters near big housing estates, there weren't any other big centres like the one at home where she could hang around.

What was she going to do? Her stomach was hollow with hunger. All that running had rubbed the side of her little toes so that they bled and hurt. It was getting cold too and a fine rain had started to fall like the mist in Keats's poem about the sad knight.

Kayleigh thought with longing of the books under her narrow bed and the thin wall between her bedroom and Mum and Ron's. If only she'd realised then, how lucky she was.

"Don't be so daft," she told herself, squatting down on the corner of a road under a protruding roof, where there was a bit of shelter from the rain. "He'd got it in for you. You're far better off without the bugger."

The pain over Mum was even worse than her sore, bloody toes. "Forget her," Kayleigh tried to tell herself. But it was hard. As she sat there, head bent into her sweatshirt to try and keep dry, her mind went back down the years.

"Keep quiet, can't you"

"Don't do that."

"Give me some time to myself, for Christ's sake."

Each one of those sentences had been said so often that they were ingrained in her head. It wasn't right. When she was a mum, she wouldn't treat her kids like they were something she hadn't wanted in the first place.

Had it been like that for her half-brother? It was hard to remember. Callum had been nearly twelve when she'd been born. He hadn't known his father either.

His father and hers weren't the same. At least Mum said she didn't think they were. But it had just given her an idea. If Mum didn't want her, maybe her dad would. Perhaps she'd have another go at finding him. Then, as if it were a sign, she suddenly saw a notice on the other side of the road.

Library.

Libraries were safe places! Warm. They had nice people inside who liked you reading their books. You could sit down on a chair and lose yourself in a good story.

And you could find out stuff.

"You're looking for your father?"

The small woman with silver hair smiled at Kayleigh but it wasn't the type of smile that reached her mouth. It was a tight grimace that observed Kayleigh's sweatshirt, soaked with the rain, and her trainers which were all muddy. Her hair felt sticky. It had been ages, Kayleigh suddenly remembered, since she'd been able to wash it.

"It's not always easy to find family," said the library woman, leading her to a row of computers at the back. Someone was already on it. An old man who was fumbling through a notebook and staring at the screen blankly. "Is it, Mr Morris?"

"Eh, what's that?"

"I said, you've been doing some family research for a long time now, haven't you?"

His face lit up. "Ay, that I have. My father fought in the First World War, you know." He nodded at Kayleigh. "If it wasn't for him, youngsters like you wouldn't be alive."

She knew all about that from history at school. "Was he in the trenches?" Kayleigh asked.

The librarian with silver hair glanced at her with new respect.

"That he was."

They'd done the trenches last year. It had been really good even though she'd been annoyed with Marlene for mucking about so she couldn't hear the teacher properly. "People must have been so brave in those days. I mean, all that awful gas and post-traumatic stress."

The old man was nodding. "It was indeed. My mother had an uncle who was never the same again. But my own father would never talk about his experiences. It was his way of coping, you see."

Kayleigh got that that. There was stuff she couldn't talk about either, although she was going to tell Frankie one day. He'd understand. She knew he would. When you'd done what they had in the park, it meant there was something special between you. Especially when it was your first time.

"If you're looking for your father," said the librarian in a more sympathetic voice than before, "this site might help." She logged on to the computer and a picture sprang up of a young girl in an older woman's arms.

'REUNITED AT LAST' said the words below.

"Do you know his date of birth?"

Kayleigh shook her head.

The librarian scrawled down the page. "What's his full name?"

Kayleigh was beginning to sweat with embarrassment. "I don't know. My mum sometimes calls him Dick."

"Short for Richard?" asked the librarian.

Kayleigh laughed. "More like short for stupid."

There was a silence. Had she said the wrong thing? Still, it was true, wasn't it?

"Do you know anything at all about your father?" asked the silver-haired woman quietly.

She thought for a minute. "Only that he gambled on the greyhounds and that he went out one day to place a bet but never came back again. I was a baby at the time."

"I think," said the librarian, closing down the site, "we'll need more than that to go on. Perhaps you could find out a bit more through your relatives."

Kayleigh tried to look as though this was possible. "Thanks."

"That's fifty pence for the use of the computers, please."

"But we didn't use them." She heard her voice rising indignantly like Marlene when accused of smoking during break-time. "Hardly at all, anyway. You didn't find anything out for me."

"That wasn't my fault."

"Take this." The old man was holding out a silver coin. "I'll pay for it."

Kayleigh was overcome with relief. For a minute, she'd thought the librarian might ring the police and then she'd really have had it. "Thanks," she said. Then, picking up her rucksack, she ambled out of the library, taking care to appear as though she knew where she was going.

Kayleigh walked on for a bit, out of the town, and then down a long lane that didn't seem to go anywhere. So she turned back and went down a different road at the crossroads, passing a large farm with cows outside and a disgusting smell that tickled her nostrils.

Kayleigh didn't like cows. When she'd gone on the school inner-city trip, one of them had made a horrible brown mess right by her, spattering muck all over her ankles. Marlene had thought it was very funny.

So she turned back again and found herself outside the library once more. It had a 'Closed' sign on the door. Her stomach was so empty now that she felt really wobbly. If she had some money, she'd be all right.

Rifling through her rucksack one more time, just in case Marlene had left a spare pound coin in it, she came across a stale biscuit. It tasted like sawdust. Not that she'd ever tasted sawdust but she could imagine it all too well. Sometimes a vivid imagination was more of a curse than a blessing. That was another of Mr Brown's sayings.

Then she thought of the newsagent.

Marlene had what she called a 'habit'. It wasn't a drugs habit or a fags habit. It was a nicking habit. Over the years, Kayleigh had watched with a mixture of horror and awe as her friend had got away with lacy bras, skimpy little pants, packets of crisps and magazines. On a couple of occasions, she had nearly got caught and once she had been cautioned.

Kayleigh might only have been a witness but she'd seen enough to know that she wasn't that kind of person. On the other hand, she'd never been hungry like this before.

The newsagent's was still open but there was no one inside. Not even the shopkeeper. Kayleigh could hear someone scrabbling around at the back. There was a stack of crisps in front of her.

'Special Offer', said the hand-written sign precariously perched on top.

It would be better to take one of those than something more expensive. Maybe some water too. Nothing fancy like one of those energy drinks that Ron was addicted to. They were more expensive and she had *some* morals. Swiftly, she slipped a bottle and packet into her rucksack just as she heard footsteps coming from the back of the shop. "The trick is to act normal,"

Marlene always said. "Don't run away or look scared. Ask them something."

Kayleigh faced the newsagent woman fair and square in the face. "Have you got a copy of *OK* magazine?" She glanced looked at the shelf behind her. "I can't see one."

That was a lie. She hadn't looked. But the newsagent woman, neat and tidy in her black cardigan and matching trousers, shook her head. "Sorry. All sold out."

Lucky. She couldn't have afforded it anyway. Picking up her rucksack, Kayleigh made her way to the door, gulping in the cold air with relief. She'd done it!

Hardly able to wait, she ran back to the library. It might be closed but it had a porch outside where she could shelter. Desperately she tore open the packet of crisps and rammed each one down her throat, hardly tasting them in her hunger. Then the bottle. Never had water tasted so good.

That was a bit better. Kayleigh sat, with her back to the library door, hugging her knees. The ground felt hard and cold. But at least it wasn't a cell which was where she'd probably be right now if the policeman had caught up with her.

Kayleigh tried to keep warm with her thoughts. Poor Frankie. What was he doing right now? Watching television perhaps? That's if they were allowed to do that. Or maybe trying to contact her. That was it. That's what he'd be doing ...

Gradually, she became aware of her head dropping with sleep. As she drifted off, she felt something wet brush her hand. Instantly, she woke with a jerk. Bloody hell. It was a dog.

If there was one thing Kayleigh was scared of, it was big dogs. Next door's Alsatian had sunk its teeth into her thigh when she'd been a kid. She'd had to have a tetanus injection. Mum had promised not to split on the neighbours about the No Pet rule when the neighbour had given her a whole box of duty free fags.

"It's you," said a voice. "The kid from the library."

Kayleigh looked up through her fringe. It was the old man. The one who had been doing his family tree.

"Don't worry about Jack. He's a good 'un."

Both man and dog were looking at her closely. "Not got a

92

home to go back to, then?"

She shook her head, eyes still warily on the dog.

He sniffed. "You can come back with me, if you like. Don't worry. I won't hurt you."

Kayleigh hesitated. Never go off with strangers her mum had said once. But wasn't that what her own mother did all the time? When Ron went, it would be someone else. That was the way it worked.

'Sides there was something about this old man that seemed all right. As for his dog, it seemed quite docile too. (Another word she'd learned from the thesaurus she'd borrowed from Mr Brown.) Maybe she could have a proper shower. And she was bursting for a pee.

"OK," she said, getting up and slinging the rucksack over her shoulders. "Thanks."

NINE

"I'm not going." Alice poured herself a large glass of Chardonnay. In her nervousness she slopped some over the edge and watched, with a certain fascination, as it seeped into the walnut drinks table. At any other time, she would have rushed to mop it up before the table stained. But right now, she felt strangely wilful. "I'm not a child any more."

"No one said you were." Daniel closed his hand briefly over hers. His touch nearly made her drop the glass onto the sage-green carpet they had spent ages choosing when they'd first moved in. Briefly, she thought of Paul Black's hand patting her back. She hadn't minded that. Why? Was it because she was dirty?

There'd been a piece in one of her magazines the other month about a woman who could only have sex with a stranger. "There's no emotion," the interviewee had said in justification. "So I can't get hurt." Alice could understand that.

"That man," she said, shuddering, "ruined my life. But do you know what made it worse? The fact that no one – not even Dad in the end – would believe me."

Daniel, nursing his evening tumbler of whisky, stood by the French windows, his back to her as he gazed over the lawn with its wide border of blowsy roses mixed with oriental poppies. The tumbler, she observed irrelevantly, was part of a set which they'd been given as a wedding present. Five out of six had survived. Not bad for a long marriage. The thought that this simple glass had outlived the mild attraction that had brought them together in the first place, was sadly comical.

"I believe you," he said, so softly that she barely heard him.

He did? Never had he come straight out and said that before. Yet the incident in the park, as she kept referring to it in her mind, appeared to have suddenly changed the ordinance points in their marriage. For Daniel as well as for her.

"Thank you," she whispered, forcing herself to walk up next to him and slip her hand in his. Then she added, "I'm sorry I can't be the wife you want."

As he turned, she could see tears in his eyes. "We've been over this before, Alice." Slowly, carefully, he stroked her hair.

Alice forced herself not to move away. It wasn't that she didn't care for him, she told herself. Of course she did. Wasn't Daniel the father of her son?

Dammit. It was no good. His touch made her cringe. Furious with herself, she stepped back. Away from the feel of his skin; gulping in the freedom of being a separate non-hand holding person once more. "I should have told you before. It was wrong of me." She took another gulp of wine. "But I thought it would be all right. I thought that when we were married, I'd be able to put all that behind me ..."

"Shhh, Shh." He was holding her to him, now. Once more, Alice had to resist the urge to duck away. "It wouldn't have made any difference. You've already told me this God knows how many times over the years." His voice was weary as though he'd given up convincing himself. "I would still have married you, Alice."

Her heart was pulsing so fast she could hardly get the words out. "So you don't think I'm a slut or that it was my fault?"

"I've never said that. That's just your own imagination. But I do wish you could learn to put it behind you. See it as the past."

I can't, she wanted to say. Don't you see? It's made me the person I am now. No. What was the point? Daniel didn't get it. He never would. He might be an English lecturer but ironically, there were times when he lacked the imagination of his heroes.

"But," he started to say. Then he paused and she held her breath. It was the kind of pause where you knew someone was going to add an important caveat. "But I won't pretend," he added heavily, "that I don't yearn to have that … that other side of marriage too."

Too late, Alice wished with all her heart that she hadn't told him about the argument with her mother. Bugger Uncle Phil. May he rot in hell when he finally went. It was what he deserved.

"But we still," said Daniel, valiantly ploughing on, "have Garth."

Alice tried not to think of the months of effort that his conception had required. Every time, she'd had to force herself not to resist Daniel's advances, knowing that if she did so, she might never have a child; someone who would always love her, no matter what. When the positive result had come through, she'd swiftly used her pregnancy as an excuse to curtail any more bedroom activity. Afterwards, she was 'too tired'. When six months later, Daniel had demanded to know whether she was having an affair, she had finally told him the truth about Phil. He'd been, she recalled, shocked and hurt that she hadn't told him before.

Since then, over the years, he had suggested counselling to 'get it out' of her head. On a couple of occasions, she had given in but it hadn't done any good. No one could really understand what it had been like. Not unless they had been through it before themselves.

Eventually, Daniel stopped pushing her. Instead, he would give her a chaste kiss on the cheek at night. Sometimes, now, in the night, she would wake up and find him cuddling her from behind. Quickly, she would move away.

Indeed, there were days – weeks even – without thinking too much about what had happened. Then the smallest thing could melt that mental wall which she'd forced herself to erect. It might be the sweet smell of a certain aftershave when air kissing someone's husband at a dinner party. Or a tune on the radio that had been popular at the time. Or a phrase. *Be a good girl* …

When that happened, she would walk. Or distract herself with a particularly challenging piece of chipped china. Perhaps ring Janice, to suggest a game of tennis so she could whip her demons over the net.

But now, Mum's demand that she should see her 'uncle' on his deathbed, had resurrected the nightmare all over again.

"Don't you think," suggested Daniel, walking back towards the whisky bottle, "that it might be cathartic to see him. You could talk the whole thing through. You could make sure that …"

He stopped but Alice knew exactly what he had been going to say. "Make sure that I wasn't making it up? You said you believed me, just now."

Daniel's hand shook on his glass. "I believe there may be other factors too. Your mother says …"

"MY MOTHER? You've been talking to my mother?"

"Only after you told me about Phil wanting to see you."

Daniel put down his glass and tried to take her hands. She shook them off furiously but Daniel hung on. His grip almost hurt. "She told me, Alice. She told me about the other things before … before it happened. The tranquillisers during your A-level year because you were anxious about your exams. The diary she found at the bottom of your wardrobe."

He drew breath for a second. "She said … she thought … they were just the wild imaginings of a teenager who was under pressure. It's OK, Alice. Adolescent angst is natural. I see it all the time with the first years. But in your day, there wasn't the help there is nowadays. But if it isn't treated, it can lead to all sorts of problems. Fantasies even …"

Alice pulled away furiously. "I did *not* imagine what happened."

"Maybe misinterpret then …"

"NO." She could feel the anger burning up inside. "If that's what you think, we might as well end our marriage right now."

"End our marriage?" repeated Daniel unsteadily. "If that's what you want, then I wouldn't stand in your way." He glanced around the sitting room with its pale blue and yellow chintz sofas and the nineteenth-century gilt mirror over the peacock-blue art deco fireplace that she had sourced from an architectural salvage yard shortly after moving in. "We'll just divide all this, fair and square."

98

He spoke as though he had already thought of this. If so, she wouldn't blame him. What kind of man could put up with a sexless marriage for so long?

"But what about Garth?" Alice heard herself saying.

Daniel nodded. "Exactly. I've got a first year at the moment who's about to drop out because her parents have just split up. And she's not the first. Kids need parents, no matter how old those 'kids' are." He shrugged. "Still, the decision is yours."

His voice had a hard edge to it. "Give us a chance, Alice. Go and see this old man. Tell him what you have to. Hear his point of view too."

"Forgive him you mean? Even though you and my mother don't think there's anything to forgive him for?"

"I'm not saying that."

"Yes you are."

Then, draining her own glass because – dammit – she needed the strength, Alice ran out into the hall, grabbed the dog lead from the coat hook, and whistled to Mungo, who came bounding out from the kitchen.

"Where are you going?" Daniel looked scared. Confused. Too late, she realised she'd ripped the cleverly wrapped Do Not Open seal around their marriage.

"Out for a walk."

"What about dinner?"

She threw him a disappointed look. "It's in the Aga. You can eat on your own. I'm not hungry."

Thank God for Mungo. If it wasn't for the excuse of having a dog, she would go crazy. But a dog permitted you to get out.

The very action of walking, she told herself as she rounded the bend and walked along the sea front, helped you to escape awkward conversations or arguments. The waves that pounded against the rocks allowed you to think of something else apart from the disappointment in Daniel's eyes.

The wind blowing through the hair made her feel a bit closer to Garth. They might be miles apart but they were both breathing the same air, weren't they?

Meanwhile, the clusters of teenagers on the beach, laughing

99

merrily over their disposable barbecues, helped to convince her that that girl in the park would be all right. It was summer. Lots of kids chose to sleep outside. She'd probably had an argument with her mother just like Garth used to do before his gap years. But they'd have made up, like most families. Maybe she was back home right now. She could imagine it clearly. They'd be watching TV together or chatting. See? No need to worry.

"Good evening. How are you doing?"

Alice looked up in surprise. For a moment, she almost didn't recognise him.

"Hi."

Paul Black's eyes locked with hers. Fleetingly, she expected him to accuse her of something. Then he smiled. Now he seemed more like a friend whom she'd bumped into.

"I like evening walks too."

"They're the only time I feel like myself," she heard herself say.

"I know what you mean."

Almost immediately, they fell into a steady pace together, following Mungo who was haring along on a part of the beach that was allowed during summer months. "It's why I always volunteer for evening duty."

"Doesn't your family mind?" The question flew out of her mouth before she could take it back.

"Actually, I don't have one. Not any more."

His voice was neutral and his eyes straight ahead.

"Sorry, I didn't mean to pry."

"That's all right."

Desperately, she tried to get back onto surer ground. "Have you found the girl? I've been worried about her."

She was about to add that she knew this was silly and that Kayleigh – such a coincidence that she really wanted to be a Victoria! – was probably safely at home. Then his voice cut in.

"No."

"Oh." Hope flew out of her like released air from a balloon. She'd never cared for the latter since extracting a deflated one from Garth's mouth as a toddler at a children's party. It could have been fatal …

100

There was an edge to Paul Black's voice that suggested there was something else. "Has the boy been sentenced yet?"

She glanced sideways at him. His face looked more handsome from the side with its aquiline nose. Almost Roman-like. He bore himself well, rather like Russell Crowe in that *Gladiator* film. But his expression made her feel suddenly uneasy.

"There's been a development," he said.

Her heart quickened.

"There's a formal letter on its way to you, which will explain."

"Tell me," she said urgently. "I need to know now."

As she spoke, a woman whom she knew slightly from church walked past, giving a quick nod of recognition and curiously checking Paul's uniform. Alice felt a flash of foreboding.

"The defendant has changed his plea. To Not Guilty."

For a second, Alice didn't take it in. Then the significance dawned. "He's saying he didn't do it?"

There was a small sigh next to her. "The defence is arguing that the girl has a history of making things up."

"But if I testify in court to tell them what I saw?"

"Then that might be enough." His blue eyes locked with hers. What was it about them? Every time she tried to look away, they were there. Fixed on her.

"It won't be pleasant. The other side will try to discredit you. They will attempt to case slurs on your own character. Make you look like an unreliable witness."

They were standing now by the undercliff where generations of lovers had carved their names into the cliff. Mungo was waiting patiently; his expression clearly saying *"Isn't it time to go home?"*

"I have to ask you this, Alice. Is there anything in your life, past or present, that might make the jury doubt your word?"

Silently, she considered the waves, bursting into white crinkly lines onto the sand. The tide was going out, leaving vast tracts of virgin sand. Pure and untroubled. Just as she had been, before Phil had sullied her. It was *him* who had lied. She was innocent.

"No," she said firmly, bending down to put Mungo on the lead again. "No there isn't."

"And are you prepared to take the stand as a witness?"

She straightened, facing him fair and square. "Would it help the girl?"

Even as she spoke, Alice knew the answer.

"Not just her but others too. This youth ..." Paul Black stopped and she had the feeling he wanted to call him much worse. "This youth will continue to hurt other girls if we don't stop him."

That was it then.

"I'll testify." Her voice rang out clearly into the evening air.

"Good." He looked relieved. "I promise you, Alice, that we will offer you protection."

She felt alarmed. "But you said earlier that witnesses rarely got threatened."

He looked away. "Not usually. But that doesn't mean we don't have to be careful."

Of course she should tell Daniel. But when she returned that evening from the walk, there had been a note.

Gone out for drink.

Daniel rarely went out for a midweek drink. He hadn't said who with, either, though instinct told her it was probably Brian, Janice's husband.

Alice checked her watch. What time was it in South America? It would be expensive to ring rather than Skype but what the hell? He wouldn't answer anyway. Kids never did nowadays. They just texted every now and then; usually when they needed something.

"Garth?" She was astounded when he picked up. Usually he had it switched off. "You're there?"

"What's wrong, Mum?"

He sounded sleepy. She must have woken him.

"Nothing. I just wanted to hear your voice. Are you OK?"

"Sure." He sounded a bit spaced out. "You?"

"Yes. Garth, there's something I want to ask you."

102

This was crazy. When had she ever asked for her son's advice?

There was a heavy sigh. "If you want to know if I'm doing drugs, Mum, the answer is no."

"It's not that. I need your help."

He laughed. "You need *my* help?"

She swallowed. "If someone asked you to do something that you knew you should do, but which might make you look very foolish, would you do it?"

"Is this a test question, Mum?"

"No." For a minute, she visualised giving evidence in court. Imagined the other side discrediting her as a witness, thanks to an old man's word against hers all those years ago. "I just want to know."

There was a pause, during which she wondered if he was still there. Then he spoke. "I'd do the right thing. At least I think I would because that's the way you've brought me up."

Alice felt a flood of gratitude. So something had gone in after all during all those years. "Thanks."

"Sure you're OK, Mum?"

His concern was sweetly touching.

"Certain. What about you? You will be safe out there, won't you?"

Her son's voice in a place she could not picture suddenly struck a horrible fear in her chest. She'd been worried before, of course, but hearing him made it so much worse, instead of better. Part of her wanted to catch a plane and bring him back safely so he wouldn't end up in trouble like Kayleigh.

"Of course I'll be safe." She could tell he'd had enough nagging. "Look, I've got to go. There's a party on the beach."

"Skype at the weekend?" she said desperately.

"If I can."

She wanted to hold his voice. Cradle it as she had cradled his body as a baby.

"Love you."

"Love you too."

Reluctantly, she put down the phone. Then she picked up the receiver again; fingers shaking as she pressed the familiar digits.

"Mum? It's me."

Alice took a deep breath. "You win. I'll come with you to see Uncle Phil."

TEN

Kayleigh followed the old man down the road, past the library. The rain was lashing so heavily that she could hardly see where she was going. It pierced her skin like lots of small needles all attacking her at the same time.

Once, as a small child, Kayleigh had found a needle under her half-brother's mattress. When she'd told him, Callum had held her by the wrists fiercely and told her that if she ever, ever split on him, something bad would happen to her. Then he'd released her and given her a hug and said she didn't need to worry 'cos he knew she'd do the right thing.

"Not much further now," Mr Morris was saying.

What was she doing, going back with a stranger? But he was ancient, wasn't he? So he had to be all right. Marlene had a nan round the corner who was always slipping her a tenner and telling her what a lovely girl she was. Kayleigh would have liked a nan too but Mum didn't know where she was any more. There hadn't seen much point in asking about a granddad. "Men don't stick around in our family," her mother was always saying as though it was a fact instead of something to waste time over.

Anyway, this old man had been researching his family history. You wouldn't get a murderer doing that.

She wasn't even that worried about the dog any more. Even though it was pretty big, it seemed a lot nicer than any others she'd come across. Certainly different from the one that had bitten her as a child. This one had a rather cute white streak down its chest and kept looking up at her as though to say "Come on, then."

"Here we are!" The old man stopped suddenly outside a small metal gate. Kayleigh brushed the soaking wet hair out of her eyes and stared at the neat front garden with yellow flowers, bowed with the rain, along the borders. It was a bungalow. Really nice with lots of little stones on the wall and a tall, neat hedge dividing it down the middle.

"That's my neighbour's." He pulled out a key from his pocket. "Deaf as a post, she is, thank the Lord. The previous one used to complain about Jack barking till the council moved her. In you go."

Ahead, was a long thin corridor with doors leading off it and a smell that reminded her of a fur coat that Marlene's nan had given her for her twelfth birthday.

"Go inside, love. Make yourself at home. We'll soon get you dry. Give us a tic and I'll find you some dry clothes."

Only now, with the door shut behind her, did Kayleigh experience a twinge of alarm. Find her some dry clothes? What if he expected her to get undressed for him?

Fucking hell. The door was locked. She couldn't get out if she wanted to. A cold panic folded itself through her.

"These should do."

Mr Morris was coming out of a room at the bottom of the corridor, carrying a pile of stuff. "These belonged to my daughter before she left home." His eyes looked her up and down. "Might be a bit big for you but they're better than nothing."

Her mouth was dry with fear. "Why did you lock the door?" she said in a half-whisper.

His glasses winked at her in the hall light. "Always do, when I go to bed. It's not a bad area but you never know, do you?"

"Then why are you being nice to me?" Kayleigh still didn't get it. "You don't know me, either."

He gave a sad smile. "See that photograph?"

A girl in a long cloak and some kind of fancy hat smiled down at her. "That was my Sandra on her graduation day. She lives in Australia now. Miss her, I do, especially now the wife's gone."

He looked down at the dog who was sitting, his face fixed on

106

the old man's like he'd do anything for him. Kayleigh felt a sudden longing for someone – even an animal – to look at her like that. The closest she'd come to it was in the park when Frankie had told her she was the most beautiful girl he had ever seen.

At least, she thought that's what he had said. It was difficult to remember exactly.

"I've got a boyfriend," she said suddenly. "We're going to find a place of our own, one day."

OK. So it wasn't exactly true but it felt good to say it. Maybe when Frankie got out, it might even happen.

"That's nice. Where is he now?"

Kayleigh didn't want to admit he was in prison. It could give the wrong idea about him. "Away."

The glasses winked again under the hall light. "Let's not hang around then. You'll want to get changed. You can have the first room on the left." He pushed open the door. "It belonged to my Sandra."

Wide-eyed, Kayleigh took in the huge bed and the teddy, sitting upright on the pillow. There was a bookshelf too! Just look at all those rows and rows of paperbacks, neatly stacked in order of height. The tidiness made her feel safe again.

"Like reading, do you?" he asked, watching her face light up.

She nodded keenly. "'Specially poetry. We're doing Roger McGough at school."

"Don't know him myself. I'm a Wordsworth man. Anyway, I'll leave you to it. Bathroom's next door. Do you want to eat or wash first?"

Both, she wanted to stay but her tongue stuck to the roof of her mouth in a mixture of gratitude and shyness.

"Maybe wash first," he chipped in, handing her a towel. You'll find the lock a bit sticky, mind. When you're ready, come into the kitchen – that's the room opposite – and we'll have a bite to eat."

Kayleigh could hardly believe it. Here she was, sitting at a proper table, eating spaghetti rings with an old man who could be her granddad. The dog was sitting by her side, waiting for titbits although Mr Morris had already warned her not to give in.

"He'll give you his big doe eyes but it's all part of the act. He eats after us. It's part of his training."

Sounded a bit harsh to her but something told Kayleigh that she shouldn't disagree. After dinner, he started to wash up. "Want to dry?" he asked, handing her a cloth with a picture of an island on it and the name Ventnor written above. Was that a place or a meaning? Maybe the former, judging from the picture of the sea. Kayleigh was so busy admiring the cloth that the plate almost slipped out of her hand. She caught it just in time.

"Sorry." She flushed deeply. "I'm not used to this. Usually we just chuck out the takeaway containers."

Mr Morris's old hands, wrist deep in the suds, paused. "Live with your parents, do you?"

"Just my mum and her bloke." The glass of wine he'd given her to go with the meal made her less shy than before. "It's why I had to leave. He was … he wasn't very friendly to me."

Best, she told herself, not to mention the hostel and the running away and the shoplifting. It would only complicate things.

"I see." He handed her a plate and this time, she managed to dry it without any problems. "Sounds as though you've had a bit of a rough time."

Kayleigh shrugged. "It will be all right when my boyfriend gets out …"

Too late, she realised she'd given it away.

"In the nick, is he?" Those glasses glinted again in the light.

Kayleigh felt her body burning up with embarrassment. "He's waiting to go to court. But the thing he's accused of, well it's a mistake. It will be all right."

The old man's lips tightened as he dried his hands on a towel hanging from the side of the sink from a proper hook. "That's as maybe. Now I don't know about you but I like watching the Discovery Channel on the box." He made a little bow indicating she should go first. "Want to join me?"

It was quite cosy, really, even though Marlene would really

108

laugh if she saw her sitting on a chair, next to an old man and his dog, watching a programme on elephants. She hadn't realised how old they got or how clever they were. Just look at that small boy on top of that huge beast, steering it with his toes.

"Incredible, isn't it?" Mr Morris stood up at the end and switched it off. "Time for bed now." He looked at her steadily. "There's just one thing."

Kayleigh's heart began to pound. Of course there was. How bloody stupid had she been. Swiftly she glanced at the window. They were on the ground floor. She could smash it and run.

"My eyes are fading now." He took off his glasses, wiped them disappointedly, and then put them back. "Would you mind reading to me, when I'm in bed. It's the only way I can get to sleep."

Then he added. "It's all right, Kayleigh. I won't hurt you. Promise."

The sensible part told her not to be so bloody stupid. What if he tried to drag her into bed with him? Then again, he wasn't very big. She could fight him off. Yet deep down, she had a feeling he was telling the truth. The poor bugger just wanted someone to read to him. The way Marlene's nan had done.

"OK," she heard herself saying. "What are we reading then?"

"*Jungle Book*," he said, triumphantly. "Ever read it?"

"Saw the video once."

"The video?" He shook his head. "Wait till you hear the words. Pure magic. Poetry."

'Sounds great," began Kayleigh excitedly but she could tell the old bloke wasn't listening. Instead, his eyes were focussed on the blank wall in front as though he could see something. Then he gave a little smile and looked away. "Used to read it to my daughter, I did. Every night." Then he looked at her expectantly, his body tucked up under a blue blanket with, she could see, proper sheets underneath. "Ready?"

He was right. They *were* magic. Sitting beside the old man's bed with his shelves of books and rows of toy cars ("a hobby of mine – drove the wife mad, it did"), Kayleigh found herself in another world. Mowgli's character reached out to her and as for that horrible snake, she just wanted someone to tell it where to get off.

The reading worked too. Mr Morris found it hard to get to sleep, he said. But he was asleep now, snoring away. The dog had settled down too in his basket in the corner of the room. Kayleigh felt a bit odd, here all alone in a place she didn't know.

Still, at least she was warm and dry. Outside the rain was lashing down, even harder than before. If it wasn't for the old bloke, she'd be out in it right now. Kayleigh shivered with relief. Then, tiptoeing back to the daughter's bedroom, she couldn't resist going through some of the stuff on the shelves and in the little wooden dressing table.

Wow. Her fingers found themselves picking up a snapshot of a girl with short dark hair, grinning, standing next to a couple. The bloke had sandy hair and glasses and the woman had a plain but kind face. Was that Mr Morris and his dead wife?

Then she stopped. There was a black file in the drawer with lots of newspaper articles inside. One fell out. It was a clipping from a local paper.

MAN ON TRIAL FOR MURDER OF BRITISH GIRL IN AUSTRALIAN OUTBACK

Curiously, Kayleigh read on.

A 27-year-old sheep shearer is on trial for the murder of 23-year-old Sandra Morris who was found, bludgeoned to death, near Alice Springs last month. The student was a British teacher from Plymouth who was on an exchange year. Her parents are understood to have gone out to Australia to give evidence."

Kayleigh's eyes filled with tears. Poor thing. And poor Mr Morris. That's why it was important to have an imagination. Because it helped you get through the real, shitty bits of life.

She woke in the morning to sun streaming through the curtains

110

and the smell of coffee. That was weird. Her bedroom door was slightly ajar even though she could have sworn she'd shut it last night.

On the back of the door there was a large dressing gown; a maroon one that felt very soft. Wrapping it round her, she made her way to the bathroom. "I've left a towel out for you," came the old man's voice from the kitchen. "When you're ready, come and join me for breakfast."

The shower was really complicated. She had to turn the lever and fiddle around with a really stiff dial before the water got to the right temperature. That was nice. Kayleigh felt much cleaner now. When she got back to her room, she found her own clothes dry and neatly folded on the bed. Mr Morris must have gone in when she was in the bathroom. Still, it was his place, wasn't it?

"Thanks," she said, coming into the kitchen. "For drying my stuff."

Her host waved a hand as though it was nothing. "You look a lot better this morning, my dear, if you don't mind me saying. Now how about a nice rasher of bacon with a fried egg?"

Bacon? Bloody hell. That would be a real treat. As soon as the plate was put in front of her, she fell on it.

"What do you normally have for breakfast?" he asked, watching her bolt it down.

"Toast," she said, swallowing her mouthful hastily so she could talk politely. "But that's only if my stepdad, Ron, isn't around. If he is, I get something on the way to school."

"Why's that?"

"'Cos I don't like being near him."

Mr Morris studied her for a moment. "Are you saying he's violent to you?"

"He tried it on with me."

His brows met. Instantly, Kayleigh wished she'd kept her gob shut. "Can't you report him to someone? A teacher perhaps?"

Kayleigh laughed. "Mum would say I was making it up."

He shook his head sadly. "That's terrible."

Kayleigh shrugged. "People do make things up, don't they?"

The old man's lips tightened. "They shouldn't. It's evil."

She thought of the newspaper article she'd found last night. "What about your daughter?" The words came out of her mouth before she could take them back, Now it was too late to stop. "She didn't really die, did she? I found the article. The one that said she was murdered."

There was a silence. The dog's hair went up as though he sensed trouble. The old man's eyes hardened. For a moment, they looked like two evil balls of glass. "You had no right to go through my daughter's things."

Kayleigh leaped up, scraping back her chair as she did so. "Sorry. I didn't mean to. Just thought it might help to talk."

"I give you a bed for the night and you repay me like this?"

He picked up a knife. A bread knife on the side of the table with a big black handle. As he did so, the dog let out a low deep growl. Now you've done it, she could almost hear Marlene saying in her head.

"I'm sorry." Kayleigh's voice came out in a whisper.

"She isn't dead. She's alive." He banged the back of the table with his fist. "Do you hear me?"

Fucking hell. He was a nutter. "OK, OK," said Kayleigh hastily. "I didn't mean it. She's alive. Your daughter is still alive. Living in Australia."

Slowly he brought down the knife onto the table. His body was shuddering now, in huge convulsive sobs. "I'm sorry," he was weeping. "I'm sorry."

Part of her wanted to comfort him. The other to run away.

"The man," he was sobbing, "the man accused of murdering her got off. There weren't any witnesses, you see. He had an alibi. Said he was somewhere he wasn't. One of his friends lied for him."

"It's not fair," whispered Kayleigh.

"No, it's not." His eyes were wet. "My wife, she never got over it. It's why she died. Broken heart, though they put 'stroke' on the certificate. As for me, all I have are my books and my bloody family tree. Do you know why I bother?"

"Why?"

He straightened himself as if on parade inspection. Callum

used to show her how he did that when he was in the army; before he went Inside. "Because no one can take away the past, that's why. No one can take away the family that I used to have."

She could see that. But she could also see that she had to get out of here. The bloke was a madman, poor bugger. Even so, Kayleigh couldn't help patting him comfortingly on the back. His dry, heavily blue-veined hand came up and squeezed hers. "I have to leave now," she whispered. "Thank you."

He shook his head. "It is I who have to thank you, for your company." Then his eyes beseeched hers. "Please stay. I won't do this again." He glanced at the knife. "I promise. It's just that I get so upset."

Briefly Kayleigh was tempted. But only for a second. "Sorry."

"Where will you go?"

She shrugged. "Maybe try and find my boyfriend."

There was a reluctant nod. "Good luck."

Then he opened a drawer by the side of the sink. "Please, take this."

It was a twenty-pound note. Kayleigh eyed it longingly.

"You need that yourself."

"No I don't."

She thought of the fifty quid that the beautiful blonde woman had given her; the one that Posy had nicked. It would buy her something to eat for the next few days.

"Sure?"

"'Course I am, Sandra." He was smiling at her now. "You're my daughter, aren't you? What father wouldn't want to help his lovely girl."

Kayleigh froze. "Thanks." Her hand closed over the note.

"Thanks, *Dad*," he said, accentuating the last word.

"Thanks, Dad," she said unsteadily.

Then quickly, before any other weird stuff happened, she nipped back into the dead girl's room, grabbed her bag, and headed for the door.

"It's open, Sandra," called out the old man. "See you tonight after work, all right? Your mother's cooking your favourite

113

again. Spaghetti bolognese."

"Great," she called back. Then, walking briskly down the path, she shut the little metal gate behind her and began to run. All over again.

ELEVEN

Alice had wanted to drive herself to the nursing home in the morning but Mum wouldn't have any of it.

"I'd like to see Phil first," she'd said in that very clear precise voice of hers which had always over-ridden Alice's and had done the same to her father when he'd been alive. "We don't know how much longer the poor man has."

Poor man? Alice's knuckles clenched quietly in the passenger seat as they made the hour-long journey through leafy lanes and then on to the motorway towards Bristol. Mum had insisted on driving; as ever, needing to be in charge.

Sometimes, when Alice looked back at her childhood, she wondered how she had survived. Surely any decent mother would listen to a daughter making serious accusations? Yet even Dad hadn't been certain in the end. She'd seen the doubt in his eyes grow after his talk with Phil and knew that his friend had persuaded him into believing that his daughter was just a silly girl who made things up.

Not surprisingly, her 'daft imaginings' had left a stain. When her mother insisted on inviting Phil and his wife to Alice and Daniel's wedding, they conveniently had a 'last-minute' cruise booked. "It's all your fault," her mother had wailed. "You've made me lose our friends. They haven't been the same since the incident."

Later, when Marjorie with her cow-like eyes had died – around the time of Garth's birth – Alice had reluctantly been persuaded to send flowers although she'd put her foot down about going to the funeral. "How could I see Phil again?" she had argued fiercely. "That man ruined my life."

"Don't be so ridiculous," Mum had snapped. "If you don't stop saying things like that, you'll get yourself into real hot water. Not your made-up variety."

Now as they drove to the nursing home with her mother all too frequently exceeding the speed limit, Alice's mind went back to the day of her eighteenth birthday. The counsellor whom she'd seen later at university, had urged her not to dwell on what she called 'your story'. It was better, apparently, to concentrate on the present and learn from the 'experience' of the past.

Yet the fact remained that all these years later, it seemed as real as if it had happened yesterday.

Alice had just passed her driving test! The first in her class to do so. Despite her nerves about impending A-levels (she'd always been a bit of a 'worrier'), the driving-test triumph had really boosted her confidence. Alice was flying high, boosted by her father's obvious pride. "Well done, my girl!"

He'd enveloped her in a big bear hug. "You obviously take after my side of the family, though don't tell your mother that. You've got good spatial awareness and you're sensible too. Make a good driver, you will."

Her mother, who had only recently learned to drive herself ("in my day, Alice, it was different. We didn't have the advantages of your generation.") was less enthusiastic. "Just make sure you're careful. It's a big responsibility, you know. You've got other people's lives in your hands."

Then she'd shaken her head. "As for this car your father has bought you, I think it's quite ridiculous. Talk about spoiling you ..."

Alice had gasped. "Dad's bought me a car?"

Her mother's lips had tightened. "I'm not meant to have told you. It's a surprise. So try to act like it when he tells you."

Sometimes Alice wondered if her mother disliked her because her birth had apparently caused "problems". It was, she gleaned over the years, why her parents had never had another child. The counsellor had said it seemed as though, despite

116

working hard to gain her mother's love, Alice was on a losing wicket. "Children without siblings can be so precious that their parents wrap them up in cotton wool," she'd told her. "Sometimes, however, they unfairly take the brunt for their parents' disappointments."

It was pretty obvious that Alice had fallen into the last category.

Still, it was different with Dad. "Like it?" he'd said, after instructing her to close her eyes and then leading her to the garage where a sparkling brand new Fiesta sat waiting. She'd gasped. Even though Mum had (deliberately?) ruined the surprise, Alice's breath was still taken away.

"It's great, Dad. Really amazing."

His eyes had shone with pleasure. "I bought it from Uncle Phil's garage. He gave me a good deal. Tell you what." He pressed the keys into her hand. "Why don't you drive over and see him and Marjorie? Nothing like a solo drive to give you confidence, right at the beginning. The weekend traffic will give you a bit of practice too."

Uncle Phil and Aunt Marjorie weren't really her uncle and aunt although she had grown up, calling them that. Phil had worked with Dad once and met his wife at her parents' wedding. (Marjorie had trained as a nurse with Mum.) They hadn't had any children of their own which was, as Marjorie sometimes said while plying Alice with butterfly cakes, a "great sadness". Alice had always liked Aunt Marjorie with her tight blonde curls that she had 'done' every Saturday, regular as clockwork. But there was something about Uncle Phil with his slick brown hair, combed neatly to one side and the way he would always give her a big strong hug that had almost winded her when she was little (and felt a bit odd now she was getting older), that she didn't care for.

Still, as Dad said, she owed it to him to say thank you for helping out with the car. And it would be nice to see Marjorie and tell her about the disco that Mum and Dad were allowing her to have tonight in the local hall, to celebrate her birthday. Alice felt a flutter of excitement at the thought of seeing Gordon from the Sixth Form Debating Society again. "'Course

I'll be there," he had said when she'd given him the invitation. "Wild horses wouldn't stop me."

It wasn't a long drive to her uncle and aunt's but just enough to get the hang of the gears which were a little stiff. Dad had been right, she told herself, pulling up outside the neat chalet bungalow with its clipped lawns and windows that were always sparkling. "It's not as though she's got anything else to do," Alice had overheard Mum say once.

Carefully reversing up their drive, following Dad's instructions, she locked the door before stroking the bonnet. Her car! Her very own car! Dad had been right! The solo drive *had* given her more confidence. Flushed with excitement, she hurried along the gravel path, clutching the bottle of wine that Dad had given her to thank his old friend along with a thank you note that Mum had pressed into her hand.

It opened before she had a chance to ring the bell with its tinkly chime. As a child she had always loved to press it, time and time again; knowing as it did so that it sang of butterfly cakes and happy adult conversation which she would observe from a corner, happily ensconced in a book or – even better – making up stories.

"Alice!" Uncle Phil enveloped her in one of his bear hugs. When she stepped back, he beamed down at her. He was wearing – how clear it still was in her mind – a blue-and-white striped jacket as though he was going to the boat race; something that he, Marjorie, Mum, and Dad did every year.

"Phil went to Cambridge, you know," Marjorie would say every now and then as if she hadn't already said it hundreds of times before. Then her husband would wave a chubby hand away as if it wasn't important although the conversation would inevitably turn to who was doing what from his year at university, which often made Dad go rather quiet.

On that particular Saturday, however, Phil was less interested in his own elite academic background than the shiny blue Fiesta in the drive. "Like it, do you?"

She nodded excitedly. "Thanks so much for helping Dad choose it." Then she held out the bottle of wine and the note. "These are for you."

118

Taking them, he opened the envelope, read it briefly, and then considered the label on the bottle. "How very thoughtful of you." She was about to say that actually it was a present from Dad but he was already ushering her in, talking excitedly. "Excellent timing, I must say!" He rubbed his chin, a common gesture, Alice had noticed, when pleased about something. "Marjorie has made one of her special chocolate cakes – makes a change from those little butterfly jobs, don't you think – and we can't eat it on our own."

Phil led her, not into the kitchen as usual, but into what Marjorie called the morning room. It had a lovely view over the golf course and a very thick carpet which your feet sank into. "Take a seat," he said, indicating the huge sofa with billowing yellow roses that Marjorie had chosen from Harrods last month and was so proud of. Then he strode across to the drinks cabinet in the corner and opened a bottle of sherry. "We ought to celebrate your birthday."

Alice shifted uneasily in her seat. "I don't want to drink. Not before driving back."

"Nonsense. Just one won't hurt."

He was handing her the glass and as he did so, his hand brushed hers. But instead of apologising, he beamed. Feeling it was right to do so, she beamed back.

"Isn't Auntie Marjorie going to join us?" she asked, looking at the door and expecting her to come in any minute.

"At the hairdresser," he announced, sitting down next to her. "Someone cancelled so she had to change her usual appointment time."

His knees were pressing now against hers even though there was plenty of room on the huge sofa for him to sit further away. Indeed, there were several chairs too. Alice didn't know what to do. If she got up to sit on one of them instead, it looked rude. Maybe he didn't realise how close he was.

Edging away, she put her glass on the side table. He moved nearer, his right arm stretched along the back of the sofa. It almost felt as though he had it around her, in the way that Gordon had – unexpectedly – done after the last debating meeting on the way to the bus stop. The recollection made her tingle. Not long to her birthday party now! What would it be like when he kissed her?

Her spine tingled with anticipation. Angela from her Physics class had had her eye on him for ages and Alice still couldn't believe that it was *her* whom Gordon was interested in. Apart from the debating club, opportunities for boyfriends were few and far between, partly because her parents were so strict about not going out at weekends. Time enough for dating when you go to university, her mother had said, tight-lipped. Her father, as always, had agreed.

"So," said Uncle Phil, grinning; bringing her back to the immediate present. He'd always had slightly grey teeth but today they seemed whiter. They smelt of mint as though he'd just cleaned them but there was also a whiff of sherry, suggesting he'd had one before she'd arrived. "Got a boyfriend, have you?"

Gordon promptly swam into her mind; as if he had ever been out of it. Tall, blond, slightly gangly, but who was pleasingly shy and reserved like her. "Not exactly but there is someone I like." Shifting, she tried to move a bit further away but she'd come to the end of the sofa. Don't be silly, she told herself. This is Uncle Phil.

"Done much with him, then?"

He was grinning even more now.

"No. I mean, I wouldn't."

Overcome with embarrassment, Alice made to get up but Uncle Phil placed a large hand on her shoulder. "Don't go, dear. I want to talk." His eyes travelled down to her breasts unashamedly. "You've grown up into a beautiful young lady, haven't you?"

Alice flushed. She was feeling really uncomfortable now but it was difficult to move with the way that he was sitting. "You know, your Auntie Marjorie and I haven't been, shall we say, close for a very long time."

This wasn't right. She could see that now. "I have to go," said Alice, trying to get to her feet.

"Not so fast."

Oh my God. His hand was actually cupping her right breast.

His mouth, smelling of sherry and toothpaste was coming down on hers. "No," she said, struggling to get away. "No."

"Come on." Phil's hand was going further down. "You know you want it. I've seen the way you look at me."

"I don't. It's not true. Stop. Please. STOP."

It was all over so fast that she could hardly believe it had happened. There was no blood, the way everyone at school said there was. Just a horrible throbbing between her legs. Weeping, she stumbled for the door, her pants still half down.

"If you tell anyone," slurred Phil from the sofa, "I'll say you made it up. I'll tell your parents that you had a drink even though I told you not to and that it made you imagine all this. You've always told stories, haven't you? Ever since you were little."

Almost hysterical, she ran to the car, turned on the engine, stalled it, and then drove home, her eyes blinded with tears. Crunching to a halt, she sat there for a minute before going in. "Mum! Dad!" she called out.

No answer. Just a note on the kitchen table to say that they had gone shopping for her party. Falling over the stairs in her distress, Alice ran herself a long hot bath. By the time her parents got back, she had made herself a strong sweet cup of tea but was still shaking.

"I knew it," said her mother, taking in her distressed appearance. "You crashed the car, didn't you?"

"No." Alice burst into tears.

"What's wrong, love?" asked Dad.

"It was Uncle Phil." She began to shake. Huge convulsive sobs that washed through her body. "He ... he tried to do something."

She was right, thought Alice grimly as her mother swung into the grounds of the nursing home. They hadn't believed her. At least Mum hadn't. "How could you make something up like that?" she'd lashed out. "It's wicked. Pure evil."

Dad said nothing but his eyes had shown that he was finding it hard to accept what she'd said. "Let me sort this out," he said.

"Don't you dare!" Her mother had clutched his arm. "I'll

never be able to look Marjorie in the face again. We'll lose them as friends, all because of our daughter's silly head."

Later, after the party was cancelled (Alice refused to go and her mother was left with the 'humiliating' task of ringing everyone, not to mention the 'terrible unnecessary expense'), Dad had taken her to one side. "Are you sure this all happened?"

She'd nodded.

He'd gone out the next day 'for a drive' or so he said. But when he returned, his face was set. "Did he admit it?" asked Alice.

Dad had shaken his head. "He said you tried to … to get familiar but that he'd had to push you away."

"That's not true."

Looking at her sadly, Dad had patted her on the shoulder and then walked away. The following month, Gordon – fed up no doubt by her failure to return his calls – started dating Angela.

Somehow, she got through her A-levels; spurred only by the thought of getting away. During her first year at uni, her mother's letters occasionally referred to joint jaunts with Uncle Phil and Auntie Marjorie. The very look of his name in her mother's writing made her feel sick and Alice made sure that she was never around if they came to the house during the holidays. Eventually, the strain grew too much. At her tutor's suggestion, she left after her first year to have a break and never came back. Far easier to rent a room in London, join an employment agency, and carry on running.

If only she'd run away from Phil before anything had happened.

My fault. My fault.

"This way, please." The cool but pleasant enough nurse who met them at the door was now leading them down a corridor. Alice glanced at her mother. She was looking as elegant as always; after Dad had died, she had blossomed rather than wilted. Now, as she clicked along in her kitten heels and tailored dress, she might pass for sixty rather than seventy-odd.

"Don't upset him," she hissed. "He's an old man. And he still hasn't forgotten those silly accusations that you made."

Gritting her teeth – what was the point of arguing back now when her mother had never believed her before? – Alice followed the nurse into a small side room. Stunned, she stopped.

There, in the bed, lay an old man. His skin was grey and there was a network of tubes leading from his arm to the drip at the side. His eyelids were closed and there was a heavy rasping. Was this really the spectre who had spoiled her life? She could surely knock him down like a feather if she so chose.

"Phil," said the nurse softly. "You've got the visitor you've been asking for."

Almost immediately, the eyes snapped open. It was all Alice could do not to gasp. The outside body might have changed but those brown eyes with flecks of green were still the same ones from her nightmares, bearing down on her. Those thin hands on the bed had once been strong enough to pin her down. Was it possible that this was a joke? That any minute now, those hands might try to do the same again?

For a minute, she thought she was going to be sick. "Take a seat, dear," said the nurse, seeing her falter. Then she whispered. "I know it's distressing seeing loved ones like this."

Phil was waving a hand. "Go away," he seemed to say.

Did he want her to leave immediately? Alice felt cheated. There was so much she needed to say to him. But then she realised he was waving his hand at her mother. He wanted *her* to go.

"We'll give you and your uncle some time together, shall we?" whispered the nurse.

Alice swallowed. Yes. No. Maybe. He was here. Face to face. Finally she could tell him all the things she'd been storing up in her head. Things that the counsellor had said she ought to list in a letter to "let it all out".

But how could she? He was an old man. Frail. On his deathbed with yellow skin. Ugh! A wrinkled hand was creeping out towards hers. He was trying to say something. "I'm sorry." At first she didn't think she'd heard him properly. In disgust, she leaned towards him, noting his thin maroon lips. "I'm sorry."

There was no doubt now.

"You ruined my life," she whispered back.

"Forgive me." The eyes held hers. "Please."

What else could she do? He was dying. Terror was in his eyes. This old man was facing the ultimate. The thing that they were all secretly scared of. It would be wicked not to give him her forgiveness.

Silently she nodded, hating herself for doing so. "I ... forgive ... you."

Each word had to squeezed out of her mouth through sheer internal effort.

Then she got up and ran out of the room, past her mother, waiting by the door with mistrustful eyes. "You didn't upset him, did you?"

"Fuck off," she threw back, appalled with herself and by the look on the nurse's face. "Just fuck off."

The two of them drove back in silence, her mother refusing to speak to her after what she described as the most embarrassing scene of her life. In front of the nurse too. Whatever would she think? What was wrong with Alice? Why couldn't she be normal like other daughters?

As her mother drove through the mid-morning traffic, they went through a small village on the outskirts of Plymouth. For a moment, Alice fancied she saw the girl from the park running, her unruly pale auburn locks cascading over her shoulders; rucksack on her back.

She shook her head. Her imagination again. Both a curse and a blessing. With longing, Alice thought of the china piece at home, waiting to be restored. It was a small vase, broken by the owner's sister which needed mending before the damage was discovered. The project might distract her. Soothe her. Take away the injustice of having been denied her final say. Give her time to reflect, on her own, exactly what had happened.

But to her irritation, Daniel met her at the door.

"What happened?" he asked, taking in her face, frowning as he tried to read it. Then he observed her mother driving off. "Doesn't she want to come in?"

Alice shook her head. "It's a long story."

He tried to hold her but she broke away. His touch revolted her. Reminded her of the old man with the blue-veined hands and maroon lips who had forced her, once more, to do something she hadn't wanted.

It felt like verbal rape.

"Please Daniel, not now."

Hurt, he turned away. Alice tried to find a voice to explain; giving up, she put on the kettle and turned on the radio. Normal Radio 4. Merrily chattering away as though nothing had happened. Sweet tea. The vase waiting to be mended. A game of tennis maybe, at the club tomorrow.

Routine.

It was the only way forward.

"*This is the news at one. There have been a series of earthquakes in south America ...*"

Appalled, she dropped the spoonful of tea she'd been about to put in the teapot. Daniel, halfway out of the kitchen, shot round.

"*Several casualties have been reported ...*"

Oh my God. "It's all right," she expected her husband to say. "Stop worrying all the time. South America is a big place."

"Peru is said to be badly affected ..."

Peru? "But that's where Garth is," she whispered, half-waiting for her husband to correct her.

But instead, he was scribbling down the emergency number on the kitchen notepad before grabbing the phone.

TWELVE

Why, Kayleigh asked herself as she ran, did she always pick weirdos? First Ron – although to be fair, it was Mum who had brought him home. Then Posy from the centre who had nicked her money. And now some old bloke who wanted to pretend she was his murdered daughter.

If Callum had been around, she thought wistfully, he'd have sorted the geezer out. But he'd been gone for so long now that she'd stopped relying on him. Instead, she had her Frankie! Yet sometimes, it was hard to picture his face. Were his eyes green or bluey-green? Maybe a mixture of both.

She'd remember as soon as she saw him again. Marlene's boyfriend was wrong. Frankie wouldn't be mad at her. He'd understand that the police had *made* her give that statement. You forgave people when you loved them, didn't you? She and Frankie might not have known each other very long but she could tell from the way he had touched her that he had really, truly wanted her just like Mr Rochester wanted Jane.

"Men aren't always good at showing their feelings," Mr Brown had said when they'd read *Jane Eyre* in class. He'd said it in such a way that Kayleigh knew he was talking about him and her. But she respected him for not doing anything because he had a family. Maybe in another life, it would be different. Mr Brown used to speak about that too in RE.

Kayleigh slowed down a bit now because her chest was hurting with the running. Anyway, no one was following her, though she wouldn't have put it past the old man to have given chase, despite his age. If Frankie was here, he'd have protected her.

Frankie, Frankie. Her heart ached with longing. "He's a well-known user," the policeman with the clear blue eyes and jet-black hair had said.

That wasn't fair. Frankie had only given her that tablet to calm her down. "Are you sure?" the policeman had demanded, when she'd sworn she'd never taken anything before herself.

But it was true. She knew what some drugs looked like because you couldn't live on the estate without seeing stuff like that. Besides, she'd seen what had been under her half-brother's bed along with the crisp fifty-pound notes.

"He didn't mean to hurt me," she'd told the policeman with the clear blue eyes. "He was just trying to help me 'cos I was upset. It was my fault for taking it. Not his."

Something flickered in the policeman's face as though he understood that bit. Good. When she saw Frankie, she'd tell him that she'd taken the blame. Maybe then he'd be nice to her.

Suddenly Kayleigh realised exactly what she had to do. She needed to go back to Marlene and get her to ask her boyfriend where Frankie was now. Then she'd visit him. Talk to him face to face.

Kayleigh ran a hand through her hair. It felt quite smooth thanks to the shower she'd had at the old man's this morning. She smelt nice too after helping herself to lavender bath salts that had been on the bathroom shelf. Only now the thought occurred to her that they might have belonged to the dead wife or daughter. Ugh.

Did she look OK enough to see Frankie? Maybe Marlene would be able to lend her something nice to wear. Her friend had had enough time to stop being mad at Kayleigh now about talking to the police. It was good to give people time to cool off. She did that with Mum. Sometimes it worked. Sometimes it didn't.

Nearly there now. The city was opening up before her with its sprawl of cheap shops before you got into the posh bit. Her spirits lifted at the sight of a corner supermarket with boxes of fruit outside. Kayleigh's stomach rumbled with hunger. She was tempted to help herself to a banana but too scared in case someone ran out of the shop and nabbed her.

There was a television in the next shop. One of those massive ones that looked like a cinema screen. Callum had promised Mum he'd get her one. "We'll never have it now." It was the first thing Mum had said after the police had come to take him away.

Kayleigh paused for a moment to look at the screen. There was a picture of a town all crushed into tiny little bits and a baby with wide eyes being picked up out of the rubble.

She loved babies! Marlene was always saying it was the only way to get a flat of your own. But she said it in a way that suggested the flat was the important bit. Not the baby. Not someone to hold against you and smell and know that this little person loved you more than anyone else ever could.

There were words under the picture now.

Massive earthquake hits South America. Hundreds feared dead. British tourists feared amongst the casualties.

Kayleigh shivered. That's what came of going abroad. She'd never fancied it herself although Mum had gone 'dirt-cheap' to a place called the Canaries a few years ago with a friend.

She walked on, still feeling sorry for those poor people on the cinema screen. Say what you did about this country, but at least you didn't get earthquakes or twisters like they'd learned about in geography.

Ouch. Her trainers were beginning to pinch more than usual. She needed a rest, Kayleigh told herself. But if she stopped, Marlene might be out when she arrived. There was no guarantee that she was in anyway. If not, maybe she'd just sit on the doorstep and wait.

At last! Here she was. Why did she feel nervous, Kayleigh asked herself, climbing the steps to the flat as the lift was out of order again? Marlene was her friend, wasn't she? Maybe she'd be worried about her. Pleased that she'd turned up safe.

The doorbell wasn't working again so she banged the knocker. There was a twitch at the closed curtains. Then footsteps. Slow footsteps that weren't in a hurry to get anywhere.

"What do you want?" Marlene's face stared at her like stone.

She had her fake eyelashes on and a T-shirt that only just reached below her bottom with *Help Yourself* written on the front in black. Nothing else.

"I ... I wanted to make up," stammered Kayleigh.

Her friend's eyes hardened. "You mean you still don't have nowhere to stay."

"They wanted to put me in care 'cos I'm underage." Kayleigh caught at Marlene's T-shirt. "Please help me."

"Is that the bitch what split on me mate?"

A tall, skinny boy with tattoos down his chest loomed up behind Marlene. His eyes narrowed, making her feel suddenly scared. "You're in real trouble, know that? Frankie's out on bail now till his court hearing. And he's looking for you."

Frankie was out on bail? He was looking for her! She knew it! He loved her, just like she loved him. Wasn't that what they'd told each other in the park?

But something didn't feel quite right.

"What do you mean, I'm in real trouble?" she asked.

Marlene's face now stopped looking hard. Instead, it was pinched and scared. "Just go, Kayleigh," she said. "Please go. Before he finds you here."

Maybe she'd try home again. God knows she needed some clean clothes. The jeans that the old man had washed for her had shrunk. And the ones that had belonged to his dead daughter freaked her out.

It would be nice, after all that running, to have a shower before she went to find Frankie. No matter what Marlene said, she knew Frankie would understand. The police made you do things you didn't want. Everyone knew that.

Kayleigh walked through the concrete open area dividing her block of flats from Marlene's and looked up. Mum had the washing hanging over the railings outside, which meant she was in. No one ever just left it there or it would get nicked.

Peering through the window – there was a useful gap in the net curtains – Kayleigh could see Mum sitting on the sofa, watching the telly. No sign of Ron. That was good.

Reaching for the key on her belt, she made to slide it into the lock.

It wouldn't fit.

Kayleigh tried again.

It was like she'd got the wrong key.

Or else the locks had been changed.

Her mind went back to the day the police had come and found the notes under Callum's bed along with the other stuff. Mum had changed the locks then. "We can't have no more trouble," she'd said by way of explanation. "Else the council will throw us out."

Was that what Mum had done now? Changed the locks again because the policeman had wanted to Caution her?

"Mum," she said, hammering on the sitting room window. "Mum. It's me. Kayleigh. Please. Open up."

But the figure on the sofa remained where it was.

Kayleigh tried again. "I haven't done nothing wrong, Mum. I need some clean clothes. Let me in."

The door on the left opened. It was the young girl who'd moved in last Christmas with a double buggy and a kid whose father came to pick him up every other Saturday. "Shut up, can you? I've only just got my little 'un to sleep."

Before Kayleigh could apologise, she could hear a noise on the other side of her own front door. "Mum?"

Then the letter flap opened. Kayleigh knelt down. Mum spoke in urgent whispers, her eyes scared through the gap. Her breath smelt of booze. "I can't talk to you. Ron's asleep but he'll go mad if he knows you're here. He says I can't see you again."

"But I'm your daughter!"

"And he's my bloke. I need him. Anyroad, he's fucking furious with you for lying. He says you made a pass at him."

What! "He was the one who tried to have it on with me."

"You're lying."

"No I'm not. You just don't want to accept it 'cos you hate being alone."

"Fuck off."

Next door's window opened and the woman with twins had her head out. "If you two don't bloody well put a sock in it, I'll

131

call the police."

There was the sound of kids screaming in the background, reminding Kayleigh of the few times she had cried as a child till her mother had told her to 'bleeding well grow up'.

"Here." The front door opened briefly and a plastic carrier bag was pushed out before the door was pulled back. There was the sound of a key turning.

Kayleigh opened the bag. There was the sweatshirt that she'd borrowed from Marlene and her only spare pair of jeans. A pair of pants too. The black lacy ones that Mum had split trying to fit into them the other day.

"Could I have my books?" she called out through the flap. "I've got to return one to school before the end of term."

There was a snort of amusement. "Ron chucked the lot. Said that all that learning wasn't good for you. I agree. Not if you're going to make up evil stories about people."

This was so unfair. "I didn't. You're scared of him, Mum, aren't you? I've heard you. In the mornings through the walls. Promise me, you will leave him if he hurts you again. Won't you?"

The voice was so quiet through the flap that Kayleigh could hardly hear. It sounded like "I need him, love."

A door slammed inside the house and the flap closed. "Pauline? Are you there?"

"Please go," whispered Mum. "I'm sorry. It's you or him. He gave me the choice. And I've got to look after meself, haven't I?"

"But I don't want to go into care," she whispered.

No answer.

Only the sound of a man's raised voice and her mum, trying to calm it down. After a while, she saw them going on to the sofa. Ron was unbuttoning Mum's blouse.

Disgusted, Kayleigh turned away. There should be a rule about older people having it off like that. Her mind went back to that lovely day in the park when Frankie had told her he loved her.

He still did. She knew it. Kayleigh looked down at the bag of clothes. She'd go to the public toilets, have a bit of a wash, and then go looking for Frankie.

It was when she went past school that Kayleigh got her idea. Term might have finished but there was Mr Brown's car in the car park with its Baby On Board sticker in the rear window. She'd go in and explain about the book on the Romantic Poets which she couldn't give back. Tell him too about why she'd had to miss the end of term.

It was weird going into school when no one else was there. The door to some of the classrooms was open and Kayleigh peered in enviously. Marlene always took the piss out of her for loving school but it was great. The only place where she could get away from Ron or whatever boyfriend Mum had around at the time.

There was a noise coming from the English room. Kayleigh felt excitement running through her. Mr Brown was in then! "You can tell me anything, Kayleigh," he had said once, after she'd stayed behind to borrow a book. "Anything."

Maybe she'd tell him about not having anywhere to live. The wonderful thought occurred to her that perhaps he and his wife might invite her to stay. She and Mr Brown could read books all evening and of course she'd help out too. Maybe babysit the kids.

Fucking hell.

Kayleigh took in the girl on the desk, her skirt by her ankles and her legs round Mr Brown's waist. Dimly she recognised her as one of the sixth formers.

Mr Brown looked horrified. But there was a slow smile on the girl's face.

"Kayleigh. It's not what you think."

Not what she thought? Did he think she'd imagined it?

Her hand over her mouth in a mixture of horror and sickness, Kayleigh tore out of the gate. Not knowing where to go, Kayleigh found herself in the shopping centre again. There was a bloke by the door, sitting on the ground with a dog wearing a red and white spotted handkerchief. He was playing a Britney Spears CD and holding out an empty carton of fries for people to put money in. There was a walking stick next to him too, propped up in the corner.

"Sorry," said Kayleigh. "I would give you something but I'm homeless myself."

Even as she said the words, they didn't feel real.

A girl strutted past. "Wotcha, Jason." She waved some notes in the air. "Got a couple of tenners, I did. You'd think people would watch their stuff more carefully wouldn't you?"

It was Posy!

"You took my money," said Kayleigh furiously. "Then you accused me of nicking it. You've got me into a lot of trouble, you have?"

Posy's eyes narrowed. "What are you on? Fuck off, will you and leave us alone."

The girl dragged the boy to his feet. He could walk perfectly well, Kayleigh saw. So the walking stick was to make people feel sorry for him! How awful.

"One of those, is she?" muttered the man. "Makes things up to get others in trouble."

"Yeah." Posy was holding his arm tight as though scared he might run off. "They say she shopped her boyfriend ..."

Then she saw him! Frankie. Walking straight towards her, through the centre doors. Striding purposefully as though the world belonged to him. His eyes steadily on hers. Everything would be all right now. She just knew it.

"Frankie," she called running towards him, her arms outstretched. "Thank you. Thank you for coming to find me!"

THIRTEEN

Alice had seen emergency numbers before, flashed on the television, during an earthquake or a tornado or a tsunami happening in a far-flung part of the world. Even though she had never been to any of these places (Daniel was a 'Let's holiday in Scotland' kind of man) Alice's heart had always gone out to those families interviewed on the news, hysterical for news of their missing loved one.

And now she was one of them. Except that, to her surprise, Alice wasn't being hysterical. That was Daniel, shouting down the phone now – after waiting quite some time to get through because so many others were probably trying to do same – and demanding to know why no one knew if his son was safe.

Alice felt surreally calm, as though this was happening to someone else – another part of herself that was here but not here. Gently but firmly, she had taken the receiver from her husband and spoken to the woman at the other end.

They were doing what they could, the compassionate but prefect-like voice assured her. Strenuous efforts were being made to locate British citizens out there. Victims (the voice took on a slightly apologetic note here) were being identified but it was a slow process.

Alice had a vague picture of a film she had seen once where a mother had had to identify a son in a far-flung African morgue. Even though Garth had been barely old enough to go to the shops on his own at the time, let alone take two gap years, she had wept buckets. Maybe, deep down, she had done so in the need to prepare for what was happening right now.

Was this, she wondered, what other parents did? Or was it her cursed imagination again?

"We have your details," added the woman crisply. "We will be in touch as soon as we know anything."

Daniel was making extravagant gestures with his hands. It was, she thought with a pang, a bit like the plane movements she used to make when trying to make a small Garth eat up his food. "Ask if they are making arrangements for relatives to go out," he was hissing.

The kind woman at the other end was clear on that one. It was not to be advised. Everything was very confused and also unsafe. Trust her. The authorities were doing everything they could. However, they might like to keep a watch on the Foreign Office website. Did Mr and Mrs Honeybun have access to the internet?

Daniel began to weep. Silently, Alice put down the phone and went towards him. Forcing herself, she wrapped her arms around him. Instantly, she saw Uncle Phil in her head; clasping his heavy sweaty arms around her on the sofa. Repulsed she drew back. Even in his time of need, she couldn't help him. How awful was that?

"You're so calm," said Daniel, looking at her. His eyes were wild and red and his fists, she saw, were clenched at his side.

Was she? Alice looked across at the cluster of silver-framed photographs of Garth on the early Georgian side table next to one of two sage-green sofas. A toddler Garth, smiling gappily. A five-year-old Garth on the first day of his smart prep school in a natty little blue jacket with matching red trim. A nine-year-old Garth leaping the high jump. A thirteen-year-old Garth with a slight hint of rebellion about his features. A sixteen-year-old Garth with adolescent spots creeping over his previously smooth complexion. And after that, no more photographs because all that was, apparently, "total crap, Mum".

If she was calm, it was a dry-mouthed sleepwalking calm. The type where you pleaded with strangers on the phone: your only link to your son in a far-flung place. But at the same time, your insides were churning as if trapped inside a liquidiser. Maybe, she told herself, she was one of those people who were calm in a crisis but fussed over smaller things.

For a minute, she thought back to Garth at Departures, setting off for the second gap year. She'd been upset over his hair, which he'd had shaved down one side and dyed orange. There'd been a tattoo on his left leg, which she hadn't seen before.

"Stop fussing, Mum," he'd said. "Yes, it's clean. My friend sterilised the needle in a flame first. Anyway, it's my body."

No, she'd wanted to say. Your body came from me. I gave birth to it. But then he had gone, still cross over the fuss she'd made about the tattoo and the hair. Only now did she realise Garth had been right. There were more important things in life to get upset about.

Like missing sons.

Instinctively, Alice's mind turned to the girl on the shopping centre steps. Where was she now? Hopefully back home. But what if she wasn't? Was her mother scouring the streets of Plymouth for her? Was she ringing round her friends to see where she was, which was what Alice used to do when a sixteen-year-old Garth hadn't come back by the agreed time.

Or didn't Kayleigh's mother care? When she'd given her statement, Paul Black had suggested the girl came from a home where the girl was left to fend for herself. Perhaps that explained the tender, vulnerable air about Kayleigh that had made Alice feel so protective.

Meanwhile, Daniel had switched on the television. Alice stared at the screen. Horrified, she took in the Sky News presenter standing in front of a crumpled house. Behind the earnest woman with her clipped voice and hound's-toothed jacket, Alice could see several men scrabbling through the bricks in an attempt, as the clipped voice presenter said, to find survivors.

"British citizens," she added meaningfully, as though this was the important bit, "are known to be amongst the casualties."

Alice heard a gasp escape from her mouth. At the same time, Daniel began to sob. How could she have even thought about that girl in the park? It was their son who was important. The only person she could bear to hug. The glue in her marriage to Daniel.

"Turn it off," she heard herself say. "Please Daniel. Turn it off right now. It's not helping."

He shot her a disbelieving glare. "But I need to know what's happening."

Alice glanced back at the screen, wincing at the sight of a woman, maybe her age, who was weeping into another woman's shoulder. Their grief might be hers. But she didn't want it. Not yet. Not until she knew for certain. It was the waiting that was the worst.

"Where are you going?" Her husband sounded like Garth as a small boy.

"Where are you going, Mummy? Why are you leaving me at school?" And then, before she knew it, it had been "*Piss off, Mum*" and "*Leave me alone*".

"I'm going upstairs to work," she said now in reply to Daniel's question.

"Work? At a time like this?"

She thought with longing of the vase that needed repairing. The piece she could put back, with a certain amount of care and, dare she say, skill. Something that she could have control over, not like the harrowing scenes on the screen.

"It helps," she said simply.

He gave her a look that suggested she was crazy and turned back to the screen. As she went upstairs, her mobile firmly grasped in her hand (she'd given the emergency helpline woman both her number and Daniel's just in case), Alice felt her blood boil.

Phil Wright, she told herself furiously, was the reason for all this. If he hadn't hurt her, she might have married a different man from Daniel and had a different son from Garth. One who had taken one gap year instead of two. One who didn't tell her to fuck off or hide rolled-up joints in his bedroom. One who wasn't missing in an earthquake.

No. What was she thinking of? She loved her son. Would do anything for him. And she loved Daniel too, in her own way. Even so, that didn't take away the consequences of Phil

Wright's evil actions.

"If you weren't already dying," Alice muttered, "I'd kill you myself."

Over the next few hours, the phone didn't stop ringing. Janice. Other friends. All wanting to know if Garth was all right. Wasn't he in that area? (Yes.) She must be out of her mind with worry. (Was that really meant to help?) What can we do? (Nothing.)

Mum, unable to cope with a situation over which she had no control, rang on the hour. Whatever kind of mother she'd been, one couldn't fault her as a grandmother. She'd always been close to Garth.

That night, Alice and Daniel lay on opposite sides of the bed, their bodies rigid. The air was heavy with unspoken thoughts that should have been diluted through sharing. Tragedies, Alice told herself, either brought couples closer or widened the cracks that were already there.

In the morning, she picked up *The Telegraph* from the floor where the boy had pushed it through and placed it calmly in the recycling bin.

"Where's the paper?" asked Daniel.

She shrugged, without actually telling a lie. The thought of her husband poring over the pictures and reports was too much. The radio was bad enough with more reports of casualties rolling in.

Meanwhile, the emergency line was busy.

"If there was any news," she said, "they'd have told us."

Daniel said nothing. Had he, she wondered, remembered he was meant to be running a summer school that week at the university? If so, he showed no signs of going in and she wasn't going to remind him. For a start, he was in no fit state to drive.

Together, they sat at the kitchen table, nursing sweet mugs of tea, neither able to face anything more substantial. "I feel so bloody helpless," said Daniel.

His eyes – red raw – stirred something inside her. Instinctively, she got up and went over to him, cradling his head in her arms. "It will be all right," she said.

He broke away. "No it won't. He's dead. I know it."

"And I know he's not," she replied calmly. Hadn't she given birth to him? She would know, surely, if his life had been snatched away. There would be some chasm inside her. An emptiness.

Meanwhile, Daniel had turned on the little kitchen portable television. There was a picture of a baby and the line 'Pulled alive from the wreckage' underneath. Then he added bitterly. "Miracles like that only happen to other people."

She reached out for him again, across the table. "Do you think that helps?"

He glared at her, furiously. "Do *you* really think that just because after all this time, you're showing me some affection, it's going to bring our son back?"

Stung, she turned away. "That's not fair. You haven't even asked me what it was like when I saw ..." she stopped, unable to say the name Uncle Phil. "When I saw him."

"That's because it's not important." Daniel was pointing to the television again. "Not compared with this. Don't you see that? Or are you too frigid to have any emotions at all?"

There was a shocked silence. Never, ever, had he used that word out in the open. Only silently in his eyes. Crushed and deeply hurt, she scraped back her chair.

"Where are you going?" Daniel's voice was scared. Mungo, whom she suddenly realised, hadn't had a morning walk, began whining. Silently, Alice grabbed her bag and car keys before slamming the door behind her. Anywhere, she told herself. Anywhere.

This particular client lived in a mock-Georgian estate at the far end of town. It was very different from their own Edwardian home but there was a certain charm about it which she might have appreciated at another time.

Luckily, Alice had had the parcel already wrapped in the back of her car, waiting to be delivered. Now was as good a time as ever – she needed space from Daniel just as he needed time to cool off.

But there were balloons outside the house. A party perhaps?

Perhaps she should have rung first. "Your vase," she said awkwardly as a pretty, plumpish woman opened the door. "I've finished it."

"Oh. Right. Thanks." There was the sound of something being moved in another room. It sounded like a piece of furniture. The woman's face beamed. "I'm really grateful. My sister will want to know where that it is when she comes over. We're just getting a disco ready for tonight. My daughter. She's twenty-one." Then she laughed happily. "I can't think where the time has gone."

Alice felt a pang. Over the years, she and Daniel had often discussed how they would celebrate Garth's twenty-first when it came. Maybe a party in a marquee on the lawn. Or a private dinner for their friends. Now, despite her words earlier about knowing he was alive, she began to feel less sure in the face of the other mother's optimism. Would Garth live to his twenty-first? The possibility that he might not, brought tears to her eyes.

"Have a nice time," she said, turning away.

"I'll put a cheque in the post," the woman called out. "Is that all right?"

Afterwards, Alice still didn't feel like going home. The other family's happiness had unsettled her. She had to do something about Garth. She couldn't, wouldn't, just wait here until there was news.

Before she knew it, Alice found herself parking near the shopping centre in the city. No point in buying a parking ticket. That was for normal people. People whose sons weren't missing.

She'd go to a travel agency. That's what she'd do. Go home with a receipt for two flights to Rio that she could then slam on the table and say "*Look what I've been doing while you've been sitting moping at home. Now we can go out. Search amongst the rubble for ourselves.*"

Whoops! Alice gasped as she almost fell over something. Just in time, she put her hands out to steady herself. "That's dangerous," she began to say to the girl on the steps whose bare outstretched legs had caused her to nearly trip. And then she stopped. Was this her wretched imagination once more? Or was it possible that this was the girl from the park again. Yet she looked different.

"Hello," she said uncertainly.

The girl scrambled to her feet, shooting her a scared look. Yes. She was right. She recognised her now even though her auburn curls were matted and she had a bruise on her right cheek. There was a bowed look to her too which hadn't been there before.

"It's Kayleigh, isn't it? Please don't go." Alice glanced at her watch. Just five minutes until closing time. "There's something I need to do inside but I'll be back. Promise."

Dashing in, she tore down the left-hand side of the mall, throwing herself in through the travel agency door. "I need to get to South America," she gasped.

The girl – surely just out of school – gave her an odd glance. "Flights are restricted at the moment, due to the earthquake."

"That's exactly why I need to go." Her voice came out as a scream. At the same time, her mobile began to ring.

DANIEL

"What?" she snapped. "Not you," she added to the girl, whose face registered alarm.

"You'd better come home. Daniel's voice rang out flatly. "Something's happened."

FOURTEEN

"Wait," the pretty blonde woman with the elegant jacket but sad eyes had said. "There's something I need to do inside but I'll be back. Promise."

It had been the last bit that had persuaded Kayleigh to stay where she was. *Promise.* She'd been so certain that the woman was going to come back.

But of course she didn't.

People broke their promises, Kayleigh reminded herself, stretching out her legs again on the steps because it hurt less that way. Just like Frankie.

For a moment, she closed her eyes remembering how she had run into his arms only a couple of hours earlier.

"Get off," he'd snarled, taking her wrists with his hands and pushing her away so she'd fallen on the stone steps and bruised both her ankles as well as getting a real shiner on her cheek.

"You're fucking mad," he'd added, spitting on the ground next to her. He didn't actually spit at *her*, Kayleigh reminded herself. That was something. But he wasn't very happy. That was clear.

Then he'd grabbed her by her hoodie so his face was really close to hers, just like it had been the park. But this time, his eyes were glittering with anger. They were green, she told herself, trying to stay calm. Not bluey-green like she'd wondered when he'd been away. Not dancing-green like the first time they met. Just standing-still, scary, staring green.

"Why did you fucking make a statement, bitch?"

Kayleigh struggled to breathe. Maybe, she told herself, Frankie was one of those men who liked to talk dirty. Marlene had told her about that. It might sound like they didn't care for you but it really meant they did.

"I had to," she'd tried to say. "The policeman made me."

The grip round her neck was getting tighter. Kayleigh began to get afraid. Why didn't someone stop him? It was nearly closing time in the centre so the shoppers were beginning to thin out but there were still some people around who could have done something. Maybe they were scared too.

"Do you know what kind of trouble you've got me in now?" His breath was on hers now but not like it had been before in the park. Now it was threatening. Angry.

"I could go Inside for this." He looked at her with disgust. "And all because you kept begging for it."

Had she? Kayleigh was aware she'd felt very dreamy after the tablet he had given her but she didn't recall begging for it. Still, if that's the way he wanted it, she'd say so in court. Anything to keep him. Anything.

"I'm sorry, Frankie," she said, circling his neck with her arms, the way she'd seen Marlene do with her boyfriend. "I'll tell them what you want me to tell them. You do forgive me, don't you?"

His hands were still tightening round her neck. It had been hard to get the words out. Any minute and she would surely stop breathing. Weakly she began to pummel her hands against his body to show him she was going too far.

"Leave her alone, you silly bastard," said a girl's voice.

It was Posy. Why was she sticking up for her? "Get off or I'll slice your balls off." Kayleigh gasped at the sight of the thin blade in Posy's hands. The pressure round her neck stopped. Gasping, she drank in air.

Frankie spat on the ground again. Then he put his face close to Kayleigh's once more. "You promised, remember," he hissed. "If you ever want to see me again, you'd better tell them in court that you made up that stuff about the drugs and that you made me fuck you. Got it?"

Then he'd sauntered off, his hips swinging from side to side.

All the girls were staring at him which made Kayleigh want him even more. Then they looked at her, enviously, apart from Posy who was carefully slipping her knife down the inside of her jeans.

Kayleigh felt a flash of pride. Frankie might have spoken rather harshly to her but anyone could tell that they had something between them. It gave her one up on the others and made her feel all grown up. "Thanks," she said to Posy. The girl scowled.

"I didn't do it for *you*." She gestured to the other girls watching. "I did it for us. Don't you realise? Your Frankie has screwed the lot of us. That girl over there with the purple hair – see her? – did eighteen months for him, pretending it was her coke and not his."

Kayleigh could understand that. She loved Frankie! They'd had sex together. He was the first man she'd done it with and now she didn't want anyone else. Maybe, if she was really lucky, she might have his baby inside her right now. Then she could be his baby mother. She'd get her own place too. That's how Mum had got her first flat years ago.

"I don't believe you," she said to Posy. "I don't believe he slept with you and all the others. And even if he did, he only wants me now."

Posy stared at her. "Are you fucking mad? You've got a crazy mind, know that? I was going to tell you where to find a bed for tonight but now I'm not going to bother. You can bleeding well look out for yourself."

Kayleigh felt a twinge of apprehension. She'd been worried about where she was going to stay. What if the police found her? Scared she sat down on the steps, stretching out both legs because that seemed to help her bruised ankles. And that's when the blonde woman with sad eyes had come along. The one from the park with the dog. The one who had given her fifty quid the other day. The one who had promised to come back.

Maybe if she waited long enough, she might just do exactly that.

By nightfall, she was the only one left on the steps. The other girls had melted away into the evening light. Posy had got into a car that had pulled up at the kerb.

"What's your name?" she'd heard the driver say.

"Tara," she'd heard her say before stepping in.

Clearly Posy had changed her name again.

It was getting really cold. Kayleigh sat with her back to the wall, just inside the bit where there was a roof above. Every now and then, when the security guard came round, she scuttled into a different part so as not to get caught.

She'd seen the others do that earlier.

Pulling her hoodie tighter around her, Kayleigh picked up a newspaper that someone had dropped on the ground. She tried to wrap it round her shoulders like a shawl but there wasn't enough of it. So instead, she read it.

BRITISH GAP YEAR BOY FEARED MISSING IN EARTHQUAKE

They'd done earthquakes in geography. They were caused by plates in the earth sliding over each other. Marlene and some of the others had made jokes about dinner plates. One of the girls had been the same one she'd seen in the school, snogging Mr Brown.

If he was going to have an affair with anyone, Kayleigh told herself, it should have been her. Not that it mattered now 'cos she had Frankie. Her old teacher would get over it. Men always did. Look at Ron. Mum said that all you had to do was ignore their moods and then they'd be all right again.

The thought of Mum felt her feel sad. Kayleigh looked down at the paper where a woman was holding her baby.

REUNITED AT LAST said the headline.

Would Mum feel that way about her if she'd got lost for three whole days under rubble? Kayleigh hoped so but if she was honest, she wasn't sure. Her stomach began to rumble but although it felt empty, she didn't feel that hungry. Not any more. She was still cold though and the stone step was making her bottom ache. Her ankles were throbbing too. Loud music floated along the street. Maybe it was a club. She'd like to go clubbing, one day. Maybe, after he'd got nice again, Frankie

146

would take her and they could leave their baby at home with a responsible babysitter. She'd be a good mother. She just knew it.

Marlene said the best clubs were in Eye Beetha. It cost a lot of money to get there but you could sleep on the beach. Her eyes began to droop. She was feeling really sleepy right now …

"Kayleigh?"

Dozily looking up, she saw a pair of clear blue eyes looking down.

"It is you, isn't it, Kayleigh?"

Great. It was that policeman from the park, the one who had wanted to caution her in the hostel. Scrabbling to get to her feet, she fell. Ouch. Her ankles were bloody killing her.

"That's some bruise you've got on your cheek," said the policeman. He had a kind voice on this time but that was probably a pretence. The policewoman who had come to the flat when they'd found the drugs and money under Callum's mattress had sounded kind at first.

"How did you get that then?"

"I fell," said Kayleigh promptly.

"Is that so?" He sat down by her side. Kayleigh hoped the others weren't going to come past right now. It didn't do to be seen talking to the scum. People might think you were grassing.

Someone had grassed on her half-brother. That's why the police had turned up. When Callum found them, he was going to tear them apart. 'Course he didn't mean it.

"We've been looking for you, Kayleigh. There was no need to run off, you know. We want to help you."

Who was he kidding? According to Marlene, that's what they always said. They didn't really want to help you. They wanted to get bonus points for having nicked you.

"You can't live out here for ever, you know," said the policeman. His voice was smooth. She didn't trust him. But on the other hand, he had a point. "Like I said at the hostel, you're under-age."

She thought of her birthday which wasn't far away. "Not for long."

"But in the meantime, you've got to go into care."

Kayleigh summoned up all her strength to get up. But her ankles were really throbbing now and it was hard to move. They were swollen too. Frankie must have pushed her harder than he'd realised. Not that she'd tell the policeman that. Frankie hadn't meant it. Not really.

"What are you going to do? Run off again?" the policeman actually looked sad for a minute. Must be a good actor. She'd thought of being an actress once but then Mum had told her not to be so bloody daft. "Start working for one of the other kids and sell stuff. Become a dealer? Come on, Kayleigh, think about it. They all get caught in the end."

A picture of Callum's smiling face as they led him to the van, came back to her. *It'll be OK, Kayleigh. Don't worry.*

"What's that?" he said, more sharply this time.

"I said you can't make me."

Before she knew it, he had his hand on hers. "That's where you're wrong, I'm afraid. We *can* make you. Your social worker's found you a good family to go to. You can stay there while you give evidence in court too."

His cool blue eyes were locked on hers. "You're a bright girl, Kayleigh. I can see that. So you'll understand when I say that they've brought the court date forward. We need to stop Frankie before he hurts any more girls." His eyes travelled from her bruised cheek down to her ankles which had got big and puffy. "You will help us, Kayleigh. Won't you?"

FIFTEEN

"You'd better come back," Daniel had said on the mobile. "Something's happened."

Then he started to say something else but the phone cut dead. Her battery! Alice could have wept with frustration. With everything that had been going on, she'd forgotten to charge it.

"Please," she said frantically to the young girl in the travel agency in that smart electric blue suit and tiny sparkling silver nose stud. "May I use your phone? It's an emergency."

The girl looked at the clock pointedly. "I'm afraid we're closing now."

"But my son!" Alice found herself tugging the girl's electric blue sleeve like a mad woman. "He's caught up in that earthquake. The one in South America. That's why I needed the flights."

She glanced at the glossy brochure the girl had handed her when she'd first come in. The one with a picture of a beach in one corner and a rainforest in the other. It was aimed, clearly, at people who didn't mind paying a bit extra for luxurious holidays.

The girl glanced with a mixture of disdain and fear at her hand which was still on her arm; clutching it even tighter now from fear and desperation. The irrelevant thought occurred to Alice that she was more able to touch this girl's hand than her own husband's.

"Please stop doing that or I will have to call the police."

Her other hand, she could see was reaching for the phone. Alice broke away, heading for the door. "You'd understand, if you had children," she called out. Then she spotted a side exit

149

on the other side of the mall, leading directly to the car park. Breaking out into a run, she bumped into a pair of women clutching shopping bags and laughing. A mother and daughter perhaps. Her heart lurched with jealousy as both glared at her.

"Sorry," she gasped. "I've got an emergency." Yet the word seemed inadequate to describe the terror inside. Maybe Daniel had been about to tell her something terrible before he'd been cut off. Garth had been found alive, perhaps, but had died, calling out her name. "Mum!" he would have said. And she hadn't been there.

By the time Alice had reached the car and peeled off the yellow and black parking fine sticker, flinging it on the ground (what relevance did it have to a dead son?), her hands were shaking so much that she could barely start the car, let alone reverse it.

Bang. Out of the rear window, she could see she'd hit something. A red car. Garth had done this once; in the same car park, strangely enough, when she'd been giving him 'driving practice' before his test. It had struck her at the time that dual control was something which should be fitted on all children from birth.

They'd left a note with their details because that had been the right thing to do, as she'd explained to her son. Now, as she glanced in the rear mirror at the not-insubstantial bump in the red car's bumper, she didn't have time to do the same. She needed to get back and find out what had happened. Swerving round the corner, she shot out in front of traffic from the left to get through the orange lights. There was a massive fanfare of horns. "All right, all right," Alice shouted, waving a hand at the other drivers.

"Always stick to the speed limit," she had told Garth before he'd passed his test. Yet now, here she was, well over the 40mph sign, ignoring the DRIVE SLOWER neon sign. "Garth," she moaned, "where are you?"

The radio! Of course! There might be some news. She could hear it now.

British boy found alive after days under rubble in earthquake.

No. That was in her head. Besides, it was usually babies who survived impossible odds; something, she'd read once, to do with their lack of fear and supple bones.

But maybe, just maybe, Garth had been found lost and bedraggled. Wandering, stunned, without anywhere to go. *Lost and bedraggled.* With a jolt, Alice remembered the pale, auburn-haired girl on the stone steps. *"Wait there,"* she had said. *"I'll be back. Promise."*

But she hadn't. She'd got distracted by Daniel's call in the travel agency and now the girl would think she'd forgotten her. How awful. But Garth had to come first! He was her son. Heart beating in her throat, she pulled up sharply on the drive, leaving skid marks in the gravel. Not bothering to lock the car or rifle through her bag for door keys, she hammered the heavy black knocker with the lion's head.

Where the fuck was Daniel? Alice, who rarely swore, began hammering again. At last! "What's happened?" she demanded.

Daniel had the phone to his ear, motioning to her to be quiet. "I see," she heard him saying in a tight voice. "Right. Thank you. I'll tell my wife and then we'll come back to you."

He spoke calmly and evenly as though discussing a household matter like insurance or a quote for a new kitchen. Alice yanked on his arm, much as she'd yanked on the girl's arm in the travel agency. "For God's sake, tell me what's happened!" she yelled.

Mungo, who always hated conflict – and was capable of sensing unspoken distress as much as out in the air arguments – began whining, pawing at her.

"They've found Garth." Her husband's voice was steady, as if about to tell a child something serious.

"Is he ..." she stammered, tugging his sleeve even harder. "Is he ..."

Daniel's eyes were wet. "He's not dead."

A huge wave of relief washed through her, followed by doubt. But why wasn't Daniel ecstatic? Dancing around with joy even though he wasn't the dancing around type?

"Injured?"

Daniel shook his head.

"Then *what*?"

Her husband took a deep breath. "It seems that Garth went to the airport just before the earthquake happened."

"So he's safe!"

"Not exactly." Daniel took off his glasses and put them on again. "He was stopped at security for carrying drugs. He says he didn't know they were there and that someone must have slipped them into his rucksack from behind. But he's in prison. That was the Foreign Office on the phone. They've advised us to find a good lawyer."

"But he's alive!" Alice sank on to the floor, weak with relief.

"Alice." Daniel crouched down next to her, his face close to hers. Mungo, misinterpreting this as an invitation for a joint love-in, began licking both their faces. "I don't think you understand. Garth was carrying a serious quantity of heroin." He faltered. "Out there, the penalty can be death."

How could he have been so stupid? That's what Alice had expected her husband to say. Wasn't that what she'd been thinking to herself? Hadn't she told Garth, over and over again, not to carry anything for anyone – and not to have your rucksack on your back at airports where someone behind you in the queue could slip something in and then retrieve it at the other end.

She'd read a piece about that in one of her women's magazines, written by a mother warning others, and had dutifully reported it to Garth. But like all her other advice (*keep emergency money separate so you have something left if someone takes the first lot)*, it had been met with a wave of the hands and a "Stop fussing, Mum".

And now he was in some horrible South American jail, waiting for them to get him out. "Can't I talk to him?" she'd pleaded to Daniel again and again as if the repetition might somehow bring about a change.

"I've told you. He was allowed just one phone call and it was imperative that he spoke to Brian." Daniel rubbed his face which was grey with exhaustion. "If anyone can get him out of there, it's him."

Through sheer good luck, Janice's husband Brian was a lawyer specialising in crimes committed by British nationals abroad. "But he hasn't committed a crime," Alice protested when Brian came round for an emergency meeting in the drawing room. There was still a stain on the walnut table, she noticed, from her argument with Daniel a few weeks ago. Now both seemed totally trivial.

"Alice," Brian had said solemnly, "in some countries, you are guilty until proved innocent. I know it's hard but try to leave it to me."

Hard? Impossible, more like. In some ways, it would have been better if Garth had stayed just a few more hours longer in South America before getting to the airport. The chances of her son surviving an earthquake now seemed, in her mind at least, greater than getting off a serious drugs charge.

Over the next few days, there was a flurry of phone calls and emails and text messages. The news in the paper had moved to more unrest in the Middle East. The earthquake only occasionally merited a mention with the odd worthy article on famine relief.

There was no reference at all to a British gap-year kid on drugs charges.

"Good," declared Daniel briskly. "The less publicity the better, Brian says. The worst thing that could happen is a piece on a middle-class kid with too much money and not enough sense."

He was angry, she knew, to hide his fear. Was this how the girl in the park's mother had reacted, she wondered, when she knew her daughter had been taking drugs? Or, as Paul Black had implied, didn't she care? Maybe she hadn't understood what was happening, rather as she, Alice didn't understand what was happening right now.

"There will be a trial of some sort," Brian had tried to explain during another meeting. "But it won't be like one in this country. The judge might well be biased." He gave a little sigh. "You can appreciate that they've had enough of young kids smuggling drugs."

"Can we go out to the trial?" she'd asked.

"We don't know when that is, yet."

"Then surely I can visit him?"

Brian shot Daniel a look across their whisky glasses. "It's not as simple as that. Trust me, Alice, we're doing everything possible. And, I have to say, the Foreign Office has been pretty helpful."

Over the next few days, Alice tried to distract herself through mending a pretty little blue and pink china pot that an old lady had brought in. It had belonged to her father's second wife, she'd explained, and she'd 'stupidly' dropped it while washing up. The stepmother hadn't been an 'easy woman to live with' but the old lady felt she ought to try and sort it nevertheless as it had been a favourite.

Yet the pot, as though sensing Alice's distress, refused to be mended. Again and again, she painstakingly matched up the jagged fragments and smeared the tiny amount of glue required. But it wouldn't stick. There were some pieces, she'd discovered, that weren't meant to be fixed.

Giving up, Alice rang Janice to suggest a dog walk. "I'm going mad, waiting for the phone to ring. I need some air. I've got my mobile anyway."

Janice was quiet as they ambled along the river, watching Mungo tear ahead and rub noses with other dogs. Perhaps, thought Alice, she'd understandably run out of the "*It will be all right*" phrases that her friends had used during the earthquake scare.

In truth, she had told very few well-wishers about Garth's true location apart from Mum.

"Prison?" There had been a silence at the other end of the phone and an almost audible pursing together of the lips. Then Mum had quietly said that she would remember Garth in her prayers even though Alice knew she wasn't religious.

"Look," said Janice suddenly as Mungo returned with another dog's ball. "Isn't that your man from the coffee shop?"

Alice's heart did a little flip. It was indeed Paul Black, striding towards them. Ironically, they were almost at the very spot where she'd seen Kayleigh and the man. It gave her a slightly queasy feeling. Since the incident, the park had felt sullied in her mind.

"Alice," he said, pleasure written all over his face. Don't be so friendly, she wanted to say. Janice, she could see, had clocked the look along with his familiar use of her first name. Nervously, she observed his brown cord trousers, casual yet smart Barbour jacket, and sturdy walking shoes. Was this plain-clothes or was he off-duty? It struck her that she hadn't thought of him since the news about Garth. For some unknown reason, she now desperately wanted to tell him.

"I was just coming to see you," he added as if reading her mind.

To her deep embarrassment, Alice felt herself flush deeply so that her cheeks stung with the heat. "Mind giving us a few moments?" she said, turning to her friend. "Could you keep an eye on Mungo?"

Janice gave her a hard look before shrugging as if to say "*Do you really know what you're doing here?*" and walking a short distance away.

Paul Black's clear blue eyes were alive with excitement. "We've found her. The girl. Kayleigh. I thought you'd like to know. She's in a foster home now. Safe."

Instantly Alice felt guilty. If she'd gone back to her at the shopping centre, might the girl have been allowed back to her real home instead of a foster place?

"There's another piece of news too." A date has been set. For the trial."

For a minute Alice thought she was talking about Garth's trial. Don't be silly, she realised. He wouldn't even know about that. "They've brought it forward," he said eagerly. "Apparently the judge is very keen to nail this man. As I said before, he's caused a lot of trouble."

Paul Black glanced across at Janice who was coming back to them now. Close enough to hear. "You're still prepared to be a witness, aren't you?"

It might have been phrased like a question but it came out like a statement. So that was why he had come to find her! Not to tell her about Kayleigh. Or to see how she, Alice, was. But to make sure that she would still play his game.

Not for the first time, an uneasy feeling crawled through her. Paul Black had talked about boys like Frankie grooming girls like Kayleigh. But was he doing the same? Keeping her sweet just so that she would keep her promise to be a witness? It made her feel used, all over again.

"I've got a lot going on in my own life," she started to say. Then she stopped. Maybe it wasn't a good thing to tell him about Garth, held for drug charges. No. Perhaps that had been her trouble before. She'd been too open. Too gullible. Too keen to please. "I'm not sure that I can be a witness now, I'm afraid."

Those blue eyes held hers in disappointment. "Then Frankie may well go free to do exactly the same to another girl."

She shivered, yet at the same time, she was angry. "This is blackmail."

"No, Alice. It's not. It's doing the right thing as a responsible member of the public. As a parent."

He'd got her. And he knew it. Either Paul Black was a very clever manipulating policeman. Or else he knew her better than her own husband and mother. Yet if it was the former, whose fault was that? Hadn't she encouraged him to call her Alice the first time they'd met? Hadn't she made the classic mistake of a lonely woman, unhappy with her marriage, clinging to the first man who seemed to 'understand her'?

How stupid, Alice told herself furiously. She should have kept a distance right from the start; both with the girl and the policeman. But now it was too late. She was in too deep, both legally and emotionally. With both of them.

"I'm not keen," she conceded grudgingly. "But I will if you think it will make a difference."

He nodded, relief washing through his face. Was that, she wondered, relief for the girl? Or for his own career which, doubtless, could be affected by all this. "It will. I promise."

Promise. The same word she had used to Kayleigh outside the shopping centre.

Promise. The same word that Garth had reluctantly used when she'd asked him to be careful before setting off.

"That thing you said earlier," she said urgently. "About girls being seen as … as loose because they don't have enough self-esteem to stand up for themselves. Do you really think that's true?"

He nodded. "I do. You know, there's a saying, Alice. You've probably heard of it but every now and then I say it to myself to remind me why I do this job. It goes something like this. 'Evil happens when a good man does nothing.' His eyes met hers. 'Makes you think, doesn't it?"

Despite her doubts, she found herself nodding. This is your chance, Alice, she told herself. This is your chance to put things right. Maybe not for yourself but for other people.

"There's an official letter in the post to you," he added. His confidence that she would go ahead was both empowering and irritating at the same time. "It gives the date of the trial and the practical things you need to know." Then he stopped as though he was going to say something else. There was a tight pause. He put out his hand in a sort of handshake but took it back before she had a chance to reciprocate. "Thank you," he said simply.

"Do you want to tell me what that was about?" breathed Janice after he'd gone. "Come on, Alice, we've known each other long enough. Anyone can see he fancies you." Then she looked sad. "Poor Daniel." Her eyes grew fierce. "How could you do this to him?"

Alice began to laugh. Tinnily. Manically. "It's not what you think." Then she grew serious. "You see that hedge?"

Her friend frowned. "Yes. Why?"

"It's where I saw them. That young girl who was having sex with the older man a few weeks ago. The couple everyone was talking about."

Janice's eyes widened. "You *saw* them?"

She nodded. "I didn't want to tell anyone because I was embarrassed. But the policeman tracked me down and got me to give a statement. Daniel knows all about it."

Janice shook her head. "I knew something had happened. You've been acting all strangely and that was *before* Garth."

Alice felt a shiver going through her.

"Sorry. Didn't mean to be thoughtless." She touched Alice's arm. "Listen. I'd think twice about being a witness if I were you. I knew someone once who was attacked after they stood up in court and described seeing a robbery. Mind you, that was in Hackney before we moved down here. She was under some protection programme too but it didn't help her."

Alice's throat went dry. Hadn't she voiced similar concerns when giving her statement? "Paul … the policeman, said I'd get help if I needed it."

Janice snorted. "They can't look after everyone, can they? Honestly Alice, if I were you, I'd tell him you've got enough on your plate and refuse to do it. After all, that girl has nothing to do with you, does she?"

For an instant, Alice could see Kayleigh clearly in front of her. Looking up at her trustingly when she had 'promised' to return. *I always wanted to be called Victoria.*

"I'd like to think that someone might help Garth if they could," she ventured. "Paul says the man involved was a predator of young girls. He drugs them and then has sex with them."

Janice shuddered. "Don't. And I'd watch out for the 'Paul this and Paul that', if I were you."

Alice pretended she hadn't heard the last bit. "He says that I'm the only witness who saw the whole thing. By the time someone else got there, they'd … they'd finished. The only other evidence they've got is an anonymous phone call, tipping them off in the first place. Someone else who saw it, although they can't trace the call because it was from a pay as you go. My evidence is crucial in sending the man down. I've got to do it, Janice. I have to. Not despite Garth. But *because* of him."

Her friend shook her head. "You're a braver woman than me, Alice. I'm not sure I could do that. It's not just the fear of being attacked. It's the embarrassment bit too."

"I know." Alice bit her lip. "I'm scared too."

How she would have loved to have confided in her friend about Phil. But it was no good. Janice, with her secure childhood that was now carrying her confidently through life, would never have understood. There was no point in even talking about Garth in prison. No one could understand the cold terror inside; the 'what ifs' and the fears that were whirling round her head; far more important, surely, than some girl in care whom she hardly knew.

Instead, they walked back home in silence; Janice leaving her at the front door with a kiss on each cheek. When she went in, placing her keys carefully on the hook behind the hall curtain, Daniel was talking on the phone. His face was rigid as he put the receiver down.

"That was Brian." His lips tightened. "It's not great news, I'm afraid."

"What?" Alice could hardly get the word out.

"He's been trying to get a date set for the hearing but the authorities are stalling. It could be years before Garth is tried."

"But he can't just waste away there." Alice felt sick to the core. "It's not human. There's got to be something you can do."

Daniel shrugged. "It's a different world there, Alice. Different rules. Different regulations. A different way of thinking. We did warn him."

There was a crash. The sound of splintered china. Red and blue china. Appalled, Alice looked at the segments of the old lady's stepmother's pot around her, just like the glass the other day.

Daniel stared at her. Once more, like the other day, it wasn't difficult to see what he was thinking. *Are you quite mad? On top of making things up and being a slut?*

Numbly, Alice knelt down to pick up the pieces, cutting herself as she did so. She couldn't even remember throwing it. How scary was that?

"What did you do that for?"

His voice boomed out over her.

"What did you do it for?" Mum had asked again and again when accusing her of lying about Uncle Phil all those years ago.

"I don't know," Alice repeated now to Daniel. "It just sort of happened."

Hold me, she wanted to say. Hug me. But he was just looking at her as though he'd never seen her before.

"When all this is over," he said slowly. "I think you ought to get some help. For the sake of all of us. You do agree, don't you, Alice?"

SIXTEEN

Marc (with a 'c' apparently) and Angie had been fostering teenagers for years. Kayleigh would like them. They had children themselves. Five to be precise. One was a girl, a bit younger than Kayleigh. It would be someone to talk to. In fact, they'd be sharing a bedroom.

Kayleigh listened to all this shit with half an ear while the social worker drove along the road that led to Exeter. They weren't going as far as that, the social worker explained. No way! Instead, they were going to a little village about forty minutes from town.

The social worker, a bouncy woman with stupid orange dangly earrings and piggy eyes had said all this as though it was something to get excited about. But Kayleigh felt sick. Forty minutes from the shops? That was her idea of hell. Even though she couldn't afford anything, she liked looking at stuff in windows and imagining where she might go in them. She loved browsing through book shops too.

'Sides, there was no way she wanted to share a bedroom with a stranger.

"Are you religious, Kayleigh?" asked the bouncy woman, her earrings swinging wildly as they took a sharp left, bumping uncomfortably along a mucky farm track.

Was she kidding? If God existed, he'd have done something about Ron instead of abandoning her. "No," Kayleigh muttered.

The social worker looked disappointed. "Pity. Still, maybe you'll think differently after living with Marc and Angie."

Orange earrings beamed as she did another sharp left, next to

161

a 'Ducks For Sale' sign. "It's amazing what magic they do. We've had some fantastic success stories."

Magic? Success stories? She didn't need crap like that. Not unless it was in a book – and it wasn't. This was real. Kayleigh's heart ached with longing and grief. She needed to be with Frankie. Not here in the middle of nowhere. If she only had a bit longer with him, she was sure he would love her again.

For a minute, Kayleigh allowed her mind to wander back to Frankie's kisses in the park on the day they had met. They had been soft at first and then hard in an exciting way. She had tasted *his* excitement too. It had made her feel powerful and also humble at the same time, because someone loved her. Otherwise why would he have made love to her?

Marlene said no one called it 'making love' any more. It was 'having sex' or 'having it off' or 'getting in the sack'. But Kayleigh knew that she and Frankie had done much more than that. He was just in denial, that was all. That was another of Mr Brown's phrases.

"Here we are!" The orange earrings craned forward enthusiastically as the car stopped suddenly – only just avoiding a duck – by a bungalow with bright blue windows. It looked like something out of a nursery rhyme book. Not that Mum had ever bothered buying her one. Maybe that's why Kayleigh still felt drawn to them in the kids section at the Library.

"Isn't it sweet? You're going to love it here. I just know you are."

Gingerly, Kayleigh stepped out of the passenger seat, right into a pile of muck. Appalled, she stared down at her trainers. They were ruined.

"Oh dear." The social worker frowned. "Better not go into the house wearing those. Angie is quite particular. There she is! And Marc too."

Kayleigh stared as a tall, very black woman with long glossy hair glided towards them. She was just like that supermodel who was always on the telly. Surely it couldn't be? Then she noticed. Angie had a limp. Just a slight one but it was definitely there. She had a long thin silver scar down her right cheek too. So it wasn't the supermodel after all.

"Welcome!" Angie said it in such a warm, welcoming way that Kayleigh wondered if this vision had got her muddled up with someone else. "It's lovely to meet you, isn't it, Marc?"

She turned to the man next to her. As she took him in, Kayleigh felt a twinge of apprehension, just as she had when Mum had introduced her to Ron. He was very tall and thin too, with a floppy brown hat that went down right over his forehead and almost covered his eyes. His jeans were turned up at the bottom and his open-necked blue checked shirt revealed a hairy chest with a small gold crucifix round his neck. Angie, she suddenly realised, had one too.

"It certainly is," he replied in answer to his wife's question. His voice was harder than hers, though, and colder. "However, I have to say to you right from the start, Kayleigh, that we have house rules here which we expect everyone to adhere to."

There was a short pause. "You do understand, don't you," said the social worker nervously, touching her right earring as if to check it was still there. "Adhere means ..."

"I know what it means," said Kayleigh crossly. Did they think she was stupid just because she'd been slammed into Care? "It means 'stick to'."

The man looked grudgingly impressed. "Exactly. We expect our own children to obey the rules too." He waved a hand towards the bungalow. "Come on in. They're just finishing off their lessons."

Lessons? Kayleigh's spirits lifted. "Is there a school here and all?"

Angie's eyes shone. "We do home schooling here, don't we, Marc? So we have classes all through the holidays. You'll be expected to take part too, Kayleigh. But don't worry. You'll love it. Won't she, Marc?"

I see, thought Kayleigh. She's nervous of him. That's why she keeps deferring to him. Mum did the same with Ron. Shit. She had a bad feeling about this place. Couldn't the social worker see there was something weird going on here?

"I'll be back to see you in a few days, Kayleigh!" chirped the orange earrings. The piggy eyes were bright as though she'd just dropped Kayleigh off at a birthday party; something she knew all about from the Kids Section in the library. "And of course I'll be taking you to court before long. Meanwhile, put that out of your mind for a bit. Enjoy your stay here. Bye-eee!"

And she was gone, in a flurry of dirt from the track, just about avoiding another suicide-happy duck, waddling straight out in front of the car. Distraught, Kayleigh stared after her. Come back, she wanted to say. Take me home.

Then she remembered. She didn't have a home any more. Mum and Ron didn't want her. Marlene wouldn't let her in because her boyfriend was mad at her for grassing on Frankie. And, as the policeman had said, she couldn't sleep on the shopping centre steps for ever.

"Everyone finds it a bit strange at first," said Angie kindly, touching her arm and gently leading her towards the front door with its 'Welcome' sign on the side in the shape of a sun and a pair of praying hands. "But you'll be all right."

Marc nodded curtly. "Not got any luggage then?"

Kayleigh shrugged. "I didn't have time to pack."

She didn't add that she didn't have any stuff anyway apart from the hoodie that Callum had given her last year ("*Don't ask where it came from, sis*"). The colour had run in the wash anyway. "Never mind," said Angie soothingly. "We'll find you some clean clothes. Won't we, Marc?"

Thank God, Marlene wasn't here to see her. Or Frankie. Kayleigh shuddered. They wouldn't recognise her. Not in this stuff. Fucking hell. She didn't even recognise herself.

The girl in the mirror was wearing jeans that flared out, instead of being thin at the bottom. The T-shirt was a really boring muddy brown colour with what Angie had called approvingly, a 'scoop' neck, instead of a 'plunge'. Here, Angie had looked disapprovingly at the pink T-shirt that showed off Kayleigh's bustline, which Marlene had lent her months ago and forgotten to ask for back.

Instead of trainers, she had to wear padded slippers because it was "better for the floor". But the worst thing of all was that make-up wasn't allowed. "God wants us to look natural," Angie had sung brightly.

It was all right for her with those amazingly black long lashes! Kayleigh's were so fair that, without mascara, they faded into nothing, making her look a bit piggyish.

"That's my T-shirt you're wearing," said the girl on the bunk bed below hers. Kayleigh had been introduced to her earlier. Her name was Hope and she was thirteen. That's all Kayleigh had managed to get out of her. She was incredibly shy.

"You can have it back, if you want," said Kayleigh hopefully.

The girl shrugged. She had a sour disappointed face. "It's OK. I never liked it anyway."

Kayleigh stared. "Mind if I ask you something? Why aren't you black like your mother?"

There was another shrug. "'Cos I'm not hers, that's why. God sent me here."

What was she talking about?

"That's what they say, anyway." There was a scowl. "Truth is I'm adopted. I don't know who my real mum and dad are. But one day, when I get out of this place, I'm going to find out."

There was the sound of footsteps outside. The girl put a finger to her lips. She was scared, Kayleigh realised. Just like she'd been scared of Ron.

"Hi there! Everything all right?"

Marc opened the door without so much as a knock. A few minutes earlier and she could have still been changing, thought Kayleigh indignantly.

"Good." His eyes flickered over her briefly. "That's much better. By the way, we don't have locks in our home. Angie and I think they encourage deceit." Marc smiled tightly at Hope. "A certain person is on kitchen duty tonight if I'm not wrong. Why don't you show Kayleigh the ropes?"

She'd never seen so many carrots before. Or potatoes. It was like feeding an army. She didn't even like vegetables anyway. And as for the table, it was so big that it had taken her ages to put out the knives and forks. When she'd lived with Mum and Ron, they'd each got their own stuff – usually from the chippie if Mum gave her some money – and scoffed it in front of the telly.

"Thanks, Kayleigh," said Angie turning round from the cooker where she was stirring a huge bowl of mince. "Mind putting the forks on the left side instead of putting them next to the knives on the right?"

Who was coming to dinner? The Queen? Bloody hell. What was that? Kayleigh jumped as a deep hollow sound rang round her ears. "That's the gong," said Hope sullenly. "Marc always strikes it when it's meal time or lessons are starting."

"Do you call him Marc because he isn't your real dad?" whispered Kayleigh.

But Angie heard. "Hope has probably told you she's adopted which means that, in law, Marc *is* her real father." She smiled brightly. "But we encourage our children to call us by our first names. Marc thinks it's healthier. Right, both of you. Ready?"

Kayleigh hadn't seen the other kids earlier as they were all busy "doing their jobs or homework". But now they were trooping in. Two were very black like Angie and the other two had ginger hair like her. Were they adopted too? There was no knowing what colour hair Marc had because he showed no sign of taking off that hat, even in the house.

Meanwhile, he was sitting at the top of the table, waiting expectantly for them to all sit down. For five kids, they were very quiet. "Silence please for grace."

Grace? There had been a girl at school called Grace who had left after one of the others had stabbed her with a penknife. Kayleigh looked at the door, expecting another child to come in.

But then she noticed that everyone round the table had their eyes shut, apart from Hope who was shooting her daggers. What had she done now?

"Dear God," Marc was saying. "May we appreciate every mouthful of this feast which you have prepared for us. And let us not forget those who have nothing."

Kayleigh almost laughed out loud. *God* hadn't prepared that pile of potatoes and carrots on the table. She and Hope had. But instinct told her that it might not be a good idea to say so.

'Sides, she was starving. And even though she would kill right now for a burger and chips, she gingerly took a bite of the carrot.

"Good, isn't it?" beamed Angie.

She was nice, Kayleigh decided. But the husband was weird.

"After dinner," announced Marc, "it's games night."

One of the younger kids, a sweet little girl with tight black curls, clapped her hands together. "I love games nights! Can I go first?"

Angie leaned across and touched Kayleigh's hand lightly. "Do you like Ludo?"

What was that when it was at home?

"It's a board game," muttered Hope. "Really boring."

Marc's face darkened. "What did you say?"

"Nothing,' mumbled Hope.

The table fell silent. Angie began twisting a long strand of her hair as if nervous. They were all scared of him, Kayleigh realised. She didn't like this. Didn't like it at all.

How was it possible that she had only been here for a week? It felt like a month at least. Marlene would die if she was stuck in this place.

Every day, in Angie and Marc's house, Kayleigh was meant to check the rota that was pinned up on the kitchen cupboard. It told her what jobs she had to do. So far, she'd had to scrub the kitchen floor, wash all the windows, and clean the toilets (that was her least favourite task).

There were lessons too, though she liked those. Marc might be a bit of a weirdo but he had loads of books on every wall. For English, she was allowed to read as much as she wanted and then write a short summary. Cool. Maths wasn't too bad either. Angie was in charge of that. She didn't get all narked like her teacher at school when Kayleigh couldn't understand something. She explained it really patiently.

They had their lessons at the big kitchen table. All the kids did different things but it wasn't noisy. They all just got on with what they were doing and if they didn't understand something, they'd put up their hands and Marc or Angie would come round and explain something. No one ignored them or passed notes or made crude jokes.

They were encouraged to read the daily newspaper too although sections of it were cut out "because they're not suitable." One day, she stopped short. There was a picture of a woman who looked just like the one who had seen her in the park. Below it was a line that said: BRITISH PARENTS CLAIM SON WAS INNOCENT IN SOUTH AMERICAN DRUGS SCANDAL

Was it Alice Honeybun, like it had said on the card that had been stolen with the money? Kayleigh couldn't be certain. Maybe it was her imagination again.

One morning, just after a maths lesson, when Kayleigh had been there for nine days, Angie touched her arm. She was often doing that, she'd noticed. "Can you stay behind a bit?"

She waited while the other kids filed out. There was a brief rest period now, according to the timetable on the cupboard. Then lunch. And then jobs.

"How are you settling in?"

Kayleigh hadn't expected that. Instead she'd been waiting for a *"Please straighten your duvet cover properly?"* or *"Can you remember to put out napkins for lunch today please?"*

"OK," she shrugged.

Angie glanced at the door. She's worried Marc is going to come in, Kayleigh realised. "I just wanted to say that my husband might seem a bit strict at times but he means well. Very well, in fact. He rescued me, you know."

Kayleigh stared at her. "From a fire?"

One of their neighbour's flats had burned down last year. Arson, the police had said, though they couldn't prove anything.

Angie smiled. "No. From the streets."

Had she heard her right? Had this woman who was so picky about putting forks on the left-hand side of a proper table mat, really been on the game? You couldn't grow up on an estate like hers without knowing about that.

"That's right." There was another smile. "I was a prostitute. In Bristol." She touched the long thin silver scar on her cheek.

Was that how you got it? Kayleigh wanted to ask. But Angie had continued talking.

"One night, Marc turned up. I thought he was another client but he didn't want to do anything. He started telling me about Jesus and how he wanted to save me."

Angie was grasping Kayleigh's hand firmly. She wasn't sure whether to feel flattered or not. "At first, I thought he was a bit of a nut. But he kept coming back. He paid to see me but he didn't want to do anything. Just talk."

The grasp grew tighter. "I was mad for him, Kayleigh. I wanted him. He wanted me too. I could tell. But I was also beginning to realise there were more important things, like helping people. So we got married and began fostering. Marc used to be a social worker, you see. He knew how important it was to help people like you."

Was she a bit touched? There was definitely a strange glint in her eyes that reminded her of a horror DVD she and Marlene had once nicked from her nan.

"He saved me." Angie was clutching both her hands now. Her nails were digging into Kayleigh's flesh. "Just as he can save you."

Kayleigh pulled away. "I'm not on the game. I loved Frankie. And he loves me. I know it."

Angie smiled sadly. "I used to think that way about men who hurt me. It's all to do with self-esteem, you see."

"But you're scared of Marc," burst out Kayleigh. "I can see it."

Angie's face stiffened. "Shhh," she put a finger to her lips. "You must never say that, Kayleigh. You understand? Never."

She leaped to her feet. "Please go to your room now. It's rest period."

For two pins, she'd leg it now. But the front door was locked which was weird, given what Marc had said earlier about doors always being open. Confused, Kayleigh went back to 'her' room. That was odd. She'd made her bed that morning – not very well, it had to be said – but now it was a real mess with muddy footprints on it.

Hope was sitting on the top bunk, glaring down at her.

"Did you do that?" asked Kayleigh.

Hope shrugged. "Might have. Might not have. You'd better clean it up before Marc sees it."

"Why?" Kayleigh felt ridiculously hurt. "Why did you do it?"

Hope sniffed. "'Cos I don't like sharing my room with strangers, that's why. I always do it. Nothing personal, like."

Fair enough.

That night, after playing Ludo (which was quite good fun, actually), Kayleigh lay awake. "Not long," she told herself. "Not long until I'm sixteen. I can do what I like then."

The thought reassured her enough to eventually fall asleep. The following morning, there was a knock on the door. Had she missed roll call? That's what Marc called it when he rang a bell before breakfast and they all had to line up and check their jobs for the day.

"Kayleigh? Are you awake?"

It was Angie. Her face was apprehensive. There were red marks on her wrists. Fucking hell. Marc must have hurt her.

"It's your mum."

For a second, her heart leaped. Mum had finally come to get her. She loved her after all. She'd got rid of Ron and …

"She's on the phone," whispered Angie again. "It's urgent."

Cursing the fact they'd taken her mobile away when she'd arrived ("another rule, Kayleigh"), she picked up the receiver. It wasn't even a cordless so she had to stand there, in the kitchen, with Angie pretending not to listen.

"Kayleigh? Are you there?"

Mum's voice was scared. Not scared as in 'Don't, Ron' through the wall, scared. Or scared like the day the police had broken down the door to get Callum who'd been hiding under his bed. But scared in a way she'd never heard before.

"Listen. Did they make you record your statement so it could be played in court instead of you actually going there?"

"No."

"Thank Christ for that."

"The police said I could give evidence on an interview screen – I think that's what they called it – but I said I'd rather

170

go to court myself. Then I could look the jury in the eye and tell them that Frankie didn't mean any harm."

"You daft bitch."

That wasn't very nice. Kayleigh was glad Angie couldn't hear.

"They put a note through the door in the night," continued Mum breathlessly.

"Who did?"

"Your friend Frankie and his mates. They say that if you give evidence in court against them, they'll do something to me."

No. That couldn't be right. "My Frankie wouldn't do that."

"He's not *your* Frankie, you silly cow. When will you realise that? He's some bloke that got your knickers off in a public place and more fool you for letting him. He doesn't love you, Kayleigh. Not like I do. Please, love. If you care for your mum, don't go to court to be a witness. Don't cough. Promise?"

SEVENTEEN

There was a parking fine in the post. And a legal letter because
someone had seen her bump into that red car in town the other
day – with everything going on, she'd forgotten to report it.
And now this. Her appearance in court. All because she'd been
in the park at the wrong time.

Someone could go with her, apparently. There was a charity
that liaised with the police to support witnesses. A volunteer
could show her the way round the massive court building. Go
over the protocol. Sit with her before she gave evidence.

But Alice didn't want that. The very thought made her feel
like a child. Vulnerable. Exposed. Just like she'd been before.

Besides, all she had to do was tell the jury what she'd seen.
When Paul Black put it that way, it didn't sound so difficult.
But then she thought of the faces in the public gallery and the
local reporter – there was bound to be one – and all the
publicity that was bound to come out.

The girls in the book club would have a field day, especially
as she'd been foolish enough not to admit, right at the
beginning, that she'd seen the scene in the park.

The tennis club lot would make jokes (some had quite a
raucous sense of humour) which would make her really
embarrassed. A passionate scene on television was capable of
doing that, so heaven knew how she was going to cope with
something like this.

Daniel, too, would come in for ribbing at the golf club and in
the pub. He'd bear it manfully, she knew. In fact, she could just

visualise his lips tightening while trying to smile at the innuendoes. "Hear your missus saw a couple having it off, did she? Gave her some ideas to spice up your sex life, did it?"

It would give him an even keener sense of injustice as he climbed into bed with her at night. What irony! His wife, who had been unable to bring herself to have sex with him for years, was now a witness to an 'indecent act in a public place'.

Ironically, all this troubled her more than the thought of the man who would be in the dock. After all, he deserved to be there.

Just as Garth surely didn't deserve to be in prison in some foreign hell-hole.

Meanwhile, Daniel and Brian were constantly conferring either on the phone or in Brian's office. "Leave it to us," said her husband when she asked what was happening.

It made her feel stupid. As though she was the little wife at home. But what could she do? Brian was the expert after all. "Perhaps you could write to him," suggested her mother, who had been surprisingly nice to her since they'd found out about Garth.

Alice dismissed this initially but then, when she mentioned it to Brian, he'd declared it might not be a bad idea. "There's no guarantee the letters will get through, of course." Then he'd patted her lightly on the back. "But it might well help you get some feelings off your chest."

So she did.

Dear Garth,
We're all thinking of you ...
No. That sounded like a sympathy letter.
I wish you'd listened to me and been more careful ...
Don't be daft.
I hope you have enough to eat ...
But what if he hadn't?
Do you have your toothbrush on you ...
There are more important things than that, Mum! His voice was so clear in her head that she'd turned round to see if he was there.
You'll never believe what has happened to me ...

174

Alice's hand paused over the writing paper with their address neatly and expensively embossed at the top. Garth had always been 'wired differently' as Daniel said. You never know. The whole thing might amuse him. Not, of course, that there was anything remotely funny about being a witness.

In a strange way, Alice wanted to tell Paul Black about all of this. To describe the fear of being mocked and the dreadful every day terror about her son. But no. She mustn't lay herself bare again; allow him to use her vulnerability and ask her how she'd feel if this was Garth in the dock. (If only he knew!). Time to be strong now, she told herself. So instead, she signed the paperwork and said yes. She would be there. At court. On the following Tuesday morning.

It was on Saturday that she heard the letter thud through the post-box. Mungo had belted to the door, beating her to it as usual. Alice, who'd been was writing another letter to Garth (it was the only thing that helped), picked up the brown envelope with the childish writing.

They'd already received the morning's post, which had contained a hefty phone bill from all her calls to Garth (and that was before his arrest) so she initially presumed that something had been delivered to one of the neighbours by mistake.

As she drew out the sheet of A4, Alice stared at the jumble of pasted-on words, clearly cut out from magazines and tabloid newspapers.

IF YOU GO TO COURT, YOU WILL GET HURT

Mungo pawed at her, sensing her confusion.

The last word, 'hurt' was slightly askew on the page as if the writer had almost thought twice about putting it there.

IF YOU GO TO COURT, YOU WILL GET HURT.

Alice read it again. Was this some kind of joke? Quickly, she opened the front door. "Mungo. Come back!"

The dog had ripped down the drive, suggesting that the person who had delivered it wasn't far away. Alice followed him, running in her bare feet but as she reached the beech hedge by the gate, she heard an engine rev up. By the time she got there, the car – it had sounded like that, rather than a bike – had gone.

"You shouldn't have gone after them – you could have got hurt," said Paul Black reprovingly.

He had come round as soon as she had phoned the mobile number he had given her. There had been no point in ringing Daniel who'd left earlier that day for a 'round'. Her husband never had the phone on at the golf club. It wasn't considered etiquette – something that the younger members apparently had little regard for.

Besides, this was police business. That was why she'd called Paul Black. Not because of the man himself and the strange emotions he aroused in her, that made her feel both protected and used at the same time. But because of his position. He was the policeman in charge of this case. He needed to know.

As for not going after them, she'd done what felt right at the time. Just like now it suddenly felt right – despite what she'd thought earlier – to come clean about her own situation. Not totally clean of course. But part-way.

"My son is in prison," she said slowly, handing him a cup of tea. They were sitting in the garden, at her suggestion, because she'd found it hard to breathe inside after what had happened. "A South American prison. They found drugs on him at the airport."

Paul Black put down his cup and looked at her. Waiting.

"He didn't do it." She focussed her gaze on a pot of azaleas which were drooping. It had been a hot month. In more ways than one.

"Excuse me." She stood up and walked slowly across to the garden tap, filling up the red watering can.

"Distraction can be very helpful."

His voice came from behind her.

"May I take that?"

She shook her head. "I need to feel the weight, thanks. It makes me feel … normal. As though Garth isn't in prison and as though that letter had never arrived."

He walked with her towards the azalea pot. The surge of water made a satisfying dent in the dry earth. She should have done this earlier but there'd been too much going on. The park. Phil. Garth. And now the trial.

"He didn't do it, you know," she added, returning to the tap to refill. There were other pots too which she'd neglected. "I know he wouldn't. But then again, maybe the mother of the man you've accused would say the same thing."

She turned to look at him. Something had changed in Paul Black's face. It had hardened. "I'd like to think so. But I doubt it."

Alice was aware of water splashing her ankles. The can was overflowing. It had got Paul Black's ankles wet too. "Sorry."

He smiled. "You know, I usually go swimming on a Saturday morning so it's quite funny really."

"You go swimming?" Somehow she hadn't ever thought of policemen swimming. A funny picture came into her head of an old-fashioned British bobby, fast crawling down a pool, still with his helmet on.

"We are human, you know." He smiled again and Alice felt her mouth lifting slightly at the corners; something that hadn't happened since the news about Garth. For a crazy minute, she thought of telling him about Phil. No. He might think badly of her then, despite what he'd said about vulnerable girls and self-esteem. And somehow she couldn't bear that.

"Do you go on your own?" The question – a deflection from the temptation to tell him her own story – escaped from her mouth before realising its impertinence. "Sorry. That's none of my business."

"No. It's all right." He watched her as she soaked the same azalea, forgetting she'd filled the can to relieve the others. "I used to go with my son, actually."

Used to? Instinctively, Alice glanced at his bare left hand. So he was divorced. Probably only saw his son every other weekend or less. Maybe less.

"I'm glad you were on duty today," she added.

He put his head to one side. "Actually, I wasn't."

The significance hit her. So he had come out here in his free time. "I'm so sorry. Your son must be disappointed."

There was silence.

This was even worse! She'd deprived the poor man and his son of each other's company during a precious custody day. Occasionally, when Garth had been younger and Alice had contemplated leaving Daniel (just as he must have contemplated leaving her), she had come to the reluctant conclusion that she couldn't possibly do so because she couldn't bear to lose him even for a day a week in some custody arrangement. As for the thought of another woman taking her place, it was impossible.

Does he have a stepfather, she wanted to know. For goodness sake, what was wrong with her? Didn't she have enough to worry about in her own life without feeling for someone else?

"It can't be easy for you to go through all this," said Paul Black, looking down at the letter with its garish sentence, "and cope with your son in prison."

She shook her head as the word 'prison' jolted her back to her senses. "It isn't."

"How long has he been there for?"

Alice put down the can. "It happened just after I saw … saw the couple in the park."

They both looked at each other for a second as if registering the significance. Then she realised. "You came round in person to make sure I wasn't going to cop out, didn't you? You're still worried I might not take the stand."

He hesitated. But it was enough. "I was also concerned about you. As I said, we like to look after our witnesses."

"But you can't stop this, can you?" She jerked her head at the letter. "What if it was a firebomb that torched the house and hurt your son or wife?"

He winced and she could see she'd hit a nerve. "We could arrange for you to have protection, if you like. Someone could move in and be there for you until the trial."

Alice couldn't imagine anything worse. A stranger witnessing the cold arguments between her and Daniel? Watching her anguish as she waited for news about Garth."

"No thanks. What about after the trial, anyway? Someone could try and hurt me then. What do you do about that?"

"I'm going to be honest, Alice. We do our best but it's a big thing to change your identity …"

"I don't want that," she broke in, appalled. "I'm not a child murderer." Then she thought of something else. "Hasn't it ever struck you that ordinary witnesses like me have to cope with threats, maybe for the rest of their lives, whereas people who've done terrible things are sometimes given expensive rehabilitation programmes?"

"Yes." His eyes held hers. "Yes it has. But I can't change the law, Alice. I can only try to make it work. And actually, experience has told us that in most cases when threatening letters or phone calls are made to witnesses, nothing ever happens to them."

He patted her hand. So lightly and quickly that she wondered if it had occurred at all. "I'll do my best to look after you, Alice. I promise."

"How can he say that?" thundered Daniel when he got back from the club later that day. "Can't you see he's getting all chummy so you do what he says? And why didn't you ring *me* instead of calling him when you got the letter?"

His words – reinforcing everything she'd already told herself – made her angry out of guilt and self-recrimination. "I didn't want to disturb you. It was the first time you'd had a break from all the work you've been doing with Brian. Besides, what could you have done?"

They spent the rest of the day hardly talking to each other. Not for the first time, Alice thought of the sum of money which her father had left her. It wasn't a great deal but enough to see her through a year or two on her own. Once, Alice had read a piece in a magazine declaring that every woman needed a secret 'Running away' money-pot. Of course, she'd never leave Daniel but the fact that she could, if she wanted, made her feel stronger inside.

The following day, when sitting outside in the summerhouse, attempting to repair the vase she had shattered in her outrage a few days earlier, Mungo ran barking to the door. A letter lay silently simmering on the mat.

Daniel got there before her. "Is this what the other one looked like?" he said, silently handing it to her. Alice took in the envelope with its first-class stamp and local franking mark before forcing herself to consider the garish cut-out letters.

YOU HAVE BEEN WARNED.

She nodded.

Daniel's lips tightened. "That's it. I won't let you give evidence."

His words gave her a sense of relief – so she didn't have to do it after all! – closely followed by a niggling feeling in her chest. "The girl," she began. "She was so vulnerable. I have to help her. If someone was able to help Garth, wouldn't you want them to?"

There was a second of hesitation. Daniel never hesitated. "That's not the point."

"Yes it is." She followed him into the kitchen where Garth's schoolboy photographs were still on the wall, grinning down at them. "See?" Her eyes filled with tears. "If someone was able to protect him, wouldn't you give them anything – anything at all – to keep him safe?"

Something gave in her husband's face. "Look, Alice. If something happens to his mother, how do you think Garth is going to cope?" He had both his hands on her arms now. Tight enough to make a point. Yet loose enough to indicate affection. "I know we haven't had an easy marriage, Alice, but if you think I'm going to stand here and let my wife put herself in danger, you're wrong. Look at this."

He thrust today's newspaper at her. It showed the face of a woman with horrific scars below a headline reading: ACID 'HONOUR' ATTACK.

"That's different," she said weakly, thinking of her previous fears about exactly this. "That's a woman whose brothers didn't want her to marry someone."

"It's all the same. Don't you see? There are people out there whose minds are wired differently. If you won't think of yourself or me, Alice, think of Garth. He needs you."

Maybe he had a point.

Ironically, there was a small piece too in the paper about

180

Garth.

BRITISH GAP YEAR BOY STILL AWAITING TRIAL DATE.

That had been Brian's influence. He had a nephew who worked for a press agency. "The more we can keep Garth in the public eye, the more chance we have of not getting him lost in the system."

That night, Alice tossed and turned, with weird dreams about Garth and the girl from the park, lying together on a beach. When she woke, Mungo was barking wildly at the door. Instantly awake, she glanced at the bedside clock. 5.30. Far too early for the post.

Daniel was still asleep. Racing down, she saw the brown envelope on the mat.

THIS IS YOUR LAST CHANCE.

Alice's heart raced. She could open the door. Run down the drive. Find whoever was there perhaps. But supposing she got hurt? Maybe Daniel was right. Her first duty was to be there for their son.

Putting on the kettle – she was far too awake to go back to bed – she placed the letter in the kitchen drawer so as not to see it. Later today, she would go down to the station with it as well as yesterday's. She wouldn't ask to see Paul Black, just as she had refused to let Daniel ring him yesterday. If she did, she might change her mind again.

Instead she'd tell the duty sergeant and …

Alice froze. The telephone. At this hour? It had to be Garth! She just knew it was him. Someone, somewhere had allowed him to ring. His time was different from theirs.

"Mrs Honeybun?"

Alice's heart plummeted at the sound of a woman's voice.

"I'm sorry to ring so early for you but I've just been reading the newspapers and I think I might be able to help you."

Alice looked at the drawer containing the letter. "Are you threatening me?"

"Threatening you?" The well-spoken voice sounded offended. "Not at all, Mrs Honeybun. I hope I might be able to help you. My name is Sheila Harris. I was behind a young man at an airport in South America a few weeks ago and saw someone behind him slip something into his rucksack."

Alice gasped but before she could say anything, the caller rattled on. "I regret now that I didn't say anything and then, I have to say, it slipped my mind. Afterwards, I had another trip and with one thing or another, I just forgot about it. Then, last night, I was up most of the night – insomnia is a devil at my age – catching up on the papers. Lucky I did! Out of the corner of my eye, I saw a small piece about your son's plight and looked you up. Just as well that Honeybun is an unusual name or I might not have found you. Anyway, here I am. Just thought my evidence might be helpful."

Alice's eyes were still on the drawer with the threatening letters inside. She should be feeling elated, she told herself. Should be feeling relief. But instead, there was a weird sense of obligation. If someone else was helping her son, how could she not help someone else's daughter?

"Thank you," she said, picking up a pen. "May I take your phone number?"

EIGHTEEN

"Don't go to court if you love your mum."

The words rang round and round Kayleigh's head. Of course she loved her mum, even though common sense told her that she had every right not to. Hadn't Mum thrown her out in favour of Ron? But something, deep down inside her, couldn't throw Mum out of her heart.

Just as she couldn't get rid of the hope that a bit of Mum loved her too.

Wasn't that why she'd rung? Not just because she was scared of being hurt but because she was worried for her own daughter? That was it! Mum had never been great at showing affection, apart from all that lovey-dovey stuff she showered over the various men she brought back. But she proved it in different ways. Look at the time she'd come back from the market and casually tossed a pair of trainers over to her.

They had been a bit tight but Kayleigh gratefully wore them anyway. It had been the first time Mum had bought her anything for years! That's why she still wore them.

Kayleigh thought all these things, and more, as she tossed and turned in the bunk bed above Hope on the night before the trial. She'd thought, briefly, of telling Angie about Mum begging her not to go to court. But then she might tell Marc who would spout off about doing the right thing because that's what "God would want". He'd probably tell the social worker too and the police might come and put her in handcuffs to force her to give evidence.

That had happened to one of Callum's friends at his trial.

Even if she gave her evidence on a screen, away from people's faces like the policeman had said she could, she'd still get Mum into trouble.

No, Kayleigh told herself as the early dawn light poured in through the window. The best thing to do was to fool everyone. To go to court and then run off before they made her say anything. She'd just have to find somewhere to hide, that was all.

There was a knock from the bunk bed below. "Stop moving around, will you?" hissed Hope crossly. "I can't sleep."

Even if it wasn't for the trial, Kayleigh told herself, she'd have to run away. There was no way she was sticking this for much longer.

"Ready?" sang out Angie through the door.

She spoke as though they were going on some kind of picnic. They'd been on one of those the day before yesterday. Marc had made them trek through all these muddy fields and kept stopping to point out some flower or creepy green insect. Then Angie had got them to sit down, right next to a pile of cow poo, and brought out a plastic box of something called hew moss. It was made of chickpeas apparently and had made Kayleigh throw up.

Right now, Kayleigh would have given anything to go on a picnic instead of court.

"Are you dressed?" Angie sang out again.

"Yes," lied Kayleigh, looking at the black dress Angie had put out for her the night before. There was no way she was wearing that even though Marc had said it was 'advisable' to wear something 'conventional'. The dress was made of a coarse material and came down well below her knees. It would make her look like a laughing stock. That had been a phrase she'd used in an English essay: Mr Brown had given her an A but it didn't seem so special now, after seeing him snog that girl.

"She's not," yelled out Hope. "She's still in her pyjamas."

They were rubbish too. All baggy with a hole at the front that had been clumsily sewn up.

Kayleigh glowered at her. "I'd rather wear my own jeans."

"Sorry," sang out Angie. Was she listening on the other side of the door? "They're in the wash. I'd like you to wear the dress, Kayleigh. I made it myself."

She could believe it. "That's better," exclaimed Angie clapping her hands together when she finally came through the door. "Isn't it, Marc?"

Marc's eyes followed her up and down. It gave her a weird shiver. "It will do." He was holding the car keys. "Right. Let's get going."

So Angie wasn't coming with them? Kayleigh felt a twinge of alarm. "We're meeting your social worker at court," he said, as she climbed into the front seat of the old jeep outside. His knee brushed hers, making Kayleigh edge away. If he so much as touched her, she'd open the door and jump out.

But maybe that knee brushing had been an accident, because he didn't do it again during the hour or so journey into the city. Instead, he had the radio on and was singing along, using his own words above the real lyrics.

"We've got a friend in Jesus,
We've got a friend in Jeeesus."

At one point he slapped the dashboard with his left hand, keeping his right on the wheel. "Go on, Kayleigh. Don't be shy. You sing along too."

So she did, just to keep him quiet. He was as mad as his wife. Kayleigh's hand gripped the handle on the inside of the car door, ready to open it if he did something. Not long now, she told herself. Not long now.

They parked alongside loads of smart cars next to a sign that said 'Parking for Court Only'. "This way," said Marc, putting on a tie as they walked along. Kayleigh tried to fall behind. There was a cafe on the corner there. She'd run in there and lock herself in the Ladies. He couldn't get her there.

"Come on. Don't dawdle."

She'd lost her chance. Mouth dry with fear, Kayleigh had no option but to follow Marc in through the revolving doors, past a man in blue uniform who gave her a hard stare. I'm here as a witness, she wanted to say. But she could tell from his disdainful expression that he wouldn't have believed her anyway.

"Wait there." Marc motioned to a row of plastic chairs. "I'm just going to find your social worker. She said she'd be here by now."

Trembling, Kayleigh did as she was told. As soon as he was out of sight, she told herself, she'd run. There was no way she could risk Mum being hurt. No way at all.

A tall, thin-faced youth came through the revolving doors and slid into the seat next to her. Kayleigh was aware of a slight smell of perspiration. "You was warned," he muttered. Then before she had a chance to turn towards him, he thrust a piece of paper into her hands and legged it out through the doors.

What the …?

Kayleigh stared at the photograph on the paper. For a minute, she didn't recognise it. Then she took in the new hair-do that Mum had had the other month. It was the rest of her face she didn't get. The distorted nose, the eyes that were closed and the cut that ran from her left ear right down to her throat.

OH MY GOD.

They'd got her. They'd got Mum.

Leaping to her feet, she headed for the doors, almost colliding with someone coming in the opposite direction.

"Wait!" called out Marc's voice behind her. "Wait. Grab her someone."

Too late. She was off. Running faster than she'd ever run before. Bumping into people coming into the court and others walking past. There was a bus. Desperately, Kayleigh leaped on, fumbling in her pocket for the pound coin that Angie had given her for 'refreshments' at the court.

The doors closed just as Marc reached them. Kayleigh stood at the back, shaking. The bus was going the wrong way but it didn't matter. She'd wait a couple of stops to make sure Marc was left behind and then she'd run home.

"Mum," she moaned, not taking any notice of the woman beside her giving her strange looks. "Mum."

Her chest was hurting so badly from running that Kayleigh could barely draw breath. But there wasn't time to stop. She'd been jogging ever since the bus had stopped and she had to keep running. Mum. She had to find Mum. Hopefully Ron would have got her to hospital or maybe he'd just left her there, beaten into a bloody pulp. Perhaps he was scared the police would presume he was responsible so had scarpered.

Kayleigh felt cold with fear and anger. How could Frankie do such a thing? For the first time since she'd met him, Kayleigh was surprised to find that she hated him now. No one hurt her mum. No one. Not even Ron. Only now did she realised that she should have made a stand when she'd been at home.

At last! Kayleigh ran into the big square yard outside the block of flats and right into a group of kids in hoodies. "Watch where you're fucking going," said one.

"Yeah," scowled another. "Show some bleeding respect."

Kayleigh flew up the concrete staircase and along the landing of the third floor to the familiar blue door. Shit. It was open. They'd definitely been here, then. Maybe beaten up Ron, too …

Gingerly she pushed it open. Something was obstructing it. A suitcase. A big blue suitcase.

"Mum!" She took in her mother shoving a giant size packet of crisps into a bag. So she was all right. Her face was normal! Relief was swiftly followed by confusion. "You're not hurt?"

If her mother was pleased to see her, she didn't show it. "Hurt? 'Course I'm not bloody hurt. What the fuck are you doing here?"

Kayleigh held out the picture on the paper which had got torn while she'd been running. "One of Frankie's friends gave me this," she said, breathlessly. "I thought they'd beaten you up."

"Nah," said Ron, coming in from the lounge door with more giant packets of crisps. "It's just the way you look, isn't it, love?" Then his eyes narrowed at the picture. "Fucking hell. They've photo shot you. Look. They must have taken your mug and then put stuff on it. Clever, innit?"

So they'd done it to scare her. Frankie hadn't really hurt Mum, after all. The flood of relief was tempered with disappointment and hurt. Frankie had frightened her. Badly.

And that wasn't nice.

"I haven't given evidence," she began, before stopping. Wasn't that a twenty-pound note poking out of one of those crisp packets? Then she realised.

"Frankie gave you money to make that phone call, didn't he? He told you to act all scared so I wouldn't get him into trouble."

There was a brief silence. "'Course he didn't," snapped Mum. But she looked at the suitcase as she spoke. Did Mum think she was daft? Frankie must have been desperate to have given her such a big bribe. Maybe his friends had helped …

"You're going to do a runner with all the money he paid you to call me."

Mum exchanged glances with Ron and then dipped into one of the crisp packets and held out two twenties. "Just take these, love, and get out, can you? Or we'll miss our flight."

Kayleigh fought back the tears. "You stopped me giving evidence so you could go off and leave me. Where are you going anyway? Spain?"

Mum didn't have to say anything. She could tell she'd guessed the truth from her expression.

"You're disgusting, both of you. Know that?"

She kicked the suitcase angrily. "You deserve each other, you two." Then giving the suitcase another kick, she headed for the door.

"Don't bother troubling your friend Marlene," Ron called out. "She's not there any more."

Kayleigh felt a cold chill descending. "What do you mean?"

For a second, Mum actually looked sorry for her. "She o-deed. Last week."

Over-dosed? She'd taken an overdose? Kayleigh clutched the side of the door for support. "She's not …"

"Sorry, love." Amazingly they looked like real tears in Mum's eyes. "It was your Frankie, they say. Palmed her off with some cheap stuff."

Marlene was dead? No. She couldn't be. Funny, fearless Marlene; always egging her on to do things she didn't really want to? Always there – until the last few weeks – to tell her it

188

would be all right when Mum was a bitch or when Callum got taken off to prison.

Kayleigh wanted to cry but the tears wouldn't come. Instead, she felt a searing hot rage inside. Frankie had killed her Marlene. She could see him for what he really was now. No good kidding herself any more. He didn't love her any more, either.

But what should she do now? If she went back to the court to give evidence, Frankie's lot might try to kill her. She might end up dead like poor Marlene.

Sinking down on a bench near the bus stop, Kayleigh tried to get her head straight. Why had she ever agreed to go out for the day with him? If only she could turn the clock back ...

A bus arrived and without thinking, she got on it. "Where do you want to go, love?" asked the driver.

Did it matter? "To the end," she said flatly. It sounded, she couldn't help thinking, like a line from one of the novels Mr Brown had lent her.

Somehow, she just had enough money in her pocket for the ticket. Pressing her forehead against the window at the back, Kayleigh tried imagining that the last few weeks hadn't happened. If she did it hard enough, she could just open her eyes and everything would be all right.

Ron wouldn't have made a pass at her. She wouldn't have met Frankie. And she wouldn't have been taken into care.

"Everyone off," said the bus driver. "Oy. You there at the back. Wake up."

Kayleigh opened her eyes. Through the window, she saw a park. A pretty green park, just like the one where she and Frankie had made love. There was a hotel just up the hill. And over there, past a line of posh-looking houses, she could see the sea.

Bloody hell. This was it. The place where it had all begun ...

190

NINETEEN

Alice had only been in a court room once before. It was during a school trip when their Politics teacher had taken them to the Old Bailey in London. She remembered giggling with a friend as they'd ogled the enclosed space where a criminal would stand – although, as their teacher told them sharply, everyone was innocent until proved guilty. That hadn't made much sense to a rather unworldly fifteen-year-old Alice. Surely the police must be pretty certain the person had done it, otherwise they wouldn't have arrested him, would they? (Most criminals, when she thought about it – which wasn't often – were male.)

The young Alice had been reprimanded, she recalled, for running her finger along the grainy wood of the witness box. "Don't," the teacher had snapped and for a few minutes she had tasted a guilty feeling in her mouth, reminding her of liver, which she'd always hated, and iodine; another disgusting smell from the hateful science labs. Was that how real criminals felt, she wondered?

Later, after lunch at a Wimpy – a real treat since her mother disapproved of fast food – she and a friend had mildly flirted with some boys from another visiting school, miles from her own. One, with dark floppy hair, had been on the verge of asking for her number (so exciting!) when their teacher had rounded them all up for a visit to the Public Gallery "where you are all going to see a real trial".

Alice would rather have stayed with the floppy-haired schoolboy who was giving her a regretful wave. It wasn't fair! Everyone else was beginning to get boyfriends, although opportunities were mainly limited to the boys' school since Alice's parents didn't approve of the local disco. Why were they so strict?

Then, just as she and the rest of her class had begun to wriggle with boredom on their seats, a policeman had led in a small, bowed, grey-haired man who was surely old enough to be a grandfather. She'd watched in a mixture of horror and inexplicable sympathy as he slumped in the dock, his head on the side, eyes closed, as a litany of charges was read against him. They included something called 'procurement' which caused a ripple of murmurs throughout the court.

What does it mean, Alice had wanted to ask, but felt too foolish to do so. Later when she'd got home, she'd looked up the word in the one of the red and gold Encyclopaedia Britannica volumes which lined her parents' lounge wall. No! That sweet old man had made women work as prostitutes? Thank heavens she hadn't said anything; the others would have thought she was stupidly naïve.

All that had been before Uncle Phil, in the days when the word 'boys' and 'sex' had sent an illicit excited thrill through her.

And now, here she was, all over again. Not in the dock (where one of her classmates had clambered in after the case had ended and been sent back to the coach for punishment instead of continuing on to the theatre). Or in the gallery where she had stared down with a thrilled mixture of horror and fascination as the old man had been sentenced to ten years. But in the witness stand, her hand on the Bible, promising to swear the truth.

Now, as Alice reached the end of her oath, she could have sworn something else too. The courtroom door was still open. Wasn't that the girl from the park, rushing past in the outside corridor? Or was that her mind playing tricks?

Certainly, she hadn't been able to think straight since that thunderbolt phone call from Sheila Harris who might, Brian had said grimly, save Garth's bacon. Lady Harris – titled! – was the mother of someone quite important in the British Embassy. "Her word counts for a good deal," Brian had told them. "We might just be in with a chance."

Lady Harris's words against the South American authorities ... Alice's own word against the tall, thin, skinny youth with jet-black hair and green eyes in the dock opposite, who appeared to be chewing something and shooting her cold steely looks. His smart suit – a cheap-looking one with a maroon sheen about it – seemed at odds with that stare. He was, Alice suspected, more used to jeans. Maybe the slashed-knee variety that Garth favoured.

Garth ... What would he wearing now? Would the authorities have taken his clothes away? Would they be feeding him properly? Dear God, please don't let them be beating him ...

"Not guilty," growled the youth in the cheap maroon suit opposite her. His Irish accent and challenging stare, directed straight at her, forced Alice to concentrate on what was happening right now instead of thinking about her son.

Was this really, she wondered, the anonymous person who had posted threats through her door with their garish cut-out alphabet letters? Daniel had told her to take them down to the station and make a bigger fuss but she hadn't. What was the point? It might make it worse. Besides, it was easier this way to pretend they hadn't been put through the door at all. To imagine that Garth was still free ...

The prosecutor was talking to her now. Concentrate, she told herself again, fiercely. This was not the time to think of Garth, who might be slumped on the floor of a prison cell, thinking that she'd abandoned him (Brian said that communication was very difficult and that the paperwork required for a visit could take months).

Listen to what the lawyer was saying. It was her duty. She had to do right by Kayleigh, the girl in the park and all the other girls in the park; just as Lady Harris was going to do the right thing by Garth. An eye for an eye. One witness statement for another.

"Can you describe exactly what you saw, please, Mrs Honeybun?"

His voice was kind. Reassuring. That was of course, because

he was on her side. The prosecutor would start first, Paul Black had explained. He would outline the case against Frankie Miller of the maroon suit in the dock and then call witnesses to 'substantiate' the case.

Originally, there was going to be another one, a young girl who had been with Kayleigh earlier in the day. But she was unable to be here apparently.

Paul Black had said this in a dark sombre tone that had discouraged further questions on her part. Now he was sitting in one of the benches, his face on hers, waiting for her reply. Oh God. Why had she allowed herself to be involved with this? It was all very well wanting to help others. But this was horrible. Like being in a shop window with everyone staring.

Alice began to sweat. Glancing up at the Public Gallery, she saw Janice looking down. Monica from the tennis club was there too. So were some of the others. But where was Daniel?

"Mrs Honeybun," repeated the lawyer with a hint of concern in his voice. "could you please tell us what happened on the day of June 9th please?"

"Of course." Aware that her voice was shaky, she tried to steady herself. "I was walking our dog in the local park when I became aware of a couple sitting on a bench. They weren't talking. Just sitting there."

"Were they touching each other, Mrs Honeybun?"

"Objection, m'lord."

A short, red-faced woman had leaped to her feet. She was the defence solicitor, Paul had explained beforehand. "The prosecution is encouraging the witness to embellish her description."

Startled, Alice turned to the judge. He was younger than she'd expected; about her age. Indeed his face was familiar. She might well have sat next to him at a dinner party, she mused.

"Objection overruled. You may continue Mrs Honeybun."

She paused. Everyone's eyes were on her, reminding her of a time when she'd been chosen to play Dido in the school play and had seized up on the first night. Afterwards, the understudy had taken over.

"Then they got up and went towards a hedge. The boy

194

remained standing and the girl … the girl bent down as though … as though she was going to put a plaster on his knee."

There was a general titter round the court. This was awful! Alice began to feel resentful towards Paul Black. He had warned her this might be difficult but this was like being on display; a sort of human cockfighting sport. "I didn't realise at first," spluttered Alice, "what she was doing."

The titters became a roar of laughter from up in the public gallery. Alice felt her cheeks burning furiously. Mortified, she turned to Paul Black. Keep going, his eyes said. Ignore them. Tell the truth.

He just wants you to help him do his job. That's what Daniel had said. The laughter grew louder and someone cat-whistled from the gallery. Why hadn't she listened to her husband?

"Quiet please," said the judge sharply. "Please, Mrs Honeybun, go on."

Her mouth was so dry that the words could hardly come out. "I went on walking but then, when I returned with my dog, I saw them … I saw them on the ground."

"And what were they doing?"

The prosecutor's voice was kind but firm. Alice's face was so hot she felt it was going to explode. "They were … they were making love."

"Objection!" The short woman leaped to her feet. "How did she know?"

"You will have your chance to question the witness in a moment." The judge was glaring. "Objection overruled."

The prosecution lawyer looked pleased. "And this was a public place at the end of the afternoon where parents often play with their children?"

Alice nodded, grateful to return to safer ground. "Yes. I was worried that someone else would see them."

"And how else did you feel?"

"Sullied." The word flew out of her mouth before she even thought about it. "The park felt tainted after that. Every time I walk in it, I can't help looking at that place where … where it happened."

"No further questions, m'lord."

Alice felt a wave of relief but only for a second. The short fat woman was already on her feet. "Mrs Honeybun, how far away were you from the defence?"

Alice hesitated. "It's difficult to remember."

The woman was waving a piece of paper. "It says on your statement that you were about five to six metres away. Do you wear glasses, Mrs Honeybun?"

"No."

"And when did you last get a sight check?"

Daniel had been nagging her about that for ages. I don't need one, she always retorted but the truth was that, just like her husband, she was in middle-age denial over glasses too. "Not for a few years."

"A few years, Mrs Honeybun? So is it possible that you were mistaken in what you saw?"

"No. I mean, I don't think so."

Desperately, she looked across at Paul Black. His face was impassive. Taut. Waiting. Save me, she wanted to say. Please. Save me.

The defence lawyer smiled tightly, reminding her of a crocodile in a book that Garth had loved as a child. It was her son who was important. Not this. Why was she even here? "In a minute, m'lord," continued the lawyer, "I intend to show that the defendant had indeed cut his knee from splinters on the bench and that Kayleigh Long could have been putting a plaster on it."

There was a roar of laughter from the gallery.

"Objection, m'lord."

"Overruled."

"I also question Mrs Honeybun's impartiality on the subject. Is it not true that as a teenager you accused an innocent man of sexually assaulting you?"

Alice froze. How did they know?

"Yes. No. "

"Please be clear, Mrs Honeybun."

"Yes," she whispered. "I accused him but he wasn't innocent."

"In your opinion?"

She grew even redder before repeating his words faintly. "In my opinion."

There was a taut hush as the defence lawyer then turned to the jury. "And is the court aware that Mrs Honeybun's potentially slanderous accusation, even though it was kept within the confines of the immediate family led to a great deal of embarrassment on the behalf of the innocent man in question?"

Sweat began to pour down her back and she became aware of a deep heat burning her face and body. Who could have told them? Mum? Surely not even she would do this to her.

The defence lawyer was waving a sheet of paper; a nasty grin on her face. "I have evidence here from the accused himself. A Mr Phil Wright. He isn't able to be here himself as he is in hospital." A murmur of sympathy ran round the court. "But it is part of my argument that Mrs Honeybun has a vivid imagination especially when it comes to sex and what she has and hasn't seen."

"That's not true!" Her voice rang out in a scream, just as it had all those years ago when her mother had said she'd 'either imagined it' or led Phil on.

"Please Mrs Honeybun." The judge's voice was sternly reproving. "I must ask you to remain silent until directly questioned."

The defence lawyer's eyes glittered as if with pleasure. "And is it also not true that the witness has not had marital relations with her husband for nineteen years? So it is possible, that her statement is the result of a woman who is sexually frustrated and makes things up in order to feed her physical cravings?"

Alice felt the room blurring around her, dimly aware of the gasps and the rustlings from the public gallery. How did the lawyer know? Had Daniel told her? Was that why he wasn't he here? Her eyes stung with tears. How could her own husband betray her like this?

"Objection, your honour."

The judge glanced in her direction. Was it her imagination or did the judge look mildly sympathetic? "Objection overruled. Mrs Honeybun, please answer."

She tried but once more, the words stuck in her dry throat; trapped in a net of fear and embarrassment.

"May I remind you that you are under oath, Mrs Honeybun."

"Yes. No. I mean, it is true that my husband and I do not ..."

She couldn't say it. She really couldn't.

"But I didn't make up that scene in the park. I didn't."

Her voice came out as a cry, ringing round the court. But the lawyer on the boy's side smirked as if to say to the jury "Surely you don't believe this mad woman."

Only Paul Black continued to look steadily at her, his face soft with understanding and sorrow. "I'm sorry," he seemed to say. "I'm so sorry to put you through this."

Did he mean it? Or was it an elaborate charade? Did he even care providing he got his conviction? Dimly Alice recalled reading something about policemen being promoted on account of the number of 'guilties' they achieved.

"STOP!"

A voice rang out from the public gallery. For a moment, Alice thought it was Janice. But then she saw a tall woman with immaculately styled silver hair, resembling a well-groomed fox, rise majestically to her feet. "I can't keep quiet any more. I saw what happened that day. And I want to give evidence."

Everyone was turning round to look at her. Voices rose like a tidal wave around her. Even Paul Black appeared unsettled. The two lawyers were approaching the judge now and talking, urgently, in low tones. What was going on? Who was this woman? And where was Kayleigh? Shouldn't she be here to give evidence too?

The judge struck the bench with his hammer. "Jury out please. I am declaring a recess of half an hour."

Alice sought refuge in her car, not wanting to speak to anyone. Time and time again, she rang Daniel on both his mobile and landline. Each time it went straight through to answer-phone. Where was he? Did his betrayal – only he knew they hadn't had sex for years – mean he'd given up on her? That he no longer wanted to continue with the marriage? The idea was both terrifying and yet strangely exciting. Maybe this was finally her chance to break free and be the person she really was, whoever that might be. Yet on the other hand, she couldn't imagine life with Daniel. Even grown-up children needed two parents. *Garth ... Garth ...*

As for Paul Black, Daniel was right. He had simply thrown her to the lions. Now she'd done her bit, he hadn't even bothered to come and see if she was all right. If he'd been really worried, surely he'd have checked out the court car park?

When she returned, she found the court was about to convene. "What's happened?" she asked someone.

"Seems like they're going to allow that woman to be a witness."

Paul Black was nowhere to be seen. It was both a relief and disappointment. Glancing around the public gallery, acutely aware of the stares and pointing, Alice continued to search for Daniel. No. He definitely wasn't here. All the anger which she'd been trying to repress ("It's not nice to get angry," her mother had told her as a child) now shot round her body in hot tidal waves. Again and again she kept asking herself the same question as if it might somehow re-write what had just happened. How could her husband have betrayed her like that, telling the police about their private life?

"I call Mrs Patricia Williams to take the witness stand," said the prosecutor. He sounded smug, Alice noticed. As though he'd already won. Despite the anger and embarrassment, she was curious.

Everyone turned as the smartly dressed woman in her fifties clattered across the courtroom floor in red high heels. Despite her own distress and apprehension, Alice could not help taking in the woman's elegant appearance. Her silver hair had that feathery cut which only looked right when professionally blow dried (which it appeared to have been) and she held her head high as though she may well have done something wrong but was not ashamed to admit it.

The new witness took her oaths loudly and clearly, rather like an actress, Alice thought. Once more there was a hush about the court; as if the curtain was about to rise on the first act.

"Can you tell us what you saw on the evening in question?" asked the prosecution lawyer. He spoke, Alice noticed, as though he didn't care for the woman very much.

She nodded. "I was staying at the Hotel Regent overlooking the park. I had just had a shower and was looking out of the window to cool myself. It had been a hot day."

There was an appreciative murmur from one or two of the male members of the jury. "I saw a couple sitting on a bench and then moving towards the hedge. The man stood very straight as though he was in another word and the girl bent down to perform oral sex."

There was a gasp.

"You are sure of that?"

The woman smiled. Her lipstick was glossy and appeared to shine in agreement. "I am very sure. The man then proceeded to take the girl's clothes off below her waist and have intercourse with her."

Another gasp.

"Did she seem willing?"

"Extremely willing."

Another hushed silence.

"But that might have been because of the pill I saw him give her on the bench."

"Yet you were some distance away."

There was a foxy smile. "I always carry my opera glasses in my handbag. One never knows when one might need them."

The noise around her in the gallery almost deafened Alice's ears.

"Silence," roared the judge.

The prosecutor's eyes glinted. "And may I ask why you didn't come forward before as a witness?"

The elegant woman's gaze stiffened. "I was having an affair with a married man. That was why we were in the hotel. But now that is over. I felt it was time that his wife should know the truth." She smiled. "And that the real story should be told about the young couple too, of course."

Alice felt sick. So this woman had come forward as a witness, not out of the goodness of her own heart but to wreak

200

revenge on a man who had, quite possibly, let her down.

How awful.

"Objection." The defence was on her feet. "What proof is there that Patricia Williams hasn't made this up?"

"I thought you might ask that." The woman smiled thinly. "I took the precaution of taking photographs on my phone. Don't get me wrong. I'm not some kind of a voyeur." She laughed as if the idea was highly amusing. "Something told me they might be needed."

"Objection," said the defence leaping to her feet.

"Overruled," said the judge smartly. "You were made aware of these photographs during the recess and I made it quite clear they could be used as part of the evidence."

The lawyer sank back in her seat with a sullen expression.

The youth in the dock was looking at her, Alice suddenly realised. He had a smile playing on his lips. I know something you don't, he seemed to say. Alice shivered.

Meanwhile, the court was in uproar. It looked as though they were going to win if the expression on the prosecutor's face was anything to go by. But at what expense to her? The whole world knew now that she and Daniel hadn't had sex for years. They also knew about Phil, even though in her view the full story hadn't been told. She was a laughing stock. It was almost, but not quite enough to make her forget about Garth.

There was another witness too. A teacher at Kayleigh Long's school. A Mr Brown with a brown ponytail; what kind of school did he teach at? Alice was still too upset to take it all in. But his evidence clearly implied that Kayleigh made things up. *Vivid imagination ... natural storyteller ... potentially dangerous ... even said she saw me in an inappropriate situation with a pupil ... her statement not to be believed ...*

Something about the man rattled Alice. She didn't like him. And why wasn't Kayleigh herself here to give evidence? Maybe they'd allowed her to do it on video but if so, they hadn't shown it yet. Perhaps there was no need now that the silver fox woman had stolen the show with her recorded film on her mobile.

At last! The judge was allowing them to leave while the jury debated. She'd go outside again. Quietly. Get some air.

"Are you all right?"

Paul Black's voice was behind her.

She shook her head, not wanting to turn round; to face the man she'd trusted. "Not really."

"I'm so sorry you had to go through that."

"Are you?"

Alice heard her voice come out sharply; not like her own. To her satisfaction, there was a flicker of unease in Paul Black's eyes. Good. He'd know now she wasn't an easy pushover. "Who told them. About me and … my husband? And … and that stuff about me as a teenager?"

He shook his head. "I can't say, I'm afraid."

"Can't say because you don't know or because you're not legally allowed to tell me?"

His words slid into the space between them, locking them together in complicity. "The latter." For a brief second, he touched her hand. "I'm sorry. More sorry than you realise."

He meant it. She could tell. Either that or he was a good actor and she was even more stupid than she'd thought.

Alice looked down at the spot on her bare arm where his hand had been seconds earlier. She waited. Waited for the all too familiar wave of revulsion. Where was it?

"We'd better go back inside." Paul Black made as though to offer her his arm but then seemed to think better of it. "Something tells me the jury won't be long."

Her head spinning, Alice returned to her seat. No point in looking for Daniel now. He'd abandoned her. Thrown her to the dogs. Maybe he was right. Perhaps she deserved to be punished. As Daniel had said often enough, a man has physical needs in a marriage. It couldn't survive alone on breakfast marmalade and other domestic banalities. Not if sex wasn't involved.

Damn you, Uncle Phil. *Damn* you. Too late, Alice wished with all her heart that she hadn't been weak enough to forgive him in the nursing home. She should have forced him to make a confession to her mother – to the whole world – instead of allowing her better nature to pity a dying man.

The judge was rapping the bench with his hammer now. "Do you find Frankie Miller guilty or not guilty of rape and the supplying of drugs?"

"Guilty, my Lord."

There was the sound of a hammer. "Frankie Miller. I hereby sentence you to ten years."

Good, thought Alice, as she tried to weave her way through the crowds and snapping cameras. At least she'd done something right. But at what cost to her? Not to mention her marriage ...

TWENTY

Kayleigh stumbled off the bus, still in a daze. Was she really here or had she made it up the way she often made things up to get away from what was real? Forcing herself to concentrate, she tried to take in her surroundings. There was the park on the other side of the road which seemed to go on and on for ever. There was the boating lake at the far end: she'd remembered that because Marlene had said she wouldn't mind a go, later.

Her friend had said the word *later* with a giggle, suggesting that they were going to do something much more interesting first. That was when she and Pete had gone off on their own, leaving her and Frankie alone.

Poor Marlene. If only she could change the past. Kayleigh stopped, looking down on the bench where it had all begun. There was still that sign on the back, that she'd noticed before. "Look, Frankie," she had said, pointing to it.

The words still got her now, second time round.

'In memory of Betty who loved sitting here.'

"Isn't that sweet?" Kayleigh had looked up at Frankie. "Isn't it nice to think someone cared enough about her to put a sign up like that? Maybe they bought the bench too." She'd looked at it admiringly. "Must have cost a lot. That person must really have loved this Betty."

That was when Frankie had pulled her down onto the bench next to him. She could remember it as if he was doing it right now. "I love you, Kayleigh," he'd said, those green eyes dancing. "One day, I'll put up a sign for you like this one."

She'd gasped with the shock. Frankie loved her? Even

though they'd only just met? Every time Mum found someone new, she talked about love at first sight. It usually meant a different noise on the other side of the wall.

But this was different. Frankie was the man she'd been waiting for. Kayleigh just knew that. She could tell from the way her heart had started to beat wildly when he'd slid his arm along the back of the bench casually and then lowered his lips gently onto her hers.

"Feeling nervous, are you?" he'd whispered. "This might help."

That was when he'd kissed her and the pill had slid down her throat. After that, everything had become a bit of a blur …

Kayleigh now shook herself. How could she have been so stupid? Sitting down on the bench, she gripped the side arm. She should have been brave enough to go back to the court, after finding out that Mum was all right. She should have stood up and told them that she stuck to the statement she'd made to the police at the time.

It would have been the right thing to do. But she'd bottled it.

Kayleigh threw a look at the sign on the bench. This Betty wouldn't have bottled it. She would have been brave and strong. That was why someone had loved her and bothered to remember her after she'd died.

Not like her. I'm unlovable, Kayleigh told herself, getting up and walking towards the boating lake. No wonder no one wants me. I'm not really beautiful like Frankie said. I've got orange hair, white skin, and freckles. Even worse, I'm a coward. And the only time I'm really happy is when I'm pretending something else is happening. Even Mr Brown, who'd acted so keen, didn't fancy her any more. Hadn't she seen him with her own eyes, getting into another girl's pants?

A woman walking past with a bicycle, gave her an odd look like she recognised her and Kayleigh felt a weird shiver go through her. It would only be a matter of time now before she was nabbed by the policeman with the cool blue eyes or the social worker with the bouncy orange earrings. They'd take her back to that crazy Marc and Angie or maybe they'd send her somewhere else.

Perhaps, thought Kayleigh in a burst of optimism, she could just hide away until next Wednesday. Her sixteenth birthday. Her knowledge of the law was a bit hazy but Marlene always said you could do what you wanted then.

Perhaps she could live on her own! She might even be able to get a flat if she got pregnant. That's what Marlene had always planned to do. Kayleigh's mind went back to her period that had finally arrived, a bit late. In some ways, that was just as well. She didn't want his kid now. Not after what he had just done. But maybe she could get pregnant by someone else. It was a way out, wasn't it? 'Sides, she'd give anything for a kid. A baby who would love her unconditionally. She could build herself a real family.

As if on cue, there was a burst of laughter from the family on the boating lake. Kayleigh eyed them enviously. The laughter came from the woman who was sitting at one end while one of the kids rowed and the dad was showing him how to do it.

Had her real dad ever shown her how to do something before he had walked out? If so, she couldn't remember. Kayleigh walked on past the boating lake a little faster now, glancing over her shoulder. Bloody hell. What was that noise?

Ducking under a tree, she waited until it had passed. An ambulance, she noticed with relief. Not a police car. She reached a gate now, leading out of the park on the other side. There was a sign.

'To the beach'

She'd like to see the sea. They were going to do that, her and Frankie and Marlene and Pete, when they'd first set out that day. But they'd never got there because the other stuff had happened instead.

Now, as Kayleigh made her way uncertainly down the dusty footpath, she gazed at the water in front of her. How beautiful! You could almost touch those sparkly bits with your finger. You could run into the water and feel it splashing up around you.

It would wash her clean. Take away the horror of Marlene and Mum and Frankie and everyone else ... Wow! The sea was so cold! Running out again, Kayleigh realised too late she'd forgotten to take off her trainers in her keenness to get in. Maybe if she sat on that rock over there, she could put them in the sun and let them dry.

"Kayleigh? Is that you?"

She stiffened at the sound of a posh voice coming from behind. Whipping round, she stopped. And gasped. Wasn't that the woman from the park? The one who had given her fifty quid in the shopping centre?

"No. Please. Don't go." The woman caught her by the sleeve. "I'm not going to hurt you or call the police. I've come straight from the court, Kayleigh. I've got something to tell you. Frankie got ten years. You're safe!"

Anyone looking at them, thought Kayleigh, might think they were mother and daughter. Lots of kids had different-coloured hair from their parents, didn't they? She'd have liked a mother like this. Someone who had time to sit down with her and talk to her like an adult. To tell her exactly what had happened.

"People got hurt," said the woman, her beautiful eyes filling with tears.

Kayleigh gasped. "Stabbed?"

The woman gave a funny smile. "Not in court."

"It's not funny," said Kayleigh fiercely. "If you lived where I did, you'd know that. People get stabbed all the time."

Alice – "you must call me that, dear" – stopped smiling then. "I'm sorry." Then she looked away towards the sea. "I got hurt, actually."

"You did?" Kayleigh looked at her arms and neck. She couldn't see anything.

"Inside." The woman was talking to the water. "Someone said something unkind to me in court."

Kayleigh felt a sharp pang of guilt. "Because of me?"

"No."

"Yes it was. If you hadn't gone to court to give evidence, this wouldn't have happened."

The woman reached out and touched her arm kindly like Mr Brown used to do after school. "No one blames you, Kayleigh.

208

So you mustn't blame yourself either. It's a lesson I'm still learning myself." She stared dreamily towards the horizon where there was a small boat bobbing. "You know, I often come down here to think."

"I would too," said Kayleigh quickly, "if I lived here. It's really cool, isn't it? But where I come from, you can't do much thinking. There's always an argument or someone wants you to do something you shouldn't."

The woman frowned. "My son has been accused of doing something he shouldn't have."

"Drugs?"

She nodded.

"I wondered it was him. I read about it in a newspaper. Recognised your name."

"You read the papers?" Alice Honeybun seemed surprised.

Kayleigh felt offended. "Why shouldn't I?"

"No, it's just that ..."

"Forget it." She felt protective towards this woman who had tried to help her and was now so upset. "Tell me more about court. Why you were hurt?"

Alice 's eyes deadened. "They said I made things up. Told lies about something that happened when I was younger." She paused abruptly, before adding. "When I was abused."

Kayleigh hadn't realised things like that happened to women like this. Weren't they too posh?

"I was about your age." She spoke very slowly. Very deliberately, like every word was a stone you had to walk round carefully. "I should have told someone – someone apart from my mother. She didn't believe me, you see."

Kayleigh was riveted. "My mum doesn't believe me either. What happened to the bloke who did this stuff to you?"

There was a funny little laugh. "Uncle Phil? He's dying. But he made me forgive him."

Kayleigh felt a rush of indignation on her new friend's behalf. "Why did you do it?"

"Because sometimes there's no point in fighting."

That's not true, she was about to say but Alice was now giving herself a little shake and looking directly at her. "What

209

about you, Kayleigh. What are you going to do now? Where will you live?"

Kayleigh shrugged. "I don't know." She bit her lip. "Can I trust you to keep a secret?"

The woman nodded uncertainly. "Provided it's legal."

"Sort of. I'm meant to be in care but I've run away. Don't look like that. I had to. They were weirdos. If I can hang out a bit, I'll be sixteen and then no one can stop me from living on my own."

Alice Honeybun's eyebrows rose. It was cool, the way they looked. Maybe she plucked them like Marlene. "Isn't that rather young?"

"Nah!" Kayleigh spluttered. "Loads of girls do that where I live. There's a kid who's twelve in the block below us. She hasn't seen her mother since last summer and she manages. Better off without her, if you ask me."

There was a murmur of 'How awful' although that might have been the kiss of a wave. Once more, Kayleigh looked around, admiring the red cliffs and the pretty houses on the hill. How come some people got to live in a place like this while others, like her, ended up in shitty flats with mould on the walls and Rons in the kitchen. It wasn't fair.

Alice seemed to be deep in thought now. Not wanting to disturb her, Kayleigh picked up a shell. It was white with a pink tinge. She slipped it in her pocket, hoping no one would notice.

"Kayleigh?"

She flushed. Shit. Now Alice would think she was a thief.

"About that secret I just told you. The thing about my uncle." She went bright red. "I'd rather you didn't mention that to anyone else."

Kayleigh crossed herself – something she'd never done before but somehow it felt right. "Hand on heart. When I like someone, I'll do anything for them. Anything at all."

She meant it too. Alice looked a bit startled. "Right. Thanks. Now why don't you come back to my house for a cup of tea?"

Had she heard her right? Women like this one didn't ask girls like her back to their house for a cup of tea.

"Please." To her surprise, Alice's voice was trembling. "To

be honest, I don't particularly want to go home on my own. That's why I came here, after getting back from court. My husband is out and ... well let's just say I could do with the company until he gets back. There's something I've got to talk to him about, you see and ..."

She broke off.

"You're scared of him, aren't you?" Kayleigh suddenly realised.

"Yes. No. I don't know." Alice gave a sort of smile that wasn't really a smile at all. "Part of me thinks our lives might not be as different as you might think. No. Don't ask me more. You'll see."

Kayleigh's heart went out to her. Besides, she thought, as they walked through town, past some really pretty shops with surfboards and pictures of beach huts in the windows, it wasn't as if she had anywhere better to go, was it?

A police car went past and they both stiffened. Then it rounded the corner and disappeared out of sight. Shit. What if Alice Honeybun was trying to get her back to her place so she could turn her in to the police or the social worker? Kayleigh was about to leg it when suddenly Alice stopped outside one of those huge tall white houses she'd admired from the bus with a gravel drive leading down. There was a great big car at the bottom.

"My husband's back," she heard her say in a hushed voice. "Look. Please don't leave me, Kayleigh. Please don't."

If there was one thing Kayleigh could recognise, it was fear. Real fear.

"OK," she said, walking nervously down the drive with her. The promise made her feel special. Important. "But what ..."

She broke off as suddenly the front door swung open. This place was so big! It must be a whole load of flats bunged together. But then this thought was replaced by apprehension as she took in the man's stern face which looked first at her and then Alice.

"What the hell have you got us into this time?" he yelled.

Alice, next to her, had gone pale. "You mean, what have you got *me* into? You didn't even have the guts to come to court to hear all those nasty things you told the police."

"What are you talking about?" His eyes were wet, Kayleigh realised. This grown man was crying!

Alice noticed it too. "Something's happened, hasn't it?" She clutched his arm. "Is it Garth?"

"Mungo." There was a loud sob. "I couldn't be in court because I was at the vet's. They've poisoned him."

TWENTY-ONE

When Alice had first seen Daniel glaring from the front door, she'd presumed he was going to defend himself for having told the court about their sex life. After all, who else could have done so?

But now, Daniel's words blew the ones she had prepared in her head (like "how could you?" and "do you want a divorce?") out of her head.

"I couldn't be in court because I was at the vet's. They've poisoned him."

"The vet poisoned him? Alice stared incredulously at her husband. Impossible. Yet things happened like that, didn't they? Mistakes were made. A dim but horrible memory came back of a neighbour whose cat had died during a routine neutering operation.

"Not the *vet*." Daniel's eyes were watery. She'd only once seen him cry and that was when Garth had been born. He turned away but not before Alice saw a tear trickle down his right cheek. "It was that lot," he said angrily. "Friends of the boy whom you were testifying against. Those letters you were sent. We should have taken more notice of them. None of this wouldn't have happened if you hadn't been so keen on being a bloody witness."

I wasn't keen, Alice tried to say. I felt I had to do it. But instead her knees began to knock together as though some unseen force was moving them. Unable to stand, she sank onto the bottom step in the hall, right below the framed photograph of Garth in his blue and red uniform, on his first day at school.

"How did it happen?" Her voice didn't belong to her. It was surely owned by another woman. Someone else whose dog had been poisoned. Not her. Not Mungo who would come racing any minute, out of the kitchen, pawing at her for a walk.

"They slung a piece of poisoned meat through the cat flap." Daniel's back was to her and she knew from the choked sound in his throat that he was desperately trying to control himself. "I heard the noise of a car from upstairs while I was getting dressed to come to court." He whipped round. "To support you."

Daniel spat out the word 'support' like a stone in anger; making her flinch. "I found Mungo chewing at a piece of meat." He covered his face with his hands. "I tried to make him sick by putting my fingers down his throat …"

Alice heard herself let out an anguished cry.

"So I just grabbed him and the meat that he hadn't eaten and bundled him into the car." Daniel's knuckles were white on the back of the big wooden hall chair which still bore puppy teeth-marks from the days when Mungo chewed everything in sight. "But he began fitting before we got to the vet's."

"No," whispered Alice. "No."

"Is he dead?" asked a voice.

She'd forgotten the girl was there. Still standing by the door; face tight; eyes wild and searching.

"Who's that?" demanded Daniel as if he hadn't noticed her existence earlier on.

His question seemed superfluous in the light of Kayleigh's. Alice had presumed Mungo was dead but now a glimmer of hope hung before her like the thin cobweb which, she noticed irrelevantly, glimmered in the dusty sunlight from the staircase above.

"IS HE DEAD?" thundered Alice in a voice which came from a place inside her that she hadn't been aware of before.

"They've pumped out what they can but it's still in the system. So they …"

Alice sank to her knees in thankfulness. "Then he's still alive," she whispered.

"The vet doesn't know if he's going to make it." Daniel's

eyes were narrowing at Kayleigh. "Does *she* have anything to do with this?"

Alice prided herself on not telling lies. Before Uncle Phil, she had told the odd white one but afterwards – when her mother had declared her to be a 'wicked little liar' – she'd taken care to tell the truth about everything. Apart from the one secret she'd had to keep back.

But now, still on her knees, she looked from her husband's furious glare to Kayleigh's fearful eyes, and wondered, just for a minute, whether to omit yet another crucial fact.

Then the girl spoke. "I'm Kayleigh."

Daniel's eyes hardened. "The girl from the park?" He switched his gaze to Alice. "The one you gave evidence about?"

"What kind of car was it?"

"What?" They both spoke in unison, turning to her.

Kayleigh's voice was calm. "You said you saw a car when you was upstairs. What kind of car was it?"

"Some beaten-up piece of rubbish," said Daniel, tightly in a what-the-fuck-does-it-matter voice.

She nodded. "I reckon that belongs to Frankie's mate. They killed my friend Marlene too."

"*Killed* her?" Alice stared at the girl.

There was a vigorous nodding of the head. "They gave her an overdose. She's dead. Mum said so before she got me put into care with these weirdos. The bloke hurt his wife – well I think he did – and kept looking at me like he might touch me up. He took me to court this morning but then Frankie's lot sent me a picture of my mum and I thought they'd beaten her up. It's OK. They hadn't – they'd done stuff to the photograph to make it look bad like they'd thrown acid at her – but I was too scared to go back to court in case they hurt me. Now I don't know where to go."

The girl's words came out like a torrent with barely a breath in between, as though she'd been bottling it all up. Alice's head was beginning to spin. Acid attack ... abusive foster parents ... friend dead from an overdose ... It was too much to take in. But one thing at least was clear.

"She must stay here, mustn't she, Daniel?"

"Are you joking?" Daniel let out a hoarse laugh. "If these people think we're looking after a girl who could put them in prison, they'll do something far worse than poison the dog."

"Like tell the world we don't have sex, you mean?"

The words flew out of her mouth, regardless of Kayleigh's presence.

Daniel eyed her as though she was nuts. "What are you talking about?"

"Don't try that on me." Alice felt fury burning through her like a great rage. It made her throat feel sore. "You told the other side that we didn't have sex. The lawyer stood up and said that I ... I was messed up and frustrated and that I *imagined* the whole thing taking place in the park. And they knew about Phil. They brought him up too, making me out to be some teenage fantasist ..."

Her voice tailed away. Either her husband was a very good actor – like Paul Black – or else he really was shocked. "Alice," he began to say. "I didn't ..."

He stopped as the phone broke the silence from the hall table, chirping brightly. "Leave it," croaked Daniel. "I haven't finished."

Too late, Alice wished she'd listened to him. Not Mum. Not now. Purposefully, she hadn't told her about the court case. She certainly wouldn't have approved of Alice's involvement; in fact, she'd have somehow turned it round so it was all her fault in her first place.

"Alice?" Her mother's voice boomed imperiously down the line. "I thought you ought to know that Uncle Phil is on the mend, dear. Amazing, isn't it? Something must have brought him back from the dead. Perhaps it was your visit. No. Don't say anything. He told me you'd finally apologised. Perhaps now you've learned your lesson. Have you any idea what damage you caused over the years?"

"What?"

"Don't try to pretend, dear. We've all had enough of your stories. By the way, how did your court case go?"

That was it. That really was it.

"Who was that?" Daniel's face was apprehensive as she

216

slammed down the phone.

"Mum." Alice looked from Kayleigh to Daniel and to Garth's picture on the wall and then back to Daniel again. Despite her earlier thoughts, she could see now that she needed her husband for stability. Everything that had happened in the last few weeks – their son, her court case and now Mungo – had thrown life into perspective. Thank God it hadn't been Daniel after all who had told the world about their sex life.

Otherwise she couldn't have stayed.

"What did she want?" Daniel, who knew her all too well, could tell something was up. Something else to throw into this equation of wild turmoil.

"Just a chat." There was no way she could talk about it now. Uncle Phil and his games belonged to another time. Not now. Not with Mungo ill and Garth in prison.

"Ta ra, then."

The girl's voice startled her. The child had a way of staying so silent you forgot she was there.

"No. Stay."

"You can't do this!" Daniel's voice was outraged. "She's in care. It's illegal and …"

The girl cut in. "I'm sixteen tomorrow. I can do what I want. " She looked around. "I wouldn't mind staying here for a bit. But only if it's not too much trouble."

Alice looked at Daniel. The thing about being married for years, she suddenly realised, was that you didn't always need to talk. You just knew. Maybe she shouldn't take that for granted any more. Please, said her look. Please don't throw Kayleigh out. She could be Garth, desperately needing a stranger's help. And if you do make her leave, she could be hurt like her friend and Mungo.

He held her plea for what seemed like several minutes. Then he turned, his back disapproving. "Do what you want," he said, sharply. "Isn't that what you usually do?"

Then he headed for his study, clicking the door quietly behind him. Alice would have preferred it if he'd slammed it. There was a low murmur on the other side. He was using the phone. Maybe ringing Brian to see if there was any news on

Garth. Or perhaps calling the vet.

Alice's nails dug into the palm of her hand. There was a noise from beside her. Once more, she was taken by the girl's silent presence. "Shall I put the kettle on?" Kayleigh said. "My mum says she can always think better when she's having a cuppa." Then she added "Or a fag."

Alice felt her mouth twitching despite herself. "Well I don't smoke. So it had better be tea." She remembered her manners. It was soothing to do so; it helped to distract her from the uncertainty around her. "Please. Sit down." She flung open a kitchen cupboard. "What would you like? Lapsang? Earl Grey? Darjeeling?"

The girl's eyes flickered from one packet to another. "Just tea, ta."

"Do you take sugar?" asked Alice.

Kayleigh's eyes widened as though it was a daft question. "'Course. Three, ta." She patted her skinny waist. "I'm trying to cut down."

"Really?" Alice felt a flicker of alarm, remembering how she had come very close to anorexia after Uncle Phil. Relief that Daniel hadn't betrayed her and that he was still here almost made her feel high. Slightly manic, in fact. Over-keen, perhaps, to make their visitor feel welcome after her husband's cool reception.

"I think you look great as you are. In fact, you could do with putting on a bit more weight. By the way, I do hope you don't think I'm interfering but I've got a brilliant hairdresser. Would you like your hair cut into a bob?" She gave Kayleigh what she hoped was a reassuring smile. "I think it would suit you."

Looking after Kayleigh helped to distract Alice from both Garth and the empty dog basket, in a way that her broken china could no longer do. The latter gave her too much time to think. But the whirlwind left in the girl's wake refused to allow Alice to dwell on Mungo who was still 'poorly' in the veterinary hospital or her son who was 'bearing up under the circumstances' according to Brian.

Her new 'guest' either needed something (*how does that*

posh shower work in my bathroom?) or constantly offered to help (*let me wash up – it's cheaper than using a dishwasher*) or simply wanted to chat. It turned out Kayleigh had already read the thriller they were doing at Book Club. "Got it from the library. They look out stuff like that for me."

Silently, Alice reproached herself for feeling surprised. Why shouldn't a girl from the council estate with matted red-gold hair (she'd turned down the offer of her hairdresser, much to Alice's disappointment) and a bluebird tattoo on her shoulder, be well-read? *"You're too judgmental, Mum"*. Wasn't that what Garth was always saying?

Garth, Garth. Be safe. Please. Alice didn't need Daniel to tell her that she'd taken in Kayleigh because she could help the girl in a way that she couldn't help her own son.

Meanwhile, the stories that were coming out of Kayleigh's mouth were riveting in their horror and other-worldliness. There was a half-brother who was Inside for cannabis dealing, whom she clearly hero-worshipped. Alice decided she'd keep that one from Daniel. Then there was a teacher called Mr Brown who had said she was clever enough to go to uni one day. Was that the same teacher who had stood up in court and declared Kayleigh to be a fantasist? If so, she'd keep that one back too.

But despite this, the uncertainties still kept tormenting Alice, reminding her of a seaside amusement arcade that her parents had once taken her to as a child. You had to stand in front of a table with holes in it, holding a hammer. Every few seconds, a toy worm would pop out of one of the holes and you had to hit it to make it go down again.

Even at the age of nine or so, Alice had thought this was a bit like bashing the bad thoughts that came into your head; like whether Mum and Dad might get divorced after the last argument or whether she might not be selected for the school netball team.

Now, as she ran around after Kayleigh (*yes, please, do help yourself to whatever you want from the fridge*), she was, at the same time, mentally hitting down the worms popping up from the table. Brian, who was still waiting to hear from the 'other side' after Sheila Harrison's statement. Uncle Phil, who was now out of hospital; back in his nursing home; and 'his usual self again'. Daniel who had started going back to the university every day even though term didn't start for another month. Her mother, whose idea of support was to ask her vicar to pray for her grandson's 'safe delivery' and continue to talk about 'how wonderful' it was that Uncle Phil had made such a miraculous recovery. And Mungo, who would be here now if it hadn't been for her witness statement.

Then of course, there were her friends. "What did they mean in court about that man you accused as a teenager?" Janice had asked curiously.

"I can't talk about it," Alice had retorted. "It's private."

Her friend had looked hurt but it was true. She couldn't talk about it. Not yet, at any rate. But she needed to find out who had told the defence lawyer about the lack of sex in their marriage.   It   meant   speaking   to   her   lawyer … how embarrassing. Still, it had to be done.

Reaching for her phone, it began to ring on its own accord. 'Alice....' "Alice Honeybun?"

The voice was pleasant. But not like anyone she knew. "Who is this?"

"Hi! I'm Lisa from the features desk of *Charisma* magazine. The local news agency has just passed us your very moving story. Poor you! Listen, we wondered if you were interested in being interviewed for a piece on how child abuse can wreck your adult love life …"

Click. Alice cut her off in mid-sentence. Was this was it was going to be like from now on? A never-ending intrusion into her private life because she'd tried to help someone else? A witness. That's all she'd promised to be.

But now she'd become the victim.

Carry on. It was the only option, Alice decided. At least until Garth returned. Despite everything, she had to keep life going so it was normal when he returned.

'When'. Not 'if'. The alternative was unthinkable.

Meanwhile, she could at least help Kayleigh in a way that any decent person would help her own child. And if that meant taking her in, despite Daniel's deep disapproval, so be it. As for the invasion into her own life, that damage had already been done. She'd just have to deal with it.

The girl from the park, as Alice privately called her in her head, had been with them now for two days. Yesterday, she had made her a Victoria sponge which Daniel had reluctantly watched her cut. "No one's ever made me a birthday cake before," Kayleigh had said, disbelievingly. Today, she was teaching the girl how to make a quiche in the Aga when Paul Black called round. Did he always turn up unannounced, wondered Alice as she opened the door. It was really rather rude. Then again, perhaps that's what policemen did to catch people on the hop.

"Sorry to arrive without an appointment," he said, as if reading her mind. "But I was passing and wanted to make sure you were all right."

His clear blue eyes were fixed on hers just like they'd been from the beginning. Did he do that to others too? If so, it was a clever trick. It made you feel like you were the only person he was interested in talking to. For God's sake, Alice, what are you thinking? Say something. Don't just stand there like a moron, on the doorstep.

"Those things that were said in court," he continued. "They were cruel."

She gripped the tea cloth she was holding. "But you're still not going to tell me who said them?"

He had the grace to look abashed. "You know I can't."

"It was cruel." She faced him fair and square, wanting him to squirm. To know what she was feeling inside. "Cruel but true."

Good. He looked shocked. "True?" he repeated.

"Not all of it. I'm not a fantasist when it comes to sex. But it *is* correct that my husband and I haven't had … haven't had that kind of relationship for years. And I did accuse someone of something when I was a teenager. But I'm not sorry and no, I don't want to discuss it."

"I respect that."

Really? Somehow she'd expected those piercing blue eyes to challenge her. "I also came round to see about your dog. I'm so

221

sorry."

"Do you know *everything* about our lives?"

"Your husband reported it. It's on your files along with … with everything else."

"You sound like a lawyer."

He looked away. "Actually, I used to be one."

"Who's the fantasist now?"

"Alice." He looked as though he was going to take her hand but then stopped. "You're upset and understandably so. You're not yourself …"

"How dare you? How do you know what I'm really like?"

His eyes held hers. "Because I've seen this before. I've met other Alices. Not just young girls but women. Older than you. Younger too. Women whose lives have been tarnished by someone who hurt them. Brave women, like you. I can help, Alice, if you let me …"

Phil's silky words slipped into her head. *Help you. Let me help you, dear* …

'No. NO. I'll sort myself out. And don't, for one minute, think I believe your story about coming round to check on my dog. You're just feeling guilty because you said you'd protect me if I testified."

He looked alarmed. "No one's hurt you, have they?"

She laughed. "Not physically. Only mentally."

The flush on his cheeks grew. Deservedly so. Alice began to feel anger; not a fury that she had felt towards her husband earlier but a slow burning resentment. What had got into her? Until all this happened, she'd never been an angry person.

"We try to look after our witnesses." His voice shook slightly. "But there are times when … when it's not easy."

"I trusted you." Tears began to wet her eyes. "I believed you when you said it was important for me to give that statement."

"It was …"

She ignored him, rushing on. "But now I don't feel safe in my own home. Yes I know this Frankie got ten years but he's still got friends out there, hasn't he? Kayleigh says …"

Alice stopped.

Too late.

Paul Black's eyes had turned from empathy to suspicion. "You're in touch with Kayleigh?" Instantly he turned from confidante to policeman again. "If you know where she is, you must tell me."

Alice's hand began to sweat on the door. How could she betray the girl? Yet at the same time, she had to comply with the law. Was it possible she had broken it, unwittingly, by taking in Kayleigh?

"You'd better come in," she said, aware, too late, that she sounded ungracious. Then, prompted by an innate courtesy, she added. "Would you like a cup of tea?"

He followed her in, admiring (she could see) the walnut hall table with its silver-framed photograph of Garth on his christening day. "Any news on your son?" he asked with exactly the right tone of empathy mixed with professionalism.

He's good at his job, thought Alice. He shows empathy to get what he wants. Or maybe he's simply a decent human being. Why couldn't she tell the difference?.

"Yes. We have a witness." She took down two Emma Bridgewater mugs from the big old pine Welsh dresser which she and Daniel had bought on their honeymoon in Somerset; a time when they had both still hoped for other things. "Someone who saw someone else slipping drugs into his rucksack at Lima airport. She's made a statement and is prepared, apparently, to stand up in court. Just like I did."

Horrified, Alice heard herself laugh. Hysterically. There was the sound of a smash. One of the mugs lay in bits around her feet. This time it was an accident – it had just slipped through her fingers – but she could see, just from looking, that it would take a great deal of time and patience to repair.

"That's what I do!" The laughter came out even more hysterically in great splutters like a silly schoolgirl. "I mend china but I can't mend the cracks in my own life."

Someone was putting a pair of arms around her. It couldn't be Paul Black because policemen weren't allowed to do that kind of thing. But the arms had a stiff serge feel to them. Maybe it was her imagination again. That cursed imagination which was both her refuge and her chain.

"You've been through a lot. It's understandable if you're upset."

Then the arms were gone. In their place was an empty vacuum. I didn't flinch, Alice realised with amazement. *I didn't flinch. I didn't flinch,* she told herself.

"I'm sorry." Paul Black's blue eyes weren't locked on hers now. They were focussed on the floor. "I shouldn't have done that. It was unprofessional."

Did that mean he cared? Or that he was sorry he'd touched her? Confused, she clutched the surviving mug in her right hand, willing him to lift his eyes to hers. "I'm glad you did. It was … it was comforting."

For a minute, they both stood in awkward silence. Then the kettle began to sing (she'd always liked the old-fashioned variety) and at the same time, the phone began to ring. As if in tandem, there was the sound of footsteps coming down the stairs.

Kayleigh! For a while, she'd forgotten why Paul Black had come in, in the first place. So too, from his face, had he. The phone stopped before she could reach it. At the same time, Kayleigh came into the kitchen. Clean. Hair freshly washed. Pale. Scared.

"Kayleigh, I believe you've met PC Black before."

The look on the girl's face was matched only by that of her other visitor. "He's just come round to … to see how I am," she added, aware that it sounded odd. "Would you like a cup of tea? Paul's having one. Sorry. I meant to ask. Darjeeling or Lapsang? Kayleigh takes builder's although she did try a sip of Russian Caravan at breakfast, didn't you, Kayleigh?"

Aware that she was babbling with nerves, Alice came to an abrupt halt.

"Breakfast?" repeated Paul Black, incredulously. "Are you *staying* here then?"

Kayleigh folded her arms defiantly, jangling the charm bracelet which Alice had given her from her own jewellery box; privately, without telling Daniel. "Yes. I'm sixteen now. You can't stop me."

Paul Black's eyebrows met. "Actually, I'm afraid we can."

Really? Alice began to feel nervous. "We met ... bumped into each other ... on the beach after the trial. Kayleigh was worried ... we both were ... that Frankie's friends might hurt her. So she came back here because she didn't have anywhere to go ..."

Her voice tailed away as her visitor's face grew even more serious.

"She *did* have somewhere to go. She had a foster family and ..."

"That lot was weird!" Kayleigh cut in furiously. "Marc was a right creep. Have you seen the bruises on his wife's arms?"

"Frankie's friends gave her a picture of her mother looking as though she'd been attacked," added Alice, shooting the girl a 'Let me take over here' look. "That's why she skipped court. She had to check her mother was all right."

"And was she?"

Kayleigh nodded.

Paul had his notebook out. "Can you describe his friends?"

"You kidding me?" Kayleigh snorted. "I'm not going to give you any bleeding statement. If I hadn't given you the last one, I wouldn't be in this mess. And if Alice hadn't blabbered to you, her dog would be all right."

Dear God. Maybe the phone call earlier had been the vet. Why hadn't she thought of that? "Excuse me," she began, picking up the receiver and dialling 1471. It *had* been the surgery and now it was engaged. Her heart began to beat faster with a pulse that didn't know if it was hope or fear.

"I don't think you've got your facts quite right," said Paul Black clearly, looking first at Kayleigh and then her. "The local authority is still responsible for you until you're twenty-one."

Kayleigh's face crumpled. "You're kidding me."

"However, this doesn't mean you have to go back to your previous foster family." Paul looked up at the huge Welsh dresser studded with Victorian and Edwardian china that Alice had collected over the years. When Garth had been little, he had saved his pocket money for weeks to buy her a cup and saucer for her birthday. Now she was lucky if he even remembered the date.

"We need to set up a meeting with your social worker who will work out a Pathway Plan."

Alice almost laughed. Pathway Plan? Who thought of these titles?

Kayleigh's eyes were sullen, dull. "What's one of those when it's at home?"

Paul started to speak but as he did so, the phone rang again with the distinctive Ring Back tone. "Veterinary Centre speaking," said a voice.

"This is Mrs Honeybun, speaking." Alice's throat thickened. "I believe you rang, just now."

She stopped. Waiting. This was it. This was the time when she would know if ...

There was a knock at the back door. The top half was already open Alice favoured stable doors as it made the kitchen less stuffy in summer with the Aga. Another irrelevant thought, she mentally observed, to puncture the drama around her and lessen the shock. Perhaps her brain was acting as a sort of screen saver.

Dimly, she took in Janice, standing there uncertainly, the local newspaper under her arm. Her friend's eyes darted to Paul Black and promptly widened with interest. Then she glanced at the girl and visibly shrank back. Kayleigh's dreadlocks and small silver stud in her lower lip probably weren't to everyone's taste.

"May I come in?" said Janice quietly. "There's something I need to tell you." Then she gave Paul Black and Kayleigh another glance. Steelier than before. "Alone, if that's all right."

"Mrs Honeybun. Are you still there?"

For a second or two, Alice had forgotten she was still holding the phone. "Thank you for calling back." The voice was carefully neutral. "We have some news about Mungo ..."

TWENTY-TWO

If she kept very quiet and very still, no one would remember she was there. Over the years, Kayleigh had developed this art into a fine skill. She still had a vivid memory of crouching behind the kitchen door while Mum and some bloke – whose name she couldn't remember – threw stuff at each other.

Afterwards, they had inexplicably, made out right there on the ripped lino. She'd given herself away when Mum had started to make a terrible moaning noise like a cow she'd seen once on the telly.

"What the fuck are you doing there?" Mum had yelled. Kayleigh, stricken into silence by the sight of a naked man, had burst into tears and run off into the toilet, locking it behind her.

There'd been the sound of a door slamming, followed by Mum hammering on the door. "Look what you've done. He's gone. How are we going to bleeding well eat now?" After that, Kayleigh learned to stay quiet, no matter what happened. Even when the police had come to take away Callum.

Now, in Alice Honeybun's amazing kitchen, she stood very quietly by the fridge (never had she seen one so big!) and simply observed. So what if that woman who'd turned up at the door with the newspaper under her arm was eying her suspiciously! Nosy cow. Kayleigh knew that look. It was the type that some snotty shop assistant would give her when she and Marlene would rifle through the sale rails, pretending they might actually buy something.

Marlene ... for a minute, Kayleigh's mind wandered. It still seemed impossible that her friend was really dead. How could Frankie's mate have done that to her? He'd seemed so nice. Her body prickled uncomfortably. Maybe Callum was right when he said Kayleigh was too trusting. "Too bloody naïve for a world like ours," he'd said, chucking her under the chin, just before the police had come for him. "You don't belong here, know that?"

If only he could see her now! At last, she *did* belong somewhere. In Alice Honeybun's home with its cosy cooker that you called an Ah-ger where you lifted up a lid to put saucepans on (she'd got that wrong to begin with), not to mention her beautiful bedroom with a real wardrobe instead of coat hangers on the door and proper curtains that met in the middle. As for the bathroom that led off it – an 'on sweet' apparently – she'd never seen anything like it. There was even a funny little sink on the ground with a tap that you could wash your feet in. Then there were all the books! Wonderful stories with leather spines. She'd taken one down the other night to have a look until Daniel had told her to be careful. "It's valuable,' he'd said sharply, as if she was going to nick it instead of reading it.

Sometimes Kayleigh felt as though she'd died and gone to heaven. The only problem was Alice's snotty husband and this friend of hers, Janice, with the smart, crisp haircut like a shampoo advert. Her suspicious eyes, sweeping her up and down. But then Alice said something that made each of them stop throwing daggers at each other and listen instead to the conversation on the phone.

"You are sure? Really?"

Alice's face was shining. She'd had some good news! Kayleigh felt happy for her. Mrs Honeybun had been nice. She deserved something good back in return.

"Is it Garth?" asked this Janice as soon as Alice put down the phone.

A slight cloud passed over Alice's face, masking her earlier smile. "No. The vet. Mungo's going to be all right."

The woman frowned. "I didn't know he was ill."

Kayleigh watched Alice's hands shake. Mum's hands did that when she had too much to drink but Alice had only had tea, hadn't she? Unless she'd been at the bottle early. Mum did that too. It made her do silly stuff. That's why Kayleigh had decided, ages ago, not to drink even though Marlene took the piss out of her for it.

"It's … it's complicated," said Alice, looking at the policeman. That had been the other reason why Kayleigh hadn't so much as twitched a muscle. If she attracted attention to herself, he might take her away. Make her go to this Pathways woman perhaps.

Too late. He was looking right at her now. "I'm glad your dog is recovering." He spoke stiffly, Kayleigh noticed. Was he nervous of the woman with the newspaper who was shooting him curious looks as well. "But I'm going to have to file a report about Kayleigh."

Alice's friend eyed her with open suspicion now.

"File a report? Why? Who is she, Alice? Has she stolen something?"

What cheek! "I'm no bleeding thief. Get your facts right before you start accusing people of stuff."

Alice threw her a reproachful look. "Kayleigh. Please don't swear like that."

"Well it's the truth." She tried to talk as though she wasn't quaking inside but really she was shit scared. She wanted to stay here, Kayleigh realised. Desperately wanted to remain in this safe house with proper towels instead of torn up strips and a bed that was big enough to stretch out in. She liked Alice and her kind face and way of listening to her without putting her down all the time. OK, the husband was rude but he wasn't here all the time, was he? Maybe he'd bugger off like Mum's blokes.

"Can she stay here for a bit until something is sorted?" Kayleigh heard Alice say. Yes! Yes!

"It doesn't work like that."

Kayleigh felt a crash of thudding disappointment followed by a glimmer of hope as he added "Let me phone social services to see what we can do. It might be possible to arrange an emergency care order."

She'd heard of one of those. The kid next door had had one. It meant you didn't have to go to court to get put into care. It was all arranged for you.

"That would be wonderful." Did Alice realise how lovely she looked when she smiled? She ought to do it more often. "Please use the landline if you prefer." Then she looked at Kayleigh. "Do you want to make your bed? Janice and I are going to have a little walk in the garden."

Kayleigh slipped back to her room (it already felt like 'her' room just like it had seemed really cool when Alice had said 'make *your* bed'). Hastily pulling up the duvet with its pretty pink roses, she looked out of the window. There was a bit of lawn outside and then a bench, where the women were talking, and then a hedge and through that, an opening that led down to a field. Surely that couldn't all be theirs?

The woman with the newspaper had one of those loud voices that carried through the air.

"In the newspaper …"

"Everyone talking …"

"Something I've got to tell you …"

"Daniel …"

"Monica …"

"NO!"

Kayleigh almost fell out of the window as Alice's cry reached her. Instantly, she flew down the stairs, rushing through the kitchen past the policeman who was still on the phone and out into the garden.

"What's happened?" she said, taking Alice's hands. A stream of tears were running down her cheeks and her eyes were red and swollen. Then she rounded on the woman with the paper and posh haircut. "What did you say to her?" she demanded.

"What business is it of yours? Alice, for goodness sake, tell this girl to go away."

"No." Alice, Kayleigh noticed with a flush of pleasure, was gripping her hand as though needing the comfort. "No. I want you to tell me again, in front of her, so I know I haven't imagined this. I insist, Janice. Tell me again."

Alice's mate spoke in a quieter voice now. "I said that Daniel has been having an affair with Monica. That's how they knew in court about you and … about you and Daniel not sleeping together any more. She told someone.'

So Alice's boring bloke with the grey bits in his hair was having an affair? Still, posh people did it all the time. That's what Marlene always said. They just pretended they were better than anyone else but inside, they were as randy as the rest of them. "Who's Monica?" she couldn't help asking.

Alice gave a laugh that didn't sound right. She'd stopped crying, Kayleigh noticed, but her eyes were still red and puffy. "She's a scrawny cow from the book club."

Kayleigh was shocked. She didn't expect women like Alice to use the word 'cow'.

"I don't get it," she said, squeezing Kayleigh's hand so hard that her wedding ring pressed against her skin. Not that she minded! Alice needed her. "How could he do this to me? And why did he tell the court?"

"He didn't." Janice was puzzled by the hand holding. She could see that. Kayleigh straightened her back with importance.

"It was Monica who told them. She wants to cause trouble, don't you see? She wants you and Daniel to split up."

Kayleigh frowned. "How do you know?"

Janice glared.

"Yes," repeated Alice. "How do you know?"

"Because," said Janice stiffly, "Beverley told me."

Alice nodded, closing her eyes briefly before opening them again. "Beverley's in the book club too," she told Kayleigh. She was really confiding in her like a proper friend! Then Alice dropped her hand, leaving Kayleigh with a horrid sense of loss and emptiness.

"What are you doing?" demanded Janice.

"Ringing Daniel." Alice's voice had an unnaturally high squeak. "I need to find out the truth."

"Don't be daft!"

Janice tried to grab the phone. "That's playing into Monica's hands. Don't you see?"

"She's right." Kayleigh heard her own voice. "That's what happened in this book I read. The woman who's having an affair tells the woman whose bloke is cheating on her and then it all goes tits-up even though the bloke is sorry and wants to

231

get rid of the woman he's having the affair with, 'cos he's had enough of her."

Janice's mouth was open but she was nodding. "See," she said weakly.

Alice was shaking her head. "I don't know. Nothing makes sense any more. Daniel ... how could he do it. How could he ..."

"Face it, Alice. If he hasn't had sex for years, he'd going to look elsewhere, isn't he?"

Kayleigh had been about to say the same thing. Frankie might have been her first but she'd learned the theory side from Marlene years ago. If you didn't sleep with a boy, he chucked you. It was as simple as that.

"But I thought he'd accepted it ..."

Janice snorted. "You were deluding yourself then. Brian and I ..." Then she stopped and looked at Kayleigh. "Are you sure you want this girl here?"

Alice paused. "This girl, as you put it, needs a safe haven."

Janice's lips tightened. "If you hadn't tried to help her in court," she said quietly, "Monica wouldn't have been able to have stabbed you in the back. Now she's got you where she wants. Don't you see? Daniel's been made to look like a fool in front of everyone and men don't like that. I told you about my friend. She said that when you're a witness, it's not just you that's on show. It's your family too."

There was a cough behind them. The policeman was standing at the back door. Talk about snooping! How much had he heard? Kayleigh suspected from her face that Alice was wondering the same thing.

"I'm sorry to bother you but I finally managed to get through to the right people." He spoke directly to Alice, his eyes never leaving her face. He liked her! Kayleigh could tell. He fancied Mrs Honeybun! Even though her eyes were still red and raw, she still looked pretty. For a second, Kayleigh felt a touch of envy. She looked a right mess when she cried. Mum always said so.

"The Pathways co-ordinator needs to meet Kayleigh." Here he looked at her briefly. "And you too, if you're certain about having her to stay."

Alice nodded firmly. "I am."

"Are you touched?" The friend grabbed Alice's arm but she shook it off.

"I know what I'm doing. This girl needs help and I'm the right person to give it to her."

"And you don't think you've got enough on your plate?"

"That's my affair." There was a hysterical laugh. "Affair? Get it?"

So she could stay. She didn't have to go. Kayleigh wanted to hug Alice. "Thank you," she whispered. "Thank you."

"I've managed to set up a meeting tomorrow." The policeman sounded as though he'd done them a huge favour. What would he want in return, Kayleigh wondered, suddenly worried. Men never did you a favour for nothing. Marlene always said that.

"We're very grateful. Aren't we Kayleigh?"

For a minute, it felt as though Alice was her mum. A real proper mum who involved her daughter in decisions and did stuff with her like mums in books. "Yes," she said, playing her part. "We are. Thank you."

But she managed to say it in such a way and with a certain look so that the policeman knew. Don't expect anything from Alice for doing this, she said. If you try to hurt her, you'll have me to deal with.

If there was one bit of advice that Kayleigh remembered, it was the thing Callum had said before the police came to get him. "Always look out for people who look out for you," he'd told her.

"What about the others?" she'd asked. "The ones that don't."

"Get rid of them."

His reply, swift and crisp, had shocked her.

"You don't mean that, do you?"

He'd nodded. "Yes I do."

No one, decided Kayleigh as she put the kettle on (because they both needed another cuppa after this), would ever hurt Alice again. She'd make sure of that.

It was what a daughter would do.

TWENTY-THREE

In the past, Alice had flicked past magazine articles along the lines of "What would you do if your husband had an affair?"

The answer, or so it seemed to her, was so blindingly obvious that it wasn't worth reading. How could you trust that person again?

Anyway, the articles were irrelevant because Daniel wasn't that kind of man. If he had been, she wouldn't have married him. Surely women whose husbands had affairs only had themselves to blame for marrying irresponsible, thoughtless, Jack-the-Lads.

And now it was happening to her – at least, if Janice was to be believed. Yet instead of having it out with him, she'd decided to ignore it. For the time being. "There's too much going on," she said quietly. "We've got to work together to get Garth out of prison. How can we do that if we split up?"

"You're in denial," said Janice, putting her arm around her. "It's a shock. I'm sorry. But someone had to tell you."

Did they? Paul Black had already gone, and Kayleigh was in her room tidying up. "Frankly, I'd rather not have known."

"Alice. Get real." Janice stood back, as if looking at her for the first time instead of speaking to an old friend. "You've been different in the last few weeks – and not because of Garth. It's ever since you came across that fifteen-year-old druggie runaway."

That wasn't fair. "She's sixteen now and she doesn't do drugs any more. It was a one off."

"If that's what you want to think. Come on, Alice. Think

about yourself for a change and not someone else. Forget this waif and stray you've taken in. Start battling for your marriage. Monica's going around telling everyone she's having it off with your husband and then swearing each person to secrecy."

She tapped the local newspaper under her arm. "Besides, you've got to tackle the stuff in here. Look."

Alice turned away at the headline.

LOCAL WOMAN ACCUSED OF HIDING HER OWN PAST WHEN GIVING EVIDENCE IN HIGH PROFILE SEX CASE

Alice felt sick. This was a small town. How was she ever going to hold her head up again? Everyone read the local paper. Everyone would look at her. In the shops. At the tennis club. At Book Club. At the gym. At the local community centre where she did voluntary work every now and then. They'd have to move and even then they might follow her. Look at the national magazine that had rung her up the other day. Your story will strike a nerve, the girl had added, before Alice had cut her off. There are a lot of women like you out there …

"Fight for him," added Janice firmly. "Talk to Daniel and make him see how much he has to lose if he gives you up." She looked Alice up and down. "Buy yourself some sexy underwear. Flirt with him. Do something to make him want you again."

"But he's the one who needs to make it up to me! He went off with …" Monica's name stuck in her mouth. "With that woman."

Janice was giving her a pitying look. "That's not how it works, Alice. Trust me."

There was something odd in the way she spoke. "Did you …?" began Alice hesitantly.

Janice made a sweeping action across her face. "Don't ask. We don't talk about it. Not any more."

So her friend – or Brian – had had an affair too? She'd never have guessed it. They had always seemed … well, so together. Alice's head began to spin. Was the whole world going topsy-turvy or was it just her? Suddenly, her eye was drawn to a broken plate lying on the sideboard: her latest commission. It

236

had slipped out of her hand, the tearful owner had explained, handing her the fragments. "I know it's not worth it in monetary terms but it has huge sentimental value for me." Then she'd stopped, clearly embarrassed.

She, Alice, had understood, though. Had she not heard it all before? Broken cups or plates which had belonged to long-deceased mothers or husbands or – in one case – an estranged son – who had given them as birthday or Christmas presents until some careless accident had broken their souls. Each shattered fragment represented a piece of the departed one. No one could restore the latter but miracles could be performed on the china; and, in so doing, the breaker would feel less guilty. Partial relief could be restored at the bringing back of a broken vase or cup which symbolised the loved one.

Alice now stared at it hard. Sometimes she wondered if she was doing the right thing, putting broken pieces back together. They might look almost the same but even if you'd done a great job – and Alice prided herself on doing that – she knew that the crack still existed. So did the owners.

Did she want that for herself? To mend a crack which would always be there; no matter how carefully she disguised it? Wouldn't that be cheating her own soul? Or was it the practical thing to do, in order to restore the set; to keep the family together.

"I'll think about it," she now said, aware she sounded firmer than she felt. "But after my meeting tomorrow with social services."

"Social services?"

"It's about Kayleigh and ... and us giving her a home. Temporarily."

Janice snorted. "Get your priorities right, Alice. This girl isn't your daughter."

Alice whipped round. "But she could have been *me*."

Janice frowned. "Are you talking about that stuff they said in court? About you accusing a man when you were younger? You can tell me. I'm your friend. "

But she couldn't. No one could really understand unless it had happened to them. "It doesn't matter. Look, thanks for coming round."

Janice gave her a hug. The type you only kept for big awful occasions. "Don't do anything stupid, will you? I know far too many women who've kicked out their husbands and then regretted it. But talk it through. You can both learn from your mistakes."

Then she stepped back, still holding her hands. "Think of Garth. Kids need two parents, however old they are." She looked away briefly. "Why do you think I've stayed put? No. Please don't say anything or I will cry." Her eyes sought Alice's. "They always say the quiet ones are the worst, don't they?"

So Brian had cheated on Janice! The shock revelation – or as good as – still reverberated round Alice's head the following day as she sat at a conference table in a room that seemed to be made entirely of glass. Concentrate. Concentrate.

It wasn't just what Janice had said, or rather hadn't said. Nor was it Daniel and Monica. A combination that seemed so unbelievable she could scarcely take it in. Nor was it the surreal knowledge that her son was in a South American jail. Or the relief that Mungo was going to be all right.

It was also this. Being here at a conference with Kayleigh's social workers and various other people who had introduced themselves. Doing something that didn't seem quite right, yet would be definitely wrong if left undone.

Through the huge windows, Alice could see ordinary people doing ordinary things in the street below. Not long ago, she'd been one of them. But thanks to a chance sighting in a park, she was now agreeing to take in a child – well, as good as – as if she didn't have enough on her plate.

"I am happy for Kayleigh to live with us until she finds a job and gets settled," she declared, clenching her fists under table; grateful that Daniel had chosen not to be here.

The social worker gave her a wry look. Her earrings bobbed like floats on the water, observed Alice. Frankly, she never trusted women whose earrings were too youthful. They looked cheap too. The type you made yourself. "Have you ever done anything like this before, Mrs Honeybun?"

Alice thought back to all the teenage arguments with Garth. "I've got experience of young people. I have a son. He's nineteen."

"And where is he now?"

Was this a trick question? Did she already know?

"In South America," replied Alice carefully.

"I see." She wrote something down on the page. "And is your husband happy to give Kayleigh a short-term home?"

Alice crossed her fingers below the desk, thinking of the cold evening she had spent with Daniel last night. She should have talked to him about Monica. Asked him if it was true. But something inside had stopped her. Whatever Janice had said, blind eyes seemed safer. Less likely to rock a boat that was already in troubled water.

"Mrs Honeybun," repeated the voice. "I asked if your husband is happy to take in Kayleigh."

"Yes," she nodded. It wasn't exactly a lie. He just didn't know. That way, he couldn't refuse. Then she glanced at Kayleigh, next to her. The girl was trembling. Slowly, she reached out her hand and squeezed hers briefly. If only Mum had done the same when she'd needed support over Phil.

"And what about you, Kayleigh," said the social worker silkily. "What are your long-term plans?"

"I want to go to college if my GCSE grades are OK. I'd like to do psychology." She waved a brochure for a sixth-form college which Alice recognised. At the age of fifteen, Garth had suddenly announced that he wanted to leave his expensive private school and go to this college instead. She and Daniel had joined forces and argued fiercely with their son, pointing out that the teaching would probably be different and there was hardly any sport. In the end, he'd given in. Had that been a mistake? Would Garth have turned out 'better' if they'd let him do what he wanted? And what exactly *was* 'better'?

Her thoughts were interrupted by the next question. "How far is the college from your home, Mrs Honeybun?" asked the social worker, orange earrings bobbing.

"About half an hour. I can give Kayleigh a lift but there's

also a bus."

"And how long is the course?"

"Two years." Kayleigh cut in. "But if Alice doesn't want me that long – I can rent somewhere, can't I?"

She had it all worked out! Once more Alice was struck by how mature the girl could be at times – while, at others, very naïve. It was a curious combination.

The social worker was making more notes. "That depends on several factors." Alice felt a chill. Having Kayleigh for a few weeks while she sorted herself out was one thing. But two years was another matter entirely.

"If we agree that Kayleigh can live with you, Mrs Honeybun, the situation will need to be reviewed regularly."

Alice found herself nodding. There was a small gasp beside her. "So does that mean I can stay?"

The social worker was folding her papers. "We've been authorised to make an emergency care order. Kayleigh can continue staying with you, short-term, until a longer-term programme has been established. That is, if you're happy to still have her."

Alice made a huge effort to crush the doubts that were now swimming to the surface. "Of course."

"YES!" Kayleigh leaped up and gave her a big hug. Never had Alice seen Kayleigh to be so demonstrative before. Then again, she didn't really know her, did she?

What on earth had she done, Alice asked herself, gathering her coat and bag. Supposing Frankie's friends found out where she lived? What would Daniel say? And, even more importantly, what was she going to do about him and Monica?

"I'll decide tomorrow," she had told Janice, "after the meeting about Kayleigh." She'd reached that point and now she needed to talk to her husband. It wasn't just the sex bit. It was the dishonesty. The cheating. The lies. The fact that, if it was true, Daniel wouldn't be the person she'd thought he was.

Just as she hadn't been the person he had thought, when he had married her.

They drove home via the vet's. Mungo was slightly subdued

when they picked him up but delighted to see her. He covered her with licks and – to Kayleigh's horror – did the same to her. "Don't hurt me," she flinched.

"It's all right." Alice had always felt sorry for people who were scared of dogs. They didn't know what they were missing. "He's really friendly. Why don't you sit next to him in the back of the car so you can get to know him?"

That was a good sign, she told herself, glancing in the rear mirror and seeing how Mungo rested his head in Kayleigh's lap. Dogs were excellent judges of characters. Better than humans, at times. Monica! The thought of the woman filled her with loathing. How could she have been so stupid to miss the signs?

Back home, Alice handed Kayleigh a ball and suggested that she played with Mungo in the garden. Apart from anything else, it would give her space to sort out all the horrible thoughts whirling round her head.

Daniel and Monica.

Monica and Daniel.

Kayleigh, she observed through the window, actually looked like a normal sixteen-year-old in those jeans she'd found in Garth's old wardrobe – styles seemed to be unisex nowadays. She also looked fresher without all that make-up she normally plastered on. (Alice had suggested she toned it down for the meeting with the social worker and she still hadn't got round to putting it on again.)

When Garth had been that age, he had loved playing with Mungo too. Alice felt the old panic coming back; a panic which had been temporarily put to one side during the meeting about Kayleigh and her distress over Daniel and Monica. It had been a few days since Brian had heard anything from the South American authorities. What if there'd been a hitch?

"Any news?" she now texted Brian.

The reply came back promptly.

"Not yet."

Could she really trust a man who had had an affair? For the first time, Alice began to realise why MPs were often ousted from their jobs after illicit relationships. If they couldn't be true to their families, how could they be true public servants?

As she put down the phone, Kayleigh waved gaily at her. Alice turned away. Janice had been right. She must be mad. What on earth was she doing with a strange teenager in her house when her own son was on the other side of the world and her marriage was falling to bits?

Later, while Alice was chopping leeks with careful precision (cooking was such a therapeutic distraction), she kept going over and over the options. Daniel was due home shortly from a pre-term conference at the university and she still hadn't decided what to say to him. It would also be difficult to talk, she suddenly realised, with Kayleigh around. You forgot about that sort of thing when you were used to being on your own.

"Where did you say the bus stop was?"

Alice looked up from her chopping to take in Kayleigh with a full face of make-up again, wearing ripped tights under frayed shorts and a T-shirt that showed off every curve. Her long auburn hair was loosely tied into a careless knot at the back.

"Are you going out?"

Kayleigh nodded.

At least this would give her and Daniel some time together. Yet at the same time, her chest fluttered with apprehension. "Where?"

Kayleigh looked as though it was blindingly obvious.

"Just into the centre. One of my mates texted."

She cast another look at the frayed tights and shorts. "Won't you be cold?"

There was a shrug. "It's summer."

"And you've got your phone?"

"'Course."

Fleetingly Alice wondered whether she'd made the right decision to top up Kayleigh's phone credit but it had seemed sensible at the time. After all, she needed to know where she was. It had been one of the stipulations of the agreement.

"You won't be back late, will you?"

Kayleigh gave her another look. "Why?"

"Because I promised your social worker I'd look after you."

Kayleigh seemed to consider this. "OK."

"What time did your mum ask you to get back?"

"You bleeding kidding? I used to wait up for *her*."

Alice took a deep breath. "Look Kayleigh, I don't want to sound all heavy when you've just arrived. But we don't use swear words like … like the one you've just used here. And I'd like you back by eleven. All right?"

She waited for Kayleigh to say that no it wasn't bleeding all right and that she didn't want to live here any more. In some ways, maybe that might be a relief. Perhaps Janice was right. Maybe she was so confused she didn't know whether she was coming or going.

"OK." Kayleigh shrugged.

"The bus stop is down the road. On the left." Sheer surprise that Kayleigh had accepted the curfew and the moratorium on swearing, made her open her purse. "Here's ten pounds. It should be more than enough for the bus and a coffee."

Kayleigh looked at it as though she'd given her a fifty-pound note. "Thanks. See you later then."

Then she went over to Mungo and patted him. "Good boy. Nice to be home, isn't it?"

It wasn't until after she'd watched Kayleigh saunter off down the drive, her long legs all too obvious under those shorts, that Alice took in those final words. *Nice to be home, isn't it?*

She'd been speaking for herself as well as for Mungo. Alice's heart gave a little flutter. How sweet. "Wait," she called out. "Wait."

Kayleigh paused, her face stricken as Alice ran towards her. "What?"

"Turn round."

"You're not going to wallop me, are you?"

Alice's heart lurched. "Of course not. I just want to fix your hair." Gently, tenderly, she wound the loose tendrils of auburn hair – so much nicer now Kayleigh had brushed it out – fastening them with the clip. It looked familiar.

"I borrowed it from your bathroom." Kayleigh's voice trembled. "Don't mind, do you?"

Tell her she needs to ask permission first, said the voice in her head. Tell her she can't go into your bathroom and that,

243

anyway, she has her own.

"That's fine," said Alice. "Turn round now."

For a second, Victoria stood in front of her. There was no reason why her own daughter might not have been auburn too. After all, her own grandmother had had hair that colour. "Lovely." She patted Kayleigh's shoulder. "Now go and have a good time. But please be careful."

Kayleigh's eyes shone; all the earlier anger and suspicion gone. "Ta. You too." She stared at Alice. "Had it out with him yet? About that woman?"

Shocked, Alice searched for the right words. "No. Not yet. I'm not sure …"

Kayleigh tutted. "Don't let him take you for a ride. Me mam does that. I made the same mistake with Frankie. But I'm not going to do it again. And you shouldn't either. Ta ta."

Speechless, Alice stood and watched the girl saunter out of sight. How funny that a sixteen-year-old girl had tried to give her advice! Yet there was more of a grain of truth in what she had said.

Meanwhile, she hoped Kayleigh would be all right. Hadn't she watched Garth go out like this, on many an occasion? Yet somehow it was different with a daughter: even a pretend one. So much could happen to a girl; things that didn't happen to a son …

Slowly, with Mungo at her heels, Alice walked back to the house. It seemed so quiet. So empty. Even Radio 4 with its early evening chit-chat, didn't fill in the blank space. Yet it was better than having Daniel back. Better than having to decide what to say. Maybe Janice would have some ideas. Picking up the phone, she began to dial her friend's number and then stopped as Mungo began to bark.

Sure enough, there was the distant smooth crunch, through the window, of her husband's car, coming up the drive. Trembling, Alice wiped the kitchen knife on some kitchen roll, put it back in the block, and popped the seafood lasagne into the Aga.

It would be ready in half an hour.

Time enough to talk.

Or not.

Daniel was ecstatic to see Mungo back. More so than he had ever seemed to see her, Alice couldn't help thinking.

"You're all right, boy. You're all right," he kept saying.

It was almost as though he was using the dog as a buffer against the things they *should* be talking about. "Brian says there's no news about Garth yet," she said tersely, setting down the serving dish in the middle of the kitchen table. She had laid it nicely as usual with the duck-blue table cloth to match the Aga.

"I know. He emailed me this afternoon. Want some of this, boy?"

They had a rule about not feeding Mungo at the table; a rule which Daniel had introduced when he'd been a puppy. Occasionally, when Garth had been younger, he and Alice had disobeyed it. It had united them; made them a team; complicit in a rather exciting feeling of rebellion.

Alice waited until her husband had put a forkful into his own mouth. "I went to a conference about Kayleigh today. They agreed she could live here for the time being."

Daniel spluttered. "What?"

"Please finish your mouthful before you speak." She observed him with distaste, dabbing his face with his napkin. Was this really the same man who had slept with Monica?

"Don't talk to me like a child."

"Well you are one, aren't you? Children don't understand the rules of life."

Daniel put down his knife and fork. "Alice. What are you trying to say?"

She pushed her plate to one side. It wasn't too late to take it back. To pretend she had meant something else. "I'm talking about Monica."

The name leaped out of her mouth without permission. Jumped without looking. Threw itself into the maelstrom of the unknown without thought – until now – of how it would surface and swim.

Her eyes were on her husband's. If you do decide to talk to him, Janice had said earlier, make sure it's face to face. You'll get a better idea of whether he's lying or not.

"Monica?" Daniel was trying not to look away. He was rattled. She could see that. Part of her had been hoping that he would be more certain in his denial. That he could prove this had all been a terrible mistake.

"Please tell me it's not true." There was a horrible silence, broken by Mungo whining pointedly at Daniel's plate. "No," said Alice quietly, beginning to shake. "No."

Daniel sat there. Rigid. His face angry. With her. "Well what did you expect? We don't have a proper relationship, do we?"

"You know why. I told you. I can't. Uncle Phil …"

"You told me when it was too late. When we were already married." Daniel gave a nasty laugh. "It's incredible that we actually managed to have Garth."

Alice leaped up, walking towards the window. Anything to put some distance between her and him. "We've been through this. Hundreds of times. I told you. I thought it might get better. I thought I could get over it. Why did you stay with me if you couldn't handle it?"

"Because I thought I could help you." He spoke through gritted teeth. "And because we have a son. I take my commitments seriously, Alice."

"Take your commitments seriously?" She laughed out loud. "Then why did you go off with Monica? It's not just the sex, Daniel. It's the deceit. Where did you do it? When?"

She walked up to him, grabbing him by the collar. He looked scared but not as scared as she felt inside. Never before had she held a man by the collar like this. "I want to know. Everything. When did it start?"

He had the grace to look embarrassed. "At the golf club ball. Last year. She … kissed me outside when we went out for some air."

Alice felt sick. "You could have said no."

"I was starved, Alice. Starved of affection. It was nice and yes, I'll admit it, flattering that someone wanted me. For God's sake, it wasn't as though you did."

She couldn't argue with that. "When did you see each other? You're always busy during term-time …"

Then she realised. "My God. The vacation course. It didn't exist, did it? You used it as a way of seeing her."

Daniel's face was in his hands. She'd gone too far, Alice realised. Janice had been wrong. She should have kept quiet. "Do you love her?" she whispered.

"No."

A huge wave of relief broke over her.

"I tried to break it off. But she wouldn't let me." Daniel raised his face to hers, like a child desperately seeking help for a wrong-doing. "She said that if I didn't leave you, she'd tell someone about us and …"

He hesitated.

"Go on," demanded Alice.

"And that she'd also tell the defence about you not being able to …"

"To have sex," finished Alice quietly. "Something she decided to do anyway. Probably to push you into being so humiliated in front of everyone, that you'd leave me. I get it now."

Daniel nodded. "I'm so sorry, Alice. I didn't mean to tell her. It's just that …"

She sank onto her chair again, Mungo whining by her feet, jumping up at her; knowing something was wrong. "Please." Daniel had tears down his face. "I don't want to lose you." He glanced round the room.

"Or the house," added Alice sharply.

"Not just that. I don't want to lose you or Garth or our home or everything that we've built up. I'm sorry, Alice."

She gulped. "So am I. If I could do something about it, I would."

He looked scared. "What do you mean?"

Alice had been referring to her inadequacies in bed. But now she realised Daniel thought she was referring to her inability to forgive him. Both might be true.

The phone began to ring. Not now. Not now.

"Leave it."

"It could be Brian."

"Hah!" Only just did she stop herself from adding "Two

247

peas in a pod."

"Please, leave it." His voice sang with a pain of raw gravel under feet. "This is more important."

"Is it?" Never before had she felt such honesty between them. How ironic that it had taken his dishonesty to achieve this.

"This could be the best thing to happen to us."

The phone stopped ringing.

"What do you mean?"

"Don't you see? We're talking properly now. Without any pretence. We can start again. Make it right this time. You could go to a counsellor – we both could ..."

The phone began ringing again.

"Wait." Daniel was gripping her arm. "I'll do a deal with you. I'll allow Kayleigh to stay if you promise to give me another chance. I won't see Monica again. I promise."

Alice hesitated. Kayleigh's earlier words rang through her head. Once a bloke has cheated, that's it. He'll do it again.

"All right," she said. Then she picked up the phone.

"Mum," said a distant voice. "Mum. It's *me*!"

TWENTY-FOUR

Kayleigh had to pinch herself at the bus stop. Here she was, living in a real home with someone who really seemed to care about her. "Be back by eleven," Alice had said. Then there had been all that stuff about her hair.

She'd nearly shit bricks at that. Why the fuck had she nicked the clasp? Alice could have rung the police. But instead, she'd been so nice about it that Kayleigh felt really guilty. Then Alice had given her a quick hug like she'd been her own kid and said "Ring if you miss the last bus and I'll drive in to get you. I don't want you walking back."

Mum had never bothered about that.

Kayleigh's heart swelled with love towards Alice. She was so nice. So kind. But at the same time, she felt really jealous of that boy in the photographs. Alice doted on him. ('Doted' was a word that Mr Brown had used once during a lesson on the romantic poets. It had a nice ring to it so Kayleigh had looked it up and written it down in her book of words.)

Garth, he was called. The boy in the photographs that was. Strange name. Looked a bit weird too in the picture that Alice said was the latest one. He had long curly hair like a girl but you could see from the nose and the rest of his face that there wasn't anything gay about him.

Did Garth know how lucky he was to have a mother like Alice? Already, Kayleigh decided, she didn't like him.

It struck her, as she waited for the bus, that she didn't know if Frankie had a mother. If he had, she was more probably more like Kayleigh's than Alice. Otherwise he wouldn't have let her down like that. Bet Garth was a real gentleman.

Kayleigh felt a big lump in her throat. She'd trusted Frankie. But it wasn't just her he had hurt. It was Marlene too. That's why she was here. That's why she'd told Alice a lie about a friend texting. She needed to find some of their mates; see if anyone knew exactly what had happened. Find out where Marlene was buried, too, to pay her respects. Maybe she'd been cremated. The thought made her shiver.

"Want a lift?"

Looking up, Kayleigh took in a really cool red Mini had pulled up. At the wheel was a bloke with curly blond hair. He was smiling at her like she was a nice girl: not someone who had stolen Alice's hair clip. "I'm going into the city if that's where you're heading." He glanced at the bus stop. "You can wait hours at this place. Used to do it myself."

Don't take lifts from strangers. Somewhere, at the back of her mind, Kayleigh remembered a teacher telling her that. (It definitely wasn't something that Mum would say.) But this bloke's voice was really posh. Surely someone like that wouldn't hurt her?

"Thanks," she said, getting in rather clumsily. Great car. If only Marlene could see her now!

His name was Seb, he said, as they drove along the windy narrow lanes. Seb? Another weird name like Garth. Why didn't they have normal names like the rest of the world? Perhaps they belonged to the upper classes. Mr Brown was always banging on about that. He said it wasn't politically correct any more but everyone knew it happened, both in books and out of it. They had different rules, he used to say, staring at her. Different ways of eating. Talking. And of making love …

Kayleigh shook herself, not wanting to think about him and that girl bent over the desk. Meanwhile, Seb was going so fast that she wanted to grab the side of the door but didn't like to in case it offended him. He was home from uni but couldn't wait to get back, he yelled out over the engine. His parents were effing well driving him mad.

He said the effing bit in such a cool way that it didn't sound crude the way it did when Mum said it. Until she'd come to live with Alice, Kayleigh hadn't realised how much she'd picked up Mum's swearing.

"What about you?" She blushed as his eyes took her in. "I haven't seen you around before."

"Just moved here." Kayleigh tried not to look as Seb took a corner so fast that they nearly went into a car coming in the opposite direction. Then, because she couldn't resist the novelty, she added "I'm staying with Mrs Honeybun."

"Alice Honeybun? No way!"

Another corner. Another hoot.

"She took me in after something happened."

She hadn't meant to say so much but it was too late.

"After what happened?"

Don't say it was you. Don't say it was you.

"She saw this couple making out in the park so had to be a witness in court. All kinds of stuff came out about her personal life apparently and now everyone's talking. So she ... she needs some company."

Another corner. Another load of car hooting.

"Fuck off. Sorry, not you. That idiot. So how come you know Alice? Friend of your mother's, is she?"

Kayleigh had to stop herself from laughing. The thought of Mum and Alice in the same room was both funny and scary. But after what Seb had just said, there was no way she was going to tell him that *she* was the girl in the park. He might chuck her out of the car or laugh – which would be even worse. "It's complicated."

Seb laughed. He had a nice deep laugh. She rather liked that. "Life usually is. So what do you think about Garth? Banged up in some South American prison." He uttered a low whistle. "Wouldn't fancy that myself. Still, Mum says it serves Alice Honeybun right 'cos she's such a goody-two shoes."

Kayleigh wasn't sure what goody-two shoes actually meant but it didn't sound very nice. "I don't know Garth," she said tightly, "but I do know that it's not easy for Alice."

HOOT.

"FUCK OFF. Sorry. Didn't mean to speak out of turn then.

Garth's mum always seemed very nice to me. She and my mum did a school run together a few years ago. And I do know that Mum can be a bit judgmental at times."

He was slowing down, much to Kayleigh's relief. Her stomach was churning with the speed and the near misses. "Let me know where you want me to drop you."

"Here would be fine."

"By the shopping centre? But it's closed."

"I'm meeting some mates here." Kayleigh crossed her fingers.

"Well I'm meeting mine at The Half Moon. Know it? It's a club round the corner." He screeched to a halt and then turned to face her. "If you get bored, come and find us." He was looking at the bare flesh between the bottom of her T-shirt and the shorts. "OK?"

No way, she added silently to herself as she got out. Not with her stomach churning like this. They could have been bleeding killed. Then she remembered her manners. "Thanks for the lift."

"Anytime. Give your mum my regards."

Regards? It sounded like something out of a French book.

"Tell her that Monica's son gave you a lift. She won't like it." He chuckled. "One of the reasons they fell out was that Alice wouldn't let Garth come in the car with me. Something about me driving too fast. See you!"

Kayleigh shivered. Maybe she should have worn Garth's jeans after all, even if they did make her look like a right idiot with those wide bottoms.

"Spare a quid?" wheedled a girl in the corner. She was sitting cross-legged on a filthy blanket with a dog at her side. There was a sign next to her saying "Hungree".

Kayleigh put her hand in her pocket and pulled out Alice's ten pound note. "Got any change?" she asked.

The girl cackled. "Are you kidding me?"

Now she felt really stupid. "I'll go and get some."

After all, didn't she know what it was like to be hungry and cold? That had been her a few weeks ago. Second thoughts, maybe it would be better if she bought the girl something to eat.

The queue at the fast food place took for ever. The homeless girl would think she'd forgotten, thought Kayleigh worriedly. While she waited, she kept her eyes open for anyone she and Marlene knew but this lot seemed to be a new crowd. Where *was* everyone?

"Special deal, please," she said when it was finally her turn. The boy on the other side of the counter held the tenner up to the neon light above. Cheek. "Haven't you seen ten quid before?"

"Yes. But not in your hand."

She squinted at him. Bloody hell. It was a kid from her maths group.

"You knew my friend Marlene, didn't you?"

"What? I can't hear you."

It was really noisy. It wasn't just the din but also the iPod which someone was playing behind her. "Can you turn that down? I'm trying to speak."

"Trying to speak, are yer?"

The bloke behind her spat on the ground. "Well I'm trying to eat. So take your bleeding food and move out of my way."

He had a look of Frankie about him. Suddenly scared, Kayleigh did as she was told. It was only after she'd left that she checked her change. The maths kid had given her a pound less than he should have done. No time to go back or the homeless girl would think she'd gone off. And she knew that that felt like.

"Sorry it took so long."

Kayleigh stopped. There was someone else sitting in the corner. This one had her hair shaved down one side. But the dog was still there as well as the 'Hungree' notice. "Where's the other one," she said desperately. "The girl who was sitting here before."

"Gone to have a crap."

The shaved headed girl – who seemed strangely familiar – eyed the food in her hand. "Got any spare?"

"Actually I bought it for the other one."

The eyes narrowed. "Friend of yours, is she?"

"Not exactly but …"

Hang on. That's who the girl reminded her of. She'd changed her hair. That's why she looked different. "Posy?"

"Tara actually."

Kayleigh felt a wave of indignation surge through her. "If it wasn't for you, I wouldn't be in this mess now."

"Serves you bleeding right." The girl lunged at the food in her hand.

Suddenly Kayleigh was aware of a crowd gathering around them. "Cat fight," someone whistled excitedly.

"No." She backed off. "I only came here 'cos I wanted to find out about my mate." She scanned the faces. "Does anyone know what happened to Marlene? Marlene Smith."

"Isn't she the girl that took drugs?" piped up someone.

Kayleigh nodded sadly.

"Got some change now, have you?" whined a voice.

It was the first girl. The one who'd gone to take a crap.

"I bought you some food." Kayleigh gestured towards Posy. "But she's taken it."

There was a laugh. "I don't want any bleeding food. I want some fucking money."

To her horror, the dog began to give out a low throaty growl and walked towards her. "I've got some. I've got some," spluttered Kayleigh. Desperately pulling the change out of her pocket, it fell on the ground. There was a mad rush for it. But the first girl got there before the others.

"Three bleeding quid," The girl eyed her furiously. "That's not going to get me far, is it? Got any more in those jeans of yours? They've got a bleeding Ralph Lauren label on them. Bet you're loaded, really."

"GET OFF HER." The voice rose above the yells around her. Stunned, Kayleigh was aware of being pulled out of the crowd and slung over a shoulder.

"Put me down," she yelled. "Put me down."

"It's me, Kayleigh. It's me."

Gently, he lowered her to the ground by the back of the Ladies. "Callum?" She stared at him. "But you're meant to be in prison …"

"Shhh." He put a hand to her mouth. "I've broken my probation."

Probation? "I didn't know you'd been let out. Why didn't you tell me?"

"I came back for you, Kayleigh. But Mum said you didn't live there any more. One of your mates said you hung round here so I've been looking for you."

He'd come to find her! Her big half-brother had come to find her! To look after her …

"I need money. So I can get out of this place. Mum said you'd gone to live with some woman who's rolling in it but she wouldn't give me the address. "

He grabbed her hands. She wasn't sure if they were holding hers in comfort or squeezing them threateningly. The bracelet on his wrist cut into her skin and the thought occurred to her that if he was really broke, he could sell it. But she'd only upset him if she said that.

"You've got to help me, Kayleigh. You've got to. I'll meet you here tomorrow at the same time. Got it?"

What was she going to do? Kayleigh's head whirled. Poor, poor Marlene. And then there was Callum. Breaking his probation when he'd only just got out. But he was right. If he turned himself in, he'd get God knows how many more years. She had to help him. Just as he'd helped her when she'd been little.

Maybe she'd ring Alice. She'd understand. Or would she? Shit. The line was busy. To make it worse, the last bus had gone even though it was still quite early. Alice's phone was still engaged. Both her mobile and the landline. There was no option. She'd have to walk.

"Want a lift?"

It was the red and black Mini. She could smell the drink on Seb's breath from outside.

"No thanks."

"Don't be daft. Hop in."

Somehow she found herself doing so. "Had a good time?"

"Not really."

"Me neither."

A hand crept onto her knee. Kayleigh knew what to do this time. "Piss off."

"OK. Don't freak out."

"Can you go slower?"

"Getting a bit demanding, aren't we? My mum says Alice is like that. You never told me. Is she your aunt or something?"

A sharp corner.

A hoot.

"I want to get out."

"Come on. Don't be daft. Who are you ringing?"

"Alice."

"Give it here."

A sharp corner.

Another loud hoot.

Fucking hell. FUCKING HELL.

TWENTY-FIVE

"Mum," said the voice. It sounded as though it was coming from a long way away. "Mum."

"Garth?" she'd whispered disbelievingly.

As she spoke, she looked up at Daniel. His face, black from their argument, now lit up with an almost child-like amazement. Alice felt the distance falling away between them. Forget Monica. Forget Kayleigh. This was their son. Their *son*.

"Are you all right? Are you still in prison? Are they letting you out?"

Her stream of questions, falling out of her mouth in their eagerness to reach him, were met with a brief silence before Garth replied.

"I'm all right but it's not great here."

At least, that's what she thought he'd said but the line was faint.

"Are they treating you all right?"

"*Are they treating you all right?*" A parody of her voice echoed back mockingly. The time gap meant her words overlapped with his reply.

It sounded like "Don't worry."

And then there was a high pitched whine followed by silence.

"He's gone." Alice heard her voice cry out in anguish like a child's. Knowing she was being unreasonable, she reached out to Daniel. "Can't you do something? Can't you bring him back?"

He was already on the phone, holding the mobile close to his

257

ear which Daniel didn't normally do. He was walking too. Short, furious steps up and down the drawing room by the French windows. Hope fluttered in her chest. Her husband would do something. He had to.

"Brian? It's Daniel. Look, Garth has just rung us – yes I know – but he didn't make much sense. The phone line was bad. Say that again?"

There was a short agonising silence as Alice pressed her nails into the palms of her hands, waiting.

"I see."

"What?"

Alice tugged at her husband's arm. His eyebrows met with disapproval. Instantly, she was eighteen years ago. Facing her furious mother and disappointed father.

It wasn't my fault. It wasn't my fault.

"Don't, Alice. Please let me finish. Sorry, Brian. My wife is understandably distressed. Yes. I see. Of course. I'll tell her. We're very grateful to you. Yes. I'll make that clear."

"What is it? What's happening?"

Alice felt the words stream out of her mouth. Hysterically. Tearfully. The old Alice. The new one too. Still hoping that someone might believe her. Listen. Understand. A flash of Paul Black came into her mind. Don't be so ridiculous, she told herself fiercely. How could she think of *him*? At a time like *this*?

Numbly, she became aware of Daniel leading her to the sofa. Sitting her down. Holding her hand. Mungo jumped up beside her, licking her concernedly. Neither bothered to tell him to get off even though the 'no dog on the sofa' rule was normally non-negotiable. "It appears that the authorities allowed Garth to ring you as a gesture of good will."

"Good will?" she repeated. "I don't understand. I thought we had a witness. Sheila Harris *saw* someone putting something in Garth's rucksack. So why can't they just let him go now?"

Daniel took his hand away. Instantly, Alice felt a clammy relief. His touch hadn't been comforting like Paul Black's the other week when he'd patted her arm. Instead, it had irritated her.

"Brian says it's not how it works," continued Daniel in answer to her earlier question. He stood up, moving towards the window again; clearly keen to put distance between them. Mungo jumped up, pawing the glass. "These things take time."

"But they *will* release Garth?" she said desperately.

Daniel spoke, his back still facing her. "Hopefully. But we're in the hands of others. You've got to remember that."

A horrible net of powerlessness engulfed her. She needed to do something. Anything. How on earth could she sit here, while her son was in prison; maybe hungry or worse?

Alice sprang to her feet. "I can't stand this. I'm going for a walk." Running out of the drawing room, she seized the lead which was hanging in the hall. Mungo didn't need any bidding. If she didn't get out of this house, she thought to herself, she might very seriously go mad.

As she jogged out of the drive – pulled along by Mungo who had clearly made a good recovery judging from his energy – Alice spotted a pair of youths sitting in a red car on the other side of the road. Almost immediately, they pulled off, leaving a cloud of dust behind, making her cough.

Frankie's friends? Or just a pair of passers-by. Maybe she should have made a note of the number; even checked the make of car. She should be worried, in view of what had happened to Mungo. Yet in the scale of things, it came way below her fear over Garth.

To be honest, she told herself, blowing the whistle that was attached to her key ring in order to recall Mungo, she'd been surprised as well as relieved by Sheila Harris's phone call. Drug smuggling was just the kind of thing that Garth would do. Thank God that he hadn't. At least as far as they knew.

Still churning with emotion, Alice opened the little kissing gate at the top of the cliff path. Below, the sea sparkled like a magical hidden pool. How she loved this bay. It was hard to get to – these steep steps deterred many holidaymakers and quite a few locals too. It wasn't so bad going down but coming back could be a killer.

Just what she needed to clear her head. "Garth is alive," she sang out into the evening air. It sounded more reassuring than when she just said it in her head. "Brian will get him back."

He had to. Even Janice, who was always moaning about how hard it was to be married to a lawyer (you never won an argument!) was proud of the number of cases he won. Proof perhaps, that infidelity didn't have to ruin a marriage.

Mungo was nearly out of sight now, heading round the corner and on to the beach. She followed, picking her way over the pebbles towards the water. It was soothing watching the waves coming in and out. Just like life she thought, not for the first time. You lost things – like the receding wave – and then others came back to take their place.

Was Daniel right, she wondered. Could all this help them make a new start?

Alice didn't realise, until dusk began to fall, that it was so late. That was the wonderful thing about the summer and living by the sea. It was still light, even at this time.

She glanced at her watch, realising that she must have spent much longer than she realised walking through the shallow waves and then sitting on the beach, throwing a ball for Mungo. But it had calmed her. Made her feel that it was all going to be all right. She'd ignore Monica, she'd decided. She'd try hard to … to get closer to Daniel. And she'd visit Uncle Phil, who'd made such a miraculous recovery (why did the bad ones always last longer?) and tell him exactly what she thought of him. She'd persuade Daniel that they had to provide Kayleigh with a safe base until she sorted out her life. And, most important of all, she'd have faith that Brian would get Garth back.

But as she began the long, slow, climb up the cliff path, Alice felt a sense of apprehension. It began in her chest like a light weight and then, the higher she climbed, the heavier it got.

Even Mungo, who'd been so lively earlier on, was dragging back. Maybe this walk had been too adventurous after his trauma. The vet had said it was fine for him to have 'gentle' exercise but, too late, Alice realised she'd probably overdone it in her keenness to get away from the house.

"Won't be long now," she said, breaking into a jog as the

ground finally levelled out. Along the lane, round the corner, past the park – it now seemed inconceivable that anything had happened there – and up the road towards the house …

Alice's heart stood still at the sight of a police car outside. Garth. Her chest tightened with terror. Something must have happened. Something after their phone call.

Mungo surged ahead so fiercely that she dropped the lead. Flying after him, she saw with alarm that the front door was open. Then she stopped. Standing in the hall as though waiting for her, was Monica. *Monica?*

Standing very close to Daniel.

"What's she doing there?" whispered Alice. "What's going on?"

Daniel dropped his arm. Monica's face was swollen, suggesting she'd been crying. Had she come to the house? Had Daniel told her it was all over? That it was his wife, he loved?

But that still didn't explain the police car outside.

"It's Kayleigh."

Alice started at the deep voice. She hadn't noticed him. Hadn't spotted Paul Black coming out from the kitchen with a glass of water as though he owned the place.

"Thank you," whimpered Monica gulping it down.

"She's had a shock," said Daniel.

"*She's* had a shock?" Alice spluttered. "What do you think it's been like for me to find out that you've been …" She stopped, unable to say the words. "You've been seeing her behind my back."

"Alice." The deep, dark, rich voice was soothing. So too was the familiarity which, she noticed with some pleasure, had not gone unnoticed by her husband. Or Monica.

Then she felt a hand on her shoulder. Paul Black's hand. It was only for a second but it scalded her with an emotion she hadn't felt since she'd been seventeen and Gordon had first kissed her.

"Alice," he repeated again. "There's been an accident. Kayleigh was in a car, driven by Seb. Monica's son."

This didn't make sense. "Kayleigh," she repeated. "Why was she in the car with Seb?"

"You tell *me*," spluttered Monica.

Daniel was still close; as though this interloper was more in need of comforting than she was.

Alice turned to Paul Black. "Are they all right?" she asked, as though the others weren't even in the room. "Are they all right? Please. *Tell* me."

TWENTY-SIX

It had all happened so quickly. The other car had looked as though it was coming towards them and then shot past. There'd been a screeching of brakes and a terrific crunching noise. Kayleigh had felt herself being thrown forwards so that the seat belt cut into her. She put out her hands in an automatic reflex reaction just as the car came to a halt. It seemed to be dipping downwards.

In front of her, the windscreen was covered in little cracks, rather like a picture she'd seen once as school. A tessellation, the teacher had called it. She'd only remembered because she liked the sound of the word.

"Are you all right?" croaked a voice next to her.

Seb! For a moment, she'd been too stunned to remember that there was anyone else in the car.

Kayleigh nodded. Or at least she thought she did. Everything seemed so vague and unreal. "Are you?"

"My arm hurts like fuck." Turning round awkwardly – the seat belt had got twisted – she saw Seb's arm hanging at a strange angle. There was a big swelling on his right eye too. "Hit the bloody wheel. Don't know what happened to the sodding airbag."

Kayleigh wasn't sure what that was, but from Seb's tone, it sounded important. Still, the main thing was that they were all right. "What are you doing?" she asked as he picked up his mobile which had fallen on the floor beneath his seat.

"Ringing the police, of course."

Kayleigh began to panic. "Don't do that. They might send

me back to care." She tried to wrestle the phone out of his hand. "They'll think Alice isn't looking after me ..."

"What are you talking about?" He gave her a weird look. "We've been in an accident. It's against the law not to report it. Besides, how are we going to get out of here? We're stuck in a sodding ditch." He reached for his mobile with his good arm. "Police, please. Maybe ambulance too."

Shit. Everyone knew you didn't call the police. Not for anything. They weren't on your side. Not when you came from her kind of world, anyway. She could just see it now. That social worker with the swinging earrings would send her back to weirdo Marc with the wife with bruised arms. Or maybe someone worse. She'd never see Alice again. Never have the chance to live in a normal house where people sat up at tables to eat and cared about you.

And it was all her fault for getting into a car with a boy who was driving too fast.

Desperately, she wriggled out from the seat belt. Fuck. The door wouldn't open.

"Kayleigh, come back!"

Ignoring him, she flung herself into the back seat. Yes. The door opened. Flinging off her shoes – it would be easier to run without them – she shot across the road. Which way was Alice's? If she could get back there quickly, she could pretend that she was never with Seb in the first place.

Shit. There was a siren. Flashing lights. An ambulance, followed by a police car. That was quick. They never normally came this fast when there were fights on the estate.

A man was striding towards her in uniform. With a sinking heart, Kayleigh recognised him. It was the policeman from before. The one at Alice's house.

"Don't they have more than one of you?" she started to say but the words came tumbling out in the wrong order.

"This one's concussed." The policeman turned round to the figures running out of the ambulance in fluorescent jackets. He took her arm and gently sat her down on the verge. Then he looked down on her with those blue eyes that had been so keen on Alice the other day. "I recognise you, don't I? Kayleigh, isn't it?"

She was going to deny it but then the eyes softened. "It's all right. You're in safe hands now."

"Alice," she managed to croak. "She'll be worried."

"Don't worry about that," said another voice. A woman's this time. "Someone will contact your nearest of kin but in the meantime, let's get you to hospital, shall we?"

"I don't need to go," she began but as she spoke, everything dipped in and out like a fuzzy picture on the telly.

Ahead, she could see Seb being helped to the back of the ambulance, a grey blanket draped around his shoulders.

"Can you tell me what happened, Kayleigh?" asked the policeman as they followed. "Was the driver going too fast?"

Yes, she almost said. But then Seb turned round. His eyes were fearful. Pleading. Please don't split on me, they said.

Kayleigh hesitated. But only for a second. "It was the other car," she murmured, feeling really sick. "The red one. That was the one going too fast. We had to swerve to get out of its way."

"Thank you," said Seb's eyes. "I owe you one."

And Kayleigh felt a warm flush of gratitude because she'd done something that Seb wanted. Now he liked her, so she had to like him too. Because that was the way it worked if you wanted someone to love you.

"Will they let me go home with you?" she asked Alice within seconds of her arriving at the hospital.

They'd put her in a side room with a big white machine at the side that kept bleeping. There was a wire attached that led into a vein in her hand – it had hurt like fuck when they'd put it in – but the nice Irish nurse who had shown Alice in had said the readings all looked "nice and healthy".

"As soon as they're happy with you." Alice was holding her other hand, the one without the wire. "You've had mild concussion and also you're in shock." She shuddered. "You were both so lucky. The car's a write-off. You could have been killed."

There were tears in her eyes as she spoke. Kayleigh felt awful that she'd upset Alice so much. "I'm sorry. I shouldn't have got in the car with him."

"Had he been drinking?"

"I don't know but he was going quite …"

She'd about to say fast but then remembered Seb's face and the good feeling she'd got when she'd lied for him.

"Quite carefully."

Alice gave her a strange look as though she didn't believe her. "That's what you told the police, right?"

Kayleigh nodded.

"Sometimes we say things – or don't say things – to please other people," said Alice slowly. "It's because we want to win their friendship." Her hand tightened. "Real friendship is when people want to be with you, whatever you've done."

"Like us?" whispered Kayleigh, scarcely believing she had the courage to say this.

Alice nodded. "Exactly. I believe in you, Kayleigh. I want you to know that. You've had a rough deal. Just as I had … when I was your age. So I want you to be all right in a way … in a way that I wasn't."

Kayleigh tried to concentrate but her eyes were growing heavy and the curtains round her bed were looming in and out.

"You need to rest," said a voice. Was it Alice's?

Kayleigh tried to claw it back. She needed to check, just to be sure, that when she woke up, she could go back to Alice's and that the social worker with her silly earrings, wouldn't stop her.

"Mum," she murmured.

"We've left a message on her mobile," said a voice. "But we're still waiting to hear back."

"I need to find my brother," she tried to say but she wasn't sure if she was speaking out loud or in her head. "I need to help him," she murmured. "Callum's waiting."

But then she fell into darkness. Down, down and down.

It wasn't until Kayleigh woke, in the hospital bed, that she realised she must have fallen asleep. Or maybe she was still dreaming. She could hear Alice arguing angrily outside the door.

"How could you?"

Alice's voice was clearer now: like it was in the room.

"What's it to you anyway?"

This other voice was sharp and mean. If she raised herself onto her elbows, Kayleigh could just about make out a sharp-faced angular woman with a thin nose and expensive looking silver bangles on her wrist that rattled as she spoke.

"It's everything to do with me." Alice's voice rose. "Don't you realise the damage you've done to our family not to mention yours? Haven't you thought about Seb and ..."

"Don't you bring my son into this."

My son? So that was Seb's mother?

"Alice," called out Kayleigh weakly. "Please don't blame Seb. It was an accident. That's all."

The narrow-eyed, sharp-faced woman turned to her, eyes narrowing. "So that's the tart who made my son crash. Distracting him, were you?"

"No." Kayleigh started to say but Alice cut in.

"Don't you dare talk about her like that. Get out. Go and look after your son. And leave my husband alone."

Kayleigh's jaw dropped. Husband? So this was the woman who'd been having it off with Daniel? Immediately, she wanted to comfort Alice. Just like she'd comforted Mum all those times when her blokes had dropped her. "Don't take any notice of that silly bitch," she called out.

Alice gave a little laugh. It sounded shocked but admiring at the same time. "You know what I like about you, Kayleigh? You say what you think. It's what I should have done, years ago. Now let's get you ready, shall we? The doctors said you're all right to come home now."

Home? Did that mean the emergency care was over now? Or that Mum had come back from Spain? She didn't want that. Not now.

Alice was actually smoothing her hair like she was a kid. "Yes. To our house. It's yours too, remember? For the time being, at any rate."

There was a snort behind. Kayleigh hadn't realised the sharp woman with the spiky hair was still there. "You're insane,

Alice. Know that? No wonder Daniel can't cope any more."

Kayleigh was about to say something rude when Alice got there first. "Get out of my sight, Monica. Daniel is my husband. You know nothing about our marriage and I'll thank you for leaving us alone. Go and look after your own family, including your son who's lucky not to be facing charges, if you ask me. Or is he?"

Impressed, Kayleigh watched Seb's mum turn her back and flounce out. That was the way to do it, she observed. Classy. No swear words. Just straight talking.

"I wish you were my mum," she found herself saying.

Alice looked surprised but pleased. "That's really sweet. Thank you. Actually, something happened when you were out last night."

"You found your husband having it off with that cow?"

A shadow flitted over Alice's face. "No. Something else." The shadow cleared and a light filled it, in its place. "I had a phone call from my son. I spoke to him, Kayleigh. I actually spoke to him."

Her face lit up in such a way that Kayleigh felt a rush of jealousy. Then it looked sad again. "But we still don't know when he'll be back."

Good. If he did return, Alice might not want her around.

"Stay away," she willed quietly. "Stay away, Garth. And leave us alone."

It seemed both weird and normal to be back at Alice's. "Why don't you go to your bedroom for a bit of a rest?" Alice had suggested when they drove home.

But as she lay on the bed, she could hear arguing in the kitchen. Daniel's voice was loud. Furious. It reminded her of Callum when he got cross.

Fuck. In the accident, she'd forgotten. He'd be waiting for her in the centre by the toilets. He'd think she'd let him down.

Meanwhile, the voices continued. "Don't you see what you're doing, Alice? You're trying to make up for not having Garth. What's going to happen when he comes back?"

"We've got enough room."

There was the sound of a chair being scraped across the floor. "For God's sake. When will you look at the really important things in life."

"Like you and that tart?"

It was all Kayleigh could do not to clap her hands and say "Go on."

"Monica isn't a tart. She's lonely. Like me."

"So you want to leave me, do you?"

Kayleigh froze.

"No, Alice. I don't want to leave you. I just want a proper marriage, that's all. Is that so much to expect?"

There was a muffled noise then – from Alice? – and a dog barking. Then a slammed door. And then silence.

When she woke up the next day, Kayleigh stayed very still for a few minutes. Listening. There was no sign of last night's argument or anyone telling her she had to go. That was a relief.

Then she got out of bed, had a shower, and wandered along the huge landing and down the stairs. Somehow, she had to find a reason to go into the city and find Callum.

But Alice wasn't in the kitchen. Still searching, Kayleigh found herself in another room with three guitars – three! – and a music system which must have cost a bomb.

Eventually, she found her in a little room, overlooking the garden, mending a yellow and blue plate with a pot of glue by her side. Kayleigh was incredulous. "What do you want that old thing for? Can't you just throw it out?"

Alice shook her head. "It's too precious."

"Like that *Cash in the Attic* programme? Mum loves that."

Alice smiled. "This isn't worth anything. Not in terms of money, anyway."

"Then why are you trying to mend it? You can't be skint. Not with a house like this." Kayleigh looked round at all the stuff in the room. There was loads of china on the sideboard and also other plates on the wall. "If you are, maybe you can sell some of this stuff on eBay."

There was a tinkly laugh; but not an unkind one. Kayleigh loved it when Alice laughed. It made her face softer instead of

269

tight round the eyes like when Daniel was around or that bitch in the hospital yesterday. "I mend things for other people because they are precious to them. It's not about money. It's about feelings."

Slowly, Kayleigh absorbed this. "I get that." Her eye fell on a big silver bowl. That would fetch quite a lot on the market. At least a tenner. Anything would help, Callum had said. Anything.

"You know you said we could go shopping," she said slowly.

"Sure." Alice was carefully fitting a small piece of china into a jagged gap in the bowl, using a pair of tweezers. "Maybe tomorrow. I need to finish this first. How are you feeling? Sorry. I should have asked before. It's just that I get so absorbed in all this. And it takes my mind off things …"

She stopped.

Kayleigh nodded. "I know just what you mean. Books do that for me. They help me forget the shit. So do my dreams. Sometimes I imagine that my father is coming to find me."

Alice tilted her head to one side questioningly. "Where does he live?"

She turned away. "I don't know. But he'll find me one day. I know he will."

"That's wonderful." Alice smiled but it was a sad smile. "Never give up your dreams, Kayleigh. It's what keeps us going."

"Right." Kayleigh wondered how to work the next bit. "Can I go shopping this afternoon?"

Alice's eyes widened. "So soon after the accident?"

"I'm better. And the doctor said I could do normal stuff. Remember?" She held her breath.

"I'm not sure."

"There's a bus in half an hour. I've worked it out from the timetable you gave me the other day. I need to get out. You know. Forget what happened in the car."

Slowly Alice nodded. "I know what you mean. Sure you feel all right?"

"Sure," said Kayleigh fast, sensing victory.

"I'd like you back by 5 p.m."

"Promise." Kayleigh nodded earnestly, her eyes on Alice as she reached over for her bag and drew out five twenty-pound notes. "This is more than you'll need. Get yourself some new jeans and some shoes too."

She fingered the crisp notes, disbelievingly. "Ta."

"Oh, and Kayleigh?"

She paused by the door, half-expecting Alice to say she'd changed her mind. "Don't take a lift with anyone. Will you?"

TWENTY-SEVEN

The police weren't going to prosecute Seb over the crash. There weren't any witnesses and no one had been hurt. When Alice had heard this through Janice (who'd gleaned the information through someone whose 'daily' did for Monica too), she was cross.

How many injuries – both emotional and physical – never came to light simply because there wasn't a witness?

"What are you going to do about Monica?" Janice wanted to know.

Alice concentrated on measuring out the tea. "I'm not sure."

It was the day after she'd allowed Kayleigh to go shopping in Plymouth on her own. "Why did you do that?" Daniel had demanded angrily when she'd told him after dinner, while Kayleigh was playing music in her room.

"She wanted to and I thought it might be a test," Alice had replied quickly. "See if she could do it without getting into trouble." She glowed. "And she did."

It was true. The girl had come back with a pair of canvas loafers and a thin pair of jeans which had cost sixty pounds. The rest had gone on the bus fare so there wasn't any change.

Alice had pushed the little flutter of distrust to the back of her mind. How often had she been shopping with Garth, only to be appalled by the cost of an ordinary pair of jeans? The memory gave her a jolt in her chest. He had to come back safely. He *had* to.

Meanwhile, she still had to work out what to do about her marriage – if indeed, it was her decision.

"What do you mean you're not sure what you're going to do about Monica?" repeated Janice, helping herself to one of the carrot sticks she had brought along in her handbag. (Janice, who was a perfectly acceptable size twelve in Alice's view, was always on a diet.) "Haven't you got a plan? And what exactly happened at the hospital?"

Pulling up a chair, Alice joined her friend at the heavily marked pine kitchen table overlooking the lawn. She loved every one of those marks. That dig over there had been from Garth's toddler days when he was still trying to master a knife and fork. That other one – a pattern of dots – had been an angry teenage Garth, deliberately stabbing his fork into the wood during yet another 'please revise' argument. At the time, the marks had distressed her but now they were comforting reminders; especially now he was so far away.

"Daniel and I have decided to put any decisions on hold," she replied, aware that she sounded rather prim. "At the moment, Garth has to be our first priority."

Janice fixed her with a *you-don't-get-out-of-that-so-easily* look. "You're avoiding the question, Alice. What happened at the hospital between you and Monica? You said she was there. You must have said something."

Sometimes Janice was too pushy. Too familiar. Yet she had been the first friend that Alice had made when they'd come down to Devon. They'd done school runs together; watched their boys go through teenage years together (although Janice's sons had been far more biddable when it came to revision and were now at Oxford). If she couldn't tell Janice, she couldn't tell anyone.

"I told her to keep off my husband if you really want to know."

Janice nearly dropped her coffee mug with excitement. "Good for you. So what did Daniel say?"

Alice drummed her fingers on the fork marks. "I told you. Daniel doesn't want to talk about it until Garth is back."

Janice gave her an uncertain look. "*Until* Garth is back? Look, I don't want to dampen your spirits, Alice …"

"Then don't." Alice put down her mug and stood up,

walking towards the French windows. It was a mild day and the lavender bed outside drew her to it. Lavender was so soothing.

"I just felt I ought to point out that you might have to wait longer than you want to. Brian says …"

Alice rounded on her. "He's discussed our case with you?"

Janice had the grace to look embarrassed. "Not in detail. Only to say that he hoped the witness was going to be able to pull rank."

Picking a piece of lavender, Alice began to shred it to bits, carefully keeping the bits in the palm of one hand.

"They do things differently out there, Alice."

Slowly she raised the palm of her hand to her nose, breathing in the lavender. It took her back to the time when, as a child, she and a school-friend had cut up her mother's stockings into small sections and stuffed them with lavender and rose petals. Mum had been livid. The stockings had apparently been new.

"So Daniel keeps telling me. Garth rang me, you know."

Janice nodded. "Brian said."

Alice began to shred another piece of lavender. "Do you know what it's like to hear your son from the other side of the world and be unable to help him?"

Janice bit her lip. "I'm sorry."

"When did you last speak to the twins?"

"Last night."

"And before that?"

"I don't know." She frowned. "Maybe three days earlier, although they don't always pick up. You know what they're like. Alice, where is this leading?"

"I'm trying to point out that it's easy for you." Alice felt her words spilling out in anger. "Your sons aren't locked up in prison. You can ring them whenever you want. Your marriage might have had its issues from what you've said but it's all right now. You weren't abused as a teenager – something that your own mother didn't believe …"

Janice laid a hand on her arm. "Is that what the lawyer meant, in court?"

Dammit. Why had she let that slip out? Alice flung the bits

275

of lavender on the grass and began to march on down the lawn, towards the old tree-house that had belonged to the family before them and which Garth used to hide in when he wanted to smoke.

"You were abused?" Janice was running to keep up, puffing slightly. "What happened?"

"It's personal."

Sitting on the bottom step of the ladder leading to the tree-house, she gazed up at the apple tree fanning its branches over her. Janice, to her irritation, sat next to her. "Don't take this the wrong way, but sometimes people imagine things when life gets difficult. It's a sort of escape. And you have had a lot on your plate …"

Alice jumped up. "I knew you wouldn't understand. I'd like you to leave now, Janice. Please. Just go."

But her friend was shaking her head. "Don't do this, Alice. I'm trying to help you. We're worried about you. All of us. Brian, I and Daniel …"

"You've discussed me with Daniel?"

Janice coloured. "Only about this girl you've taken in. It's crazy. Don't you see it? You don't know her. She comes from … from goodness knows what kind of family. She's a drug addict …

"No she's not …"

"Well she's taken drugs anyway. Yet you're letting her sleep under your roof and allowing her the run of your house – she's there right now while we speak, isn't she? She could be stealing things for all you know. And Daniel says you gave her money to go shopping."

Alice thought of the thin jeans and loafers and the crisp twenty-pound notes. "It's none of your business."

"But it is. You're my friend. And I can't stand by and see you break down like this."

Alice pushed away her hand. "A breakdown? Is that what you think I'm having?"

Janice looked sad. "It's not a criticism. It's understandable. Many women would break down under the strain you're under. Brian is furious with Daniel about Monica, if you want to know.

Told him he was a bloody fool."

"Bit rich, isn't that? Considering he had an affair too."

Janice looked away. "I didn't say *he* did. You just presumed that."

Shocked, Alice stared at her friend. "You don't mean *you* …"

"We were very young. Just married. I wasn't sure I'd made the right decision." Janice turned away. "I don't want to talk about it now. I'm just saying that relationships can be repaired and I wouldn't want you to muck things up before it's too late."

There was a short silence before Janice turned round and touched her arm gently. "As for this other thing … this being abused …" She shivered. "That's awful! Did you ever report it?"

Alice stared up at the tree, focussing on one particular apple which was almost within reach. When they'd first moved in here, Garth had promptly shimmied right up to the top; causing her to freak out.

"My mother wouldn't let me." She gave a little hoarse laugh. "In those days, we did what our parents told us."

"How long ago was that?"

Janice's voice was so kind that the answer slid out before Alice could help it. "On the eve of my eighteenth birthday. By a family friend." She spat his name out in disgust. "Phil Wright."

"Then report it."

Alice reached up on tiptoes and pulled the apple off the branch. It came off easily, as though it had been waiting.

"It's too long ago."

"No it's not. The paper's always full of cases like that. It's often not until you're an adult that you have the courage."

Alice hesitated. Wasn't that why she was looking after Kayleigh? Because the girl had had the guts to give a statement, outlining the abuse she'd suffered at Frankie's hands?

So shouldn't she too show the same courage herself?

"You could ring up that nice policeman who's always round here," added Janice, slightly sharply. Was this a test too?

"He's *not* always round here," retorted Alice defensively. Aware of her reddening cheeks, she moved away, biting into the apple. The juice ran down the side of her face. Deliberately, she wiped her mouth on her sleeve, the way Kayleigh had done at dinner the other night, much to Daniel's disgust.

"If you say so."

"I do."

She began to walk back towards the house, Janice running beside her. "It's worth thinking about, isn't it?"

"What is?"

"Going down to the police station. I'll come with you. Goodness, what's that noise?"

Alice stared at the open window on the second floor. It was Garth's bedroom. Loud music was coming out of it. A horrible din. The kind that made your ears want to bleed. Exactly the kind of noise – and level – that Garth had played before he'd gone away.

"He's back," she called out, breaking into a run. "He's home!"

Belting up the stairs, two at a time, with an excited Mungo beside her, Alice flew into the room. "Garth –" she began.

And then stopped.

Sitting on the bed, side by side, examining a CD cover, were Kayleigh and Seb.

"What are you doing here?" Alice was so mad, she could barely speak.

Seb sprang to his feet. "I'm sorry, Mrs Honeybun. It was my fault. I came round to see how Kayleigh was doing. We got talking about music and I started telling her about Garth's amazing CD collection so we thought ..."

"You thought you'd go into my son's bedroom and help yourself."

Seb had both his hands in his jeans pocket. She couldn't work out if he was really apologetic or defiant. "Like I said, I didn't mean any harm."

"Just like you didn't mean any harm when you crashed your car."

Alice began pushing him down the stairs. "You could have killed Kayleigh."

"Please don't push me like that."

"I'll do what I like. Just like your mother."

"Alice!" said Janice, appalled. Alice glowered at her friend who was waiting at the bottom of the staircase.

"Go home." She was quivering with rage now. "Now."

"What about me?"

A small frightened voice came from behind. It was Kayleigh.

"Not you," said Alice, more gently. "You can stay."

Dinner was a terse affair that night. Kayleigh still hadn't got the hang of a napkin and blew her nose on it before helping herself to the salad bowl, using her fingers.

Alice took one look at Daniel's face and had to cough in order to hide the giggle which almost escaped. Although quite how she could giggle when Garth was in prison was beyond her. Maybe it was nerves like before, when she'd had coffee with Paul Black.

Another memory floated into her head. A more distant one, recalling a giggle of panic when her father had asked if she'd given Uncle Phil permission to do the things he had. A giggle that her mother had misinterpreted for complicity.

"This is nice," said Daniel eventually when they got to the apple pie.

"I made the pastry," burst out Kayleigh excitedly. "Alice showed me. Didn't you? I didn't know you could actually do that. Thought it just came from shops."

Daniel looked as though he wished he hadn't taken a slice. "So tell me," he said, putting down his spoon and fork. "When are you going to get a holiday job?"

"Soon as I can." Kayleigh spoke with her mouth full. Alice, who would have died if Garth had done that, watched with an inexplicable fascination. She also got a disturbing pleasure from her husband's horrified face. "But it's difficult out. There's no work round here and there are hardly any buses to the centre."

"Our son managed," retorted Daniel tersely.

"No, he didn't," Alice shot back. "He did two days' work at the garden nursery and then got sacked because he couldn't get

279

up in time."

"That doesn't mean our guest has to sit here all day, without earning her keep."

He said the word 'guest' with a heavy sarcastic emphasis.

"Daniel," said Alice horrified. "That's rude."

"Nah, he's right." Kayleigh helped herself to another slice of pie without being asked. "I do need to get a job. I'll go in tomorrow."

"I'll give you a lift," said Alice quickly. "It's no trouble. I've got something to do."

Then she stared at Daniel. "What about you. What are you doing tomorrow? Taking Monica out to lunch?"

There was a short dangerous silence. "Alice," said Daniel warningly. "We agreed not to speak about that for a bit, didn't we?"

"You agreed. Not me," muttered Alice, clearing the plates. Kayleigh jumped up to help. She was learning fast in some areas, if not in others.

"I want you to sleep in the guest room, tonight," Alice murmured as she picked up Daniel's. "Do you understand?"

"Any chance I could borrow some more money?" asked Kayleigh on the way in to Plymouth the next morning.

At first, Alice didn't hear her. She was still distracted with the fact that Daniel had left early, before she'd woken up. It had felt strange but not unpleasant waking up in an empty bed; not having to endure the touch of her husband's peck on the cheek or the accidental brush of his legs as he got out.

"I'll need about fifty quid if that's OK."

Kayleigh's words broke through. "Fifty pounds?" she repeated, looking briefly across the car.

"Maybe sixty then, to be on the safe side." Kayleigh was lying back in the car, her legs up on the dashboard. "I've got some books I need to get for my new college course."

Alice headed for the car park at the back of the shopping centre. "Don't you have to wait for your results first?"

Kayleigh sniffed. "I'll be all right. My teacher said I would be. 'Sides, I want to get going with the reading so I'm ahead of the others."

Alice was so impressed that she decided not to mention the feet on the dashboard. That could wait for another time. "All right." Pulling into a space at the top of the car park, she reached behind for her bag. Yet another handout! It was just like having Garth at home, except that he didn't spend his money on books.

"Where are you going to look for a job?"

"A job?" repeated Kayleigh.

Alice felt a quickening of doubt. "Yes. Remember. That's why we've come into the centre."

"Oh yeah. Right. I'll just get my books first and then I'll go round some places."

Alice didn't feel reassured. "I'll meet you back here in two hours. That's 12.30. All right? Have you got a watch?"

Kayleigh stared at her as though she'd said something odd. "Never had one. But I've got my phone."

Of course. Garth had never used a watch either. Not even the expensive one which her mother had given him for his eighteenth. That reminded her. Alice hadn't been able to find her own that morning when getting up. Maybe she'd left it in the garden shed again; a common occurrence after weeding.

"Where are you going?"

Alice hadn't been expecting that. The question threw her. "To see someone," she said slowly. "Tell me, Kayleigh. Are you glad you told the police about what Frankie did to you?"

"I am now. It made me realise what he was really like, telling someone else about it. If I hadn't, it would have eaten me up, if you know what I mean."

Alice's heart quickened. "I know exactly what you mean."

She walked as far as the crossroads with Kayleigh and then left her to go into the shopping centre. Then, glancing around, in case there was someone who knew her, she took a sharp left towards the library and then a right. It was a roundabout way to the police station. A place she had only been to once when Garth had lost his A-level coursework and she had gone in, in the hope that someone had handed it in. (They hadn't.)

A woman with sharp eyes and hair scraped back into a bun,

was at the desk. "Is PC Paul Black available?" asked Alice nervously.

"Who shall I say is here?"

"Alice." Her name came out as though it weren't her own. "Alice Honeybun."

She'd expected the woman to say that he wasn't available. Not on duty or out on a call, perhaps. But after a short wait on a chair, next to a woman who was on her phone constantly (she seemed to be trying to get hold of her solicitor), Alice was rewarded by the sight of Paul Black coming through a pair of doors at the far end of the desk.

"Alice," he said warmly. "Nice to see you."

His handshake was firm. They could be acquaintances meeting in a shop or a restaurant. Once more, she thought that this man with the educated voice and slightly tanned face (suggesting a fondness for the outdoors), didn't sound or look like the stereotyped image of a policeman in her head. Then again, he had been a lawyer – something, she recalled with embarrassment, that she'd disputed because she'd been upset at the time. If it was really true – and there was no reason to doubt it – why had he changed careers?

Suddenly she was aware of his blue eyes holding hers. "What can I do for you?"

The formality made her wish she hadn't come. He'd been keen enough to chat when he'd wanted her to be a witness. Perhaps she'd outlived her usefulness. Hurt, she found herself unable to speak. The fraught tone of the woman on the chair, looking for a solicitor, increased with panic. ("But she *can't* still be in a meeting. I need her.")

Paul Black's face was beginning to look serious. "Is it about Kayleigh?"

"No." She glanced at the woman on the desk who was now dealing with a teenager. The phrase 'missing phone' was clear. "It's about me. About … about something that happened when I was a teenager. The thing they mentioned in court …"

Even as her words died away, Alice was aware of a weight falling off her shoulders. Paul Black's face softened. "Let's find somewhere to talk, shall we?" he said.

They went to a room marked Interview Room on the door. "Please sit down."

Again, she was aware of his good manners and a manner of bearing himself that didn't seem to fit a policeman on a beat. "Were you really a lawyer?" she found herself asking even though it was irrelevant.

"Yes." He spoke as though they were guests at a dinner party. "My father expected it. So I stuck it out for a few years until something made me change my mind."

What, she wanted to ask. But he was picking up a pen; his voice changing from personal to professional. "Why don't you start at the beginning?"

So she spoke. Slowly at first. But then faster as it all rushed out. Details which she'd forgotten like the colour of Uncle Phil's shirt (pale blue) and his smell (a sickly aftershave). Suddenly, Alice was on the eve of her eighteenth birthday again. Young. Stupid. Naïve. Too polite.

"He told me to sit down next to him on the sofa," she whispered, her hands gripping the side of her chair. "I thought it would be rude if I didn't. Then he began to move towards me. I thought I might be imagining it. That was when he began to touch me."

Something flickered in those bright blue eyes. A flash of recognition. "You wouldn't believe how many young girls are abused," he said softly. " I think I told you that before, when you made your statement."

He understood. Relief washed over her.

For a minute, she thought she saw tears in his eyes. "You don't have to go on," he added.

"I want to." She had to force each word out. "I need to. He began to put his hands under my T-shirt so I stood up." As she said it, she began to re-live each moment as if it was happening right now. "Then he … he pulled me onto the carpet. I remember thinking that I didn't realise he was so strong. He wasn't a tall man. And then … and then …"

She was there, now. Crying out. "No, No."

Or was it a "Yes?" like her mother had insisted afterwards. Had she really led Phil along by going round, wearing a T-shirt with a low neckline? Was it actually all her fault?

"No." Paul's nails were digging into his hand, she could see. "It's what young girls think. But it's not."

"I felt ..." She stopped.

"Dirty?" His eyes were full of sorrow.

"Yes! And I was sure that somehow, without realising, I must have led ..."

Again, she couldn't complete her sentence. Paul did it for her. "Led him on? Is that what you mean, Alice?"

She nodded, choked with gratitude.

"Everything you're describing is very common. You're not alone, Alice. You must believe that."

"Then why wouldn't my parents believe me?"

"Ah. That." A resigned look came over his face. "I see that too. Parents often feel guilty themselves. They think they should have been around to protect their children. Some find the guilt so horrendous that they deny that it even happened."

Alice hadn't thought of that. "Phil said my parents wouldn't believe me. And he was right. Mum blamed my vivid imagination. I was good at stories, you see. Dad used to be proud of it – said I was a natural writer. But I wasn't making this up. I wasn't ..."

"Shhhh. Shhhh. I know. I believe you."

He believed her! He believed her even though he hardly knew her. Not like Mum. Or Dad. Or Daniel. Paul's deep, gravelly voice felt like it was holding her hand. It felt comforting. Reassuring. Solid.

"After that ..."

She stopped. "After that, I couldn't bear anyone to touch me again." A huge regret swept over her for Gordon. A decent, kind boy who would have been good to her, if only she could have let him.

"But I wanted to get married. I craved the security and I wanted children. So I married Daniel. He was older, ten years older. We met at university. I'd dropped out of my own course in Fine Arts, unable to concentrate after what ... what had happened. So I moved to London and took an admin job through an employment agency. By chance, it happened to be in his department."

For a moment, she fell silent, remembering the calm, quiet, bookish man who had asked her out to dinner. Rumour had it that this gentle, well-mannered, bookish man in his early thirties was recovering from a broken engagement. "He seemed to respect me when I said I didn't want to sleep with him until we were married."

As she spoke, Alice knew she should feel embarrassed. How could she talk about sex to a relative stranger? But it seemed quite natural.

"So you got married, not because of the physical side, but because you needed security after what had happened?" It was more of a statement than a question.

She willed him to look at her again. "How did you know?"

He gave a sad smile. "Because it's a very common pattern. So too is a delay in reporting it. Some women wait for years until something triggers them into taking action. What made you come here now, after all this time?"

A common pattern. Other women also wait for years. So she wasn't as crazy as she'd thought. That was some consolation at least. Relief began to seep through Alice and with it, the need to tell this Paul Black everything. Well, almost everything. "A friend. The one you met at my house. Janice. I told her too ... because of Kayleigh. She said I ought to do something about it."

He nodded. "It's often the way these things work. Even so, I've got a problem."

Paul Black's words startled her. His fingers, she noticed, were drumming on the side of his chair. "I'm going to be honest with you. The thing is that I've just taken a complaint from someone."

What? Alice wasn't sure if she'd heard probably. What did this have to do with her?

"Someone wants to take action against you, Alice. It's just come through on the system. It's a complaint of harassment, I'm afraid."

"Who?" she asked hoarsely.

But even as she spoke, she knew the answer.

"A Mr Wright," said Paul Black, his bright blue eyes steadily on hers. "A Mr Phil Wright."

TWENTY-EIGHT

Kayleigh fingered the crisp twenty-pound notes in her jeans pocket as the bus lurched into the centre. Alice was so nice. Too nice. The woman wouldn't last a minute on the estate. Part of Kayleigh – quite a lot actually – felt bad about taking money from her.

Correction. She'd been *given* it, hadn't she? And now she, Kayleigh, had to pass it on to Callum because the handout that Alice had given her before wasn't enough.

That's what her brother had said anyway.

"You've got to help me," he'd said when they'd met last time at the back of the toilets on the far side of the city. "You're my only hope, Kayleigh."

Yes! His words had made her feel good, reminding her of the times he'd been nice to her. Helping her forget the other ones when he'd lied to Mum about her, to get himself out of trouble. She still remembered that really big row about the cigarettes he'd nicked from Mum when they were younger. "It was Kayleigh," he'd said, even though she'd been barely twelve.

Mum had believed him. Ruefully, Kayleigh looked down on her arm. There was still the scar to prove it. But now Callum needed her. How could she let him down? Even if it meant giving him the new lot of money that Alice had given her. Or stealing some of her stuff.

Kayleigh peeped inside the designer bag that Alice had given her ("I've got too many as it is") to take another look at the silver bowl. She hadn't pinched the big one. That would have been too obvious. But there'd been a smaller bowl in the dining room on a table that was full of other stuff like photograph frames. She'd taken one of those too. They were always selling stuff like that in the market.

Better get rid of the picture first. Kayleigh looked at it. She'd seen enough of the photographs round the house to know that this was Garth Honeybun. What a name! Bet he got bullied at school for that. Second thoughts, he probably went to one of those really posh schools where bullying wasn't allowed.

Still, decided Kayleigh, as the bus jolted its way along the high street, he wasn't bad-looking with that straight nose and blue eyes like Alice's. His hair was dark, though, like his dad's. Kayleigh automatically twisted her own round her right index finger. "Your bleeding father had red hair," Mum had once said on one of the few occasions when she'd talked about him. "A temper to match too."

Here they were. Kayleigh got out of the bus, her heart pounding. The toilets were right there, next to the car park. Bloody hell, it was windy. Shivering, she walked round and then again, in the opposite direction like Callum had told her. *"You've got to make sure no one's watching."*

A bloke in a leather jacket came out and stared at her breasts brazenly. Kayleigh flushed. Maybe he thought she was on the game. Marlene used to say that public toilets were the place to hang around if you were a slut and wanted to make something.

She really missed her friend.

Meanwhile, the bag was getting heavy, what with the bowl and the photograph frame. What if Callum didn't turn up? Suddenly, Kayleigh felt scared. What should she do now?

Two hours later, Kayleigh was still sitting on the wall by the back of the toilets. Loads of blokes had come in and out. Nearly all of them had looked at her like the first one. In some ways, it was quite flattering.

"You're quite pretty," Seb had said the other day just before Alice had found them in Garth's bedroom, playing music. "Know that?" Then he'd traced the side of her cheek and looked as though he was going to snog her. That's when Alice had come in.

"Pssst."

Kayleigh jumped. She'd been so busy daydreaming that she hadn't seen the short, thick-set figure darting towards her; collar turned up and black beanie over his head. If it wasn't for his voice or the swagger, she wouldn't have recognised him. Maybe that was the point. He didn't want to get spotted, did he?

"Callum," she said excitedly.

"Shut up, you silly cow."

He grabbed her arm and pulled her into the Gents. "I can't go in here," she spluttered.

But he'd shoved her into a toilet and locked the door behind them. "If anyone comes in, stop talking," he hissed.

Kayleigh nodded, her mouth dry.

"Did you get the money?"

Shaking, she pulled out the money from her jeans pocket. He tore it out of her hand and counted it. Then his face broke into a smile. "You did well."

A lovely warm feeling flowed through her. Callum was pleased with her.

"I've got this too."

"Shut up."

They both froze at the sound of footsteps, Then she could hear someone taking a piss. Kayleigh tried hard not giggle, partly through fear and partly because it always seemed so weird to her that men could wee like that.

Callum held a finger to his lips until the footsteps had died away. Then he looked down at the silver bowl and photograph that she'd pulled out of her bag. "What the fuck's that?"

Kayleigh began to feel less certain. "I thought you could sell them. At the market, maybe."

He knocked them out of her hand so that the bowl bounced on the hard concrete. "You silly cow. There are words on it. Look. It'll get identified."

So there were.

WINNER OF THE OVER-40 GOLFER OF THE YEAR 2000
She hadn't noticed that when she'd taken it.

"I'm sorry," whispered Kayleigh.

Callum gave her a contemptuous look, like the ones he used to give her when she was younger. Instantly, she felt awful. "I'm really sorry," she repeated. "I won't do it again."

"Pick it up then." Callum wasn't tall but he still seemed to tower over her. She hesitated.

"I'm not going to belt yer."

Relieved, she did as she was told. There was a big dent in the side of the cup. "You'll have to put it back or they'll get suspicious." His eye fell on the silver photograph frame. "That's all right. You can sell that if you get the picture out. Who is he, anyway?"

"That's Garth." She spoke it like she already knew him. "Alice's son. He's got this great room, full of guitars and stuff."

Callum's eyes grew warm again. Interested. "What about the rest of the house. Is that full of stuff too?"

Kayleigh nodded eagerly. "You should see it. It's amazing."

Callum began to nod as though agreeing with himself. "What's the address?"

"I'm not sure they'd like me saying." Kayleigh began to panic in case she upset Callum again.

"Come again." He took her chin in his hands. "Don't you trust me, little sis?"

"'Course I do." But she didn't feel quite as certain as her words. "I honestly don't know the number, although I could give you directions. It's in this little town about half an hour from here. Near the sea."

Callum was stroking his beard. It was one of those short ones that merged into a moustache without a gap. "You say they're called Honeybun? Maybe I'll come and pay you a visit."

She nodded, nervously, wondering what Alice and her husband would say to Callum. He already had his hand on the door lock. "Where are you going now?"

"To see a bloke about some gear."

"What kind of gear?" She looked at his torn jeans. "I could get you some clothes, if you like. There are some jeans in Garth's room."

He laughed but it wasn't a nasty laugh like he used to give her when he'd been at home. "You don't know nothing, do you, little sis?"

She thought of Frankie in the park and the lovely happy feeling when he'd unexpectedly given her that tablet and then the warmth as he'd entered her. "I know more than you might think," she said proudly.

That made Callum laugh even more. "That's what I like about you, little sis. Chip off the old block, you are. Just like the old woman."

Kayleigh didn't like the thought of that. "Have you seen Mum?"

His eyes narrowed. "Where do you think I'm hiding out?"

She felt a rush of hurt. "But she wouldn't have me there."

"That's 'cos her bloke fancies the pants off you." He snorted. "Jealous, she is." He gave her another kind of look now. The sort that Seb had given her. "You've grown up real pretty. Just be careful. That's all."

Then he'd opened the door. "You be careful," she said quickly. "If they find you, they can make you go back into prison."

Callum patted his top pocket where he had placed the money she'd given him. "That's why this will help."

As he spoke, there was a thin whistle outside. Callum froze. "Get out," he said, pushing her in front of him. "It's the bloke I've been waiting for."

"To get your gear?"

But this time, he didn't laugh. "Just get out."

"When will I see you next?"

"Don't worry about that. I'll find you. And get some more of this, can you?"

Then he pushed her so she fell down the steps, landing on her knees. He didn't mean to. 'Sides, it was her fault, not looking out for the steps. But as she got up, she caught sight of a bloke going into the Gents with a shaved head and a tattoo of a cockerel on the side of his neck.

Pete! Marlene's boyfriend! Kayleigh almost went back into the Gents to have a go at him. But then she stopped. If he was Callum's friend, her brother would be cross with her.

And she didn't want that. Not when she'd just found him

291

again. He loved her! He might be a bit rough with her. But that was families. Wasn't it?

"How much?" repeated Kayleigh,

The market trader with thick dirty fingers gave her a hard stare. "You heard me. Three quid."

But that wouldn't be enough to buy some clothes. Then Alice would want to know what had happened to the money. She'd have to pretend someone had nicked it. Still, at least three quid would get her a bus fare home.

Funny how the word 'home' seemed so natural.

"OK," she said, reluctantly handing over the frame.

"You can take that snapshot out and all."

Garth stared up at her pleadingly. She ought to rip him up to get rid of the evidence but he was too nice. Quickly, she folded him in two and put him in the bag along with the bowl that she'd have to sneak back somehow.

"Kayleigh?"

She whipped round to see a small woman with big pearl earrings and a really smart red jacket. She knew her from somewhere … of course. Marlene's nan.

"I'm so sorry," she spluttered. "About Marlene. I was really upset when I heard."

Marlene's nan gave her a cold glare. "She got into a bad crowd. So did you, from the sound of it." She looked her up and down, taking in the designer bag. "Looks like you've done all right for yourself. Heard you got taken into care?"

Kayleigh nodded, not wanting to say more. "I'd have liked to have gone to the funeral." Tears filled her eyes. "But I didn't know Marlene had died."

"*Died*?" Marlene's nan stepped away as though she'd been hit. "Who told you that?"

"My mum."

"She took an overdose." Marlene's nan's lips tightened. "Those boys you two were hanging around with were bad news. But she's all right now."

"She's not dead!" Kayleigh felt an enormous wave of relief tempered with disbelief.

"No." Marlene's nan's lips were so thin now that you could hardly see them. "Her mum's sent her to London to live with a cousin. Don't try and contact her. We want her to have a new start."

"But I *need* to see her!"

Marlene's nan's eyes grew grey and hard. "I don't think you get it, Kayleigh. She told us how it was your idea. Going off with those boys for the day. We blame you for what happened. She was lucky not to be nicked along with you and that boyfriend of yours."

"It *wasn't* my idea," began Kayleigh.

But Marlene's nan had gone, swallowed up in the crowds.

Still, at least her friend was alive! That was amazing. But at the same time, it was horrible that she'd lied about something so important. A memory of her mother's eyes glinting with malice came back when Kayleigh had found her with the suitcase stuffed with notes. Had she wanted to upset her? Or had she just got the story wrong?

There was the sound of a smart silver car pulling up alongside her. "Kayleigh?"

Alice! There were black smudges under her eyes as though she'd been rubbing them. But she was smiling. She looked really great. Much better than when she'd said goodbye to her earlier that day.

"I had to go into the centre. Want a lift home?"

Aware that everyone was looking at her, Kayleigh slid into the front seat. "Ta."

"Did you get anything then?"

Kayleigh wished she'd had time to get her story straight in her head. "No. I got mugged."

"Mugged?" Alice's voice rose in alarm. "Are you all right?"

"Yes." She began to feel bad now. "They didn't hurt me. They just took the money out of my hand."

"You didn't have it in your bag?"

" I was … I was counting it."

"Kayleigh." Alice's voice was reproaching but kind. "You have to be careful, you know."

If only she knew.

293

"Sorry."

"But you bought something." Alice took her eye off the road in front for a second and it rested on the bulge in her bag.

Shit. The silver bowl.

Then she got a brilliant idea. "Actually," said Kayleigh, taking it out, "it's yours. I'm afraid I was looking at it this morning and dropped it on the ground. It's got a dent. See? So I thought I'd take it in and try and get it mended. But it was too expensive."

For a minute, Alice's face hardened as though she didn't believe her. Kayleigh held her breath. Then she smiled. "How very thoughtful. But don't worry. Don't worry. Daniel's got loads of them. We'll just put it away in a cupboard. He won't notice." Then her eyes tightened. "But we ought to report the theft to the police."

"What theft?"

"The money those boys took from you. At least, I assume they were boys."

"No. They were girls."

"Can you describe them?"

"Big. Scary. Tattoos. One of them was called Marlene."

Why had she said that?

"We ought to tell the police."

Kayleigh's chest quickened. "Do we have to?"

"Of course. Otherwise they'll just keep stealing from others, won't they?"

She needed to change the subject. Fast. They stopped at some lights; next to a big poster with an advert for condoms on it. Kayleigh saw Alice looking at it; flushing and then looking away.

"When people get married, do they still have lots of sex?"

There was a little laugh. "Actually, I don't really like …"

Her voice tailed away but it was too late.

"You don't like it?"

"No." Alice went bright pink as the traffic began to move again. "I mean, well, it's personal, isn't it?"

"Marlene, that's my friend – well she was – and I used to talk about it all the time."

"Really?" Alice seemed to be considering this. "Maybe more people ought to."

"I like it. I mean, when you saw me in the park, it was my first time but I don't regret it. It made me feel good about myself. Powerful. Able to give him something he wanted."

There was another short silence. "I hadn't thought of it like that."

"It's the only way to get them to do what you want. That's what Mum says."

"But surely that's not a very nice way to look at it."

"Why not? Anyway, it makes you feel good too, doesn't it?"

Was she laughing? It sounded like a sort of stifled giggle. But what was so funny? Sex *did* make you feel good. And it was free. Not like booze or fags.

Then Alice turned into their road – *their* road! – and a passing car flashed them. "That looked like Brian."

"Who's Brian?" Kayleigh started to ask as they pulled into the driveway. They both saw him at the same time. A tall, lanky boy with a shaved head, on the doorstep. Just staring at them. For a minute, she thought it was Frankie. But no. This one looked posh. You could tell it from the way he stood there, one hand in his pocket. Smiling. Confident.

Then Alice made a funny sound in her throat, screeched to a halt and ran out of the car, leaving the engine still running. Should she turn it off? At first Kayleigh did it the wrong way, making a grinding sound Then, awkwardly, she got out and hovered by the passenger side, feeling horribly left out. Abandoned.

"Garth," Alice was calling out. "Garth!"

The boy had his arms around Alice. He was taller than her. From a distance, they looked like boyfriend and girlfriend. Then he looked up. Straight at her.

And she realised he was the smooth kid in the photograph. The one that was folded in half inside her bag.

TWENTY-NINE

Garth was home. In her arms. Hungrily, Alice breathed in her son. He smelt different and yet the same. A mixture of sweat, BO, cigarettes, and stale clothes and something else she couldn't put her finger on. His narrow shoulders were thinner and his rib cage dug into her body as she hugged him.

At last she felt whole! Complete. Only now did she realise that the grief she'd felt since he'd gone away, was akin to having a great gaping hole in her body.

"Why didn't you tell me?" she whispered into his chest, unwilling to let him go. "Why didn't you say you were coming?"

Garth's voice was gravelly; much deeper than before, unless that was hoarseness. He must be tired. He certainly looked it with those dark circles under his eyes. "It happened really fast, Mum."

Mum! The word filled her with joy. A sense of worth. She had a job again. A reason to keep going.

Daniel's voice cut in. "Brian managed to get a judge to agree to bail. So we got him out on the next flight."

We? Alice rounded on her husband from the safety of her son's arms. "So you didn't think of telling me that all this was happening?"

They were standing, still on the doorstep; Alice unwilling to move away from Garth. If she did, he might go away again and that was unthinkable. "I didn't want to raise your hopes."

"What am I? A child?"

"Please, you two. Don't argue."

297

It was the voice of a man. Not the teenager who had gone away in a strop because he hadn't 'felt ready' to go to uni.

Flattened, Alice stepped back to appraise him. Garth was definitely thinner. But there was something else that was different about him. There was a maturity to his manner. A certain firmness in his tone, combined with a gravitas that made him seem more in charge than she was. "Come inside, Mum," he said, putting his arm around her waist.

She tried to remember when he'd done that before. A dim and distant memory came back of a small Garth, in his prep-school uniform, trying to hug her because he didn't want her to leave. The school had been for weekly boarders: Daniel had insisted it would be 'good' for him but the separation had killed her. Garth had loathed it too (she often thought this might explain why he had rebelled later on) and she'd used the move to Devon as an excuse to put him in a good day school instead.

Now, they sat together on the squashy lemon sofa in the sitting room; Alice leaning into Garth while Daniel sat some distance away on the chair by the French windows. Questions were flying round her head. If someone had woken her up and told her she'd been dreaming, Alice would have immediately agreed.

"Tell me everything," she said, nestling her head into her son's shoulder, basking in his arm around her. Then, before he could start, she added, "Have you really been pardoned?"

"Don't bombard him with questions, Alice."

Don't treat me like a child, she almost snapped back. But Garth did it for her; reproachfully firm but kind at the same time. "Dad! Don't be so condescending."

Thank you, she wanted to sing. Thank you.

"It's all thanks to that witness. She was pretty influential. Brian said we were really lucky not to go to trial."

Alice felt her heart swell with love and gratitude for the unknown Sheila Harris. "We need to thank her," she murmured. "Thank God she saw you." Nestling even deeper into her son's shoulder, she realised this was the closest she had ever got to cuddling him. That awful holding back on her side – that reluctance to invest too much emotional trust – was still there

298

but not as strongly as before. Briefly, Paul Black flashed into her head. Swiftly, she batted him away. "What really happened at the airport, Garth? Before they arrested you."

Her son stiffened and lifted his arm, edging away to the end of the sofa. Instantly, she wished she hadn't said anything. "I met these New Zealand friends on the beach. We'd seen each other before in Ecuador. Everyone meets up again when they're travelling." He shrugged. "I thought they were all right. One of them had done me a favour …"

He stopped. "What kind of favour?" asked Daniel sharply.

"It doesn't matter." Garth's voice had a Keep Out edge. Before he'd gone away, Alice would have interrogated him. Insisted he'd told them what he meant. But this wasn't a boy any more. This was a man and she mustn't – couldn't – drive him away.

"Anyway, they asked me to take this package with me on the plane. Said they couldn't fit it into their own bags because they'd been overweight. It's all right, Mum. Don't look like that. I said no."

Alice breathed a sigh of relief.

"They seemed a bit pissed off about it but I just thought, sod that. Anyway, they must have slipped this package into my bag at the airport. That's what that woman saw, thank God, though the first thing I knew was when I got stopped at customs."

"What happened to the New Zealanders?" demanded Daniel before she could ask.

Garth shrugged. "Disappeared into the crowd, when they saw I'd been pulled to one side."

It all sounded so plausible. Just as convincing as the time when Garth had insisted, hand on heart, that it hadn't been him who had stolen a twenty-pound note from Daniel's wallet at the age of fourteen. The same Garth who, a year later, had come home, stinking of cigarette smoke, declaring it was his friends ("It sticks to your clothes, Mum"). The boy who had come home early from his last A-level exam, proclaiming it had "finished early", only for her to discover later that he'd simply walked out half way through because he "couldn't be bothered". If it hadn't been for the complex points system and the fact he'd done really well in the other papers, he might have lost his uni place altogether.

Alice tried to banish these distrustful thoughts from her mind. "What was it like in there? In ... in prison."

He laughed. "Basic."

She moved closer, yearning to feel his arm around her again but he just gave her hand a quick squeeze. Back off, it said. I'm not a kid any more.

"Did anyone try to hurt you?" she persisted.

"No, Mum."

His voice had a raw edge.

"Alice." This time her husband's voice had a distinct note of sympathy. "He's tired. Needs a break."

"You don't have to talk about me as though I'm not here, Dad."

The old argumentative Garth was back! The one who'd insisted he needed the second gap year because he wasn't ready to do another "three bloody years of studying". In one way, his anger was a relief because it felt normal again. In another, it made her heart sink at the thought of all the familiar arguments starting again. That hadn't helped her relationship with Daniel, she thought.

"What about you, Mum?" Her son was looking her up and down, just as she had him. "What have you been doing, apart from mending your old china?"

That had always been a bit of a joke between them. Garth had found it 'bloody stupid' that she 'could be arsed' to mend stuff that ought to be 'binned'. Rather like Kayleigh's initial reaction, she thought, amused.

There was a snort from Daniel's direction. "What's your mother been doing? Apart from looking after waifs and strays, you mean?"

Only then did Alice remember. Kayleigh! She'd been with her when she'd got out of the car, after picking her up at the bus stop. But then Alice had seen Garth and – she was ashamed to say – she'd forgotten Kayleigh altogether in her urgent need to put her arms around her son and breathe him in.

She must have just slunk off to her room.

"I don't get it." Garth looked mildly amused and confused at the same time.

Alice stood up, aware that she was flushing. Blast Daniel for introducing the subject so early. Maybe he'd hoped to deflect the attention away from him, in case she told Garth what his father had been up to in his absence.

"It's a long story. You don't want to hear it now. You must be hungry."

"No." Garth shook his head. She missed his hair; his long hair which she was always nagging him about because he didn't wash it. Had they shaved it like that in prison? "Brian got me something on the way back from the airport. By the way, he said to tell you that he'd call later. He reckoned we'd want time together first. Now tell me, Mum. What's this about waifs and strays?"

There was no getting out of it. "I saw something ... saw a couple getting ... getting intimate in the park when I was walking Mungo." Alice felt herself heating up with embarrassment.

"No way!" Garth's eyes widened and Mungo, woken up by the sound of his name, began pawing at her knees. (Surprisingly, she'd noticed, he'd been ignoring Garth altogether.) "So you reported it?"

Daniel snorted. "If only it was that simple."

"Please. Both of you. Let me explain." She felt even hotter. "I thought they might be in love so I just walked on."

Garth gave her a quick squeeze. "You didn't interfere? That's so cool, Mum. Really mature. I'm proud of you."

See, she wanted to say to her husband. *He* understands even if you don't.

"But then this policeman knocked on the door." Alice felt herself burning up even more. Had Daniel noticed? She hoped not. "Someone had told him that I'd seen them. It turned out that the man, who was much older than the girl, was a known drug dealer who preyed on teenagers. So I was persuaded to give evidence in court."

Garth whistled. "Shit, Mum. That must have taken some courage."

"Thank you." This time she couldn't resist shooting a triumphant glance at her husband.

"And now this girl is living with us," cut in Daniel.

"*What?*"

"It's only short term. Just till Kayleigh gets on her feet." Alice braced herself.

"That's amazing of you, Mum!" Garth picked her up and spun her around in his arms. So unexpected! "Was that the girl I saw getting out of the car just now?"

Alice nodded, breathlessly, glad to be back on the ground. "She's only just sixteen and she's had it tough. But if you want, I can ask her to leave so we can have some time together …"

"No." Garth was shaking his head emphatically. "You need to help her. *We* need to help her, just like that woman helped me. If it hadn't been for her, I'd still be in that cell."

Exactly. She couldn't help shooting another triumphant look at Daniel. But something wasn't quite right. Garth sounded like he was on a high. She tried to take a look at his pupils. They seemed the right size. Maybe it was the excitement of getting back. Besides, he didn't do drugs, did he? Just like he hadn't smoked when he was younger. Oh God. Who was she kidding?

"What about you, Dad? What have you been up to?"

Alice felt a nasty little laugh coming out. "You wouldn't believe it."

Instantly Garth's eyes froze. "What do you mean?"

There was a short silence. A silence during which Alice could hear music floating down from Kayleigh's room. So that's where she was. Alice registered a wave of relief combined with fear at what she'd just unleashed.

Daniel's face was rigid.

"Nothing."

They both spoke at the same time.

"Your father's been very busy."

Daniel was nodding energetically. "Summer school. You know. The usual thing. International kids who want to have fun instead of learning anything."

Garth wasn't fooled. She could see that from his eyes. That had been the thing that had bound the two of them together all those years, despite the teenage arguments. They'd always been able to understand what the other was thinking. A wise head on young shoulders, despite the rebellions. "Is everything all right, Mum?" Garth spoke softly as his father got up and crossed the room towards the phone which had begun to ring.

No, she wanted to say. Your father's had an affair with that sharp-faced bitch from Book Club. Seb's mother. And Uncle Phil, whom I never let you meet, has filed a complaint against me for harassment, because he's scared I'm going to take action against him for what he did all those years ago. Oh and by the way, there's something about a policeman that I don't get. All I know is that he makes me feel ... different. Though I still don't know if he's just been using me.

"Everything's fine," she said in the same voice that she'd used when he was younger. And then, because he clearly didn't believe her, she added, "Honestly. You need to ring Gran. She's been worried about you."

"In a minute. I want to talk to you first."

They waited until Daniel, making signs that he needed to take this call from another room, went out. Was it Monica, she wondered? If so, she almost didn't care any more. She had Garth now. The two of them were together, talking conspiratorially. It was like the old days, when she'd hidden things from her husband. A poor school report. Another complaint from a neighbour about loud music from Garth's bedroom.

"Are you sure everything's OK? Because if not ..."

He stopped. Looked up. Saw her before Alice did. The girl at the door looked like Kayleigh. Yet at the same time, she didn't.

She'd washed her hair. Twisted it in a different way – with one of her clips again, Alice noticed. She was wearing a pretty top in an apricot shade that suited her blonde hair. And her eye make-up wasn't as heavy as usual.

"Hi." Garth's voice was thick and heavy with interest. "You must be Kayleigh. Mum and I have just been talking about you. Welcome to our house. It's crazy here at times. But nice crazy."

Alice felt a flush of pride. That was a compliment. She

started to say something but Kayleigh got in first. "I've been playing your music. It's cool."

Alice tensed. No one was allowed to touch Garth's music. He'd thrown a complete paddy, just 'like a baby, when she'd decided to dust his CD collection last year. Just don't mention, she prayed, that you listened to his stuff with Seb the other day.

"What do you like best?"

Kayleigh's eyes were on her son. Big, wide, doe eyes. "Great Cynics."

"No way! They're my idols. Been following them since they started."

They were going to get on! Alice felt a mixture of relief and also apprehension. No. Surely not. Kayleigh was only sixteen. And Garth was just being friendly. A vision of Seb on the bed next to Kayleigh came back to her, along with that scene in the park. She might just be a kid but she'd already done a great deal. And Garth already seemed smitten ...

The phone rang. Again? That must mean Daniel had finished. Maybe Monica was trying to cause trouble. An anger began to boil up inside. She wouldn't allow anything to spoil Garth's homecoming. Nothing.

"Who's speaking?" she said sharply.

"Hello?" Daniel's voice, on the extension, cut it in at the same time.

"I've got it," Alice snapped.

But he was still holding on. Both Garth and Kayleigh had stopped talking. The room fell silent.

"This is Paul Black." There was a click as Daniel finally put down the phone. "I'm sorry to bother you. Is this a good time?"

Alice smiled at Garth. The kind of smile she'd perfected over the years to try and fool him into thinking that Dad and her hadn't been arguing. "Yes. Absolutely."

"I've been thinking about our discussion earlier today. It's none of my business. But the CPS – that's the Crown Prosecution Service that acts on behalf of the law – thinks you've got a case even though Phil Wright has filed a complaint against you." There was a slight pause. "There are some people, Alice, who need to be taught a lesson in life. However old they

304

are."

She gulped.

"It's not my place to say this, but …."

Another heavy pause.

"If you do this, Alice – if you take Phil Wright to court – I have the feeling that you'll be able to get on with the rest of your life. Does that make sense?"

"Yes," she whispered, aware of a wonderful warm light feeling floating through her. He believed in her. This policeman with the startling blue eyes, believed in her!

"Yes," she repeated. "It does."

306

CHAPTER THIRTY

She was in love! Garth had only been home for a few days but Kayleigh was sure of it. Every time he came into the room, her heart gave a little skip and she went all red and tongue-tied.

What was more, he felt the same way. She was certain of that too. When Alice started asking him questions (like what had it been like out there in prison and wouldn't he let her make an appointment with the doctor because he was so thin?), Garth started talking to her, Kayleigh, instead.

"So amazing that you like Great Cynics too! Been to any of their gigs? I hitchhiked to Milan to see them last year."

Alice had made a surprised noise at that.

"Don't fuss, Mum. That's why I don't tell you everything. You just freak out."

Garth had given her a wink and Kayleigh glowed with pride. He was telling her that they were on the same side. She wasn't the outcast any more.

Alice didn't like them talking so much. Kayleigh could tell that. She wanted her son to herself but she was too polite to say so. Part of Kayleigh knew she ought to give them some space together but she couldn't leave Garth alone. It was like she was connected to him by a piece of invisible string.

This was the real thing. She just knew it.

Every morning, now, Kayleigh spent ages getting herself made up. Then she'd hang around, pretending to apply for summer jobs on the computer Alice said she could use, while waiting for Garth to get up. "He needs to lie in," she overheard Alice saying to her husband last Saturday, when he complained about his son still being in bed at lunchtime. "He's been through a lot." Then, she'd added, in a low voice. "Like me."

"Don't start that again, Alice. I told you. I'm sorry. Monica didn't mean anything. Now Garth is home, I just want everything to be back to normal."

Hah! How often had she heard one of her mum's boyfriends saying the same? "Don't listen to him," Kayleigh wanted to tell Alice. "He's lying. They're all the same."

Apart from Garth and Callum, of course. And maybe Seb although she felt rather confused about him now. When Garth had found out about the car accident, he'd gone very quiet and told her to 'steer clear' of 'the bloke'. Seb, she recalled, had spoken about Garth in the kind of way that suggested he hadn't liked him either.

Funny really. She'd quite fancied Seb until Garth had come home. But now there was no contest. Garth was really funny; he'd roll his eyes whenever Alice asked if he'd been smoking in his room again. And he'd open a bottle of wine from one of those racks in a room off the kitchen that was as big as their flat at home, pretending that Daniel had done it earlier.

Meanwhile, at the back of her mind all the time, was that worry over Callum. "I'll need more," he'd told her when she'd handed over the money that Alice had given her.

How was she meant to do that?

"Come back tomorrow with it," he'd told her.

But she hadn't.

It wasn't just that she'd been distracted by Garth's homecoming (something that made her feel really guilty because here she was, living in this really cool place while Callum was on the streets). It was also because she didn't dare nick any more stuff.

Alice, she was sure, was getting really suspicious about the mugging story. She'd insisted on calling the police to report it. But when she'd put her on to the phone to give more details, Kayleigh had found herself stammering and blushing and getting the second version wrong.

"I thought you said there were *three* girls," Alice had said when she'd finished. "Not two."

"One of them legged it," she said quickly. It was scary how the lies came out. "I don't want to give a statement. I've had enough of the police. They freak me out."

Alice had reluctantly agreed. But then she decided to give the house a 'jolly good dust' and that's when she noticed the missing photograph frame. "It can't just have disappeared," she kept saying, looking under the sofa and even behind the chair cushions with those fancy fringes.

Kayleigh thought uncomfortably of the creased photograph in her handbag. It wasn't as though she'd got much for the bloody thing anyway.

In fact, the more Kayleigh liked Garth, the less she was beginning to like his mother. Instead of being kind, Alice now seemed annoying and pushy and also wet at the same time. Who else would put up with a husband that had had it off with one of her mates?

Alice was also up to something. Kayleigh was sure of it. Only this morning, she'd gone into the kitchen to help herself to some muesli (she'd got really into the stuff since coming here) and found Alice on the phone, talking really quietly.

Perhaps she was having an affair to get back at her husband. Kayleigh wouldn't blame her if she did. The thought also passed through her mind that she might be able to blackmail her. "Give me some more money," she might say, "and I won't tell your husband."

But Garth wouldn't like that. And if there was one thing she wanted to do, it was to keep Garth sweet. (That had been one of Marlene's phrases.) Every now and then, Kayleigh began to imagine what it would be like to move in with Garth. They'd have plenty of money. He was pretty spoiled right now, with all those CDs and that posh music system.

Maybe Callum was right. Some people had too much. Just look at Alice. She didn't have to work (that china stuff didn't count – not like an office job). She spent ages having coffee with friends like that Janice who was always over here. She did a bit in the house but she also had "Mrs M", as she called her, to help her. And she had a bloke that came in to do the garden.

Recently, Kayleigh had been having a daydream in which

she took over Alice's life. Not that she'd want Daniel Honeybun. Ugh! Mind you, she'd seen the way he'd looked at her the other day when she was coming out of the bathroom with just a towel wrapped round her. If she'd wanted, she was pretty sure she could have had him.

The thought made her feel really powerful inside.

"Would you like another cup of coffee?" asked Alice, interrupting her thoughts. She'd given up looking for the photograph, thankfully. Maybe, with any luck, she'd forget about it.

"No thanks." That powerful feeling she'd had just now, had disappeared. In its place, came a niggling, nagging feeling. Callum was in trouble. She just knew it. When he was living at home, she always sensed when there was something wrong. Mum always said it was like they shared the same father, they were so close.

"I need to go into the centre again."

Alice's face tightened. Sometimes Kayleigh felt like she was in a prison.

"Why?"

"None of your bleeding business."

Alice's head jerked up, shocked. Instantly, Kayleigh knew she'd made a mistake. "I'm sorry. It's just that I'm not used to people asking me where I'm going and what time I'm going to be back."

Alice still looked uncertain.

"I've got a job interview," she added.

Instantly, Alice's face softened. It was so easy, thought Kayleigh, guiltily.

"I'm sorry too, Kayleigh. And it's great that you've got an interview. But the thing is that I've got a responsibility to look after you. And after last time, I'm nervous for you."

"Last time?"

Alice put her head on one side and gave her a funny little look. "When you were mugged."

Shit.

"Oh that. Yeah. Sure. Whatever."

Alice gave a nervous little laugh. "You're beginning to

sound like Garth."

"Someone mention my name?"

They both turned round as he sauntered in. Bloody hell. He looked even more gorgeous this morning. His hair was beginning to grow a bit; it suited him. And he had a great body! Clearly he wanted to show it off. That's why he wasn't wearing a T-shirt with his jeans. Kayleigh tried not to look at the crop of dark hairs running down the middle of his chest and round his tummy button, but it was difficult not to.

She was sure Alice could see her trying not to stare.

"Kayleigh was just saying she needed to go into Plymouth." Alice was handing her son a mug of coffee at the same time. Kayleigh couldn't ever remember her own mum fussing round her like that.

"Me too." He grinned at her. A lovely friendly grin which made her feel like she was gorgeous. "Want a lift?"

"That would be great." Kayleigh took a deep breath. "I need to buy some stuff. The only thing is that I don't have any money."

Alice's face went stiff again. "I thought you had a job interview."

"I do." Kayleigh felt herself getting hot. "That's why I need some more clothes. So I look smart."

Alice nodded slowly. "She got mugged the other day. Thank goodness she was only robbed and not hurt."

Garth gave her a meaningful look. "Yeah. That *was* lucky, wasn't it?"

Kayleigh felt herself burning up inside.

"This should be enough." Alice was opening her purse and peeling out some notes.

"Thanks, Mum," he said casually, winking at Kayleigh but in a way that Alice didn't notice.

Kayleigh stared at the money in her hand. It wasn't right. She'd got tenners. Garth's were twenties. Callum wouldn't be happy with this.

"Let's hit the road, shall we? Don't look like that, Mum. I'm a good driver. You know that. Not like that idiot, Seb."

"Why don't you like him?" she asked as they drove through the narrow lanes towards town. Garth had been right. He *was* a safe driver; waiting patiently for someone to pass and then spending ages at the crossroads until it was OK to go over.

"Who?"

"Seb."

"Never have. He's a complete and utter prat." Garth's lips tightened. "Our mothers were friends when we were at school but we weren't. Not after he told Mum that I'd been caught smoking."

"I don't think your mum and his are friends now," Kayleigh said, without thinking.

"Really? Because he nearly killed you in his car?"

"No. It's because ..."

She stopped, remembering what it had been like when some woman had rung to tell Mum that her bloke was having it off with someone else. She'd literally crumpled. Broke Kayleigh's heart, it had, to see her so upset.

"Sorry. You'll have to ask her."

"Come on, Kayleigh. Give me a clue."

Garth was so persuasive when he looked at her like that, head on one side, his eyes twinkling. "OK. I heard her talking to her friend. Janice. She said that your dad and Seb's mum were ..."

Fuck. That was close. The car nearly went into a ditch.

"Were what?" Garth's voice was raw. "WERE WHAT?"

His shout was right in her ear. It scared her.

"You know," she mumbled miserably. "Were having a thing. He told her it was only once – least that's what she believes."

She glanced nervously at Garth. His hands were white on the steering wheel. "I hate the bastard," he was muttering. "It's not the first time, you know."

Kayleigh felt a little thrill passing through her. She liked the way he was taking her into his confidence. "What do you mean?"

"I saw Dad with another woman two years ago. They were in a pub, holding hands. He pretended she was just a friend but I made him tell me the truth. He made me swear not to tell Mum so I didn't." His eyes filled with tears. "I couldn't bear the idea of hurting her. That's why I went away. It messed with my head."

Then he looked across at her. "Anyone ever messed up your head, Kayleigh?"

She nodded. "Frankie. The one your mum saw me with in the park. He gave me a tablet and it made me do stuff that … that I hadn't done before."

Garth's hand stole out and patted her on the knee, sending little thrills through her. "He gave you drugs?"

"Yes."

"Then he had it off with you. In the open air."

She felt awkward. "Your mum told you?"

He nodded. "It's how you met, isn't it?"

She nodded.

"She's a good person." Garth was still looking straight ahead at the road but there was something different about him. His eyes were steely hard. "I'd do anything for my mother, Kayleigh. If we're going to be friends – and I hope we will because I can really talk to you – you need to know that. She gets on my nerves but she means the world to me. I'd do anything for her. Anything."

Kayleigh felt her heart bursting. If Garth could feel that way about his mother, what would it be like if he learned to feel that way about her?

"Did you do drugs before this Frankie?" he asked, just as they pulled into the car park.

She shook her head, vehemently.

"It's just that, well if you feel like anything to help you relax, all you have to do is ask me."

Kayleigh swivelled round in her seat to face him. "So you did? You did what they said you did in South America?"

Garth shrugged. "I didn't say that. I'm just saying that if you fancy a smoke, you know where to come. Listen, forget I said that. OK?"

He seemed nervous now, opening the car door like he wanted to leave her. Kayleigh's heart began to quicken with fear. "See you here in two hours. And good luck."

"Good luck?"

He winked. "With the job interview. The one you pretended you've got. You can't fool me, Kayleigh. I know all the tricks because I've done them myself. See you. And try not to get mugged either. They stop believing you after the first time. Trust me."

Confused, Kayleigh wandered round the city, looking for Callum. Was Garth going to grass on her to his mother about the money or the job interview? If he did, she could tell Alice that her son did drugs after all.

But she had a feeling that Alice wouldn't believe her. 'Sides, she didn't want to cause trouble. There was no way she wanted to get thrown out of the house. It was nice there. With any luck, she might be able to carry on living there, even when she went to college.

Perhaps she and Garth might have a baby. Then they'd be able to stay there for ever.

"Hiya."

It was Seb! Sitting outside one of the pavement cafes, his arm in a sling. Next to him was a really pretty girl, with those high cheekbones you only usually saw in magazines, giving her a dirty look.

"Hi," said Kayleigh uncomfortably.

"Sorry about the other day." He was grinning as though he hadn't nearly killed her.

"What other day?" said the pretty girl smoothly. She had bright pink lips, noticed Kayleigh, and a nose that tilted up at the end like a model. Posh voice too. The sort that looked down on others.

"Just a bit of a problem with the car. Come on. Sit down and I'll buy you a drink."

She didn't want to but somehow she did. "Lucky you didn't hurt more than your arm," Kayleigh found herself saying.

The pretty girl pouted. "I thought you did that playing cricket."

"Don't believe a bloody word he says. Seb wouldn't know the truth if it hit him in the face."

They all turned at the voice. Kayleigh's heart plummeted as Garth stood there. His eyes fixed on hers, disappointed.

"That's not very fair …" began Seb.

"Fair!" Garth had Seb by the collar. "Learned the meaning from your fucking mother, did you?"

There was a gasp from the pretty girl with the pouting pink mouth. "Let's go," cut in Kayleigh quickly.

"I see." Seb's eyes narrowed. "So you too are together now are you? What's it like being out of prison, Garth?"

"Leave him," said Kayleigh urgently. To her relief, Garth began to stride along the street. She had to run to keep up with him.

"He saw me in the street," she began. "I didn't want to sit down but he made me."

"Made you? Really?" His eyes hardened.

They were standing by the car. So close that she could almost lean up and kiss him. But at the same time, she felt angry with him too.

"We understand each other, you and I," he said softly. "I must admit, Kayleigh. I was privately a bit hacked off to find you at home at first. But now I think we could make good allies."

Then, to her disappointment, he moved away to open the car door. "Get in then," he said.

They wove their way in and out of the traffic in silence. Kayleigh stared out of the window. What a mess! She hadn't been able to find Callum and now she and Garth were … were what? Friends? Boyfriend and girlfriend? She didn't know.

"Get out of the fucking way," growled a male voice.

Kayleigh gasped as a man in a black T-shirt walked right in front of the car just before they turned off to take the road home. If it hadn't been for Garth's quick thinking, they'd have hit him. Shocked, she stared back and that's when she saw it. The tattoo on his neck.

Shit. It was Frankie's friend. Pete. The one who'd gone out with Marlene. And he'd recognised her too, judging from the way he was standing there, staring.

Garth had noticed too. "Know him, do you?"

She didn't want to lie this time.

"He's Frankie's mate."

Her voice trailed away but Garth seemed to know what she meant, judging from his face.

"Mum said he got ten years."

So he knew more than he'd let on.

She nodded.

"No one will hurt you, Kayleigh. I won't let them."

She could hardly speak for the lump in her throat. "That's why Mum took you in." His voice was soft; like his left hand which was reaching out for hers. "Mum and I are both the same. We're loyal to the people we like. And I like you, Kayleigh. You're clever even though life's dealt you a rough card. And you're drop-dead gorgeous too."

Drop-dead gorgeous? No one had ever called her that before!

"Really?"

"Sure." He took his eyes off the road and grinned at her. "I love your hair. It's a really cool colour. And your eyes are like a witch's! Maybe you are a witch! You've certainly bewitched me!"

They were almost back now. Kayleigh wanted Garth to stop. To take her in his arms and snog her. "I love you," she tried to say but the words stuck in her mouth.

She tried again.

"I …"

"Fucking hell."

She leaned forward, staring at the flashing police light. Garth leaped out of the car, leaving the engine running; tearing towards the front door which was open.

"Mum," he yelled out. "Are you all right?"

Kayleigh followed, not sure if it was OK to leave the car like that. Her eyes widened as she took in the mess. Stuff was everywhere. Broken china on the floor in the hall. Silver cutlery on the ground in the kitchen as though someone had just pulled open the drawer and rifled through. Coming down the stairs with something in her hand, was Alice. Her face white.

Garth had his arm around her. "What happened?"

"We've been burgled," she said in a weird voice that sounded like Mum's when she'd taken a sleeping tablet. "Mungo and I were only out for an hour. Someone got in, even though I set the alarm."

Kayleigh felt dizzy. *Even though I set the alarm.*

"Who else knows the code?"

Alice was looking straight at her. As though seeing her for the first time. "No one. Just me and your father. We changed it when you were away. The police said it had to be done by someone who was very good at that kind of thing."

But Kayleigh turned her gaze away. It wasn't that she was trying to avoid Alice's anguished face. It was because her eye was drawn to something in the corner. Bending down, on the pretext of picking up some broken glass next to it, she slipped the small brass link into her pocket without anyone seeing.

It was just like the one from Callum's bracelet.

THIRTY-ONE

Until she'd come back from the walk and discovered the break-in, Alice had felt quite positive. She'd done it at last! Summoned up the courage to finally do something about "Uncle Phil".

"Yes," she'd told Paul Black, on the phone after she'd slept on his suggestion. "Yes, I *will* take him to court."

"It will be hard," he'd warned her. "You'll be cross-examined by the defence who will try to blame you."

"I've been humiliated in court already," she said tersely. "I can do it again, if necessary."

Yet inside, she was shaking. Hadn't there been a piece in *The Times* recently, about a teenage girl who had tried to kill herself after cross-examination during a case where a gang of men had been accused of raping her?

The jury, according to the report, hadn't been told of the attempted suicide. The men had got off.

"Phil will probably deny it, just like he did before," she told Paul Black. "But I still want to go ahead. You were right. If I don't, I won't be able to get on with the rest of my life. How do we start?"

Come down to the police station to give a statement, he'd said. They'd arranged a time later that morning. In the meantime, Alice had decided to give Mungo a walk, partly for his sake and partly to clear her head. So many of the questions were buzzing round her head that she needed the air.

Could she remember exactly what had happened, even though it was so long ago? (Yes.) What would her mother say?

319

(It didn't matter any more.) What about the publicity? (Sod that.)

Alice rarely swore but this time it felt good. Mungo seemed to agree as he tore ahead, foraging in rabbit holes and looking back to check that she was still there.

And then she'd returned to find the front door open and mess, everywhere. Papers on the floor. Her collection of cranberry glass lying in fragments on the kitchen floor; beyond repair. Daniel's desk opened with more papers spilling out. Her jewellery boxes, empty upstairs. The box for emergency cash, hidden under the bed, emptied. It must have contained at least two hundred pounds, if not more, although that was nothing compared with the jewellery. Garth's room in a mess too – although now he was back, that was quite normal. When he'd been at home as a teenager, it had always looked burgled anyway.

"Did you set the alarm?" said the police when they'd come, amazing fast, after her shaky call.

Yes. Of course.

And then Garth and Kayleigh had turned up, looking for all the world like an item. Oh God, she thought. That was all she needed. Judging from the way the girl was giving her son adoring looks, even in the midst of this panic, it looked serious already. A flash of her legs upside down in a v-shape shot into her mind. It was one thing giving Kayleigh a home. But it was another to see the girl making a play for her own son.

Making a play.

Such old-fashioned words, she reprimanded herself. The same words that her mother had used when she'd accused her, Alice, all those years ago. "Admit it," she had said when Alice had come back in tears after Uncle Phil had abused her. "You made a play for him, didn't you? Either that or you imagined the whole thing."

"Mrs Honeybun?"

The policewoman's kindly voice jerked her back to the present. "Would you mind coming down to the station to give a statement?"

Alice began to laugh. A strange hollow laugh that felt as

though it was coming from someone else's mouth. Both Kayleigh and Garth who'd been helping to clear things away, looked up. "I've already got an appointment to make a statement about something else."

The policewoman gave her a distrustful look. Not surprising. She probably thought she was one of those loony tunes who brought cases against people all the time. Brian had talked about that during a dinner party once. "Usually women," he had told his rapt audience. "Bored women with nothing else to do."

Nothing, thought Alice, as she left the chaos of her home for the comparative peacefulness of a police station, could be further from the truth.

Paul Black was ready for her. She could tell from his eyes that he already knew about the burglary. "I'm sorry about the theft."

"Do you know everything?" she couldn't help asking.

"It was on your file."

To hide her embarrassment, she tried to make light of it. "Must be getting pretty big now."

He smiled. "Not nearly as big as some, believe me."

Then he touched her arm briefly as he led her into a side room. Were policemen meant to touch people's arms, Alice wondered. Was it something that he did to everyone to demonstrate empathy? Or just to her?

"I gather," he added, "that fingerprints have been taken so we'll do what we can."

Alice sat down in the chair he indicated. "It's not the stuff that was taken," she said tightly. "It's the invasion of my personal space."

"I know."

"In a way, it's like being ... being abused."

"I understand that too."

Suddenly she felt a wave of anger. "*How* can you know? *How* can you understand? You know all about me but I know nothing about you." Even as she spoke, Alice realised she was being ridiculous. Policemen didn't tell you about themselves. It wasn't their job.

"I was burgled after my wife left me. They took everything,

including the photographs of our son."

Was this one of those things that the police were trained to say? To make up something, perhaps, to show they weren't that different from Joe Public? "Photographs can be duplicated," she snapped.

"But not people."

Shocked, she watched his eyes move from hers to the floor and then back to her again. "My wife and son were killed by a drunken driver. She was on her way to meet me, to discuss a reconciliation."

"But I thought you were divorced … that you saw your son every few weekends …"

"That's what you presumed. Perhaps I chose not to put you right." Paul Black's voice was steady as if holding back the pain. "Sometimes it's easier to pretend they are still here than having to cope with the awkward questions and inevitable sympathy."

She could see that. At the same time, she felt flattered he'd confided in her.

"Her mother blamed me, even though my wife was the one who had left – for someone else. She said I was a workaholic who didn't spend enough time with his family." He gave a small sad smile. "She might have had a point. Lawyers work notoriously long hours."

Alice's voice came out all cracked. "How old was he? Your son?"

"Ten."

A flash of Garth at the age of ten, proudly holding up a certificate for cricket, came into her head. "What did the driver get?"

"Six years which meant three. He's coming out next summer."

Mentally, Alice quickly did the maths. So Paul Black's life had changed for ever about the time that she was nagging Garth to revise for A-levels. For some reason, it was important to know what she'd been doing in her own life at the same time as his.

"Six years is nothing for a life," she whispered.

322

He held her gaze steadily as if willing himself not to break. It reminded her suddenly of a documentary about an explorer determined to get to the top of a notoriously lethal mountain. There had been the same look of grim resolve. "He might have got longer if there'd been a witness. But his counsel was able to argue 'extenuating' circumstances. It turned me away from the law. Made me realise it didn't always do its job for ordinary people. So I became a policeman." He gave a short laugh. "I had to start all over again but at least I'm on the coalface. I can do more good that way." His face clouded. "I think my wife and son would have liked that."

She wanted to hold him. Comfort him. But it didn't seem right. How could anyone offer comfort in circumstances like this. Even a simply 'sorry' would have been trivial.

"Why are you telling me this?" she whispered instead.

Paul Black's eyes never left hers. "Because I can talk to you, Alice. I shouldn't be saying this. But it's true. You're in pain over something that happened and can never be put right. I'm the same."

Briefly he closed his eyes. When he opened them again, his voice was crisp and professional again. "I need you to tell me exactly what happened on the day that you claim Phil Wright abused you."

"Claim?" she repeated. "I'm not claiming it. It's the truth."

"Alice," he said, his voice wobbling slightly. "You're going to have to remember that not everyone will believe you. Now let's start at the beginning, shall we?"

He switched on a tape machine.

Alice hadn't expected this. She'd thought he'd write it down just like he'd written down her statement about the park on the kitchen table.

This time, it was her turn to close her eyes. To take herself back to that day when she went round to Uncle Phil's.

By the time she'd got to the bit about her mother insisting that she had made it all up, Alice was drained.

"You've been very courageous," said Paul, switching off the tape. "Too many kids kept quiet in our day," he added quietly.

Our day? Fleetingly, Alice wondered how old Paul Black was.

"I'm forty-five," he said, as if reading her mind.

She blushed. Just a bit older than her then.

Then he looked at the tape machine again. "Is there anything else you want to add?"

'Want', he had said. Not 'should'. Alice forced the nails of her right hand into her palm to stop herself saying any more. "No."

There was a short silence. Did he know she had left something out? The most important bit.

Nonsense. How could he?

"May I give you a lift home?" Those blue eyes were fixed on hers again; they drew her to him. Or was that her, again? A silly little girl, masquerading as a woman. Desperate for affection, even though she couldn't return it. Come on, Alice, get a grip on yourself.

"I drove here, thanks."

"Right."

His voice had gone cold. Why did this feel as though they were playing first-date games? Not that she'd had much experience of this. Was it part of the police psychology?

"What happens now?" she asked, getting up.

"The Crown Prosecution will try and gather witnesses."

"But there weren't any."

"There might have been other girls abused by Phil Wright ... Girls who are now women and willing to come out and make a stand."

She hadn't thought about that. "Like the recent celebrity cases, you mean?"

He took a deep breath. "They might prove to be just the tip of the iceberg."

"What makes people behave like that?" she asked suddenly.

"I don't know." For a minute, they were back to that easy-to-talk level. "What makes a young man have too much to drink and drive into a woman and her son?"

"I'm so sorry," she said. To her amazement, Alice found herself putting out a hand in comfort.

He looked down at it for a minute as though considering it. Then, slowly, he walked away and held out the door for her. "Someone else will take your statement about the burglary."

They were back to that polite distance again. Alice felt stunned by the rejection. Stupid too.

"By the way, how is Kayleigh getting on?"

She nodded. "Fine. She … she seems to be making herself at home."

Too much so, she almost added, thinking of Garth.

"You did a good thing there." He smiled. "You're a decent person, Alice."

Then he put out his hand. His handshake was firm. His skin warm. "We'll be in touch. Meanwhile, if there's anything else you think of – about either case – let me know."

The burglary statement was relatively straightforward. Simple questions about what she'd found, put to her by a female police officer. There was a box of tissues on the desk but to her surprise, Alice didn't need them. In the scheme of things, a burglary seemed one of the lesser evils compared with infidelity or teenage abuse.

"We've changed the alarm code," she told the officer.

The woman had given a wry smile. "Unfortunately there are a lot of people out there who are good at by-passing them."

Afterwards, Alice, made her way to the centre because she couldn't face going home just yet. It wasn't her home any more. Not after that person or those people had been through it.

Just like her body hadn't felt like her own any more after Phil had touched it.

Meanwhile, thoughts continued to whirl round her head. Why wasn't there any justice? How could that old man in the nursing home bed continue to cheat death, just as he had cheated her of her peace of mind? Should she have told Paul the rest of the story? Or should she continue to pretend the sequel had never happened. Wasn't that what Mum had said? If she wanted to get on with the rest of her life, she had to blank it out. Ironically, it was the one piece of advice that had seemed to make sense at the time.

But now Paul Black's story was making her question this. Perhaps this was the time to be brave. To make a stand. About everything.

Alice's mouth tightened as she parked the car. With a jolt, she realised she hadn't even told her husband about the robbery. Was this the extent to which they had drifted apart? How crazy that she had tried to sort out the mess and give a statement to the police without ringing her own husband. Still, she probably wouldn't be able to get through anyway. He'd be lecturing.

"Hi. This is Daniel."

His smooth voice unexpectedly slid onto the line; a voice which belonged to someone who claimed to be her husband but was in fact, an adulterer. Despite their agreement to 'try again for Garth's sake', the questions wouldn't leave her mind. Where did they go? What had they said about her? Was it just sex or did Monica with her sharp face and Essex accent have something else that she wasn't able to give? Did they each have a private mobile number, just for each other?

Hurt combined with anger, now made her curt. "We've been burgled," she said on the phone. "Your desk is a bit of a mess." She felt a certain satisfaction in saying that. "And things have been smashed. Someone managed to get past the alarm." Then she added. "I did tell you it needed servicing."

There was a pause. Somehow Alice had expected Daniel to cut in. "And by the way, I've lodged a complaint against Phil Wright. The police are taking it seriously."

Without waiting for a reply, she slammed down the phone and, fired with courage, dialled her mother's number. Why not? Why stop now?

"Sheila speaking."

Her mother always answered the phone with an air of expectancy.

"Hi, Mum. How are you?"

"Oh. I was hoping it was Garth. He'd promised to come round."

"Well I'm sorry to disappoint you. How is *Uncle* Phil doing?"

She laced the word 'uncle' with disgust.

"Amazingly well." Her mother's voice was guarded. "Back home again. Incredible really."

"Good. So he'll be well enough to face police charges then."

"I beg your pardon?"

Alice hand tightened round her mobile. "I've filed a complaint against him, Mum. Just as he has against me, apparently."

"What are you talking about, you silly girl. You'll withdraw it immediately. Alice, do you hear me …"

Cutting her off, Alice turned the mobile to Off. Her mother would be frantically trying to ring her back now. But she couldn't. Maybe she'd never turn her phone on again. That was a thought.

Feeling oddly strong now, Alice put an hour's worth of parking into the machine and wandered off into the crowds. She should be at home tidying-up, she told herself, but it was strangely therapeutic to be somewhere where she shouldn't.

Pausing at the market stalls, she began to browse through a stack of CDs. Jazz. Blues. She used to love them all as a teenager but Daniel had different tastes. Serious tastes like classical composers whose scores left her feeling empty. He also refused to buy second-hand CDs on the grounds they might hurt his expensive music system. Perhaps it was time to ring the changes.

Handing over a five-pound note for an Ella Fitzgerald CD, her eye fell on a box of silver photograph frames. Perhaps she should buy some replacements as a start for the ones that had been stolen. This one looked rather nice. It actually had a silver mark on it.

Picking it up, Alice took the back off it to check it would click into place. She caught her breath. Inside, was a sticker. A school sticker. From Garth's old school. There was an order number too with the name Honeybun on it.

Surely this was the same photograph frame which had gone missing the other day. But where was the photograph? "Excuse me," she said. "Where did you get this from?"

The old man, manning the stall, shrugged. "Someone brought it in. Why?"

"Was it a young girl?"

His eyes grew cold. "Can't remember. Do you want it or not?"

"I want it."

Slowly, she headed back to the car, her possession wrapped in newspaper. Kayleigh had taken it. Of that, she was sure. And if Kayleigh could steal a photograph frame, she might also be responsible for the burglary. Perhaps the girl had found out the alarm code (which was, after all, written in the back of the kitchen diary) and told her mates. And what about her watch, which she still hadn't found? Had Kayleigh sold that too?

Oh God. How stupid, how bloody stupid, she had been. Kayleigh wasn't an innocent, wronged teenager. She was a viper. And one whom Alice had welcomed into the nest …

THIRTY-TWO

Kayleigh had had a heavy dead feeling in her chest ever since the burglary. Or, to be more precise, since she'd found the brass link from Callum's wrist chain.

How daft had she been? She should never have given him the address. It was obvious what had happened. He'd got tired of waiting for her and decided to do the place over.

Kayleigh's mind flitted back over the various sentences Callum had got through the years. Handling stolen goods. Drugs. Burglary. "I'm good at alarms," he'd once told her with a grin. "Needs a special touch, it does."

At the time, she'd been impressed but then again, she'd been a kid. Easily taken in by a big brother who gave her presents and looked after her when Mum was on a bender.

"I've changed," he said, when he came out of prison the time before this. Honest."

Mum had laughed at that but she, Kayleigh, had believed him. And now look where it had got her. Somehow Alice blamed her for the robbery: she'd seen that in her eyes when she'd come back yesterday from the city. She'd been all quiet and hardly spoke a word. Kayleigh could have wept. "I didn't mean it," she wanted to say. But if she did, the police might take her away.

Then Alice had called Garth into her little room next to the sitting room where she did all her china stuff and although Kayleigh had tried to listen in at the door, she couldn't hear anything. So she'd gone back to her room and played music really loud to block out the scared thumping inside her chest.

At dinner, no one spoke to her. Kayleigh, who had grown

used now to sitting round a table and making proper conversation, instead of making do with a bag of chips if she was lucky, felt really awkward.

Even Daniel, who had recently started to talk books with her (he'd been surprised that she'd read *Measure for Measure* and had laughed out loud when she'd told him that the plot was "rubbish"), ignored her.

"What's up?" she said to Garth when Alice told her that no thank you, she didn't need any help in clearing away.

He looked away. "Nothing."

"Yes there is." She went to tug at his sleeve but found herself holding the bare skin of his lower arm instead. They'd never touched before; only accidentally. Now, the feel of his flesh on her made Kayleigh feel giddy.

He felt the same. She could see it in his face. "Let's get out of here," he said in a low voice. Then, calling out, he yelled "Just taking Mungo for a walk, Mum."

Together, with the dog bounding ahead down the lane (she wasn't so scared of it now), they walked in silence.

Kayleigh wanted to say something but she could feel the tightness between them. Part of it was threatening. The other part held them together. In the end, she had to break it.

"You've got to tell me why no one's talking to me."

Garth threw her an expression that made her feel small again; like the time when the kids at school bullied her for being Mr Brown's pet. "Mum found a photograph frame in the market. It was hers. She recognised it from the markings. She thinks you're stealing stuff. And she thinks you were behind the burglary."

"No. NO."

Kayleigh broke into a run to keep up with Garth who was now striding ahead. "It's not true. I mean, yes it's true about the frame but I just did it to get my bus fare back."

Garth laughed. A nasty low laugh which scared her and reminded her a bit of Frankie. "Come on, Kayleigh. I've told you before. You're talking to someone who knows all the excuses. Don't you think I've used them myself? Money for the bus fare. Money for new shoes. Money for a school trip that didn't exist. Money for anything just so long as it helps you score."

"Score?"

"You know what I mean. Drugs."

"So you do take them?"

He nodded. "'Course. When you've got a habit like us, you've got to have ready cash, haven't you?'"

"I don't have a habit," said Kayleigh quietly.

"You could have fooled me. What were you doing in the park with that bloke then? And before you try to lie again, I know about it. Not just from Mum but from Seb too. Why else do you think he's trying it on with you? He thinks it's cool to be with someone who hung around with the tough guys. It turns him on."

There was something about the way Garth was looking at her with that cheeky smile, that suggested he felt the same. Kayleigh felt uneasy. "I needed to sell the frame to get home because I gave away the other money your mother gave me."

"Sure." Garth was throwing a ball to Mungo. "You gave it away. That was my favourite excuse. Who to? A wildlife charity? Or the *Big Issue* woman. I've used both of those."

"To my brother."

Garth stopped. "Your brother?"

She nodded, her mouth dry in her desperation to explain. Anything to show Garth – and his parents – that she wasn't what they thought she was. "Callum. He's my half-brother, actually and he's older than me. He's been in and out of prison and he's out now but he's broken his parole. Callum needed my help or else he'll go back to prison."

"So you gave him our address," said Garth slowly.

"I didn't know he was going to steal stuff."

He laughed. "Don't be so naïve."

She grabbed his arm again. "I didn't mean to, honest. I love living here. I like Alice. Your dad …"

He pushed her away. "Don't. He's a prat."

"I know," she said defensively. "I don't like the way he treats your mum."

Until then, she hadn't realised how much she meant that.

331

Only a few days ago, she'd felt jealous of Alice; wanting the things that she had. But now Alice didn't trust her, Kayleigh felt lost. Abandoned. It was like losing a mother all over again. Somehow she had to build up that trust again.

And the only way to do it was through her son. To tell him everything. "There's something else, too," she added. She took his hand, lacing her fingers through his. He didn't pull away which was a good sign. "It's not nice but I need to tell you."

"What?"

"Your mum was abused when she was a kid."

Garth gave a loud splutter. "You must be mad."

"No." She held on to his hand tightly. "It's why she gave evidence at my case. She said someone had to stand up to bullies."

They were standing so close now that she could smell his breath. "Who abused her?" said Garth in a low dangerous voice.

Kayleigh's skin began to prickle. "Someone called Uncle Phil. I don't know much more. But she did say that her mum wouldn't believe her." She looked away. "That's the kind of thing *my* mum would say."

Garth had gone very red. "Uncle Phil? Uncle *Phil?* That's Gran's friend. I'm met him. At her place. Shit. I've got to talk to Mum."

"No." Kayleigh began to panic. "She told me that in confidence."

"Too bad."

He was walking determinedly back to the house, shaking Kayleigh off. She shouldn't have told him. She should have kept her big mouth shut.

"Go to your room," he said when they reached the back door. "I need time with my mother. His eyes hardened. "Without anyone else."

He didn't want her. Just as Frankie hadn't wanted her any more. Or Mum. Or Marlene.

Crawling into bed, Kayleigh pulled the covers up over her head. Then she began to hear the voices. Raised voices. Angry ones that reminded her of the voices through the wall between hers and Mum's.

"You should have told me."

That sounded like Garth.

"I'm taking action against him."

That was Alice.

"Don't be so daft. It's too late. You'll be a laughing stock."

That was Daniel.

"How can you say that, Dad? He's got to pay for what he did."

Garth.

"You won't be able to prove it."

Daniel.

"You don't believe me, do you?"

Alice.

It wasn't fair! Why was it that people believed you when you told lies and didn't believe you when you told the truth?

Kayleigh wanted to run out there and tell Alice to tell her sodding husband where to get off. But Garth had told her to keep out. Family only, he had said. That had hurt.

For a bit, she'd been able to kid herself that she was family.

Finally, the voices stopped. Had they hurt each other? A couple next to Mum's flat had stabbed each other to death a few years ago after a row. It had been before they'd moved in but people still spoke about it.

Kayleigh lay still. If she didn't hear anything in half an hour, she'd go out there. Check everything was all right. After all, she was responsible, wasn't she? If she hadn't said anything, Garth would have been none the wiser.

What you don't know, won't hurt you. Mr Brown used to say that. Then again, you couldn't trust what he said. Not after what she'd seen.

Then the door opened.

"Kayleigh?"

It was Garth. He was crying.

Kayleigh opened up the duvet to let him in. It seemed natural. He lay there, his head against her shoulder, shaking. "My fucking father doesn't want her to go to court."

"Of course he doesn't." Kayleigh stroked his head like a baby. "But as long as you're behind her, it's all right."

"But I'm scared she's going to get hurt." Garth raised his head and she could see his eyes were red and raw. "Dad could be right. She might not be able to cope if she has to stand up there and tell them what happened. And even then this horrible old man will probably lie."

He shook again. A huge judder that sent waves through them both.

"We could go and see him," Kayleigh heard herself saying. "Make him tell the truth."

Even as she said it, she realised this was daft. How could they make him?

"You're right." Garth stopped stroking her head. She felt bereft. "We'll go right now."

He was buzzing. She could feel it. Maybe he was on something.

"Wait until the morning." She drew his hand down below her waist. She needed to distract him.

"Maybe."

Sensing his hesitation, she put his fingers inside her.

Instantly, she sensed his interest. "I'm sorry," he mumbled. "I didn't mean to sound off at you earlier."

He still liked her!

"That's OK."

Taking his other hand, she cupped it across her breast.

"You're so beautiful," he murmured thickly.

Beautiful? Kayleigh's heart sang. Right at this moment, she would do anything for him. Anything.

"I need you," he murmured again. "It's been such crap. The prison. Mum. Dad."

"But not me?"

He paused for a second and looked down at her. "No, Kayleigh. Not you. You're brilliant."

And then he entered her.

It didn't hurt like it had with Frankie.

"I love you," she gasped as the waves overtook her.

"I love you too."

But he was crying at the same time.

"Help me, Kayleigh. Help me get revenge on the bastard."

334

They had to do it fast, said Garth. She wasn't to worry about the silver frame. He'd make up some excuse to his mum to get her off the hook. And no, he wouldn't blab about Callum. Not if Kayleigh helped him.

They needed to go now. Before anyone woke up.

He said all this the next morning, as soon as they woke. Part of her wanted to have a shower. The other part hadn't wanted to wash him off.

"How do you know where this Uncle Phil lives?" she whispered.

"I texted Gran. Said I wanted to send him a get well card." Garth snorted. "She believed me. Said I was a nice boy." His mouth tightened. "I can't believe she didn't take Mum seriously. But she's always been hard on her. I thought it was just her generation."

Kayleigh wished he'd stop talking about his grandmother and tell her, instead, how lovely it had been in bed last night. Had he forgotten already?

It took ages to get there. Garth drove fast, not talking. At times, she nodded off; it was still so early! Then she woke just as they stopped outside a pink and white building. Quite nice really. "It's a care home," said Garth. "Care!" He spat out the word with disgust. "I'll show him what *care* is."

Kayleigh began to feel scared. "What are you going to do?"

"I don't know yet."

Defiantly he rang the bell. A nurse arrived in blue and white uniform. Instantly, Garth looked like the charming boy she'd first met. He was like her, she realised with a shock of recognition. He could be two people when he wanted. "We're here to see my great-uncle. Phil Wright. I'm sorry we didn't ring first but my fiancée and I were driving past and we decided to pay a spur of the moment visit."

Fiancée! Kayleigh felt a surge of excitement. Garth wanted to marry her! She could move into the house and be part of the family. Alice would forgive her and …

"We shouldn't really allow it as visiting hours aren't until this afternoon." The nurse beamed at him. "But poor Phil has been a bit under the weather recently. Might do him the world of good."

"Thank you."

Together they followed her down a corridor, stinking of antiseptic, and into a side room. Kayleigh tried to keep quiet but couldn't stop the gasp escaping from her horrified mouth.

The little old man sitting up in bed was shrivelled. His head was bald with brown spots on it and there was saliva dribbling down from his maroon mouth. "Visitor for you!" chirped the nurse. "Just ten minutes, mind. Don't want to overtire you, do we?"

"Who are you?"

The old man's words were blurred. Confused.

Garth knelt next to him. His voice might sound gentle, Kayleigh thought, but his eyes were glittering with fury.

"Alice's son."

"*Alice?*" The old man glared. "Get out. Don't you think I've got enough trouble with this?"

His shaking hand fumbled under the pillow for a brown envelope.

Garth pulled out the letter, read it and tossed it to her.

Bloody hell. It was a court summons. She'd seen enough of these for Callum over the years.

"It was all so long ago," whimpered the old man. "But it wasn't my fault. She came to see me, you know and she looked so pretty. Just like her mother."

His words came out in great gasps.

"What do you mean?" asked Garth in a low dangerous voice. Kayleigh shivered.

"Her mother. Sheila. We had an understanding. Went on for years. My wife … didn't know. Then Sheila tried to break it off after her husband had a heart attack. Felt guilty, she said. So I tried to show her what she was missing. Tried it on with her daughter to make her jealous."

"You did *what*?"

The old man's eyes misted. "I didn't mean any harm. Don't you think I've felt bad about it all these years? And now I'm scared. Not because of that bit of paper. But because soon I'm going to die and then I'll have to account for what I did."

He spat out the words. "It's all right for you kids. You think you do it right. But your mother was asking for it. Why do you think she wore a low-cut top?"

"SHUT UP. SHUT UP!"

Kayleigh gasped with horror as Garth grabbed one of the pillows from behind the old man's back.

"What are you doing?"

Struggling, she tried pull it away but Garth was too strong. The old man was mewing like a kitten. His arms beat weakly. It was like watching an injured bird. Then the arms flopped to the side of the bed. The mewing stopped. The pillow fell to the ground.

In horrified silence they looked at each other.

The old man was lying there as though asleep. Maybe he *was* asleep, thought Kayleigh desperately. Perhaps he'd just nodded off. Old people did that, didn't they?

"Time up," chirped the nurse, bouncing in. Then her eyes took in the old man lying there and the pillow on the floor.

"What have you done?" she whispered.

Kayleigh looked at Garth. His eyes were full of tears.

"He hurt my mother." His tone was defiantly shaky. "I'd do anything for the people I love."

I love you, Kayleigh.

This is my fiancée.

So he would do anything for her too. Just as she would for him. Then she thought of Alice, who had been so kind to her.

Alice, whom she'd wronged, by telling Callum about the house. Alice who had risked her own reputation in court so Frankie could get what he deserved. Alice who had introduced her to Garth. Alice who'd been more like a mum than her real one had ever been.

Suddenly, Kayleigh realised she hadn't repaid her very well. She shouldn't have nicked that stuff or told Callum about the house.

But this was her way out! Her chance to make up for everything. Because if she could take the blame for Garth, both mother and son would both love her for ever.

"Actually," she said clearly, turning to the nurse. "*I* did it."

THIRTY-THREE

Alice had been unable to sleep. How could Kayleigh have betrayed her like that? The girl had clearly told her brother about the house. She could see it now. Lots of antiques. Silver. That sort of thing. There for the taking. Why should this wealthy couple have it all?

So Daniel had been right after all. But not about the other thing. Not about her determination to take Phil to court. "I don't want to see you being made a fool of, in court," Daniel had said fiercely, before turning his back on her in bed last night. "How can you prove something that happened over twenty years ago?"

He'd faltered. "Besides, you might be considered to be unreliable …"

"Unreliable?" She'd sat up in bed, switching on the side light so she could see him face to face. His eyes had winced at the sudden brightness. "You're a fine one to talk about being unreliable."

Just then, they heard firm, heavy footsteps coming down the landing. "Garth," said Daniel warningly.

But the footsteps had continued past their son's room. There was the distinctive creak of the guest room door opening and shutting. Then low murmuring followed by the unmistakable sound of something more intimate. Murmurings. Gasps of pleasure. Small at first and then louder.

"Satisfied?" said Daniel.

She shook her head. "How can you be so nasty?"

"How can you be so naïve? You've taken in a teenager with

a record who might or might not have had something to do with the burglary. And now she's having it off with our son."

"You're jealous! I can tell from your voice."

Daniel gave her a sad look. "Jealous? No. Envious, maybe. A man has needs, Alice. For nearly twenty years, you and I haven't slept together. And I'm not counting lying next to each other in bed. Do you honestly think that's normal?"

The light was too honest. Turning it off, she slid down under the covers, putting them over her head. "If it wasn't for Phil, I would have been normal," she whispered.

"What did you say?"

Her husband's voice was hard.

"It doesn't matter."

But it did. She would take him to court, vowed Alice. It didn't matter how old Phil was. He had to pay.

Daniel's slow steady breathing showed he'd managed to fall asleep soon after the argument. If only she could do the same. But something was beginning to niggle away at her inside. A force which was – how odd! – encouraging her to explore herself. To rhythmically move up and down; silently, so as not to wake Daniel. To find, to her surprise, that her body had taken on a life of her own. A rhythmical pulsing down below. Short, sharp breathing that surely didn't belong to her. A wave which took her with it, filling her with … with pleasure? Really?

Kayleigh had been right, Alice, thought sleepily as she fell into a lovely peaceful space. Sex – even with yourself – did make you feel powerful. If she could enjoy what she'd just experienced, maybe she was getting stronger.

Meanwhile Phil Wright still had to pay.

Because it had taken so long to fall asleep, Alice woke much later than she normally did. Nearly ten o'clock! Mungo would be desperate.

Then all the events of last night came flooding back with a low horrible thud. Looking across the bed for Daniel, she saw with relief that his side was empty and his shoes (always a well-polished brogue) were gone from their usual place beside the bed.

Good. So she'd escaped a sullen husband at breakfast. He must have gone to the college or maybe to Monica. Strangely, the prospect of the latter didn't hurt as much as it should.

Then she remembered something else. Garth sneaking into Kayleigh's room. Kayleigh, the thief; something she would have tackled her about last night if it hadn't been for the row over Phil.

Quickly slipping on her jogging bottoms, she hovered outside her son's room. She needed to talk to him. Tell him what he was letting himself in for with that girl. Nervously, she opened the door.

Empty.

So Kayleigh was still with Garth in the guest room.

If it was anyone else, she would have told herself that Garth was old enough to have a girlfriend sleeping over. But Kayleigh wasn't their type. It wasn't the correct thing to say yet it was true. She might be surprisingly well-read but she had a record. She'd been in care. She stole things. Alice had only taken her in out of pity and because she'd wanted to give her the second chance that she, Alice, had been denied.

Now this was the consequence.

"You've only got yourself to blame," Alice told herself as she put on Mungo's lead and walked out across the lawn towards the sea. "You've tried to make things right but really, maybe that's impossible."

Perhaps that applied to her as well as Kayleigh. Despite her fierce words last night, she actually felt sick with apprehension at the prospect of taking the stand in court against an old man.

As if on cue, her mobile rang with her mother's name on the screen. Maybe if she ignored it, it would go away. No. It was ringing a second time.

"Alice? I just can't believe you're actually going ahead with this case against poor Phil. Daniel's just called me. He's worried too. Why didn't you tell me?"

Holding the phone away from her ear, Alice made her way down the slope towards the beach. Mungo was already racing ahead. It must be nice to be a dog, she suddenly thought. No real worries apart from when you were going to be fed and walked.

"I didn't tell you because I knew you wouldn't approve."

"He's an old man, Alice. How can you put him through it? Besides, it's not really his fault …"

Her voice tailed away.

"Then whose fault is it, Mum?" demanded Alice. "He might be old but he's ruined my life."

"You're so hard! Did you know that your own son …"

She cut her off; too late, wondering what Mum had been going to say about Garth. No doubt she'd find out soon enough but at the moment it wasn't important. Turning the phone to Off, she tried to concentrate on the thoughts whirling round her head.

By the time she came back to the house, with a wet but happy Mungo alongside her, Alice felt more in charge of herself. Despite that argument with Daniel last night, she would definitely go ahead with the case against Phil. She would kindly but firmly tell Kayleigh that she knew she'd stolen the silver frame and that this was her chance to confess about any involvement with the burglary before she told the police. And she would tell Daniel that she wanted to start again. Somehow, for the sake of the family, they had to put Monica behind them.

Maybe she'd have some counselling to help.

The phone rang as she came through the back door. "Wait," she instructed Mungo whose paws needed wiping. She picked up the handset noticing that the house was still quiet. So Kayleigh and her son were still in bed … Some rules needed to be set round here. They both needed summer jobs for a start.

"Yes?"

"It's Brian. We have a problem, I'm afraid."

"But they've released him! They can't go back on their word."

Brian's serious voice cut in. "It's not South America this time. It's to do with a Phil Wright."

Alice went cold. Paul Black had said the Crown Prosecution would handle her case. How did Brian know about it? Of course. Janice. She had spilt the beans even though she'd said it was confidential.

"Janice had no right," she began.

"Janice?" Brian sounded genuinely surprised. "Janice hasn't got anything to do with it. Listen, Alice. I need you to prepare yourself. I've had a phone call from Garth. He couldn't get hold of you and he didn't want to ring his father. Kayleigh's been arrested. For murder."

This couldn't be happening. Dazed, Alice listened to the story – as far as Brian knew it – while he drove her to the police station.

"Garth is trying to take the blame. He says it was him. But Kayleigh says it's her."

His lips tightened. "I know who my money would be on. Janice has told me a bit about this girl and I have to say that it sounds like you've taken on more than you can chew."

He reached out and patted her knee. It seemed a peculiarly intimate gesture, given that he was talking in the role of her lawyer. Briefly, Alice thought of Janice's admission that they'd gone through a difficult patch. Stiffly, she moved out of reach.

"What were they doing at Phil's nursing home, anyway?"

But instinctively, Alice knew. The girl had either murdered – or got involved with the murder – for *her*.

"*When I like someone, I'll do anything for them. Anything at all.*" Wasn't that what she'd said on the beach, on the day Alice had given evidence against Frankie? The girl's strength of feeling had startled her. Scared her, to be honest.

"Garth wanted to fight your battle." Brian shook his head. "He told me about it. I'm sorry, Alice. It sounds as though you went through a lot as a teenager."

Victoria. Victoria ...

"So has Kayleigh," she found herself saying.

"I'm afraid," replied Brian pulling up outside the police station, "the law may not be so ready to see that as an excuse for murder. However, we do have one thing in our favour. Turns out that your son had the presence of mind to record Phil's confession on his mobile. We've got it safe." His face turned to hers with compassion. "He admitted to raping you, Alice."

But at what price? Shivering, she got out, and allowed Brian to steady her elbow as they made their way in. Paul! He was there. Uncomfortably, she watched his eyes take in Brian's hand on her elbow.

She moved away.

"Mum."

She hadn't seen Garth, sitting on a chair. Springing up, he flung his arms around her. She breathed him in. Her boy. Her man. The one good thing to have come out of her marriage.

"I did it but they won't believe me,"

"Don't say any more," snapped Brian.

"Where is Kayleigh? Can we see her?"

Paul's eyes were on hers. The same hypnotic blue gaze. Warm this time with a look that said "*I'm here for you.*" Unless she was imagining it.

"She's waiting for the duty solicitor."

Alice looked at Brian. "I'd like you to take on her case."

He nodded. "Do you want to clear that with Daniel first?"

"No." If necessary, she'd pay for it out of her own money.

"Then I would like to see my new client," said Brian heavily.

"This way," said Paul. "Alice, could you stay here for a bit? There's something I need to talk to you about."

He sat her down in an armchair with a wooden frame. It was more comfortable than the steel-rimmed ones in the waiting room. Then he gave her a cup of tea in a proper china cup and saucer.

"The thing is," he said steadily, "that I genuinely don't think Kayleigh did it."

That lump of fear which had formed in her chest when Brian had first phoned came back.

"What do you mean?"

"Well, the nurse swears that the pillow was in Kayleigh's hands. But I've seen enough of people over the years to know when they're guilty. And I don't think she is."

She could hardly get the words out. "You think it was Garth?"

344

"She's protecting him," he said, ignoring her question. "She adores him. Anyone can see that. And I suspect he has a thing for her too."

Slowly, she nodded. "I know."

Paul put down his mug. "When people have low esteem, they will do things for others – extraordinary things sometimes – to win approval. I think that's what Kayleigh's doing."

"But if you're right and it's Garth, he'll go to prison for murder?"

His eyes were on hers. "Maybe manslaughter. It will be argued that he did it out of love for you."

"So it's my fault again?"

He put a hand on hers. A hand that surely shouldn't be there. "I can't bear to see you beating yourself up like this, Alice."

Was this an act? And if so, why did her body tingle like this?

"What can I do?"

"Talk to her. Wait until your lawyer friend has finished and then talk to her."

He said the 'lawyer friend' bit with a touch of sharpness. Was he jealous? No. That was ridiculous.

"My husband has been having an affair with someone from my book club." She blurted out the words before knowing it.

An expression of surprise flitted across his face.

"I'm sorry."

"I'm going to try to make a go of my marriage."

Why was she telling him this? Was it a warning? As if there was any need for one.

He nodded. Briefly. Disappointedly?

"You've got a lot going on in your life at the moment, Alice. When that was happening to me, someone told me to do the next thing first." He smiled. A lovely comforting warm smile. "It's another way of saying 'One step at a time' but it helped."

"Thanks." She drained the tea. It felt sweet. Comforting. Someone had put sugar in it even though she didn't normally take it. There was a knock on the door and a voice. "The lawyer's finished now."

Paul looked at Alice meaningfully. "Are you ready?"

345

"There's something else." She could hear Victoria's voice in her head. *Tell him, Mum. Tell him.*

"After … after what Phil did to me, I got pregnant." She closed her eyes, finally allowing herself to meet the past. The bit that really mattered.

Two months after her eighteenth birthday, Alice had had to face the truth. Her period was late. Which meant …

"Positive." The nurse at the student medical centre, had taken her into a side room to give her the news and hand her a box of tissues. "No doubt about it, love. You're pregnant." She put a motherly arm around her. "Now, now. Don't panic. I know it seems the end of the world in your first year but there are things that can be done." Her eyes were milky with sympathy. "Is your boyfriend likely to stand by you?"

Alice had shaken her head vigorously. "He's not my boyfriend." Pausing, she tried to tell the nice nurse what had happened but failed. Maybe she'd blame her. Think that Alice had been responsible.

"Ah, it's over, is it?" The nurse sucked in her breath. "Well, you have other options. There's lots of help here for single mothers and …"

"I don't know what to do." Alice heard her voice ringing out. "I can't have this … this man's baby. " She shook with sobs. "But I don't want to get rid of a life."

Someone was holding her hand. Not the nurse. That had been years ago. Not Daniel because she'd been too ashamed to tell him. But Paul. Paul Black who had nothing to gain this time from her confession. Paul whose eyes were wet with understanding.

"What did you do?" he asked quietly.

She nodded, swallowing back the tears in an attempt to sound lucid. "I made the mistake of asking Mum's advice. She had to accept Phil had … had sex with me then, although she still said it was my fault; that I must have led him on. She told me that I had no choice. A baby would ruin my life and Dad's too. He was beginning to have chest pains then … I couldn't add to that. I wanted to consider adoption but Mum persuaded me it would be difficult to hide a pregnancy.

" 'Far better to get rid of it and wait until you're married to someone,' " she said. At the time, it seemed to make sense. I was so young … I didn't know what I was doing."

Alice closed her eyes. "Afterwards, I tried not to think about it. But then I started seeing prams in the street, when I'd never noticed them before. Someone in my year got pregnant and I began to wonder what would have happened if I'd kept my own baby."

She opened her eyes and smiled wistfully. "In my head, I knew it had been a girl. Victoria, I would have called her. Finally, I couldn't cope with all the stuff going round my head. So I dropped out of my course and started work."

"That's how you met your husband."

Paul said the word stiffly.

"Yes. You remember."

"Alice, I remember everything you say."

"Because you're a policeman?"

"Yes. And because …"

He stopped.

She waited but to her relief or disappointment – Alice couldn't decide which – he said nothing. So she went on. "I've never told anyone else before."

"Then I'm flattered." His hands dropped hers. "You have to decide something now, Alice."

Her heart fluttered.

"Do you want to include this in your statement?"

Yes. No. Yes. But not before she'd done something she should have done a long time ago. Daniel wasn't the only one who had hidden things. Now was the time to make amends.

Or try to.

THIRTY-FOUR

"I told you. I did it. I put the pillow over his face."

Kayleigh tried to make herself sound like a woman in a film she'd seen once with Marlene. Her grandmother had taken them and had chewed toffees all the way through.

The rustle of the sweet papers had made it difficult to hear and even now Kayleigh didn't know why the character in the film had said she'd killed the man in question. It had been with a knife, rather than a pillow. But she could remember the hard way the actress had sounded and her unrepentant facial expression.

So Kayleigh tried to copy that too even though she still felt shaky after the lawyer's probing questions and patronising manner.

"Why?" asked Alice, who was sitting next to her. But she said it in a nice way. One that almost made Kayleigh want to tell the truth.

"It was like I just said to your posh lawyer friend. I did it for you. I remembered the name from when we talked on the beach. Uncle Phil, you'd said. Then I heard you arguing with your husband about him. I could see he was still upsetting you so I decided to do something about it because you've been good to me. Garth found out where he lived from your mum – he pretended he wanted to send a get well card – so I made him drive me there."

It sounded real, even to her.

Alice leaned forward and took her hands. Was this what it would be like to have a real mum who loved you? "Kayleigh, sometimes when we care for someone, we try to protect them. I think … I think you have learned to care for Garth and that you are protecting him now."

"Why?" Kayleigh heard her words ring out sharply. "Why do you think that?"

"Because my son told me what really happened."

Kayleigh felt cold even though Alice's hot hands were still there. "Then he's lying."

Alice leaned back in her chair and closed her eyes briefly before opening them again. Her mascara was smudged, Kayleigh noticed. Marlene had taught her a good trick to deal with that. "You can't buy someone's love, Kayleigh," added Alice softly.

Standing up, Kayleigh kicked the table. Shocked, she looked down at her foot as though someone else had done it. "I'm not. How dare you say that?"

"Because I understand." Alice looked away. "I tried to buy my husband's love by flattering him when we met. I told him that I liked the same kind of books he read and the same kind of music. I also made him want me even though …"

Her voice tailed away but Kayleigh knew what she meant. "Even though you didn't fancy him?"

Alice gave a half-smile. "Something like that. The thing is, Kayleigh, that you have to be honest. Otherwise, the lies will eat you away."

Kayleigh thought about Mr Brown in the classroom with the woman who wasn't his wife. Were his fibs eating him away? It hadn't looked like it.

"Don't you want me to save Garth from going to prison?" she demanded disbelievingly. "Blokes on my estate get loads of money for doing that."

Alice shook her head. "Not if my son really did it." Then she looked away but not before Kayleigh saw a tear slide down her cheek. "If anyone should go to prison, it ought to be me."

"No." Kayleigh reached out for her. "You're a good person. You gave me a home. You took me in and I … I wasn't truthful to you. I stole something."

Alice looked sad. "I know."

"But it wasn't what you thought. I stole a frame to buy my fare home 'cos I gave the money you gave me, to Callum."

Alice frowned. "I don't understand."

So Garth hadn't told her then.

"He's my brother. Half-brother really. He saw me in the centre and said I had to get him some money. He'd just come out of prison, you see, and he was in trouble again."

Kayleigh felt sick. Alice was looking at her in a way that suggested she despised her. "So you helped him burgle our house?"

"No. I didn't know he was going to do it. But I did give him the name of the house. I'm really sorry."

Alice was shaking her head. "It doesn't matter any more. Not compared with this." Then her voice hardened. "We've all done things we shouldn't have done, Kayleigh. And yes, if I'm honest, I would rather you went to prison than my son. But I also know that I would never be able to find peace in myself if you took the blame. And nor would Garth. So if you really love him, you'll tell us what really happened."

Kayleigh hesitated. She'd told her story so many times, to the police and to that lawyer, that she could almost feel that pillow in her hand. Hear the old man's mewing as she pressed it down over his face.

"I don't know," she said, turning away. "I don't know nothing any more. I can't properly remember."

When she came out, Daniel was waiting in the interview waiting room with Garth. So too was Brian. Daniel's face was stone. "I told you not to let that girl into our house."

"Daniel." Brian's tone was mildly reproachful. "Recriminations aren't going to help."

"Aren't they? What will help then?"

"Shut up, Dad." Garth enveloped her in a big hug. "Mum's had enough to cope with all these years."

Daniel stood up and began pacing round the room. "I don't know what to believe any more."

Phil Wright got me pregnant, Daniel! It was on the tip of her tongue to say so. But now they were face to face, she began to

351

doubt her earlier resolution to come clean. It might only make things worse. He might not believe her. Or he'd think even worse of her than he did already.

"Calm down everyone." Brian had his lawyer voice on. "We all need to take stock here and ..."

He stopped as the door swung open. Alice's heart began to thud. Paul Black wasn't looking at her. He was addressing Brian. But he wanted to look at her.

She just knew it.

"A new witness has come forward," he said.

Alice's heart quickened. Garth, she noticed, looked scared. "Someone saw what happened?"

"Not for the recent incident." He still faced Brian. "For the complaint which Mrs Honeybun made about an alleged rape twenty-three years ago."

Alice's heart caught in her throat.

"Who?" she asked hoarsely. "Who?"

Finally, he turned to her. "We've been making our own enquiries; interviewing people who knew the Wrights. A Mrs Patricia Cross was their cleaner at the time. She saw what happened and she's prepared to testify that Phil Wright abused you. She also claims she was bought off by the man and that it's been weighing on her conscience for years."

"But I didn't see anyone," Alice began to say, just as Daniel interrupted.

"Great. But how's that going to help my son? You've got to see that he's just pretending to have smothered Phil Wright out of a misguided sense of loyalty towards this girl."

"I *did* ..." began Garth.

"Don't say anything," said Brian quickly. Then he turned to Daniel first and then Alice. "If I'm not mistaken, this new piece of evidence might make all the difference. Whoever murdered Phil Wright could argue they did so out of loyalty to the rape victim."

He coughed delicately. "Especially if the victim is the mother of the accused. The tape isn't enough on its own because Phil Wright is a sick man. It could be argued that he made his confession when he wasn't of sound mind."

352

Alice groaned.

"No. It's not as black as it sounds. Now we have a witness, the tape assumes greater significance. The two pieces of evidence combined, might be enough to reduce the sentence. Substantially."

THIRTY-FIVE

"See!" said the woman in the white coat. "Baby's sucking her thumb!"

Kayleigh gripped Alice's hand as they both stared at the screen in awe.

"*Her?*" she squeaked.

The woman who'd smeared all that gooey stuff on her stomach, made a cross sound with herself. "Sorry. I should have asked if you wanted to know."

"Yes," said Kayleigh, vigorously. "I did, didn't I? I told you that on the way, Alice." Excitement racing up through her throat. She was having a daughter. A girl! A doll she could dress up and teach her stuff like how not to do daft things with men who didn't really care for you. A real person who would love her for ever.

Then she looked up at Alice, suddenly unsure. "Can we ring the prison to get them to tell Garth? Or should we wait till visiting time?"

A scared look flitted across the face of the woman who was doing the scan. A radiographer, she was called. That's what it had said on the door. "It's OK," Kayleigh added hastily. "My partner's a really good bloke. He just …"

Alice put a hand on her shoulder. "Let's leave it at that, shall we, Kayleigh?" She was still looking at the screen. "It's amazing. A miracle."

Her eyes were wet. She cared, Kayleigh realised. Really cared. She'd waited until visiting time before telling Garth that her period was really, really late. He couldn't run off, she told herself. 'Cos he was already in prison, waiting for his case to be heard.

But he'd been pleased. Really pleased. "That's amazing," he'd breathed, leaning across to give her a seriously heavy snog until one of the prison officers stopped them. "That's fucking fantastic. I quite fancy being a dad. It will make me change my ways. Have you told Mum?"

At first, Kayleigh had been frightened of that. What would she do if Alice threw her out? They'd only just moved out of that big cold house and into a sweet little cottage near the sea front. It was really nice, just the two of them.

Daniel was welcome to Monica, Alice kept saying. He'd done her a favour. "So much for him saying he didn't love her," she told Kayleigh. "Still, at least I know where I stand now."

Kayleigh liked it when Alice confided in her. It made her feel important. Respected.

So she'd taken the plunge, after talking to Garth, and told her about the kid. Kayleigh had thought she might go mad. But instead, Alice's face had lit up in a way she'd never seen before. "A new life," she kept repeating. "A new life."

POSTSCRIPT

It hadn't been what Kayleigh had been expecting. Then again, everything that had happened in the last few months had been weird. First there had been Garth who had told her that if she didn't tell the truth about what had really happened to the old man in the nursing home bed, they couldn't have a future together.

"You've got to stop saying you killed him," he'd told her. "I need you to back me up, to agree that I did it."

She hadn't been sure of that but then he'd added a sentence which she would remember for the rest of her life. "Will you wait for me, until I'm out?"

"You really want me to?" she'd asked, hardly daring to believe this was possible.

He'd nodded, stroking her hair. Alice had been right even though it had taken Kayleigh a while to get used to a shorter style. A bob *did* suit her. Everyone said so. She'd even been approached in the street the other day by a scout who wanted a model for some pregnancy magazine. But she'd turned down the offer so she could concentrate on her studies.

"You're different, Kayleigh. You understand me, like no one else." Then he pressed his lips against her forehead. "Besides, we've been through stuff together that no one else has."

Then there had been the murder trial which was horrible. Alice had cried in the witness stand when the lawyers had brought up all that stuff about Phil Wright raping her.

Lots of other people in court had cried when the cleaner woman told the court what had happened. "I only came round

357

to get my money. I have a key you see and I didn't normally go round on a Saturday so he wouldn't have been expecting me, but Mrs Wright had agreed to pay me early. So I let myself in and that's when I saw him. Forcing herself on to that poor girl. I should have said something. I know I should have done. But I was that shocked, I went and hid. After she'd gone, I came out and told him what I saw. I know I shouldn't have taken the money he gave me but I was desperate. And scared. Haunted me for years, it has. So when I read about the case in the paper, I felt I had to come forward. Better late than ever, you know …"

And there'd been more tears when Alice had described how she'd got pregnant and she'd had an abortion out of fear. "I'm sure it was a girl," she kept saying. "I've felt guilty ever since."

How bloody unfair. Kayleigh's hands crept protectively round her own stomach. No wonder Alice had been so supportive. She was a good woman. Nicer than Kayleigh deserved. But she'd show her. She'd do everything she could to make Alice's life better.

Mrs Honeybun's mother was in court too. There was something about a letter which she'd given Alice that day but Kayleigh didn't really understand that bit. She'd been too engrossed looking at the jury, hoping they might let Garth off.

When he got six years, she'd burst into tears.

"It could have been more," the lawyer kept saying outside the court. "Better than I had hoped for, to be honest."

Alice had been pale and quiet. Daniel stood some way off from her.

"Can we go and see him soon?" Kayleigh asked.

Daniel glared at her. "The best thing you can do is stay out of our lives."

She'd felt really small then.

"Actually," said Alice. "Garth told me that if he was sent to prison, I was to bring Kayleigh with us to visit."

Her heart had leaped at that but then Daniel had then given Alice a really nasty look. "Us?" he repeated. "You really think there's an *us* still? You hid things from me Alice. You didn't tell me about the abortion."

"You hid things from me too," Alice had whispered. "What about Monica?"

It was clear that things weren't great between them. "It's all right," she'd whispered, reaching out her hand to Alice. "I'll be there for you."

"And I'll be there for you too," Alice had said back.

It was true. They'd gone to court. Made it formal. Alice was allowed to look after Kayleigh until she was twenty-one now. Mum hadn't even bothered to turn up at the hearing. When Kayleigh had written to her, at Alice's suggestion, the envelope had come back with 'Not known at this address'.

To be honest, she hadn't been surprised.

As for Callum, she was beginning to wonder if she'd got him wrong too, like she had the others (apart from Garth of course). A proper brother wouldn't have got her into trouble, would he?

Kayleigh continued to stare at the screen. Not that any of this mattered any more, now there were two of them. Three, counting Alice. Maybe four if that policeman came back although none of them had seen him for a while. No. Make that three.

Three of them, waiting for Garth to come home.

"When you have a child," Alice had said with a strange look in her eyes, "you are never alone again. There will always be someone for you to love who, touch wood, will love you back. Whatever happens."

She couldn't wait!

When she was a mum, Kayleigh told herself, she was going to be the best one in the whole world. She just knew it.

"It's going to be a girl," said Alice down the phone. "A girl!"

She'd rung Janice as soon as she'd got back from the hospital and sent Kayleigh to have a lie down. "Isn't that exciting?"

"I don't get it." Her friend's voice was tight. "You really are thrilled about this girl having Garth's baby?"

"Of course I am."

"And how do you know that …"

359

"How do I know it's his?" Alice had asked herself this a few times and always come up with the same answer. "Because Kayleigh says it is and I believe her."

Janice made a despairing noise at the other end. "You're too trusting, Alice."

"Maybe."

For a few moments, Alice allowed herself to think about how she had trusted Daniel. How she'd believed him when he'd said the affair with Monica had started at the golf club dinner.

After the trial, when he had told her he didn't want to stay married any longer, he'd admitted that it had been going on for years. "What else was I meant to do?" he'd said angrily. "I'm a man, Not a monk. It wasn't as if you showed any interest."

In a funny way, she could see his point. It wasn't the act of sex that was important, Alice was beginning to understand. It was what it represented. Love. Respect. Attraction. Something that she'd like too.

At first, Daniel had blamed her for 'being deceitful' too. "*Why* didn't you tell me about the abortion?" he had demanded during the same horrid, turbulent argument.

"Because I felt dirty. When we had Garth, I kept looking at him and thinking of the baby I got rid of. That's why I couldn't cuddle or hold him. I felt too guilty."

To give Daniel his credit, he'd seemed to understand that. "I'm sorry," he'd said. "If you'd told me, it might have been different."

Would it, she wondered, looking at him. They'd never had anything in common, to be honest. Only a mutual desire to find a mate. There hadn't been the lust. The passion. Daniel had never aroused the feelings she'd had for Gordon, her first boyfriend; whom, ironically, she had never allowed to go further than a kiss. Nor had he precipitated the strange stirrings she now felt in the night as she lay, spread-eagled, alone in her new double bed.

Then there had been her mother. Alice had forgotten about the letter until her mother had been called as a witness. It had been the defence lawyer who had asked why she'd instructed Alice to go round that day.

"I needed her to take a note."

"And what was in it, that was so important?"

"None of your business."

But the judge had intervened. Told her mother that she had to answer.

"I told him I was breaking it off." Mum's voice had been so low that she'd barely heard it. "Phil and I had been … close. I felt guilty at betraying my husband, especially after he was ill."

"And you think that's why he abused your daughter – to get back at you."

Appalled, along with the rest of the court, Alice had watched her mother nod her head. "I'm sorry," she whispered.

"But you refused to believe your daughter when she told you she'd been raped," persisted the lawyer.

"I was scared," her mother had whispered. "I thought that if I allowed my daughter to make a complaint, the truth about Phil and me would come out. As for her being pregnant, I couldn't cope with that." She glared at the judge. "He was mine. It was inconceivable for my daughter to have my lover's child."

Alice had felt sick. How could a mother do that to her daughter? But according to Brian, her mother's evidence had had the effect of making the jury even more lenient towards Garth.

"Have you heard anything from Daniel?"

Janice's voice broke into her thoughts.

"Only that he and Monica are renting a cottage in Dartmoor." How odd. It didn't hurt as much as it should do, to say that. "Did I tell you that I've also promised to help Kayleigh find her father?"

Janice let out another *I-don't-believe-it* laugh at the other end. "That could open up a real bag of worms, couldn't it?"

"Maybe. Maybe not. But it's part of her moving-on process. Her social worker thinks so too."

"I have to say, Alice, I take my hat off to you but …"

The rest of Janice's voice was obliterated by the sound of a car pulling up outside and Mungo's frantic barking. "May I call you back? Someone's arrived and then we've got Visiting."

"You make it sound so normal," said Janice admiringly.

"Give Garth my best, won't you? Ask him if he'd like me to visit too."

"Thanks."

Normal, wondered Alice as she opened the front door. That wasn't how she'd describe the shock at going into a prison twice a week to visit her son. But she had to pretend it was normal, to reassure him as much as herself.

In reality, it terrified her. All that security. Being frisked. Asked questions. Sitting in a room with a real mixture of people; some of whom you might expect to find there and others whom you wouldn't. Seeing his scared face as the prisoners came in. Knowing that he was there because of *her*. There was nothing as strong, she had learned, as a son's sense of loyalty towards his mother.

"Hi," said the tall, good-looking man on the doorstep.

Paul? Paul Black?

It had been weeks since she'd seen him. She'd almost forgotten how he reminded her of a middle-aged Steve McQueen with that all-weather glow to his skin, that 'let's-go' look in his face, and the enthusiasm in those bright blue eyes. "Is this a convenient time?"

The formality of his words took away her initial surprise and, to be honest, excitement. Suddenly a curtain of awkwardness hung between them.

"I've been on a course," he added, falteringly.

"You don't have to explain," she said firmly.

"I want to."

"Why?" She felt powerful. Stronger than when she'd last saw him. "It's not as though you need me to give any more statements, is there?"

His eyes clouded. "Is that why you think I paid you attention?" He flushed. "More attention than I should have done, professionally."

Now it was her turn to flush. "I don't know."

There was another silence. Alice could feel that strength disappearing. Instead, she felt eighteen again.

Then he spoke. "This is nice." He waved towards the small, neatly laid-out cottage garden with its stone walls, wrought iron arch, and rows of wall flowers.

Gratefully, she seized the lifeline of normal conversation. "Thank you. I have to admit I miss the old house at times but I love being on the sea front."

When it all gets too much, she almost added, all she had to do was walk along the gravel beach and watch the waves come in and out. Riding whatever life threw at it. Just as she was finally learning to do.

It was the case that had done it. Not the one against Phil which she had hoped to wage; his death had cheated her of that. But the case against her own son. "*Murder is always wrong*," as she'd told *Charisma* magazine later in an exclusive feature. "*But never underestimate the bond between mother and child. My son wanted to avenge what had happened to me and although I don't approve of the way he did it, his actions have shown how people like Phil Wright and Frankie Miller have ruined women's lives.*"

The fee for the feature had, at her request, been donated to The Passage, a charity for the homeless.

What she hadn't added, because it was too private, was that Phil Wright's confession on tape – played to a stunned court – had shown that a teenage Alice had not been responsible for her abuse. The clearing of her name, in turn, had released an unseen switch inside; allowing her to become physical and responsive again. It was as if her body had had to wait for a formal condemnation of Phil Wright before it could move forward again; to take all the risks that a modern loving relationship demanded.

How ironic that she had Kayleigh to thank for that. If she'd never come across the 'girl in the park' as some of the papers had called her, none of this would have happened.

"How are you doing?"

Paul Black's deep, gravelly voice brought her sharply back to the present. Alice hesitated for a moment, taking in the blue eyes. The strong rugby nose. The cords. Open-necked shirt. All suggesting that he was off duty. Was this a social call or not, she wanted to ask. "How am I doing?" she repeated. "Better. Much better thanks."

There was another moment of silence but this time, it felt different. More like the type that was comfortable between friends. "I have to be honest," he said, eventually. "There was a reason for my visit."

She couldn't resist a joke. "You want me to be a witness again?"

He smiled. The laughter lines crinkled. "No. I think you've done enough of that. Actually, I've got some news."

"Good news?" She stood to one side, gesticulating that he should come in." Her heart quickened. "Is it about Garth's appeal?"

"Afraid not. Your solicitor will tell you about that, anyway."

"Of course."

"I've brought you this." He handed her a form. It was a list. "We've found some of your possessions – the ones from the burglary."

"Really?" She'd almost forgotten about that.

"The watch you mentioned wasn't there."

Alice felt herself go scarlet. "Actually, I found it during the move. Turned out I'd misplaced it, I'm afraid."

To think she'd blamed Kayleigh …

"No problem. It happens. We've got the man, too. Turns out he's Kayleigh's half-brother. Did you know that?"

Alice felt uneasy. "I knew the connection. Yes."

Those eyes turned cool. "And you didn't think of mentioning it?"

She felt a flutter of unease. "Briefly, yes. But so much has happened. My own situation … you know. It sort of slipped my mind."

He seemed to be silently evaluating her words. Take them or leave them, she wanted to say. This is me. The new Alice. The one who refuses to keep apologising or feel inferior any more. "So he'll be tried soon?"

"At some point. He's been remanded in custody."

Alice tilted her chin defiantly. "I'm not going to tell Kayleigh. Not yet. She's just had her second scan."

Paul Black looked surprised. "She's pregnant?"

"Yes. And yes, it's my son's."

"How do you feel about that?"

"Excited, actually. Happy even."

He was standing close to her. So close that they could almost touch.

"I get that."

She hadn't expected his approval. Instead, she'd been prepared for the sceptical or disapproving expressions that had appeared on Janice's and Brian's faces, not to mention her own husband's.

"She asked me to go to her first ante-natal class!" Alice heard her voice ring out. "It was wonderful. I felt more excited than I had done when … when I'd been expecting my own son."

Her voice dropped. "Do you think that's awful?"

Suddenly his opinion meant a great deal.

"Not at all. Not after what you've been through." He looked as though he was going to step even nearer before thinking better of it. "I know I asked you just now but how are you managing? Really."

His gaze, she noticed, left her and instead took in the low-beamed ceiling of the hall and beyond into the bright conservatory which had sold the cottage to her. "Better than I'd thought. I've even proved that I can paint a wall or two. And when I begin to have doubts in myself, I look at this."

Alice found herself leading her guest into the kitchen and pointing casually to the little plaque on the wall.

'A woman is like a teabag. You never know how strong she is until you put her in hot water.'

He laughed. "I like that. Is that how you feel? Strong?"

"Sometimes." She turned her back, looking for the ordinary tea. Paul Black's tastes didn't run to Russian Caravan. That much she knew already.

He looked embarrassed. "I saw your friend Janice the other night. At a dinner party."

She stopped in her tracks, not sure whether to be more shocked by the fact that he was at the same dinner party as her friend or by Janice's failure to say anything.

"I went with a friend. Not a girlfriend. Just someone I know who wanted a plus one."

So he'd read her mind. How embarrassing! "Janice was surprised to see me too. But when she'd got over it and put me in a 'guest' category rather than the 'PC Plod brigade', she became quite chatty. In fact, she went as far as to say that you were an amazing person. I think her words were 'Not many people could go through what you have'."

Alice turned round. "I think we both know that's not true," she said quietly. "Anyway, I'm still going through it."

There was no need to say what. No need to talk about her mother whom she hadn't been able to speak to since the trial. Or about Garth who wasn't having an easy time of it in prison. Or of Daniel and the hurt that was still there. Even though they had never been right for each other, they shared a son. It was a cord that would be there for ever within a landscape of awkward future social situations (Garth's wedding, one day, perhaps?) which would have to be negotiated somehow.

"Your experiences will strengthen you," said Paul, studying her kitchen dresser carefully. She knew that trick. Concentrating on something helped check the emotions. "Challenges come in many forms."

"So I'm finding."

His blue eyes held hers. "I told the truth just now about being on a course. But I could have come round earlier. Instead, I felt … I needed … to give us … you … time."

He was nervous. The realisation made her excited. Hopeful. Scared.

"So tell me," he continued. "How do you feel? Really feel, I mean."

She could catch a whiff of something lemony now. After-shave perhaps? "I feel …" she paused for a moment, searching for the words. Then her eye fell on a cup which she had just mended for a woman whose son had given it to her before emigrating to New Zealand. "I feel there's a whole new world out there, waiting for me. All those lies. All that deceit. All that guilt. It's been wiped out although of course I still feel terrible about Garth. Inside. Because of me.

"He had a choice."

Paul Black was so near now, that they were almost sharing the same breath.

"We all have a choice. Alice, I probably shouldn't say this but ..."

"I'm not ready."

He stepped back, stung.

"I'm sorry. It's not the ... the physical bit." She flushed. "It's because I can see now that the only real love that matters is the one between mother and child. Don't you see? I may be just the grandmother – or 'nan' as Kayleigh puts it – but it's my chance to put things right. At last there's a baby in my life made from love. Not fear. Or lust. Or ... or rape. But a real love child. And I want to be a part of that."

He nodded. "I get that. I lost a child too, remember."

Of course he had. A son who had breathed and walked and talked and laughed.

"But do you know what else your friend Janice said to me at that dinner party?"

She shook her head.

"That she could see there was something between us. Yes. I know I'm being pushy here. And, frankly, I think Janice had had more than a bit too much to drink. But sometimes these things have to be said. I'm serious, Alice. We've got something. I can feel it and I know you can feel it too. Can we give it a chance? Take one step at a time?"

She hadn't expected this. Not so soon! Maybe at some point in the distant future. Maybe never. Maybe only in her head which, she had to confess, had played this scene more than once before. Yet now it was happening, she didn't know what to say. Could she, did she, really want to take such a gamble?. How did she know she'd changed? What if she wasn't – despite her hopes – able to let this kind, warm man touch her the way she hadn't been able to let Daniel do? And was it really possible to swap one relationship for another after so many years?

"I want to sit on the edge of the water with you," he said slowly, drawing her closer to him. Alice waited for her body to pull away.

"I want to eat fish and chips with you while the sun rises or sets."

Something began to tingle down her back.

"I want to be able to be silent with you without feeling one of us has to say something. And to say something that might sound mad to someone else but which you understand."

The warmth grew across her back. And down her arms, setting the little hairs on edge.

"I want to share the colours of the cliffs beyond the harbour and the way the sea sparkles at night as though thousands of little pin pricks are lighting it up."

"I like walking at night, too." Hers was barely a whisper but it was enough. As Paul's lips met hers – soft at first and then hard – there was a flash of an eighteen-year-old Gordon in her head, taking her back to a time before it had all gone wrong.

There were some things, she realised, which could never be seen or fully witnessed. Only felt, like this warm, all-enveloping yearning of desire that was taking over her body.

Paul Black might not last for ever, just as Kayleigh and Garth probably wouldn't last (although she, Alice, would always be there for the baby)

But along the way, she and this kind, warm funny man who boosted her confidence instead of putting her down, might help each other to move forward. And who knew? Some things did go on for eternity. You just never knew unless you tried them out.

"Are you ready to take a risk?" he murmured.

Her lips sought his. "Yes," she said with the determination and hope that had become part of the new Alice. "I am."

Katherine John

The Case Books of Wolf Mau

The Defeated Aristocrat

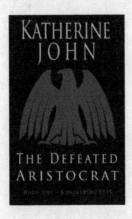

After spending the last months of the Great War as POWs, Wolf Mau and his fellow soldiers are relieved to be back in Germany. Their homeland is defeated, starving, and broken – they didn't expect a welcome home party. But neither did they anticipate murder ...

A killer is stalking the medieval streets of Konigsberg. A killer who specialises in kidnapping demobbed soldiers ... before torturing them using medieval methods and leaving their mutilated corpses in the city's red light district.

With senior police officials more concerned with politics than crime-solving, it falls to Wolf to hunt down whoever is committing these sadistic crimes – before he and his remaining friends find themselves on the growing list of victims ...

James Green
The Road to Redemption Series

Bad Catholics

Meet Jimmy Costello. Quiet, respectable, God-fearing family man? Or thuggish street-fighter with a past full of dark secrets? Perhaps the answer is somewhere in between …

After Jimmy's wife dies the conflict inside him is too much and the violent assault he commits on a gangster forces him to leave London and his job with the police and disappear for a while. Now he's back, on what you might call a divine mission … and to settle a few old scores too.

Through the eyes of his hard-boiled ex-cop, James Green takes us on a thrilling journey from 1960s Kilburn, through war-torn 1970s Africa to the modern streets of a London that seems to have cleaned up its act … until you scratch the surface.

Bill Kitson
Eden House Mysteries

Silent as the Grave

A chilling tale of murder, madness, and what happens when ghosts from the past won't stay in their graves.

When former journalist Adam Bailey agrees to spend Christmas at ancient Mulgrave Castle, he knows there is an ulterior motive behind the invitation. His old flame, Harriet, and her husband, Sir Anthony Rowe, want Adam to investigate the legend of an old family curse – a curse said to have claimed several victims, and which may be due to strike again ...
Soon, heavy snow cuts off the castle from the outside world, and the guests become aware that the curse has indeed claimed a new victim – but how? Adam, aided by Harriet's feisty sister Eve, seeks to discover if the death is linked to the mysterious disappearances that have occurred over the centuries.

Is there the usual foul play afoot – or is someone powerless to resist the force of a far older evil?

For more information about **Jane Bidder**
and other **Accent Press** titles
please visit

www.accentpress.co.uk